TWISTED TEA CHRISTMAS

Tea Shop Mystery #23

LAURA CHILDS

BERKLEY PRIME CRIME
New York

BERKLEY PRIME CRIME
Published by Berkley
An imprint of Penguin Random House LLC
penguinrandomhouse.com

Copyright © 2021 by Gerry Schmitt & Associates, Inc.
Excerpt from *A Dark and Stormy Tea* by Laura Childs copyright © 2021 by
Gerry Schmitt & Associates, Inc.
Penguin Random House supports copyright. Copyright fuels creativity, encourages
diverse voices, promotes free speech, and creates a vibrant culture. Thank you for buying
an authorized edition of this book and for complying with copyright laws by not
reproducing, scanning, or distributing any part of it in any form without permission.
You are supporting writers and allowing Penguin Random House to continue to
publish books for every reader.

BERKLEY and the BERKLEY & B colophon are registered trademarks and
BERKLEY PRIME CRIME is a trademark of Penguin Random House LLC.

ISBN: 9780593200889

Berkley Prime Crime hardcover edition / October 2021
Berkley Prime Crime mass-market edition / November 2022

Printed in the United States of America
1   3   5   7   9   10   8   6   4   2

TWISTED TEA
CHRISTMAS

1

❧

'Twas the week before Christmas, and all through the house, a Victorian Christmas party was stirring in a genuine Victorian mansion at one of the swankiest addresses in all of Charleston, South Carolina. The original owner of the mansion had been a signer of the Declaration of Independence, and the current resident, a certain Miss Drucilla Heyward, was signatory on a bank account that contained more money than the GDP of a small European country.

Picture it this way: a group of well-heeled women in St. John Knits and low-heeled Manolos, wearing stacks of bangles, diamond-stud earrings, and subtle hints of Chanel No. 5. All quite tasteful and genteel as they sipped Lapsang souchong from bone china teacups.

The men at the party leaned toward portly and were beginning to get ruddy-faced from nipping brandy. The rent-a-bartender in his snug red rent-a-jacket was pouring Hennessy X.O tonight, so that was what they were drinking. Talking stock markets and sailboats and business and family, dressed in conservative Corneliani suits from M. Dumas & Sons on King Street, here and there a few of them sporting tartan plaid vests or Christmas bow ties.

And down the hallway, in the palatial dining room . . .

Theodosia Browning would never consider herself a member of this well-heeled, fairly insular group. But she knew what they liked. Which is why she'd orchestrated a spectacular menu for tonight's party. Rare roast beef on rye with dabs of horseradish, steamed blue crabs pulled fresh from local tidal creeks, Capers Blades oysters on the half shell, goat cheese crostini, and spicy chimichurri steak bites.

And then there were the tea sandwiches.

"I hope the guests love these little sandwiches as much as I do," Theodosia said as she arranged her offerings on polished silver trays.

"The crab salad on brioche?" Drayton asked. As Theodosia's tea sommelier at the Indigo Tea Shop, he was also her partner in crime for tonight's catering gig.

"And lobster salad accented with fresh tarragon. Haley whipped up both fillings using her famous homemade mayonnaise recipe—or receipt, as she calls it."

"Yum," Drayton said. "No wonder Miss Drucilla asked us to serve champagne along with Lapsang souchong." He paused. "I do love that tea. The gently twisted leaves impart such a delicious smoky flavor."

"I'd say it's all rather perfect," Theodosia said.

She stepped back to admire their buffet table, an amazing amalgam of food, flickering candles, crystal vases filled with red and white roses, and some silver angel figurines that had somehow snuck their way in. As proprietor of the Indigo Tea Shop on Charleston's famed Church Street, Theodosia was used to serving cream teas, luncheon teas, and afternoon teas. But anytime she could land a fancy catering job—and this one sure was fancy—it was a happy addition to her shop's bottom line. Theodosia also knew that happy, satisfied guests often led to new bookings, which led to more business for her tea shop. And, really, wasn't that a good no-brainer kind of marketing?

Theodosia normally wore T-shirts, khaki slacks, and a long black Parisian waiter's apron. But tonight she was glammed up in a red velvet hostess skirt and a pink ruffled blouse that set off her complexion to perfection. Her English ancestors had blessed her with fair peaches-and-cream skin, startling deep blue eyes, and an inquisitive face. And some distant-distant relatives (from perhaps even farther north?) had gifted her with masses of curly auburn hair. In her mid-thirties now, Theodosia had worked in marketing, traveled a bit, dated enough men to know what type she preferred, and set up her own tea shop. In other words, she knew enough to be dangerous.

Drayton Conneley, also a born-and-bred Southerner, was sixty-something, a tea fanatic, and most definitely a world traveler. Drayton was smart, stylish, droll, and exacting (some might say *demanding*) in everything he did. His tastes ran from Shakespeare and Dickens to Baroque music, and he lived in a historic old house—in the Historic District, of course—that had once belonged to a Civil War doctor. Tonight he wore black slacks, a Brioni jacket, and a red-and-green-plaid bow tie.

"Can you believe this place?" Drayton asked, glancing around the dining room. "It's like something out of *Architectural Digest*. Only the castle and manor house version."

"If the Great Gatsby lived in Charleston," Theodosia said.

And who could have argued with her, given that they'd arranged their buffet on a twenty-foot-long antique Sheraton table in a dining room where a marble fireplace occupied most of one wall, a crystal chandelier hung overhead from a domed ceiling, and colorful hand-painted Venetian scenes decorated the walls? Lavish garlands entwined with red roses, greenery, and fairy lights highlighted the tall, narrow windows that looked out over the back gardens, and an enormous fifteen-foot-high gilded Christmas tree sat next to a glass-fronted cabinet that held silver and crystal treasures.

"You hear that?" Drayton asked.

Theodosia stopped to listen for a moment. A string quartet had begun to play a rousing rendition of "God Rest Ye Merry, Gentlemen" in the front parlor.

"That's our cue," Theodosia said. "When the music starts, we're supposed to light the candles and pop a few champagne corks."

"Happy to oblige," Drayton said. He grabbed a bottle of Moët & Chandon, twisted off the metal cage, placed a towel around the cork, and eased it out. There was a gentle resounding POP.

"I'm thinking we should open four or five bottles," Theodosia said. "Once the music concludes and the guests come streaming in . . ."

The rest of her words were drowned out by a loud, unpleasant buzz that seemed to blast out of nowhere. The sound not only startled her, it filled her ears like a hive of angry hornets.

"What's that?" Drayton asked. Only the noise was so loud, Theodosia wasn't able to hear him; she could only read his lips and see the consternation on his face.

Suddenly, Miss Drucilla fluttered into the room, wearing a coral silk caftan and dripping with diamonds. She held up a finger, darted around a corner, and then, mercifully, happily, the buzzing stopped.

"What was *that*?" Drayton cried.

Miss Drucilla returned, and her laughter filled the room.

"Oh, don't worry, kittens. It's only my crazy security alarm. Sometimes it pops off for no reason at all."

At eighty-five, Miss Drucilla Heyward was still a force to be reckoned with. Tiny as a bird, pixie white hair cut short to show off her favorite Tiffany Victoria earrings, she was spirited, fun-loving, and social to the max. She served on the board of directors of the Charleston Opera Society and the Charleston Symphony, and contributed money to dozens of charities. She was also known to occasionally join the men after dinner to smoke a cigar and enjoy her whiskey straight.

"Thank you," Drayton said. "But what an awful sound."

"Kind of gets your attention, doesn't it?" Miss Drucilla said.

Though she was still, technically, Mrs. Everett Heyward, she was generally addressed as Miss Drucilla. That was how it was done in the South. Women of a certain age and charm often had the moniker *Miss* added to their first name: Miss Kitty, Miss Abigail, Miss Drucilla. Like that.

Miss Drucilla surveyed the table. "I love it," she said, clapping her hands together. "Everything's perfect."

"Thank you," Theodosia said. "And I sure do love—I mean, *really* love—your jewelry."

Miss Drucilla brandished an arm. "Look here. I even wore my Verdura cuff tonight. Took it out of the vault just for this special occasion."

"Gorgeous," Drayton said. "A show stopper."

"That's not all you took out of the vault," Theodosia said. She couldn't help but notice the array of diamond rings that glittered on Miss Drucilla's tiny fingers.

"Oh, these?" Miss Drucilla fluttered her hands to show off her rings, sending brilliant flashes of light everywhere. "Tonight I'm wearing five diamond-and-gold rings in honor of Christmas—you know, like the song." She giggled as she half sang, "Five *gold*-en rings." Then she folded her hands to her chest and added, "All were gifts from my dearly departed husbands, Gerald, Charles, and Everett. All three of whom I've managed to outlive. Knock on wood."

"Love the manicure, too," Theodosia added.

Now Miss Drucilla studied her fingertips. "Jolene over at Fantasy Salon did them. Kind of trendy, don't you think? Tipped my nails with fourteen-carat gold."

"Fun," Theodosia said.

"But not all that expensive. Anyway, enough with my tiny indulgences." Now she leaned forward and said in a conspiratorial whisper, "I've decided to part with some of my money. That's why, along with a bunch of friends and neighbors, I invited executive directors from six of my favorite charities tonight. They're all going to be getting a wonderful Christmas present."

"That's fantastic," Theodosia said. She served as a board member for Big Paw Service Dogs and knew firsthand that nonprofits were constantly on the lookout for funding.

"Okay, you two open a couple more bottles of champagne, and in a few minutes, I'll start herding my guests in," Miss Drucilla said. And she hurried off in another quick burst of energy.

"She's amazing," Theodosia said to Drayton. "I hope I have that much energy when I reach her age."

"You will," Drayton said. "Look at your aunt Libby. How old is she now?"

"Eighty-three," Theodosia said.

"And she still gets up at five every morning to feed the birds."

"I guess that's called commitment," Theodosia said as a loud bray suddenly filled the air for a second time.

"There goes that annoying alarm again," Drayton shouted, pursing his lips in dismay. "I hope Miss Drucilla punches in the code before the security company gets nervous and sends an armed response." He touched his bow tie and fidgeted. "That's all we need: a couple of rent-a-cops rushing in to upset our lovely buffet."

"Everyone going head over teakettle," Theodosia said. But even as she tried to make herself heard, the alarm continued its terrible buzz.

"Can't they *hear* that in the parlor?" Drayton asked.

"Apparently not. Probably because the quartet's still playing."

Drayton walked around the table to shout in Theodosia's ear. "Well, that noise is driving me batty!"

"I'll see what I can do," Theodosia said. She nipped around a corner, intending to run down the wide center hallway that served as a sort of art gallery and led to Miss Drucilla's front parlor.

But Theodosia had taken only a single step when she saw a crumpled body sprawled halfway down the hallway on the marble tile floor. Then she recognized the filmy coral caftan and cried, "Oh no!" running as fast as her high heels could carry her.

"Miss Drucilla!" she cried, bending over the small body. But the woman lay ghostly still.

Is she breathing? I don't think . . .

Theodosia sprinted back to the dining room.

"Drayton!" she cried. "Miss Drucilla's fallen down and I'm afraid she might have had a stroke or something!"

"Dear Lord!" Drayton went running while Theodosia stepped into the butler's pantry, located the security system panel, and randomly hit a couple of buttons. That seemed to do the trick, thank heavens, and stopped the noise. Then she rushed back out, shouting for help as she ran down the hallway, dropping to her hands and knees next to Drayton. And poor Miss Drucilla.

"What do you think? Did she have a stroke? Is it her heart? Is she even breathing?" Theodosia asked.

"I don't know," Drayton said. "She's facedown and all crumpled up. I'm afraid to move her."

Theodosia's cries had alerted a dozen or so guests and now they poured into the hallway, one man immediately pulling out his phone and calling 911, directing the dispatcher to hurry up and send an ambulance.

Thank goodness. Theodosia breathed a huge sigh of relief. At least help was on the way.

"Passed out," another man behind her said. He spoke with a high voice and sounded concerned but calm. "Probably too much excitement."

"Let's try to turn her over, make sure she's breathing," Theodosia said. She was keenly aware of the buzz of voices behind her and realized that more party guests had spilled into the hallway.

"Theo?" a woman's voice called out. "What happened?"

Theodosia allowed herself a quick glance over her shoulder and saw her friend Delaine Dish, her brows puckered, expression solemn, eyes scared and jittery.

"I don't know," Theodosia said. "She just collapsed. She's . . ."

"Slide your hands under her shoulders," Drayton said. "We'll try to change her position and see if we can make her more comfortable."

"Okay," Theodosia said. Miss Drucilla was hunched up and still facedown. Not moving a single muscle.

Drayton was deeply shaken but still gamely hanging in there. "Okay. Ready?"

Theodosia nodded. She tried to gather Miss Drucilla up gently, like you would a sleeping child, then turn her over carefully.

"Oh my, I'm not sure about this." There was a momentary hesitation as panic flared in Drayton's voice. "We'd best be careful."

"Let's try to shift her very gingerly." Theodosia knew something had to be done—and fast. But as she started to move Miss Drucilla, the woman's head lolled heavily onto one shoulder and her eyes remained tightly shut, as if she'd experienced some terrible horror.

"Okay . . . easy." Drayton was trying his best but Miss Drucilla's face was a washed-out pale oval, and there was a terrible finality about her.

"Drayton!" Theodosia cried as they began to slowly turn Miss Drucilla. "Look at . . ." Theodosia's heart lurched crazily, and she gasped, words logjamming in her throat. Finally, she lifted a trembling hand and pointed.

Reacting to the shock on Theodosia's face, Drayton widened his eyes with worry. Then he saw what she was pointing at.

"Oh no," he groaned.

Someone had plunged a bright orange syringe deep into Miss Drucilla's throat!

2

Screams rose up from the guests who had clustered in close. Then the entire group began to shout en masse!

"What's stuck in her throat?" one man demanded.

"Get back. She needs air!" another man cried.

"Did she faint?" a woman asked. Standing at the back of the pack, she jumped up and down, desperately trying to get a look.

"What happened?" another voice trembled.

Their shrieks and cries rose in an unholy cacophony that was almost as bad as the faulty alarm system.

Pauline Stauber, Miss Drucilla's personal assistant, was the first person to batter her way through the wall of stunned onlookers and drop to her knees. "Oh no," she cried. "What happened? What's . . . what's that stuck in her throat?"

Theodosia was still cradling Miss Drucilla's head. "Don't touch her," she warned. "Don't touch anything." Then, "Who are you again?" She'd been introduced to the woman some three hours earlier, but couldn't remember what part she played in the household.

"I'm Pauline, Miss Drucilla's personal assistant," the woman said. She was in her mid-twenties, dressed in a fuzzy white sweater and a black skirt that revealed a zaftig figure. Her hair was a streaky blond brown and worn shoulder length. Fear shone in amber eyes that, under better circumstances, were probably warm and filled with humor. Theodosia decided that Pauline looked a lot like a concerned kindergarten teacher.

Screams and cries had alerted the rest of the guests, and now nearly three dozen people—everyone who could cram themselves into the hallway anyway—pressed in around them.

Drayton looked up, his face ashen. With a mixture of shock and sadness in his voice, he said, "I think Miss Drucilla is gone."

"Gone? Gone where?" demanded a shrill voice at the back of the pack.

Drayton's voice was a hoarse croak as his hand indicated—but didn't touch—the syringe. "I think . . . I think perhaps she's been drugged?"

Pauline immediately burst into tears while everyone else seemed to ratchet up their babbling.

"Drugs? Who would do this?" a man demanded. He glared at the crowd around him, suspicion evident on his face.

"Someone killed Miss Drucilla?" a woman asked in a querulous voice.

"Ohmygosh, look at her hands!" Delaine shouted as she pushed and shoved her way to the front of the group. "All her beautiful rings are gone!" She touched a hand to her neck as if fearing she could be the next victim. "Miss Drucilla's been murdered *and* robbed!"

Theodosia blinked as she took in the scene. Pauline crying, Delaine shouting, stunned faces gaping at her. She tried to make sense of this alien scene. Tried to figure out what could have happened. Someone had attacked Miss Drucilla when the alarm went off the second time and then . . .

Before she could pull her thoughts together, loud voices erupted in the hallway. Then two EMTs, hauling a clanking metal gurney, broke through the jittery crowd. With barely a wasted motion, they were down on their hands and knees and pulling equipment from their medical packs.

"Priority one," the first EMT, a serious-looking African-American woman, said to the second EMT. Her name tag read LUDLOW; his read SLAGER.

Theodosia figured *priority one* must be code for a big bad emergency.

Both EMTs worked feverishly, following the ABC protocol of checking airway, breathing, and circulation.

Still, it didn't look good for Miss Drucilla. She wasn't responding to anything they tried and her lips had begun to turn blue.

"Naloxone?" Slager asked.

Ludlow, the lead EMT, looked up at the crowd. "Anybody know what drug she was hit with?"

Nobody knew. Or if they did, they were remaining silent to cover up a nasty murder.

Without hesitating, Ludlow grabbed a preloaded syringe and injected Miss Drucilla. "Come on, sweetheart," she whispered. "You can do this."

But in the end, after all lifesaving measures were attempted, Miss Drucilla really couldn't.

And even though the two grim-faced, tight-lipped EMTs continued to work over her, Miss Drucilla was clearly deceased.

Sobs broke out. Men hung their heads. And finally, four uniformed police officers arrived to try to clear the hallway and push everyone out of the way.

"You're not going to transport her?" Theodosia asked Ms. Ludlow.

Ludlow shook her head. "I'm sorry. She's gone."

"What now?" Drayton asked.

"That hypo stuck in her neck?" Ludlow said. "Means we have to wait for an investigator."

But they didn't have to wait long.

The slam of the front door, heavy tread on the marble tile, the crowd parting like the proverbial Red Sea meant Detective Burt Tidwell had finally put in an appearance.

Big, burly, and bristly, Burt Tidwell headed the Charleston Police Department's Robbery and Homicide Division. Not only was he short-tempered and grouchy, he was your basic evil genius. He'd cut his teeth with the FBI, then switched over to police work. His close rate was phenomenal; his staff of detectives was in awe of him and sometimes feared him. Still, they would have tiptoed barefoot across a bed of white-hot coals if he'd asked.

Tonight Tidwell was dressed in a baggy tweed jacket that barely stretched around his ample girth, voluminous drab slacks the viscous brown color of pluff mud, and clunky thick-soled cop shoes with reinforced steel toes. Presumably for kicking in doors.

As Tidwell slouched his way toward the dead woman on the floor, his beady eyes roved across the crowd that had inched its way back to the murder scene. Then he nodded at the EMTs, cast a quick glance at Theodosia hovering nearby, and knelt down carefully so as not to disturb the body. He put his face as close to the syringe in Miss Drucilla's neck as possible, studied it, then pulled back. His thick lips twisted in a grimace.

"It looks as if someone injected her with a narcotic," Theodosia said. She felt comfortable speaking up because she knew Detective Tidwell. Well, sort of knew him. They had a running battle about her getting too involved in a few of his cases.

Tidwell nodded without looking at her. "Could be a DIH," was his gruff reply.

"What is that exactly?" Theodosia asked.

"Drug-induced homicide," Tidwell said.

That dropped a terrible pall of silence over the entire group.

Tidwell beetled his brows, looked at the gaggle of subdued guests, and said, "We need to take names and interview witnesses." He turned and gazed at the four officers who were watching him carefully and said, "Get to work, boys."

"What else?" Theodosia asked as the entire group started churning and swarming like ants at a picnic.

"Crime Scene Team," Tidwell said.

"And they're . . ."

"On their way," Tidwell said. "So. Besides the syringe lodged in this unfortunate woman's neck, what else can you tell me?"

"Someone stole all of Miss Drucilla's rings," Drayton said, his voice trembling slightly as he stepped forward. "Pulled them right off her fingers."

Tidwell studied her hands. "I see that."

"This is an absolute nightmare," Drayton continued. "Miss Drucilla was so happy and carefree only a short while ago when she showed us her rings. 'Five gold rings' was how she phrased it. You know, like from that song 'The Twelve Days of Christmas.' But now . . . one can barely comprehend that some *monster* crept in and killed her! Made off with every one of her diamond rings." He shook his head, unable to process such senseless cruelty and violence.

Theodosia, who'd been eyeing the wall directly behind Drayton, suddenly spoke up. "I'm afraid Miss Drucilla's collection of rings isn't the only thing missing." She lifted a hand and pointed to a conspicuous blank space. "So is the painting that was hanging right there."

"What!" Drayton cried as he spun around. Others had overheard Theodosia's words and were staring at the wall as well.

Tidwell's mouth worked furiously for a few moments as he digested this new revelation. He took a step forward and said, "A painting?" His eyes swept the gallery of paintings that were clustered like large colorful postage stamps on the wall. He seemed to be confirming the fact that a blank space did exist.

"I swear!" A man's voice rose in stunned shock. "I think the painting that hung there . . . it was a Renoir!"

Tidwell whirled about, a fierce look on his broad face. "A what? Explain please."

"Pierre-Auguste Renoir, the French artist who was one of the leaders of the Impressionist style," the man said. He was red-faced and nervous, and a charcoal suit hung on his spare frame.

"You're telling me a valuable painting is missing?" Tidwell asked. "A genuine Renoir?"

The man nodded solemnly. "I think so. No, I'm sure of it."

Tidwell squinted at him. "And you are . . . ?"

"Harold Linder," the man said. "I live right down the block."

The discovery of a missing Renoir hit Theodosia hard. "How could this happen?" she wondered out loud. She put a hand to her head as if to still the pounding inside her brain. "One minute I was talking to Miss Drucilla—talking about her jewelry, as a matter of fact. And the next minute she's sprawled in the hallway—dead."

"Whoever did this worked fast," Tidwell said.

"But . . ." Theodosia began.

"And used a fast-acting drug," Tidwell said.

"What do you think it was? Some kind of street drug?" Theodosia knew her questions were macabre, but felt compelled to ask them anyway.

"Could've been a street drug," Tidwell said. "A baggie of heroin can be had for around twenty bucks. There are other heroin combos even more lethal. What you'd call a hot shot that goes straight to the heart. Of course, we won't know for

sure until the ME takes a look and runs a toxicology screen."
He glanced around. "Who, um . . . Is there someone who
works here?"

Pauline raised a tentative hand and said in a small voice,
"That would be me."

Tidwell motioned for Pauline to step forward. "Who are
you?"

"Pauline Stauber, Miss Drucilla's personal assistant."

"Was she under a doctor's care?" Tidwell asked.

"Not really."

"Do you know if Miss Drucilla was taking any medica-
tion?"

"Some. Yes. I can't . . . um . . ."

"No problem. I'll have one of my officers check the medi-
cine cabinet."

Because Pauline looked so devastated, Theodosia sought
to distract her.

"Pauline, how many people were in attendance tonight?"
she asked.

"Um . . . around three dozen?" Pauline said. "Mostly
friends and business acquaintances, though a few were executive directors of charities she supported."

"Can you recall some of their names?"

Pauline thought for a moment. "Sawyer Daniels, that's
Miss Drucilla's finance guy, and Majel, she's the executive
director of . . . um . . ."

"Better yet, do you have a guest list?" Theodosia asked.

"I suppose I do." Looking lost, Pauline touched a hand to
her forehead and said, "Somewhere."

Tidwell turned his attention back to them. "We'll need
that guest list ASAP." Then he frowned and said, "Besides
the guests, do you know if anybody else was here tonight?"

"Tonight? Besides the guests and caterers? I don't think
so." Pauline was still shaken and discombobulated. Then her
forehead wrinkled and she said, "Well, maybe just Smokey."

"'Just Smokey,'" Tidwell said. "Who is 'just Smokey'?"

"Smokey Pruitt. He's a guy who does odd jobs for Miss Drucilla and a few of the other neighbors," Pauline said.

"Was he here tonight?" Theodosia asked.

Tidwell made a face—he didn't appreciate Theodosia butting in—but he remained silent so Pauline could answer his question.

"I . . ." Pauline half-closed her eyes, thinking. "I don't . . . I'm not sure."

"Okay, then, where does Smokey live?" Theodosia asked. She hadn't seen any kind of handyman stumping around in the kitchen or butler's pantry. But that didn't mean one hadn't ghosted through.

"Smokey lives in my carriage house," said a large barrel-chested man in an impeccable Armani suit. "For now anyway." He stepped forward and gave a tentative smile. He had slicked-back brown hair, a broad face, and little pink pouches under his eyes. A large gold Rolex, the size of an old-fashioned alarm clock, circled his wrist. Theodosia figured him for either a banker or a racetrack tout.

"Who are you and where is this carriage house?" Tidwell asked.

"I'm Donny Bragg, one of the neighbors. My place is three houses down from here."

"The old Caswell Mansion," Drayton murmured. A history buff and longtime Charleston resident, he was well versed on the provenance of every mansion, townhome, and single house in Charleston's Historic District.

Tidwell ignored Drayton's comment. "And why exactly does this Smokey person reside in your carriage house?"

"Well, it's more like a studio apartment above my garage," Bragg explained.

"Doesn't matter. *Why* does he live there?" Tidwell asked.

"Smokey's been making repairs on my back porch. A bunch of pesky termites moved in and started messing with my Carolina pine." Bragg gave a thoughtful nod. "That's the problem with these old homes that have been around for a hundred and fifty years. It's patch, patch, patch, and then a new problem crops up."

"Yes, fine," Tidwell said. "We'll be sure to interview this Smokey fellow."

"And the three dozen guests," Theodosia murmured. It sounded like a thankless task, a long, hard slog that might not turn up anything at all. In her mind the killer was long gone. He'd rabbited out the door with the diamonds and Renoir painting in hand. Which might point to an educated, erudite killer.

When the Crime Scene Team arrived, they hustled everyone out of the hallway and set up a hard perimeter. Theodosia and Drayton lingered in the front hallway, feeling disheartened, wondering what to do next.

"The food," Drayton said. "We should pack it up and"—he shrugged—"I don't know what."

"We'll donate it," Theodosia said. "Take it to one of the food kitchens. At least it will go to good use."

He nodded. "Okay."

Theodosia turned her gaze to Detective Tidwell. Though interviewing guests, he seemed strangely upset. She'd never known Tidwell to be emotionally involved in any of his cases.

Finally, when he drifted over to give Theodosia and Drayton the okay to leave, he said, "I knew her."

"I didn't realize that," Theodosia said.

"Miss Drucilla was a wonderful woman," Tidwell said. "She single-handedly kept our Police Officers' Children's Fund going when there was no money to be had anywhere. For someone to sneak into her home and murder her—Well, he has to be the worst kind of rabid animal."

"And you intend to catch him," Theodosia said.

Tidwell's eyes blazed. "I intend to put him down."

3

At eight a.m. on a cool but sunny Monday morning, with a few pink-tinged clouds overhead, Theodosia parked her Jeep in the alley behind the Indigo Tea Shop and let herself in the back door. She dumped her coat and bag in her small, over-stuffed office, walked down the hallway that led past the kitchen, and stopped in her tracks. Drayton and Haley were sitting at one of the small tables in the tea room, talking quietly, with steaming cups of tea set in front of them. The aroma that permeated the shop was fragrant and bright. So perhaps they'd brewed a Darjeeling?

"I take it you've told Haley about our ill-fated catering event last night?" Theodosia said. Her voice carried a little louder than she'd intended.

They both turned to look at her.

"Hi," Haley said, giving a quick wave while Drayton nodded in response.

Haley gazed at Theodosia with earnest puppy-dog eyes

and pushed a hank of silky blond hair off her youthful face. "That must have been some awful Christmas party," she said.

"It didn't start out that way," Theodosia said. "It was all quite festive and lovely—until it wasn't. One minute it was 'Hark! The Herald Angels Sing,' and the next minute we were treated to blaring police sirens and the heartrending zip of a black plastic body bag."

Drayton shivered. "A ghastly end to a Christmas gala."

"Drayton was telling me about the crazy killer who snuck in and strangled Miss Drucilla, then stole all her diamond rings," Haley said.

"And plucked a painting off the wall." Theodosia pulled out a chair and sat down at the table with them.

"Was it really a Renoir?" Now Haley looked slightly more curious than scared.

Theodosia shrugged. "We don't know for sure. One man thought it was a Renoir, but nobody knows if the painting was authentic."

"Knowing Miss Drucilla's taste in art, I doubt it was a reproduction," Drayton said.

"I remember when Miss Drucilla came here for our Sherlock Holmes Tea last Halloween," Haley said. "She was really sweet, really nice. Went out of her way to thank everyone."

"She was a lovely woman," Drayton said. "Pretty much the last of Charleston's old-guard grande dames. And so charitable and civic-minded. She donated funds to countless arts organizations and nonprofit groups."

"She had a lot of money?" Haley asked.

"She was well-off," Drayton said.

"She was loaded," Theodosia said.

"So Miss Drucilla's murder was all about the Benjamins?" Haley asked. "I mean, do you think whoever stole her diamond rings and painting intends to sell them?"

Looking morose, Drayton rested his chin in a cupped hand. "I suppose."

Theodosia thought for a moment, then said, "I'm not sure that's necessarily true."

Drayton and Haley both looked at her in surprise.

"What other reason could there be, besides unmitigated greed and a total disregard for life?" Drayton asked. He was of the opinion that a nasty cat burglar had infiltrated the old mansion, been spotted by Miss Drucilla, then killed her for her trouble. After which he snuck off with the loot.

"It's entirely possible that Miss Drucilla knew her killer," Theodosia said.

"What!" Drayton cried.

"He—I'm assuming it's a he—might have had an issue with her," Theodosia said.

"What do you mean?" Haley asked.

"Well, it could have been an unsavory relative, a business associate who felt scorned, or even someone who'd asked her for money but was turned down," Theodosia said.

"So you don't think her killing was random?" Haley asked. "A break-in gone bad."

"I think it was messy but somewhat orchestrated," Theodosia said.

Drayton frowned and shook his head. "Explain, please."

"Think of it as the perfect storm. There were caterers, decorators, florists, delivery people, and house cleaners going in and out of her home all day long. You can even count us among those folks. Then evening comes and the house fills up with a new batch of people—the party guests. They're drinking, talking, mingling, wandering about. Many of the guests don't know one another."

"Surely you don't suspect one of Miss Drucilla's guests," Drayton said. He looked unsettled. To impugn one of last night's party guests felt like heresy to him.

"What I'm saying is . . . someone could have slipped in under the guise of being a guest or making a delivery," Theodosia said.

"So you're saying that somebody had a backstage pass,"

Drayton said. "But I don't remember seeing anyone like that."

"Neither do I," Theodosia said. "But that doesn't mean it didn't happen. In an enormous house with multiple entrances and exits, with lights blazing and music playing . . . someone could have snuck in or even buffaloed their way in."

"Taking advantage of the situation," Haley said slowly. Then she shivered. "The way you describe it, kind of cold and opportunistic, gives me chills. You make it sound so simple, as if we're all vulnerable if we're not careful."

"Maybe we are," Drayton said.

"Okay, now you two have managed to totally creep me out," Haley said. "When what we really need to do is make plans for our upcoming week." She reached into her apron pocket and pulled out a pink floral notebook and matching pink pen.

"To business," Drayton sighed. He still looked unsettled as he straightened up in his chair. "This would have to happen the week before Christmas."

"There's never a good time for murder," Theodosia said.

Haley tapped her pen against the table to get their attention. "Tomorrow, Tuesday," she said, "we've got our Nutcracker Tea. Are we pretty much squared away on that?"

"The menu you drew up is fabulous, the decorations are sitting in my office, and Miss Dimple will be coming in to help serve," Theodosia said. "So yes, I think we're good to go."

"Then we have another event on Wednesday," Drayton said.

"It'll be a quick turnaround for our White Christmas Tea," Theodosia said. "And then we've got . . ."

"Our Old-Fashioned Southern Tea on Friday," Drayton said. "Can we please let those plans slide for the time being? The murder, Christmas week, it's all a bit much to digest."

"*No problema*, Drayton." Haley stood up, grabbed her notebook, and headed for the kitchen. Then, in a low voice, she said, "Just don't forget about our Victorian Christmas Tea and your fancy Grand Illumination."

"I heard that," Drayton called after her.

"I meant you to," Haley said as she ducked into her kitchen.

Drayton turned to Theodosia. "It's going to be difficult to keep our heads in the game today."

"After last night, everything feels shaky and up in the air," Theodosia agreed, "especially with a stone-cold killer running around out there."

"Still . . ." Drayton stood up and brushed an invisible speck of lint off the sleeve of his Harris Tweed jacket. "We must try our best." He scooped up the cups and saucers from the table, placed them in a gray plastic tub, and retreated to his domain behind the front counter.

Theodosia watched Drayton as he got busy. First off, he selected his teas for the day. Yes, their guests generally specified which tea they preferred to sip with their scones and tea breads, but Drayton always had a few pots of brewed tea at the ready.

This morning, Drayton seemed to be favoring oolong teas, pulling down colorful tins of tea from his floor-to-ceiling shelves that held more than three hundred different varieties of tea. Often fruity and floral, oolongs were also smooth, light, and refreshing. A perfect morning libation.

Theodosia turned to gaze at her tea room and then at the clock on the wall. *Time to get cracking,* she decided. In less than twenty minutes, they'd have customers knock-knocking at their front door. Shop owners from up and down Church Street would be dropping by for their morning cuppa. She also knew there'd be spillover from Historic District hotels and bed-and-breakfasts that were full up for Christmas. And with plenty of tourists in town for the Holiday Tour of Homes, church spirituals concerts, the Holiday Market, the Holiday Parade of Boats in Charleston Harbor, the Festival of Lights in James Island County Park, and various productions of Handel's *Messiah*, some of them would find their way to the Indigo Tea Shop as well.

First things first, Theodosia covered her tables with white damask tablecloths, then added red place mats. Red and white candles in silver holders and sugar bowls and cream pitchers went on next.

Now for the china. What better than her Christmas Rose pattern by Spode? Very festive, very cute.

Theodosia set out small plates, cups, and saucers and stepped back. *Okay, what else?*

Well, Floradora Florists had delivered several bundles of red and white carnations as well as small pine boughs this morning, so Theodosia arranged the blooms and greenery in tall glass vases and placed one on each table.

Even though Theodosia's heart was heavy this morning, working in the tea shop she'd built brought her enormous joy. A few years earlier, when she'd first purchased the little cottage on Charleston's famed Church Street, she'd kept the wavy leaded windows, pegged pine floors that squeaked underfoot, and small stone fireplace—and lovingly refurbished the rest. She'd hunted through antiques shops and tag sales to find vintage teacups, teapots, goblets, and silverware. A French chandelier hung overhead lent a warm glow; antique highboys were stuffed with retail items such as tea towels, tea cozies, tins of tea, jars of honey and lemon curd, and Theodosia's proprietary T-Bath products.

The tea shop had become a veritable jewel box, with Theodosia, Drayton, and Haley working together as a well-oiled team to delight visitors, friends, and neighbors with baked-from-scratch scones and muffins, a dazzling array of fine teas, and their ever-popular special-event teas.

Theodosia had just finished folding white linen napkins into a showy bishop's-hat arrangement when she heard the telltale DA-DING of the bell over the front door.

"Guests," Drayton murmured as Theodosia flew to the door to welcome the first customers of the day with a smile.

From then on business never let up. Every few minutes the front door opened and a whoosh of chill air swept in along with a clutch of guests. Theodosia ran to the kitchen to grab orders of cream scones, strawberry muffins, and lemon tea bread. Then she swooped over to the counter to grab small pots of fresh-brewed tea.

"Got you hopping today," Drayton said as he pushed a blue-and-white Chinese teapot filled with Madoorie Estate across the counter to her.

"It's probably going to be like this all Christmas week," Theodosia said.

"Fine with me. I'm the last to complain when business is good." Drayton peered at her over his tortoiseshell half-glasses. "Is anyone talking about . . . ? You know."

"The murder? You've got to be kidding. That's *all* they're talking about."

"Well, I hate to hear that because an untimely death is definitely not proper conversation for a tea room."

"I guess you didn't catch the front page of this morning's *Post and Courier.*"

"Mmn . . . glanced at it."

"Then you know Miss Drucilla's murder was the main story. You remember the old newspaper adage, don't you?" Theodosia said.

"What's that?"

"If it bleeds, it leads."

"Awful," Drayton snorted.

At ten o'clock, Detective Burt Tidwell walked in. He stood in the entryway, hands stuck deep into the pockets of a battered and abominable-looking khaki trench coat, as he gazed out over the tea room. His eyes were sharp but the rest of him looked tired and worn out. Probably, it had been a long night for him.

"Good morning," Theodosia said to him in a semicheery

voice. "Is this a drive-by inquisition, or are you here for tea and scones?"

"A little of both," Tidwell rumbled.

"In that case . . ." Theodosia led him to a small table next to the stone fireplace, where a crackling fire gave off pine-scented warmth.

Tidwell eased his bulk into a padded captain's chair as the wood creaked in protest. Theodosia held her breath. *Everything okay? Chair still intact?* Yes, it appeared to be.

"We have cream scones, strawberry muffins, and . . . ," Theodosia began.

"A cream scone please," Tidwell said. "No, actually, I'd prefer *two* scones. And might Drayton have some of that excellent Formosan oolong?"

"I'll ask him to brew a pot straightaway."

Theodosia whispered the order to Drayton, then went into the kitchen, plated the cream scones, and added small glass ramekins filled with Devonshire cream and strawberry jam. When she came back, the tea was already steeping in a small brown Yi-shing teapot. She carried everything to Tidwell's table, arranged it carefully, and waited.

Tidwell wasted no time in tucking into his scones. Cutting one in half, slathering it with Devonshire cream, popping a huge bite into his mouth.

Theodosia stood there, waiting patiently.

After he took a second bite, she said, "So . . . ?"

His beady eyes flicked to her. "Yes?"

"Any more thoughts on last night?"

"Probably too many."

Theodosia decided that perhaps she should try a more direct approach.

"Has the medical examiner had a chance to look at Miss Drucilla?" She lifted the teapot and poured out a cup of tea for Tidwell. The oolong had probably steeped long enough. It should be nice and strong. Strong enough to carry them both through a cause-of-death report.

"There are preliminary findings, yes." Tidwell gazed up at her. "I suppose you may as well sit down. I have a few questions."

Theodosia sat. This was the game they played of course. Their own version of cat and mouse. Only sometimes, it was difficult to know who was the cat and who was the mouse.

"The ME's report," Theodosia prompted again.

Tidwell chewed and swallowed. "It appears Miss Drucilla was grabbed from the back and partially strangled. Bruising indicates the intruder put an arm around her neck and a knee in the center of her back. Then he pulled. Hard."

"Grisly. And the syringe?"

"The coup de grâce. Lab rats tell me she was heavily injected with fentanyl. So that might indicate our killer is also a drug user."

"Fentanyl," Theodosia murmured, disliking the sound of the word. "That particular drug's been in the news lately, but I'm not sure I know much about it."

"Fentanyl is heroin's synthetic little cousin. Powerful enough to take down an elephant. Probably even a woolly mammoth if scientists could thaw one. Where thirty milligrams of heroin cause death in a human, only three milligrams of fentanyl are required."

"Wow." Theodosia sat back in her chair. Then, "What about the syringe itself?"

"A single-use disposable syringe."

"Is it traceable?"

"You can buy a bag of one hundred at any pharmacy for twenty dollars," Tidwell said.

"Who uses them?"

"Anyone who administers a subcutaneous injection to themselves. Diabetics, people with rheumatoid arthritis, gym rats using anabolic steroids, whatever."

"Did the lab find prints on the syringe?"

Tidwell took a loud slurp of tea and shook his head. "None. Did you think they would?"

"I suppose not. So the killer wore gloves?"

Tidwell shrugged. "Probably. Now, on the various doorknobs and such, we found entire galaxies of prints." He aimed a sharp look at her. "Yours are undoubtedly among them."

"I'm sure they are," Theodosia said. "But I didn't kill anyone."

"Of course not," Tidwell said. "Still, we're going to spin all the prints through AFIS, see if anything clicks." He focused on her intently. "What we have is a diabolical weasel sneaking into the proverbial henhouse. In this case, a rather expensive henhouse."

"Who have you questioned so far?"

"Obviously the first person we interviewed was Pauline Stauber, the personal assistant. She was basically Miss Drucilla's constant companion. Spent almost ten hours a day with her. Knew her business dealings, friends, her comings and goings."

"And what did you find out from Pauline?"

Tidwell heaved a deep sigh. "Our girl Friday cried nonstop through two separate interviews. It was difficult to elicit even the simplest response without her completely breaking down."

"If she's that upset, it probably means she's innocent."

"Perhaps."

"Who else did you question?"

"We talked to the former housekeeper, Mrs. Fruth. She'd been with Miss Drucilla for almost twenty years."

"Do you suspect her?"

"Not particularly. I was mostly trying to pry loose some ideas." Tidwell popped another bite of scone into his mouth. "Then there's the neighbor Donny Bragg. Aptly named, I'd say. Although once you get past the hale-and-hearty good-old-boy facade, he seems decent enough. For a lawyer, that is."

"Anyone else on your radar?"

"Basically most of the party guests are suspects at this

point, so we're trying to work our way through the guest list. But we're busy. Crime never takes a holiday. We've got missing people, two carjackings, a shooting, and a woman who beaned her husband with a crepe pan. We're waiting to see if the husband recovers consciousness before we file charges." Tidwell cocked an eye at Theodosia. "I do wish a certain detective hadn't decided to take this entire week off to go visiting in the godforsaken tundra."

"Vermont is not the tundra," Theodosia said. "And besides, Riley hasn't seen his parents in ten months."

Riley, Pete Riley, was Theodosia's boyfriend du jour, fellow sailor, food-and-wine compadre, jogging buddy, and one of Detective Tidwell's up-and-coming detectives.

"And besides," she added, "it's Christmas."

Unimpressed, Tidwell let loose a Scrooge-like "Hmph."

Theodosia decided to shift the conversation away from that particular subject.

"What about the faulty alarm?"

"It was faulty," Tidwell said. "We're going through the alarm company's log right now."

"And the painting that was stolen," Theodosia said. "Was it an authentic Renoir?"

"Apparently it was." Tidwell started working his way through his second scone.

Theodosia knew that the theft of a genuine Renoir constituted a serious art heist. Though high-end-art thievery wasn't exactly commonplace, when it did happen, there were often deadly consequences. Case in point: last night.

"Wait," she said. "How do you *know* it was a genuine Renoir? I mean, Donald Trump claims to have one hanging in his airplane."

"Pauline Stauber pulled the paperwork and I already spoke to the art consultant who arranged the sale."

"Who was that?"

"An art dealer over on Broad Street named Wolf-Knapp."

"That's his name? Wolf Knapp?"

"Last name. It's hyphenated. First name is Julian."

"And this Wolf-Knapp guy sold the Renoir to Miss Drucilla?"

"I don't understand the ins and outs of the art market, but Wolf-Knapp claims he facilitated the sale. In his words, he 'located an appropriate painting' for her," Tidwell said.

"Do you have any reason to doubt him or believe he was involved?"

"Not at this point," Tidwell said. He took a sip of tea, set his teacup down with a tiny *clink*, and said, "You weren't aware of anyone who shouldn't have been there last night?"

"Not really. I knew very few of the guests. They weren't exactly"—Theodosia was about to say *in my circle*; instead she settled for—"close friends. But if you care to share the guest list with me, I could probably make a few inquiries, ask around."

"That won't be necessary," Tidwell said. He stuffed the last bit of scone in his mouth, washed it down with a sip of tea, and stood. "Best not to get too involved."

"Right," Theodosia said, even though the image of Miss Drucilla's limp, dead body was forever seared into her memory.

4

Lunch was shaping up to be just as busy as morning tea had been. Drayton was answering the phone every five minutes, jotting down reservation requests as well as orders for take-out. Theodosia knew there'd be a few drop-ins as well. There always were. So it was time to make with the magic again, whisking away dirty dishes, resetting the tables, and dashing in to check the menu with Haley.

"Haley, it smells wonderful in here!" Theodosia exclaimed as she squeezed her way into the kitchen. Between the butcher-block table, the industrial-sized range and oven, the cooler, and the dishwasher, there was barely room for the elfinlike Haley.

"That's because I'm making she-crab soup," Haley said with a grin. "That nice pungent seafood aroma kind of perfumes the air, doesn't it?"

Haley Parker was a kitchen martinet in the body of a twentysomething young woman. Besides being smart and innovative, she was tough as nails. Greengrocers feared

Haley, lest she reject any wilted lettuce they attempted to foist upon her. Fishmongers gave her grudging respect. And the sellers at the farmers market loved her because she respected their commitment to farm-to-table produce.

Theodosia didn't know what she'd do without Haley, because the girl was a true gem. Haley's skill sets included baking, cooking, putting together imaginative menus, and creating adorable fondant cakes in the shape of teapots, glass slippers, castles, and even colorful fish.

"What else have you got for us," Theodosia asked, "besides your delicious she-crab soup?"

Haley ticked off the rest of the menu on her fingers. "Two kinds of tea sandwiches today. Chicken salad on pumpkin bread and smoked turkey with Gouda cheese on rye bread. Then we've got red pepper quiche and citrus salad. Of course we still have a few cream scones and strawberry muffins left over from this morning and I've got two pans of sultana raisin scones baking in the oven."

"You're on top of things as usual, Haley," Theodosia said.

Haley grabbed an oven mitt, peeked into her industrial-sized oven, and cried, "Yes!" After pulling out a pan of golden brown quiche, she set it on the top of the stove.

"I need to stay a step or two ahead of things," Haley said. "This is a super-busy week no matter what Drayton seems to think."

"He knows we're crazy busy, and he's well aware of how hard you work. He loves you, you know. So do I. You're family."

Theodosia's basic philosophy was you always took care of family. And because she didn't have a large extended family (she had only an aunt and uncle), Drayton and Haley had become her surrogate family.

"Thanks. That means a lot to me. But I think Drayton's still emotionally overwrought because of last night," Haley said.

"I know he is."

"The thing about Drayton is, he takes things hard, but

then he tries to stuff his true feelings down his throat and put on a stoic face."

"Crusty on the outside, sweet on the inside," Theodosia said.

Haley nodded. "Kind of like my French meringues."

Lunch was busy, exciting, and exceedingly crowded. Extra chairs needed to be brought in, and for five minutes, a gang of six had to cluster in the entryway before Theodosia could clear a table for them. But it worked out (somehow it always did), and now Theodosia and Drayton found themselves (as Drayton so aptly phrased it) on the far side of lunch.

Drayton poured them each a well-deserved cup of Lady London Ceylon tea. Then he held up his teacup to toast with Theodosia, and said, "Once again, my dear, we nailed it."

"Always do," Theodosia said.

He gave a semicontented smile. "Even when we have a frantic, gnash-my-teeth week, I can't imagine doing anything else."

"You'd never want to go back to teaching again?" Drayton had once taught culinary classes at Charleston's prestigious Johnson & Wales University.

"And give up my post here as tea sommelier? Never!"

But it wasn't all unicorns and roses. Because five minutes later, Pauline Stauber came stumbling through the front door, barely able to hold back tears.

"Pauline!" Theodosia exclaimed. "What's wrong?" She didn't really know Pauline all that well. Enough to say hello to her on the street and, of course, from last night. But Theodosia knew enough to recognize when a person was in extreme distress.

Drayton grabbed a tissue from a box and thrust it in Pauline's direction.

Pauline grabbed the tissue, wiped her eyes, and said,

"That detective . . . the chubby one who swaggered in last night and tried to browbeat everybody?"

"You mean Detective Tidwell?" Theodosia asked.

Pauline bobbed her head. "Exactly. He's being needlessly aggressive and terribly mean."

Drayton made a disapproving sound in the back of his throat as Theodosia put an arm around Pauline's shoulder and led her to a nearby table. Got her to sit down.

"Mean to you?" Theodosia sat down next to Pauline and took her hand.

Pauline's chin quivered. "To *everyone*."

"Tidwell's manner is often blunt and brusque," Theodosia explained. "Believe me, I should know. His temper's been directed at me more than once. But please don't be put off by his demeanor. On the plus side, Tidwell is a stickler for getting the job done. He heads the Robbery-Homicide Division and once worked for the FBI. His close rate is nothing short of amazing."

"That's some consolation, I guess, but it's not why I'm here."

"Then what can I do for you?" Theodosia asked as she released Pauline's hand and signaled for Drayton to hurry over with a pot of tea.

Pauline folded her tissue and dabbed at her eyes. "I'm here because Delaine said you might be able to help me."

"Help you . . . how?" Theodosia asked.

"Figure out who killed Miss Drucilla?" Pauline said, her voice rising, then cracking. More tears leaked out and then she fought to get her emotions in check. "Here's the thing. Delaine Dish gave me a super pep talk about you. Told you were Charleston's own Miss Marple. That you were smart and totally unafraid to dig around and ask tough questions."

"That's generally what the police do."

Pauline gave a sad smile. "That's exactly what Delaine predicted you'd say. But she warned me not to give up so easily, told me I shouldn't take no for an answer. She said you've solved a couple of actual cases. *Murder* cases."

"Helped solve," Theodosia said. "There's a difference." Drayton set a pot of tea along with cups and saucers on the table, then quietly retreated.

"The thing is, you were there last night. You were the one who found Miss Drucilla," Pauline said.

Theodosia nodded as she poured a cup of tea for Pauline. "I did."

Pauline's brows pinched together. "Then maybe you *saw* someone or something going on? By that, I mean something out of the ordinary?"

"The only strange thing was when the security alarm went off a second time."

"That *was* strange," Pauline said.

"Miss Drucilla said it had been happening a lot lately."

"I guess maybe it had, but I didn't think much about it." Pauline reached out and put a hand on Theodosia's arm. Tears streamed down her face. "Please, I really need your help."

"Oh dear."

"Miss Drucilla doesn't really have anyone, you know," Pauline said.

Her words stabbed at Theodosia's heart. "What do you mean, no family at all?"

"There's supposedly a nephew somewhere, but I've never met him. I wouldn't even know how to get hold of him," Pauline stammered out. She sighed, then finally managed to take a sip of tea. "So it's just me and a handful of friends to . . . to honor her final requests."

The knowledge that Miss Drucilla had no immediate family saddened Theodosia immensely. Made the woman's untimely murder feel all the more tragic and poignant.

"Tell me what's going on right now," Theodosia said finally. It wouldn't hurt to stay informed, would it?

"Obviously a police investigation is underway," Pauline said. "Lord knows where that will lead or how long it'll take.

And then, once the lawyers deal with the estate, I suppose Miss Drucilla's properties will eventually be put up for sale."

"There are multiple properties?"

"Besides the big house on Legare, Miss Drucilla also owns a condo in Hilton Head. But she hardly ever used it."

"Okay."

Theodosia could feel herself being gradually pulled in, because it was, after all, a situation that was hard to resist. An elderly woman murdered. A lifetime spent as a kind and generous donor to countless charities. Missing diamond rings. A stolen Renoir. She smiled to herself. It *was* kind of Miss Marpley after all.

"Tell me about the painting. The Renoir."

Pauline shook her head. "I don't know much about it. Just that it was stolen."

"Do you think the killer took it?"

"I'm guessing he grabbed it right after he killed poor Miss Drucilla and ripped the diamond rings off her fingers." Pauline's voice was bitter, angry.

Theodosia remembered Tidwell's words from earlier this morning. "And Miss Drucilla worked with an art consultant?"

Pauline gave a desultory shrug.

"Someone named Julian Wolf-Knapp?"

"The police made me go through all her papers and that's the name we found, yes." Pauline pulled a clean hankie out of her purse and dabbed at her eyes some more.

"Is there anyone, anyone at all, who's a friend or even an acquaintance of Miss Drucilla's that's, um . . . even remotely suspicious?" Theodosia asked. After all, she had to start somewhere.

"You're asking me to name names?" Pauline asked. She seemed startled.

"No, nothing like that. Maybe just someone who was overly friendly or eager to be around her. Or just slightly quirky?"

"Well . . ." Pauline licked her lips nervously. She looked like she wanted to say something, but was afraid to.

"Okay, let's make this simple. Why don't you start by telling me about Smokey?" Theodosia said.

"Smokey's just a guy who does odd jobs around the neighborhood. I wouldn't exactly call him mentally impaired or anything like that, but he does seem a little slow."

"But as a handyman, Smokey's fairly adept at fixing things?"

"Oh absolutely. He unplugged Miss Drucilla's kitchen sink and installed a new garbage disposal."

"So not that slow," Theodosia said.

"I guess not."

"What else can you tell me about Smokey?"

"I don't know. One time Smokey rented one of those big heavy machines and polished all the wood floors. And once he helped Miss Drucilla hang a couple of paintings."

"He hung her paintings," Theodosia said in a neutral tone.

Pauline blinked rapidly, then did a kind of double take. "Oh wow. Wow, do you think that *means* something? That maybe Smokey saw a painting he liked and decided to grab it?"

"No idea." *But it might be a place to start.*

The expression on Pauline's face brightened considerably. "Delaine told me that you were the sharpest tack in the box. That's how she described you. And now I can see why. She also said that if anyone could figure out who killed Miss Drucilla, it would be you."

Theodosia leaned back in her chair and thought for a few moments.

Or maybe you killed Miss Drucilla and you're trying to throw Smokey under the bus. Maybe you were angry at her. Or jealous. Or hated your job. Or . . . maybe not.

Theodosia didn't *really* believe that Pauline was a killer and an art thief. But if she was going to look into Miss Drucilla's murder, she'd have to poke around and explore every single angle.

"I must say I'm interested in this murder case. There *are* some unusual twists and turns."

Pauline was nodding now. "Because of the stolen rings and painting."

"And the money."

Pauline shook her head, looked a little puzzled. "I'm not sure what you mean."

"Miss Drucilla had a will, I believe."

"I'm positive she did. She was very precise that way, very businesslike."

"So someone stands to benefit," Theodosia said.

"Benefit?"

Theodosia didn't think Pauline was quite that obtuse. In fact, she wondered if Pauline was deliberately misunderstanding her. So she decided to be absolutely clear.

"I mean to say that someone will benefit greatly from Miss Drucilla's death."

Pauline pulled her lips into a perfect circle. "Oh. Now I see what you mean."

"If Miss Drucilla was in the process of awarding several endowments to various charities, she must have had any number of people flocking around her, correct?"

"Lately there were quite a few. Friends and acquaintances," Pauline said.

"Such as?"

"Well, she was friendly with Donny Bragg."

"The neighbor. The one who lets Smokey live in his carriage house," Theodosia said. "What about Bragg?"

"He's always struck me as a little . . . too slick."

"Okay. Who else?"

"There's another man who helped out as a kind of independent financial review board. He owns a company called Doing the Good."

"And who is this person?"

"Um . . . his name is Sawyer Daniels."

"And he reviews charities?" Theodosia asked. She'd never heard of him or his company.

"Mr. Daniels's company runs analytics on area charities.

They look at how much money a charity is able to raise, then weigh that amount against what the charity actually spends to help people. You know, is the good that they do significantly more than what they spend on fund-raising and administration, that sort of thing."

"That actually sounds quite smart," Theodosia said.

"I think so, too."

"Who else?"

"Well, Miss Drucilla had a housekeeper, Evelyn Fruth. But she's in her sixties and was hardly ever there."

"Okay, and how many guests were there last night?"

"Maybe . . . thirty-six?" Pauline said.

"Could I get a look at your guest list?" *Because Detective Tidwell didn't care to share it with me.*

"I'll make a copy so you can have it right away. Maybe you could even pick it up tonight?"

Theodosia's brain was spinning with ideas. "Tonight . . . sure. I can do that."

"I'll be working late at Miss Drucilla's place, so you could drop by anytime." Pauline fidgeted with the handle of her teacup. "There are so many things I have to deal with."

"I'm sure there are," Theodosia said.

"The police want to see all sorts of personal papers and bank records. I'm struggling to connect all the dots. After last night it feels like my entire world fell apart," Pauline said.

"Probably because it did."

"I don't know what I'm going to do now." Pauline leaned back in her chair and went a little limp. "I mean, for a living. Wade—that's my boyfriend—says I should hang tough, help the police as much as possible, and try to tie up any loose ends for Miss Drucilla. He's got a good job at a gift shop, so at least we can pay the rent. Anyway, Wade says I need to let some time go by before I figure out my next move."

"That sounds like smart advice."

5

❦

"*What was that* all about?" Drayton asked once Pauline had left. "Besides tears and tea?"

"Take a wild guess," Theodosia said.

"She wants you to look into Miss Drucilla's murder?"

"Bingo."

"But you don't even know this Pauline person. First time you'd ever really talked to her was last night."

"I know, but Delaine had the good grace to sic her on me," Theodosia said.

"Because you were there. As a witness. How convenient."

Theodosia gave Drayton a quick tap on the shoulder. "You were there, too, my friend."

"Yes, but I wasn't born with that nagging-curiosity gene like you were." He picked up a tin of tea, squinted at the label, and set it down. "I don't plan to get involved."

"How can you say that, Drayton, when you're already involved? In fact, you're somewhat acquainted with Donny Bragg. Am I right?"

"I spoke to him last night, but only for a few minutes."

"That's close enough for jazz. In fact, what I'd like you to do is call Bragg and set up a casual meeting for tonight."

"A meeting about . . . ?"

"Tell him we'd like an introduction to Smokey, since Smokey lives in his carriage house."

Drayton looked hesitant. "I'd feel awkward doing that."

"Of course, because it's an awkward situation, a horrible situation. A woman was murdered."

Drayton fingered his plaid bow tie nervously. "But you still want me to call?"

"If you would, please."

While Theodosia waited on tables, serving her afternoon customers, she thought about Pauline's request. And decided, *Why not look into things?* After all, wasn't she more than a little curious? Hadn't Miss Drucilla's murder taken place practically under her nose? And really, the killer could have been anyone who was at the party last night. A woman with a syringe concealed inside her beaded bag, a man with a syringe secreted in his jacket pocket. Someone clever and disciplined who'd waited, watched, and then made their move.

But wait. Where had the painting disappeared to? Had it been stashed somewhere? Or had the killer escaped with it? Did that mean there'd been one less guest at the end of the evening? All good questions.

"Hello, hello!" a cheery voice called out.

Theodosia glanced up to find Delaine Dish steaming toward her. Today Delaine was dressed in a tight-fitting wine-colored velvet jacket with braid trim on the sleeves and a jeweled stickpin in the lapel. It topped a high-necked white blouse and slim black slacks. Her hair was pulled back in a tiny ponytail and she wore a jaunty hat with a feather. She was dressed, Theodosia decided, as if she were auditioning for a part in *The Count of Monte Cristo.*

"Delaine," Theodosia said.

Delaine's eyes went suddenly round as she conjured up

faux excitement. "Wasn't that *horrible* last night?" she asked. "Wasn't it the absolute *worst* thing you've ever seen? Didn't you just have *terrible* nightmares!" Delaine loved superlatives and exclamation points. Whether she was talking about a vicious murder or a newborn puppy, her delivery was generally laced with the same over-the-top enthusiasm.

Theodosia squinted at Delaine. "You told Pauline to come and see me."

"And did she?" Delaine asked, her excitement suddenly replaced by a crooked knowing grin.

"Not only did Pauline stop by. She practically begged me to investigate Miss Drucilla's murder. You apparently told her that I was the second coming of Sherlock Holmes."

"I never said *that* exactly. But I might have called you Charleston's very own Miss Marple."

"Same thing."

"Poor Pauline, I hope she was able to rope you in," Delaine said as she walked to the closest table and plopped herself down in a chair.

Theodosia followed suit. "Well, she did. Sort of. I agreed to look into things, talk to a few people, but nothing else. The police are the ones who need to lead the charge on this since it's so high profile." She stared at Delaine. "And, Delaine, you do know this is my busy week—heck, it's probably *everybody's* busy week. So why point Pauline in my direction?"

Looking flustered, Delaine tapped her burgundy polished nails on the table and said, "Because I'm still so upset about last night. There I was, having a *lovely* conversation with Majel Mercer—she's executive director of the Justice Initiative, you know—and suddenly, we heard all that awful screaming."

"Well, it was pretty horrible. People were terrified when they saw Miss Drucilla just lying there."

Delaine touched a hand to her heart. "When I saw what had happened, I almost fainted dead away. I have very delicate sensibilities, you know."

Theodosia turned her head to hide a wry smile. Delaine had the sensibilities of a storm trooper. She was the most overbearing, controlling, gossipy person Theodosia had ever met. But perhaps this was not the best time to throw those particular character flaws back in Delaine's face.

Instead, Theodosia said, "You were Miss Drucilla's guest last night. I wouldn't have figured you were in her circle." After all, Delaine wasn't exactly a dear friend or a needy charity. And then there was Delaine's ditzy quotient.

"Miss Drucilla was one of my very best customers at Cotton Duck!" Delaine exclaimed, then added a bit coyly, "It's always good to have a socialite client."

Theodosia regarded Delaine with slightly lowered eyelids. "So that explains the coral caftan?"

"A designer piece from my boutique, yes. Beaded mulberry silk, don't you know?" Delaine glanced at her dinging phone, muttered, "Pest." Then, "That one I can deal with later."

Theodosia didn't know much about mulberry silk, but that didn't stop her from asking Delaine a few more questions.

"So you weren't there on behalf of one of your favorite charities," Theodosia said.

"I wasn't fishing around for some of Miss Drucilla's money, if that's what you're getting at. Though one of my fave charities, the Loving Paws Animal Shelter, is probably in line for some of her grant money. Now I doubt that we'll ever—"

WHAP! WHUMP!

The front door suddenly blew open; then a dazzling bright light flashed on and flooded the interior of the tea shop. A woman's voice shouted, "Ready? Let's do it!"

"Oh no," Theodosia groaned. She registered what was happening as her mind bonked into hyperdrive. Then a TV camera crew rushed toward her like a herd of stampeding buffalo. The cameraman had a sleek silver camera balanced on his right shoulder with the red light blazing, signaling that the camera was live and recording. A flunky in a khaki vest kept pace beside him, carrying a boom microphone. And leading the charge was Monica Garber, an on-air personality who specialized in sensational stories and exposés for Channel Eight's six o'clock news.

Theodosia turned to warn Drayton just as she saw him turn tail and run for her office. Haley peeped out of the kitchen, then ducked back in. Delaine, on the other hand, looked utterly delighted.

"Ooh!" Delaine cried in a breathy voice. "It's the TV people." She foraged inside her Chanel handbag for lipstick, applied it hastily, and flashed her best camera-ready smile.

Monica Garber lunged toward them, looking pin thin in a hot pink skirt suit and four-inch black stiletto heels. Garber had predatory dark eyes, a pointed chin, and black hair that was scraped back mercilessly into a tight chignon. Theodosia figured the supertight hairdo must have pulled up every muscle in her face and saved her a fortune on Botox. In fact, Theodosia was vaguely amused by the whole spectacle until Garber completely crashed into her personal space and stuck a microphone a quarter inch from her lips.

With breathy, TV-manufactured excitement, Garber said, "Tell us what it was like to witness a murder victim draw her very last breath."

Theodosia recoiled instantly. "Excuse me?" *Did she really just ask me that impertinent question?*

"I want to know . . . our viewers want to know . . . what it felt like to stare a dying woman in the face?" Garber asked.

"Please leave," Theodosia said. She said it quietly, without any undue anger or ferocity.

Garber frowned at first, then reared back as if she'd been slapped. "What'd you say?"

Delaine raised a hand. "Excuse me, but *I* was there last night. *I* saw what happened."

Garber ignored Delaine, focusing all her collective energy on Theodosia. "*What* did you say?" she asked again.

Theodosia smiled mildly. "I asked you to leave."

"Wha . . . buh . . . I don't understand." Garber was suddenly a study in abject confusion. Her eyes bulged and her mouth pulled into an unhappy tight line. Apparently she wasn't used to being denied an interview.

"I have nothing to say to you," Theodosia said. She remained polite but firm.

"But this is an important story. And . . . and . . . *everybody* wants to be on TV!" Garber shrilled. She threw a fierce look at her cameraman. "Don't they?"

The cameraman, a shaggy-haired twentysomething in a brown leather jacket, just shrugged. He was getting paid either way, interview or not.

"I'm sorry, but I'm not interested in speaking on camera," Theodosia said. She continued to keep her voice at an even level, even though she wanted to scream and boot the woman all the way down Church Street. "Thank you for your interest, but I'm afraid you do need to leave."

"What if it's just you and me?" Garber pressed. "A closed interview. One on one?"

Theodosia shook her head. "Not happening."

"You're not thinking this through," Garber spit out. "Don't you realize that media attention can highlight a tough case and often help break it wide open!"

But Theodosia had already gotten up and walked away.

"C'mon," the cameraman said to Garber, dropping his camera from his shoulder. "There's nothin' here."

Theodosia watched as the film crew retreated outside, with Delaine trailing after them, hopping up and down, still hoping to be interviewed. Then she drew the blue toile curtains closed and locked the front door.

It was only when the coast was clear that Drayton crept out of hiding.

"Are they gone?" Drayton ducked his head, adjusting his bow tie and looking a trifle sheepish.

"Ding-dong, the witch is dead," Theodosia said. "I doubt Ms. Garber will be coming back anytime soon."

"What did they want?" Haley asked as she edged her way

out of the kitchen. She'd kept a low profile, too. Really, a no profile.

Theodosia sighed. "What do TV people ever want? They want you to cry, threaten, and lose your cool right on camera. They want you to *emote* and make for exciting television so the station can get better ratings and charge advertisers a premium rate for commercial time. And then, when it's all said and done and the footage is on the air, the TV people want you to buy the drinks."

"Huh," Haley said. "You know this from experience?"

"I worked in advertising, remember? I used to produce TV commercials, write press releases, and buy media time."

"Oh yeah," Haley said.

"But you kicked her out," Drayton said. He seemed awed by Theodosia's aloof, take-charge manner.

"I didn't have much choice," Theodosia said. "It would have ended badly."

"It did end badly for Monica Garber," Haley chuckled.

"Which is why I'm impressed," Drayton said. "It's difficult to manhandle the media."

"Please," Theodosia said as she waved a hand. "It was nothing."

"No, it *was* something," Drayton said. "And by the way, I made that call to Donny Bragg"—he cocked a thumb and pointed back toward Theodosia's office—"while I was hiding out."

"Thank you," Theodosia said. "So we're set for tonight?"

"Eight o'clock," Drayton said. Then he gazed at Theodosia again and said, "I *really* have to hand it to you. You kept your cool and never lost your temper."

"Oh no," Theodosia said. "I lost my temper all right. I just didn't show it."

6

Some of Theodosia's friends ribbed her about driving a Jeep Compass. But Theodosia loved her four-wheel-drive, perched-high-above-the-crowd mode of transportation. In fact, this was her second Jeep, after owning a couple of white-bread sedans. A Jeep was the perfect vehicle for taking her off road and into the fields of the low country so she could pick lemongrass, passionflower, and red clover for homemade tea. To say nothing about four-wheeling through overgrown fields where she pulled tangles of grapevines down from trees and twisted them into decorative wreaths for sale in her tea shop. And then there was the issue of transporting all her sailing gear over to the marina.

Right now Theodosia was parked at the curb outside Drayton's house, watching him exit his side door and pick his way down a narrow cobblestone walk.

"Perfect timing," Drayton said as he clambered in. "I just finished taking Honey Bee out for our nightly stroll." Honey Bee was Drayton's Cavalier King Charles Spaniel and, in

Theodosia's opinion, a dog that had basically struck gold and won the lottery. After all, how many rescue dogs lived in a historic home surrounded by antiques, handcrafted furniture, and a carefully curated library? No others that she could think of.

Theodosia drove down Tradd Street, then turned on Legare. There were lots of big mansions here in these rarefied few blocks, where old money mingled uneasily with Charleston's nouveau riche.

"So the plan tonight is to interview this Smokey character?" Drayton asked.

"First we're going to talk to Donny Bragg," Theodosia said.

"You view him as a suspect, too?"

"I think everybody's a suspect at this point."

In Charleston, if you'd acquired a fine veneer of success, it meant you were either a banker, a lawyer, or a politician. Donny Bragg was a lawyer, a senior partner at Deutsch, Hamilton, and Bragg. To go along with his vaunted status, he'd acquired a three-story Georgian-style redbrick mansion on Legare Street. It boasted graceful columns, a hipped roof, and squared-off chimneys at either end. Tonight, lights blazed from almost every window.

Bragg met Theodosia and Drayton at the front door and welcomed them into an expansive parlor that had a sexy silver-gray S-curved sofa and four matching club chairs done in shantung silk. Oil paintings crowded the walls and Theodosia could see into the wood-paneled dining room, where more paintings were hung.

He's an art collector, she thought. *How interesting.*

Two minutes into their conversation, Theodosia also decided that Bragg was well named, just as Tidwell had insinuated. Bragg expounded on his law firm and his recent trip to a five-star resort in Thailand, and he even bragged about his golfing at Turtle Point on Kiawah Island. All things considered, Bragg's name was practically occuponymous (if that was an actual word).

"And you're also an art collector," Theodosia said, the artwork being the proverbial elephant in the room.

"I dabble some. Don't really know enough about art to be serious," Bragg said.

Drayton stepped toward a painting and studied it carefully. "This landscape by Alfred Hutty looks fairly serious to me."

Bragg gazed at the painting as if he'd never noticed it before. "Yeah, I guess."

"Wait a minute." Drayton turned back and stared at Bragg. From his expression, the wheels were turning, cranking out some vital bits of information. "Now I remember you. Timothy Neville introduced us at a Vivaldi concert last September." Timothy was the executive director of the Heritage Society and one of Drayton's dear friends.

"Oh?" Bragg said with very little enthusiasm.

Drayton snapped his fingers. "Of course. You sit on the board of directors at the Gibbes Museum!"

This was a major news flash for Theodosia. "He does?" she said to Drayton. Then her head spun to look at Bragg. "You do?" The Gibbes Museum was Charleston's major repository of fine art. A Beaux Arts building on Meeting Street that offered numerous galleries as well as artist's studios, lecture spaces, and a lovely little café that served terrific French onion soup.

"I'm mostly there as a lark," Bragg said, obviously trying to downplay his involvement.

But if Bragg was on the board, maybe even involved in okaying the acquisition of major pieces of art, Theodosia wasn't about to let him off the hook quite so easily.

"I'm well acquainted with several curators at the Gibbes Museum, and according to them, it's a serious undertaking," she said. "I understand their annual operating budget hovers around two-and-a-half-million dollars."

"I suppose," Bragg muttered.

Theodosia gazed at Bragg, her curiosity growing. Could he have stolen the Renoir? Could he have seen it, coveted it, and simply taken it? And, in the process, murdered Miss Drucilla? From his snobby, snotty viewpoint, could he have seen her only as collateral damage? She supposed it could have happened that way.

"Why are you peppering me with all these questions?" Bragg asked, his feathers clearly ruffled.

"I'm just sniffing around," Theodosia said, trying to sound casual. "Mostly because Pauline asked me to look into things."

"Oh, *that* woman," Bragg said. His tone was gruff, dripping with condescension.

"What's the problem?" Theodosia asked. "You two don't get along?" Did Donny Bragg have a bone to pick with Pauline Stauber?

"I'm not usually a guy who tells tales out of school, but Pauline has a gambling addiction like you wouldn't believe," Bragg said.

"You're serious?" Drayton said. "Pauline seems so sweet and mild mannered and, well, normal."

"Hah. Get her in a game of five-card stud and she'll pick you clean," Bragg said. "That's if she doesn't bet the house and lose it all." He rolled back on his heels and favored them with a wolfish grin.

"You're sure about this?" Theodosia asked.

"Positive," Bragg said.

"If Pauline was gambling to the extent that you imply, do you think Miss Drucilla was aware of it?" Theodosia asked.

Bragg snorted. "Doubtful. Then again, Miss Drucilla always looked for the good in people."

"And usually found it," Drayton said.

"Another question," Theodosia said, "before we talk to Smokey."

"What now?" Bragg asked. He glanced at his watch as if he had somewhere important to be.

"If Pauline's a gambler, as you say, do you think she might be having financial difficulties?" Theodosia asked.

Bragg was already bobbing his head. "You're talking about gambling debts? I'm guessing Pauline Stauber never saw a line of credit she didn't try to stretch to the max." He shrugged, suddenly bored with the subject. "Anyhoo. Good old Pauline's out of a job now, isn't she? So why don't we shut this down and move along to your big confab with Smokey? I'm guessing you think he could be a legitimate suspect, huh?"

"Do you think he could be?" Drayton asked.

"Don't know. Don't think so," Bragg said. "But you people are the ones playing amateur detective and asking all the questions."

Bragg led them through his house and out the back door onto a patio. He huffed along in front of them, taking them along a redbrick path through a garden rampant with azaleas, magnolias, and mature fruit trees. It was full-on dark, but low yellow lights lit the way, which eventually led to his carriage house.

"This is a lovely old place," Drayton said when they stopped in front of the carriage house. It was a redbrick building decorated with wrought iron curlicues that snugged up to a narrow shared alley. An old-fashioned brass lamp on a post spilled enough light to illuminate the area.

"Hard to navigate back here with a large vehicle though," Bragg said. "This alley's narrow, one way in, one way out, built back when people had horse-drawn carriages. Not very convenient when you drive a Range Rover."

Drayton directed his gaze to the second floor. "Looks like a good-sized apartment up there though."

"It's not bad. As you can see, this lower level houses a

two-car garage. Then upstairs is a storage area as well as Smokey's apartment."

"You think he's home?" Theodosia asked.

"I know he is." Bragg grabbed the railing, took a deep breath, and started to climb the narrow flight of wooden steps. Halfway up, he stopped to catch his breath, then continued on until all three of them were crowded onto the small landing at the top. Light shone through a screen door and the interior door stood open even though it was a cool evening. Bragg knocked and the screen door rattled in its frame.

"Yello?" Smokey called out.

"Smoke?" Bragg said. "Couple people here want to talk to you."

"What about?" Smokey asked.

Theodosia moved around Bragg and put her face to the screen. "Smokey? I'm Theodosia Browning. I own the Indigo Tea Shop over on Church Street?"

"Yup, know where it's at," came a rumbling voice.

"I was a friend of Miss Drucilla's. Can I come in for a couple of minutes?"

"Miss Drucilla's dead," Smokey said.

"I know and I'm very sad about that. I also know you were a friend of hers. Helped out around her house." Theodosia paused.

Ten seconds went by and then the screen door opened.

"Come on in," Smokey said. He peered at Drayton. "You, too."

"I'll see you folks later," Bragg said as he turned and clomped back down the stairs.

Smokey was tall, with wide shoulders and slender hips, built like a cowboy. He dressed like one, too, in jeans, a faded plaid shirt, and boots. His shirtsleeves were rolled up to his elbows, revealing ropy muscles and a few tribal-looking tattoos. He'd probably just finished dinner since the place smelled like burgers and onions and cigarettes.

"What can I do for you?" Smokey asked. He'd taken a seat in a rocking chair while Theodosia and Drayton crowded together on a small lumpy sofa. The apartment was plain and utilitarian, the decor on the walls a poster from Darlington Raceway and two paintings. There was a small galley kitchen with a two-person dinette table and a doorway that led to what was probably the bedroom and bath.

"Well, you know about Miss Drucilla," Theodosia said.

"Yeah. Somebody killed her." Smokey pulled a cigarette out of a pack he had in his shirt pocket and lit it. Blew out a plume of smoke. "That what you're here for?"

"Pretty much," Theodosia said.

"We're asking all the neighbors if they saw or heard anything," Drayton said.

"Like what?" Smokey asked.

"Like a stranger lurking around last night. Or someone running away from Miss Drucilla's place," Theodosia said.

"Nope. Wish I could help," Smokey said. Clearly, he was a man of few words.

"Maybe you *can* help," Theodosia said. "Were you working at Miss Drucilla's place yesterday? Maybe helping her get ready for the big Christmas party?"

"Yesterday I was over at the Simmons place, replacing a chunk of their back fence. They got a new Jack Russell terrier—a puppy really—and are worried about the little guy getting out of the yard and running away."

"So you didn't see anybody who might have been acting strangely or casing nearby houses?"

Smokey shook his head. "Nope. But if I see anything like that in the future, I should . . . what? Let you know?"

"Probably call the police," Theodosia said.

"Mm-hmm," Smokey said.

Theodosia and Drayton thanked Smokey, then trooped back downstairs to find Donny Bragg lounging on his back patio, wearing a rust-colored barn jacket and smoking a cigar.

"Cohiba cigars," he said when he saw them. "Got a friend in Miami who's a broker for high-end yachts. Every once in a while he bops over to Havana and brings back the good stuff."

"Lucky you," Drayton said.

"How'd your talk with Smokey go?" Bragg asked.

Theodosia gave a shrug. "Fine. He was cooperative."

"But you're not ready to drop him from your suspect list?" Bragg asked. He sounded amused.

"Probably too early for that since we're just getting started," Theodosia said.

"Smokey's an okay guy, but he's dumb as a sack full of hammers," Bragg said.

Maybe not that dumb, Theodosia thought, *since Smokey's clearly mastered the art of playing it close to the vest.*

"Is there anyone you think deserves to be looked at?" Theodosia asked. *Besides yourself?*

"You talk to the housekeeper yet? Mrs. Fruth? She's retired but she might know something."

"We're working our way around to her," Theodosia said. "Anybody else you can think of?"

Bragg leaned back in his chair and half closed his eyes, as if he were deep in thought. Then his eyes snapped open.

"Well, there's a nephew. Miss Drucilla has a nephew somewhere."

"Pauline mentioned him to me. But said she didn't know how to get hold of him."

Bragg made a *whatever* gesture with a hand and said, "Now that you're asking, I'm not sure I'd trust that scummy Sawyer Daniels. The guy's obsessed with money."

"I thought Daniels ran some kind of charity-review company," Theodosia said, "and that he was helping Miss Drucilla decide exactly where to direct her donations."

Bragg shrugged. "Yeah, he probably was."

"Do you have any idea which charities Mr. Daniels might have been recommending?" Drayton asked.

"Or the amount of the donations?" Theodosia asked.

"Dunno," Bragg said. "No idea. I guess you'd have to corner Daniels and ask him yourself."

"Okay, thanks a lot," Theodosia said.

"Happy to cooperate," Bragg said with an unhappy look.

7

✦

Dark clouds bubbled overhead; a cool breeze wafted in from nearby Charleston Harbor. But as Theodosia and Drayton walked down Legare Street, the glow and good cheer of the Christmas season seemed to be everywhere. Strings of lights outlined the fronts of houses, giant wreaths hung on doors, and shiny brass lamps were swagged with greens, pinecones, and red velvet ribbons. Even some trees and shrubs were festively lit with gold twinkle lights.

"You think Bragg knows something?" Drayton asked as they ambled along. With Miss Drucilla's house only three doors away, it was easier to walk than drive.

"Maybe," Theodosia said. She was still processing the conversations they'd had with Smokey and Bragg, rolling them around in her mind like rocks in a tumbler, trying to polish up any important bits.

"Or do you see Bragg as a suspect?"

"I'm not sure," Theodosia said. "It's all a little foggy. You know, Pauline was the one who kind of nudged me in Bragg's direction. And then Bragg, in what felt like a retaliatory chess-player move, tried to convince us that Pauline was a problem gambler."

"Do you think she really is? A gambler, I mean."

"No idea. But I suppose it bears looking into," Theodosia said, "though my hunch is that the two of them simply don't like each other, that they're at odds for whatever reason."

"What about Smokey?" Drayton asked as they turned up the walk to Miss Drucilla's house. "He's quiet, unobtrusive, obviously knows his way around the neighborhood. Can you see him as a suspect?"

"I'm not sure. He seems okay. So maybe more of a *person of interest* at this point."

They climbed the front steps and hesitated on the wide veranda. Two Christmas trees stood in pots to either side of the door. They'd been lavishly decorated with angels and candy canes, but the string of lights that wound around them hadn't been lit.

"Okay," Theodosia said, peeking in one of the windows. "There are lights on inside, so Pauline's definitely here. We can grab that guest list and ask her a few more questions. Kill two birds with one stone."

When they rang the doorbell they heard a loud BRIIING that echoed all the way to the back of the house. Drayton's mouth twisted in a visceral reaction, the sound obviously reminding him of last night's security alarm.

They heard footsteps; then Pauline peeked out through a triangle of small windowpanes on the front door.

"Being cautious," Drayton murmured.

"Can you blame her?" Theodosia said. "After last night's awful—"

The front door whooshed open.

"Pauline!" Theodosia exclaimed.

"Theodosia," Pauline said. She was smiling. "And it's Drayton. Did I get that right? In all the furor and horror of last night, I don't think we were ever properly introduced."

"Drayton Conneley," he said. "At your service."

Managing a faint smile, Pauline said, "You'd better come in, I suppose."

Pauline opened the door wider and they stepped into a large entry with a white marble floor and cream-colored walls painted with tropical birds and banana leaves. On their left, closed double doors led to the large parlor where last night's festivities had been centered; on their right was a curved stairway. Theodosia snuck a quick look down the center hallway, where Miss Drucilla had met her demise. It was dim with just a single light burning at the far end.

"Maybe we could talk in here?" Pauline opened a hidden door and led them into a small room. It was furnished with a white sofa that had an abundant number of poufy green-and-yellow pillows, a small table, an antique secretary, and two lovely palm trees.

"This is cozy," Theodosia said. This room seemed small and delicate, so vastly different from the rest of the home that had been decorated on such a grand scale.

"This was one of Miss Drucilla's favorite rooms," Pauline said. "She loved to sip her morning tea in here and read the newspapers."

"Lovely," Drayton said. He seemed particularly interested in the small secretary with a slanted front. "Is this by any chance a Biedermeier?" he asked.

"I believe so, though I'm not terribly well versed when it comes to antiques," Pauline said.

"Even though you're surrounded by them," Theodosia said.

"I suppose when you're busy—working here every day, answering phones and such, taking notes, running errands— the decor becomes a little like wallpaper," Pauline said.

Approaching footsteps and a rattle of paper sounded outside the room and caused everyone to turn expectantly. Then a tall, good-looking man materialized and said, "Oh, they're already here."

"You must be the boyfriend," Theodosia said.

That brought a smile to his face. "And you must be the amateur detective," he said.

"Not exactly," Theodosia said. "Well . . . maybe."

Pauline stepped forward to greet him. "This is Wade, Wade Holland. He's been a lifesaver, helping me with packing, cleaning, whatnot." She gripped his arm. "Wade, this is Theodosia Browning, the woman I told you about, and her friend Drayton Conneley."

Once greetings and handshakes had been exchanged, Theodosia said, "Wade, were you by any chance here last night?"

Wade shook his head. "I was still at work, so I missed all the excitement." Then his expression turned sad. "If that's what you'd call it." Wade wore faded blue jeans that matched his wide blue eyes and a T-shirt with a nifty image of a sphinx on it. His light brown hair was fashionably disheveled and he wore black hipster glasses. Theodosia knew he worked at an upscale gift shop but decided he could have probably passed for a bass player in an indie rock band.

"Is that the . . . ?" Pauline asked him.

Wade handed her the paper. "The guest list, yeah. I just finished printing it out."

Pauline gave the paper a cursory glance, then handed it to Theodosia. "Here you go, as promised."

Theodosia skimmed the list, recognized a few names, then passed it to Drayton.

"Are you familiar with most of the people on this list?" Theodosia asked Pauline.

"Really only the neighbors," Pauline said.

"Like Donny Bragg. And Smokey?" Theodosia asked.

"And Darcy and Jordan Fitzgerald from right next door," Pauline said.

"What about Sawyer Daniels, the man who was helping Miss Drucilla select her various charities?"

"I've met him once or twice. Majel Mercer, too," Pauline

said. "Majel's with the Justice Initiative. She's really sweet. In fact, I have some papers for her to pick up."

"Is her charity receiving one of the grants?" Drayton asked.

Pauline lifted a shoulder. "I really don't know. I'm not sure that's all figured out yet. Probably up to the lawyers now."

"Has the housekeeper been here?"

"She was here today. We've been kind of crossing paths and getting in each other's way."

"How long will *you* continue to work here?" Theodosia asked.

Pauline looked glum. "That's kind of up in the air for now. I've been told two or three more weeks. After that . . . who knows?"

"Will you be helping out as well?" Theodosia asked Wade.

"I wish he could," Pauline said quickly.

Wade was shaking his head. "I work full-time as assistant manager at the King's Ransom Gift Shop over on King Street . . . so no, I won't. I can't." He gave Pauline a commiserating look. "I wish I could lend a hand, but it wouldn't be permanent, so it doesn't make any kind of sense to quit my job." He focused on Theodosia now. "But you . . . Pauline told me you'd agreed to run some kind of—What would you call it? Amateur investigation?"

"I'm going to give it a shot," Theodosia said.

"Thank you for that," Pauline said. "I'm grateful you've decided to look into things and talk to a few people."

"I think it's smart to have another pair of eyes on this," Wade said, "besides the police. They're procedural based versus someone who's more . . ." He glanced at Pauline.

"Intuitive," Pauline said. "Delaine told me that Theodosia was very intuitive."

"I hope I am," Theodosia said.

"She is," Drayton said. "Trust me."

"We talked to a couple of people on our way over," Theodosia said. "Donny Bragg and Smokey Pruitt."

"Anything there?" Wade asked. "I've been kind of picking Pauline's brain about potential suspects and . . ." He glanced at Pauline, who jumped in to finish his sentence again.

"And I haven't come up with much of anything," Pauline said. "I just don't know the key players well enough."

"This morning you were nudging me toward Donny Bragg," Theodosia said.

"That was earlier," Pauline said. "But now that I've had time to think, I'm not sure I know anyone who could be so cruel and heartless."

"What can you tell me about Julian Wolf-Knapp?" Theodosia asked.

"Just that he's an art dealer," Pauline said.

"And Miss Drucilla worked with him."

Pauline thought for a moment. "Yes, but on a limited basis. I believe she bought only a piece or two from him."

"But one of the pieces was the Renoir," Drayton said.

Pauline's face suddenly crumpled. "I wish Miss Drucilla had never brought that stupid painting into this house. If she hadn't, she'd still be alive."

Wade's brows pinched together in sympathy; he was clearly feeling Pauline's pain.

"Would there be any paperwork on the Renoir that Theodosia could look at?" Wade asked Pauline.

"Detective Tidwell already asked me about that this morning. So I went through Miss Drucilla's papers and gave him everything I could find."

"That should help," Wade said.

Maybe, Theodosia thought. She hesitated a few seconds, couldn't think of anything else to ask them, then said, "We should probably be going." She gave a perfunctory smile.

"It is getting awfully late," Drayton said, following her lead.

They all walked out into the vestibule, where Pauline said, "Just a minute. I want to show you something."

She threw open the double doors to the large front parlor

and flipped a light switch. Instantly, the room was aglow with Christmas lights and decorations.

"Look at this," Pauline said, her eyes suddenly glistening with tears. "Look at all the Christmas lights, the flocked trees decorated with candy canes and fuzzy red cardinals, all the lovely garland twined with silk ribbon. Now it's all just going to waste. Such a beautiful, special season and nobody will be here to enjoy it."

Theodosia pulled up to her back door and let out a slow breath. *Home. I'm finally home.* It had been a long day and she was starting to feel exhaustion seep in. There was also a certain amount of stress that had been generated in dealing with Donny Bragg (*What a conceited jerk*) as well as Pauline and Wade (*Poor, sad people*).

So here she was, finally, at her small cottage, which had the actual name of Hazelhurst and was tucked in between two much larger homes. Mansions, really, though truth be told she preferred her own cozy place.

Theodosia's home had been built in the Queen Anne style, which meant it fairly oozed character, thanks to the slightly asymmetrical design and rough cedar tiles that replicated a thatched roof. The exterior walls were brick and stucco, and there were an arched door, wooden cross gables, and the blip of a two-story turret. To complete the look, lush curls of ivy meandered up the sides of the house.

Theodosia's heart swelled with pride just looking at her home because she'd truly scrimped and saved to buy it. How many scones had she sold to make the down payment? How many pots of tea did she still ferry to customers to pay the mortgage? It didn't matter. This home belonged to her and so did the Indigo Tea Shop, which was always a labor of love.

She parked in the back alley, walked through her small garden, and opened the back door. As usual, Earl Grey was there to greet her.

"Hello, pup!" Theodosia cried out as Earl Grey threw himself against her, then buried his head in hands that moved gently and lovingly, patting ears, neck, and muzzle. He was a magnificent dog with a faintly dappled coat (she thought of him as a Dalbrador), expressive eyes, and a fine aristocratic muzzle.

"Sorry to be so late," Theodosia told him.

"Rrwwr," said Earl Grey.

"Good idea. Let's go out in the backyard and see what's shakin'."

While Earl Grey snuffled around the magnolias and palm trees, Theodosia checked her tiny fishpond. Yes, the fish were still there, though it was time to move them to Drayton's pond for the winter. He had a spacious backyard filled with bonsai that wore ever-changing coiffures, and a larger, deeper fishpond that also had a bubbler.

The phone started ringing the minute Theodosia and Earl Grey walked through the back door. She grabbed it off the hook in her kitchen and said, "Hello?"

"Sweetheart!" came a rich baritone voice.

"Riley!" Theodosia cried. She was thrilled to hear his voice since they hadn't talked for a couple of days. "How are you? How's the weather in Vermont?"

"Starting to get cold," Riley said. "We had a high of sixteen degrees today, but now the mercury is supposed to plunge and really hit the deep freeze."

"Excuse me, but sixteen degrees is already freezing cold," Theodosia said.

"Not when you're from here."

"Remember, you're talking to a South Carolina native." She listened to his warm laughter and said, "How's the arm?" Riley had been shot in the line of duty some two months ago, right before Halloween.

"Good. Couldn't be better."

"So it still hurts."

"Probably from the cold, yeah."

"Then don't go out in the cold."

"You're probably right." Riley paused. "On a more serious note, I received an interesting phone call today."

Uh-oh.

Riley waited for Theodosia to fill the silence. When she didn't, he said, "From the boss."

"Detective Tidwell misses you, too?" She tried for humor but it didn't work.

"No, but he did enlighten me about the recent Drucilla Heyward case."

"Okay."

"Theodosia. I see you've gotten yourself involved in another murder."

"Since you've been missing in action, I had to fill my time with something challenging," she said.

"And apparently you've done just that, which is why Tidwell asked me to pass on a message."

"Now we're playing telephone."

"Tidwell wants you to back off."

"He always says that."

"Theo-*do*-sia." Riley said her name just the way her father used to say it when he was angry and about to take the car keys away. *Oops.*

"What?" she said, still trying to project innocence.

"You simply cannot get involved in this Drucilla Heyward case."

"It's too late. I'm already involved," Theodosia said. "Besides, Pauline, the woman who was Miss Drucilla's personal assistant, kind of asked me to look into things. Actually, she begged me to."

"That's not what I want to hear," Riley said.

Theodosia took a quick breath and kept going. "I know, but . . . I already talked to a couple of people. A guy named Smokey Pruitt, who does odd jobs around the neighborhood, and a neighbor by the name of Donny Bragg. They're not exactly suspects, more like persons of interest. But I was still wondering if you could run a quick check on them."

"Theo, I'm in Vermont! It's not like I'm at a desk hovering over my computer."

"But you have an Internet connection, right?"

"Yes, but . . ."

"Can't you do that magic law enforcement thing where you access a multitude of different databases?"

"I'm not sure. What exactly are you asking for?"

"It'd be helpful to know if either of these guys has an arrest record or if their prints are on file somewhere. Maybe you could dig into the AFIS or the NCIC, or maybe even the IRS or DEA sites? And there are undoubtedly a few super-secret-covert sources that a private citizen like me doesn't know about."

"If you ask me, you sound fairly well versed," Riley said, and Theodosia could detect a grudging smile in his voice.

"Not like you are."

"Theo, my dear, I fear you have the instincts of a blood-hound."

"Is that good or bad?" she asked.

"It simply is."

"Then I'll take that as a compliment. So. Will you do it? Will you check on these two guys?"

"Let me sleep on it."

Theodosia and Earl Grey went upstairs then for the night. Soon after she'd moved in, Theodosia had converted the small upstairs into one master suite—a combination bedroom, walk-in closet, master bath, and tower reading room. It was decorated, as she liked to say, in Southern-State-of-Mind Glam. That is, Laura Ashley wallpaper, a four-poster bed, and a poufy cream-colored comforter strewn with blue-and-cream toile pillows. Her mother's old-fashioned vanity, with its desk and drawers, large circular mirror, and cushioned stool, took up one wall and was the perfect spot for Theodosia to sit and apply makeup or brush her hair. Sitting atop the vanity were Theodosia's collectibles: a Jo Malone candle, perfume bottles, a leather-covered journal, a ceramic box decorated with two jaguars, and a large white bowl with scalloped edges that held bracelets, cuffs, a strand of pearls, and a few earrings.

Earl Grey settled into his dog bed and rested his head against one of the built-in bolsters. Theodosia picked up a mystery by Susan Wittig Albert, ready to flop into her comfy reading chair in the adjacent tower room and enjoy a couple of chapters. Instead, she put the book back down and grabbed the guest list from her purse. Thinking, wondering, she carried it to her reading chair and sat down. Started looking at the names. Some of them were old Charleston names that she recognized, like Pinckney and Alston and Manigault. Could any of these people be involved in the death of Miss Drucilla? It hardly seemed likely. Of course, there were new names on the list to consider as well, such as Bragg and Daniels. Then there was the list she'd started, which included Julian Wolf-Knapp and Smokey Pruitt. All of these people were unknown, all of them wild cards.

It made for interesting nighttime reading.

8

"I talked to Riley last night and asked him to run checks on Smokey Pruitt and Donny Bragg," Theodosia said to Drayton. It was Tuesday morning and she was standing at the front counter, sipping a cup of English breakfast tea that Drayton had brewed for her. It was Harney & Sons Keemun black tea, not too brisk with a rich aroma.

"Riley is willing to help out?" Drayton asked. "Lend his expertise?"

"I *think* so, though he wasn't exactly overjoyed by my request."

"I wonder why." Drayton furrowed his brows and favored her with a stern gaze. Then, because he was a confirmed worrywart and clock-watcher, he glanced at his watch and said, "You realize we've got less than twenty minutes before we throw open our doors."

"I know. I've still got to—"

KNOCK. KNOCK.

"You hear that? Someone's tippy-tapping at our front door already," Drayton said.

But Theodosia was skipping to the door with a good idea of who it might be. Then, when she peered out and saw who was standing there, she grinned and said, "It's Miss Dimple!"

"So bright and early," Drayton said. Then, when their chubby seventy-something bookkeeper came toddling into the tea shop, he said again, "You're here so bright and early."

Which stopped Miss Dimple in her tracks. "Am I too early?" She glanced at Theodosia. "You said eight fifteen, right?"

"Your timing is perfect," Theodosia said as she helped Miss Dimple off with her fuzzy brown coat and hung it on the brass coatrack. The sharp-as-a-tack Miss Dimple didn't just tally up weekly receipts and handle their books; she also filled in as server a few days a month. Today was one of those days.

"What do you want me to do?" Miss Dimple asked. She was plumpish and barely five feet tall, and she had a cap of pink-tinged curls. She spoke in a breathy voice and used old-fashioned phrases such as *Heavens to Betsy* and *Bless me*. She was also capable as all get-out.

"Haley's put up most of our Christmas decorations," Theodosia said. "But we need to finish." She lifted a hand and pointed to a cardboard box filled with strings of lights, silver bells, giant silk poinsettias, sparkly cardboard snowflakes, and red candles.

"Gotcha," Miss Dimple said. "And you're hosting a special luncheon tea today, am I right?"

"Our Nutcracker Tea," Drayton said.

Miss Dimple clapped her hands together. "I can hardly wait!"

"Theodosia even hired some ballet students to come in and stage a mini recital," Drayton explained. "So after we serve all our morning customers, we need to push tables five and six back against the wall so the young ladies have a little dancing space."

"Can't have them pirouetting right into someone's lap." Miss Dimple laughed.

Theodosia got Miss Dimple started on the table settings and decor; then she headed into the kitchen to check with Haley.

"Okay, morning offerings," Haley said the minute Theodosia stepped into her postage-stamp-sized kitchen. Her face was glowing pink from all the baking she'd been doing. "We've got pecan scones, white chocolate muffins, apple bread, and fried coffee cake."

"What on earth . . . ?" Theodosia began.

"It's an old-fashioned recipe—actually my great-granny's—where you do coffee cake on top of the stove in a covered cast-iron frying pan. That way it's kind of half-baked, half-fried, though now that I think about it, half-baked doesn't sound so good."

"But the fried part does sound interesting," Theodosia said as she glanced at the stove. Yup, there were indeed two covered frying pans sitting atop glowing burners.

"They're regular cinnamon-and-sugar coffee cakes," Haley assured her. "But the name is fun, so I think our guests will get a kick out of it."

"I know they will."

Anytime Haley baked or cooked something slightly out of the ordinary, it tended to be a huge hit. Case in point, Haley's cat-head biscuits, French Huguenot tortes, and her famous gougères or cheese puffs. These items set the Indigo Tea Shop apart from the drive-through coffee and tea places that served cookie-cutter goodies that weren't even baked on premises.

"And it looks as if you've started prepping today's luncheon? Are you going to need some help?"

"I'm on it," Haley said. "And I'm okay as of right now."

It was back to work for Theodosia then, as she and Miss Dimple welcomed guests for morning tea, seated them, took orders, and then ferried out the steeping teapots along with baked goodies and the accompanying Devonshire cream, lemon curd, and jam.

By ten o'clock the tea room was completely filled (hopefully with happy guests) and Theodosia paused for a breather at the counter. It was also a chance to inhale the heady aroma that surrounded Drayton like some kind of wonderful aromatherapy treatment.

"Is that one of our spiced teas you're brewing?" she asked. Earlier, they'd printed up a list—a kind of tea menu—of holiday teas that included cinnamon spice, cranberry blend, spiced plum, peaches and ginger, citrus hibiscus, and a few more.

Drayton's fingers grazed the top of a yellow Chinese-style teapot. "This one's our Winter Spice house blend. And FYI, that tea list we put together is pure genius. Our customers have been ordering selections like crazy."

Theodosia tapped a finger against the counter. "What about that other list?" she asked.

"Ah, you're referring to the guest list we picked up last night? I've been perusing it whenever I have a bit of free time."

"Several of the people on the list are executive directors of various local charities," Theodosia said.

"I'm acquainted with most of them," Drayton said. "And I have to say . . . their reputations are impeccable. Not a murderer in the bunch."

Theodosia favored him with a thin smile. "What about art thievery?"

Drayton shook his head. "Doubtful."

"Well, *somebody* killed Miss Drucilla and stole that painting."

"It's a tough one," Drayton agreed.

By eleven fifteen, most of their morning customers had cleared out, probably off to do last-minute holiday shopping or explore the various outdoor Christmas markets. So Theodosia ran into her office, grabbed a second box of decorations, and hauled it out to the tea room.

"More decor?" Miss Dimple asked when she spotted the box.

Theodosia pulled out a twenty-inch-high bright red wooden nutcracker and held it up with a flourish.

"A nutcracker soldier, how absolutely perfect," Miss Dimple cried. "Drayton," she called out. "Did you see this?"

"Adorable," he said, barely looking up.

"I was wondering how you'd decorate for a Nutcracker Tea and now I can see you've given this a lot of thought."

"Here's what I'm thinking," Theodosia said. "White linen tablecloths with pink place mats, pink candles . . ."

"And pink china," Miss Dimple said. "Maybe the Royal Albert Rose Confetti?"

"Perfect." Theodosia dug into the box and pulled out a roll of pink netting and a bag of faux-pearl necklaces. "We'll tie pink netting on the backs of chairs, the pearl necklaces get strewn on the tabletops, and somewhere—here they are—these small glass ornaments should be placed at each setting as favors."

"But these adorable nutcrackers are the centerpiece for sure. And you said something about ballet dancers coming in to perform?"

"Three of them from the Grand Jeté Ballet School. Dancing to the music of Tchaikovsky's *Nutcracker Suite*."

Miss Dimple nodded her approval. "I can see it's going to be a perfect holiday tea."

While Miss Dimple set the tables and primped the tea room, Theodosia hauled out more gift items to display on her highboys. She'd just arranged a row of bright red mugs and several tea cozies—a knit panda, a knit snowman, a mouse, and a quilted floral snuffie—when her cell phone rang. She grabbed it out of her apron pocket and said, "Hello?"

"Well, I did some digging. Actually, computer investigating. And your buddy Smokey has indeed run afoul of the law," Riley said.

Theodosia was suddenly all ears. Thrilled that Riley had actually done some checking and called her back.

"So Smokey's got an arrest record? What for?"

"Stole a car," Riley said.

"Wow. Recently?"

"When he was eighteen."

"Oh." Theodosia thought for a minute. "That had to be a while ago."

"Twenty-two years, to be exact."

"So that's it? That's the full extent of Smokey's brush with the law?"

"Well, this happened in Alabama, so your buddy Smokey was given the option of serving a yearlong jail sentence or going into the army."

"I didn't know they did that anymore."

"They don't," Riley said. "That's old-school sentencing. Now the judges just give felons a slap on the wrist so they can get back out there and keep harassing the citizenry."

"Aren't you just the law-and-order martinet," Theodosia said.

"When you've arrested as many criminals as I have, then watched them get a negligible or suspended sentence, you tend to be a little jaded."

"I suppose. Anything on Donny Bragg?"

"Looked clean to me."

"Thanks so much for . . . Ohmygosh! My dancers just walked in!"

"Dancers?" Riley said. But she'd already hung up.

Theodosia shepherded the three young dancers into her office so they could change into their costumes and toe shoes; then she ran out to do a final inspection of the tea room. And with toy soldiers standing at attention, candles flickering, Christmas lights gleaming, and a decidedly pinkish sugarplum atmosphere, the place really did look adorable.

As the strains of Tchaikovsky's *Nutcracker* echoed through the tea room, Theodosia's guests began to arrive. She checked them off her list, showed them to their seats, then ran back to the front door to greet a spill of even more excited guests.

Angie Congdon from the Featherbed House arrived with Brooke Carter Crocket, proprietor of Hearts Desire. Then Lois Chamberlain from Antiquarian Books and Leigh Caroll from the Cabbage Patch Gift Shop found their way in. Hugs and air-kisses were exchanged, Drayton finger-waved from behind the front counter, and then Jill, Kristen, Linda, Judi, and Jessica came piling in, too.

And dear Delaine Dish came rushing in at the last minute, a little breathless and hanging on the arm of Majel Mercer, the woman who served as executive director of the nonprofit Justice Initiative.

"Look who I found loitering outside," Delaine squealed. "The lovely Majel Mercer!"

"My first time at your tea shop," Majel exclaimed, gripping Theodosia's hand. "I can't wait!" Majel was a cool blonde in a navy blue suit who wore her hair in a slightly retro chignon. Majel also spoke with a distinct throaty voice. Not exactly sexy but certainly enticing. Theodosia could just imagine Majel dealing with prosecuting attorneys. Cracking their hard outer shells and pulling them in with her magnetism.

"Glad you ladies could make it," Theodosia said as she led them to the last two available seats. But before she was able to make a clean getaway, Delaine grabbed her arm and hissed, "Don't forget. I've got tickets for the ballet tonight."

"You're sure you don't want to . . . ?"

"Invite a date?" Delaine stage-whispered. "No, dear, consider this a BFF moment. I want to take *you*."

"Sure. Fine." Theodosia wasn't all that excited about going with Delaine, but it was only one night. What could it hurt?

When all the luncheon guests were seated, Drayton rang a tinkling bell to get everyone's attention. As the chatter died down to a low hum, Theodosia walked to the center of the tea room, smiled at her guests, and drew a deep breath. This was the part that scared her the most; this was also the part she liked best.

"Merry Christmas, happy holidays, and welcome to the Indigo Tea Shop," Theodosia began. There was a spatter of applause and a few cries of "Happy holidays to you!" Then she continued. "Because this is our special Nutcracker Tea, there are a few treats in store for you as well as a very special menu. We'll kick off today's luncheon with fresh-baked cranberry-orange scones served with Devonshire cream." She held up a finger. "There are seconds on the scones if you'd like, but just know that your next course will consist of sweet potato soup topped with crème fraîche and accompanied by a cashew chicken salad tea sandwich. Your main entrée is Black Forest ham and Swiss cheese quiche with an apple, almond, and Bibb lettuce side salad. Dessert—that's if you still have room—will be Haley's special sugarplum cake topped with a pouf of whipped cream."

Now Drayton joined Theodosia in the center of the room. "For your sipping pleasure, you have your choice of three teas in special holiday flavors," he said. "Crème brûlée, cranberry cream, and sugarplum spiced."

"Wow!" one of the guests exclaimed just as Haley and Miss Dimple magically appeared bearing silver trays stacked high with scones.

From there it was a slam dunk as far as Theodosia was concerned. The scones were served piping hot and she and Drayton made the rounds filling teacups with the various spiced teas. When it was time for the second course, Miss Dimple cleared and Haley ferried out the soup and tea sandwiches. Making everything look . . . easy as pie.

"Having a good time?" Theodosia asked Susan Monday, the owner of the newly opened Lavender and Lace Boutique, as she slipped past tables, checking on her guests.

"This is fabulous," Susan replied. "If this is just a luncheon tea, I can't wait to see what you do for your Victorian Christmas Tea."

"It promises to be quite the extravaganza," Theodosia said. They'd gotten so many reservations that she'd had to move their big Christmas tea to the larger and much grander Dove Cote Inn.

"Well, I'm coming to your Victorian Christmas Tea and I can't wait," another one of the guests enthused.

As Miss Dimple and Haley served the entrées and Drayton poured another round of tea, Theodosia snuck back behind the counter and clicked the CD player ahead to the "Dance of the Sugarplum Fairy." Once that familiar piece of music started burbling out of the speakers, she pushed back the green velvet curtain that separated the back of the tea shop from the front, and her three dancers came bounding out in time to the music.

They were an instant hit.

"Delightful!"

"Can you believe we're watching actual ballet dancers?"

"How perfect!" came another excited cry.

Everyone pretty much turned in their chairs to follow the three adorable girls—they were all of fourteen, leggy, and clad in perfect pink leotards and tutus—as they danced and twirled their way through the tea room. They swirled around tables, arabesqued past the front counter, then turned and, dancing *en pointe*, did a perfect dip and leap as the music continued to build.

"This is going so well," Drayton whispered to Theodosia. They were both standing at the front counter, watching the dancers.

"It couldn't get any better," Theodosia agreed.

But the words hadn't died on her lips before the front door

crashed open and an angry shout rang out. Then a man in a black leather jacket rushed in, waving his arms and clomping his boots.

The dancers stopped midstride, terrified.

A few guests uttered surprised cries and shrieks.

Others were struck dumb.

Teacups were dropped hastily into saucers; silverware clattered to the table.

Only one sound stood out above the rest, the intruder shouting Theodosia's name over and over at the top of his lungs. Screaming at her in a thunderous voice that rose in pitch like steel wheels grinding against rusty rails.

Theodosia put a hand to her chest to stop her galloping heart, then gazed at the man who'd brought her perfectly lovely tea luncheon to such a rude and abrasive halt.

Smokey Pruitt stared back at her with smoldering dark eyes.

9

❧❦❧

"Smokey!" *Theodosia cried.* She didn't exactly shout his name but her voice wasn't overly soft. "What do you think you're doing?"

"Indeed," came Drayton's indignant grunt.

Smokey reached a hand out and pointed a gnarled finger directly at Theodosia. "You," he said in a voice dripping with anger. "You put the cops on me."

"I did nothing of the sort," Theodosia said, then quickly wondered, *Did Riley make a call to Tidwell? Did he urge Tidwell to check this guy out?*

But no, Riley couldn't have cared less, she decided. He'd run those checks only because she'd asked him to. Begged him to, really. And this morning, when Riley had called with the information, he'd actually sounded bored.

So what else is going on?

Theodosia hurried around the counter, blocked Smokey's path, and hustled him right back out the front door.

They stood facing each other on the sidewalk outside the

Indigo Tea Shop, Theodosia looking puzzled, Smokey fizzing with anger.

"You came crashing in and interrupted my tea," Theodosia said. "Scared the living daylights out of all my guests, to say nothing of those little girls who were dancing their hearts out."

That seemed to tamp Smokey down and put him in his place.

"Okay," Smokey said. "I'm sorry about frightening people, but I'm real upset. The cops came by to see me this morning. . . ."

"I didn't send them."

"No?" He looked as if he didn't quite believe her.

"No," Theodosia said.

Smokey shook his head. "I don't like cops. They always act like I'm guilty before I really am."

"Well, you do have a past. Or at least a semipast."

"What are you . . . ?" Smokey looked befuddled. "Oh, you mean the car? You *know* about that?"

Theodosia nodded. "I have a few sources."

"That happened a long time ago. I fell in with a bunch of jerks and did some stupid stuff I shouldn't have. But things are different now. I'm a changed man. I fix things for people in the neighborhood and I'm good at it. I found a *trade*."

"You fixed things at Miss Drucilla's house," Theodosia said.

"Sure did."

"Such as?"

"I fixed her garage door when she accidentally backed her Volvo into it."

"You also hung some paintings for her."

Smokey's eyes blazed again and he held up a hand. "But not *that* one. I don't know nothin' about that missing painting!"

"Did you know it was a Renoir?"

"I know who Renoir was," Smokey shot back. "I'm not

stupid. But I didn't steal it. I wouldn't steal anything from Miss Drucilla. She was always nice to me. Always paid me right on time, too. And a *fair* wage, not like some people."

Theodosia gazed at him. "Okay, let's say I believe you. You're innocent on all counts. But somebody snuck in Sunday night and murdered her. Stole a valuable painting as well."

Smokey's eyes burned into hers. "I wish I knew who."

Theodosia decided to take a gamble. What did she have to lose? "Maybe you have some ideas about that?"

"I don't know. I think that's a little above my pay grade," Smokey said.

"But if you were to hazard a guess, it could be helpful."

"Helpful to you or to the police?" Smokey asked.

"Just me for now."

Smokey looked down and scraped the toe of one battered brown cowboy boot against the pavement. "Maybe there is somebody you should look at," he mumbled.

"Who would that be?" Theodosia asked.

Smokey's eyes shifted nervously from side to side. "You were with him last night."

"Wait a minute. You're talking about Mr. Bragg? Donny Bragg?"

"I probably shouldn't say anything 'cause he lets me live in his carriage house."

"But not for free," Theodosia said.

"No, he makes me do work around his place. A *lot* of work."

"Why should we be looking at him?" Theodosia asked.

"Because Mr. Bragg's a big-time art guy."

"By 'art guy,' you mean he collects art. And serves on the board of directors at the Gibbes Museum. I've already figured that out. I'm already there."

"He's also a tricky devil. I know some paintings that the Gibbes curators were trying to buy for the museum ended up in his collection instead."

"You know this for a fact?"

Smokey's head bobbed. "I do."

"Okay, that's something to think about," Theodosia said, "and look into as well. If you have any more ideas about suspects, come to me directly, will you?"

Smokey thought for a few moments. "I guess I could do that."

"But no more crash landings in the middle of my tea parties."

Smokey gave a grudging nod. "Yeah. Got it."

When Theodosia returned to the tea shop, things were back to normal. Guests were eating dessert; a few were strolling around, looking at the holiday displays and selecting gifts.

"No harm done," Drayton whispered to Theodosia as she slipped behind the counter.

Theodosia did a mock swipe of her brow and mouthed a silent "Thank goodness." Then she asked, "Are the girls okay?"

"Finished their sugarplum ballet and are right now sitting in your office, noshing scones and drinking copious amounts of milk under Haley's watchful eye." He picked up a teapot, ready to make the rounds and top off a few teacups. "So all's well that ends well?"

But that wasn't really the end of it.

Delaine lingered, telling anyone who'd listen about the marvelous new pashminas she'd gotten in at Cotton Duck. Miss Dimple began clearing tables. Haley peeped out and looked bored. And Theodosia was kept busy apologizing for the interruption, ringing up sales, then bidding goodbye to guests and apologizing yet again.

By two thirty it was over.

Drayton dropped into a chair and said, "Foof. To think we're going to do this all over again tomorrow."

"I know," Miss Dimple said as she swept past him. "I can hardly wait."

"So what did the cantankerous cowboy want?" Drayton asked.

"You mean Smokey?"

Drayton looked around. "I don't see anyone else dressed like a movie stand-in for a remake of *Gunsmoke*."

"He thought I sent the cops after him."

"Didn't you?"

"No, Tidwell probably took it upon himself to question Smokey. After all, the guy's kind of a perfect suspect. A down-on-his-luck-loner-lost-soul type, if you know what I mean."

"I do indeed," Drayton said.

"Funny thing is, Smokey knew the stolen painting was a Renoir," Theodosia said.

Drayton cocked his head at her. "Smokey doesn't strike me as being a student of art history."

"No, but he's not stupid, either." Theodosia paused. "I wish Pauline hadn't given all the Renoir paperwork to Tidwell. I wish I knew more about it."

"About the painting or the painter?" Drayton asked.

"Both."

"Why don't you run down the street and talk to Tom Ritter?" Drayton suggested. Ritter owned the Dolce Gallery a half block down from them.

"That's a great idea."

"Tell you what." Drayton stood up, went to the counter, and poured a cup of tea into one of their blue take-out cups. He snapped on a lid and said, "Here. Take Mr. Ritter a fresh cup of tea. It'll help get you in his good graces."

"Mr. Ritter," Theodosia called out as she pushed her way through the front door of the Dolce Gallery. "It's Theodosia. From the tea shop?"

She dodged around an enormous easel that held an oil

painting of Charleston Harbor and gazed around the small shop. The pristine white walls were a mosaic of paintings, lots of impressionism as well as more contemporary art. Smaller paintings were displayed everywhere—on table easels and hung on half walls that made the small shop resemble a Chinese puzzle. Dozens more paintings stood upright in white wooden crates.

Ritter came to the door of his office, peeped out, and said, "I thought I heard someone come in." He had short, spiky white-blond hair and was dressed all in black. Black sweater, black slacks, black Prada tennis shoes. Like a refugee from a hotshot New York gallery.

Theodosia handed him the cup of tea. "I brought this for you."

Ritter accepted the cup and unsnapped the lid. "Bless you. I've been crazy busy all day and could use a pick-me-up. I hope there's a copious amount of caffeine in this."

"There is and the tea's actually a bribe," Theodosia said, "in exchange for a bit of information."

"Sounds interesting," Ritter said as he took a sip of tea.

"By now you've heard about the murder of Drucilla Heyward."

Ritter nodded. "It's been all over the news. Such an awful thing. For a woman of her repute to be murdered in her own home is a blight on the civility of Charleston."

"I was wondering if you'd sold any paintings to her."

Ritter frowned and tapped an index finger against his lower lip. "No, but I sure wish I had. I understand the woman had impeccable taste. But . . ."

"Yes?"

"I don't believe Miss Drucilla was a fan of contemporary art, which is predominantly the type of art and artist that I represent."

"But it sounds as if you're somewhat familiar with her collection," Theodosia said.

"I've never actually seen it, only heard about it. But I understand she had a couple of tasty pieces. A John Singer Sargent and a few Picasso ceramics."

"She also owned a small Renoir, which went missing Sunday night the same time as her murder. Or maybe it was the reason for her murder."

"I did hear about that. So how can I help?" Ritter asked.

"Do you know how many Renoirs there are? I mean, that exist in the entire world?"

"Oh, I'd have to say at least a couple of thousand," Ritter said.

Theodosia's eyes widened in surprise. "That many?"

"Renoir was quite a prolific painter. He lived to be almost eighty."

"Do you have any idea what prices are like for a Renoir?" Theodosia asked.

"I'm sure they vary widely, depending on size and subject matter. Though I do know that Renoir's *Dance at le Moulin de la Galette* sold for a record seventy-eight million at Sotheby's."

"Holy smokes! Was it sold to a private collector?"

"Actually it was a telephone bidder."

"Wow."

"Of course, most Renoirs are hanging in museums. Although the largest collection I know of is held by the Barnes Foundation in Philadelphia. I understand they have around one hundred and eighty Renoirs."

"That many? How fascinating," Theodosia said.

"And there are quite a few—like Miss Drucilla's stolen painting—that have found their place in private collections," Ritter said.

"Is it difficult to get your hands on a Renoir? At auction, I mean."

Ritter looked thoughtful. "Today, with all the newly minted billionaires out there infused with collector mania, I think it might be difficult to find one available."

"What about a stolen Renoir?"

Ritter frowned. "You're talking about the black market? That's a whole different can of worms."

"How so?"

"The thing is—when a well-known painting is stolen, it rarely sees the light of day again," Ritter said.

"Understandable, I guess."

"Stolen pieces generally find their way into private collections. And I do mean private." Ritter's face grew animated and he took a step forward. "Think about all the artwork that was plundered during World War Two: the paintings, tapestries, sculptures, and rare books. Only forty percent of that has ever been recovered. I mean, it's been more than seventy-five years and we *still* don't know where it is."

Theodosia was fascinated. "Where do *you* think it might be?"

"If I had to hazard a guess? Maybe hanging in a drawing room in Argentina? Locked in a Swiss vault? Nobody really knows for sure."

"That's very frightening," Theodosia said.

"Here's something else," Ritter said. "In some cases—thankfully very rare cases—professional art thieves are given a laundry list of what to steal."

"You mean like when that fancy museum in Boston was robbed?" Theodosia said.

"The Gardner Museum," Ritter said. "Exactly. The museum people, even the police and FBI, are still convinced that the thieves carried a very specific shopping list."

"And that happened when? Like thirty years ago?"

"Something like that. Though two pieces were eventually recovered."

"And the rest of the stolen art?" Theodosia asked.

Ritter looked unhappy. "Even with a ten-million-dollar reward, the Vermeer, Rembrandt, Degas, and Manet just . . . disappeared into thin air. Never to be seen again."

10

~❧~

With ideas about stolen artwork buzzing in her brain, Theodosia returned to the Indigo Tea Shop, breezed past Drayton at the front counter, and called Pauline at Miss Drucilla's house.

Pauline picked up on the fifth ring, sounding a little breathless. "Hello?"

"Hi, Pauline. It's Theodosia. I'm thinking about paying a visit to that art dealer Julian Wolf-Knapp. Do you have his address? Or do you by chance remember where his shop is located?"

"Give me a minute." The phone was set down, almost two minutes went by, and then Pauline came back on the line. "Wolf-Knapp has an office—he calls it a studio because it's kind of a second-floor loft—over on Broad Street. It's above that cute little antiques shop called the Dusty Hen."

"Oh, I know that building." Theodosia had called on a wedding planner who had an office there when she'd investigated another strange case a few months earlier.

"Okay, then," Pauline said.

Theodosia heard a slight hesitation in her voice.

"How are you doing, Pauline?"

"Oh, dealing with all the lawyers as best I can. They're still hounding me to pull all sorts of paperwork together on Miss Drucilla's estate, the art collection, all her investments. You know, rich-people stuff."

"I hear you," Theodosia said. But she felt like she'd detected a wistful note in Pauline's voice. Had she been jealous of Miss Drucilla's wealth? But even if she had been and sought to do her harm, what would she have gained? Well, the painting and the diamond rings for one thing. But Pauline didn't seem like the murdering kind. Besides, she'd been right there, Johnny-on-the-spot when Miss Drucilla died. Not much time to hide all that loot. No. Pauline didn't feel quite right.

"Theodosia?" Pauline said.

"Yes?"

"Thank you for caring about all of this. I can't tell you how much it means to me."

"We'll see what shakes out. Keep your fingers crossed."

"I will."

Theodosia sat at her desk thinking. Pauline probably wasn't the killer. But maybe somebody fairly close to Miss Drucilla was. The question remained . . . who could that be?

"Theodosia?"

Drayton was standing in the doorway.

"How did it go with Tom Ritter?"

"Good."

"Did you get the information you needed?"

"Maybe."

"Want to talk about the Grand Illumination?" Drayton asked.

Theodosia stood up and grabbed her coat. "You know what? I'd love to but I can't right now."

"You're off again?" Drayton sounded surprised as Theodosia hurried past him. "Where to this time?"

"I have to see a man about a painting."

*   *   *

Theodosia drove down Queen Street, turned on King Street, went past the King's Ransom Gift Shop, where Wade Holland worked, and turned down Broad. She parked directly in front of the Dusty Hen Antique Shop, took a minute to look in their window and admire a bentwood rocking chair, then hustled upstairs to the second floor. She walked down a sleek carpeted hallway and stopped outside a white lacquered door with a doorbell and a sign above it that read JULIAN WOLF-KNAPP FINE-ART CONSULTANTS (BY APPOINTMENT ONLY).

Theodosia didn't have an appointment, but she rang the bell anyway. When nothing happened, she rang it a second time. This time she heard someone rustling around inside and muttering to himself.

"Yes, yes" came a muffled voice. "Hold on, I'm coming."

The door flew open and Julian Wolf-Knapp stared out at her with flat gray eyes. He had a narrow face, a thin nose, somewhat prominent ears, and a carefully groomed goatee. Well-dressed in a navy pin-striped suit and yellow Hermès tie, he struck her as being European-looking but not in any specific way.

"Hello. What?" Wolf-Knapp said. He sounded guarded and not all that friendly. Then again, she had interrupted him.

Didn't faze Theodosia in the least.

"Mr. Wolf-Knapp, I'm Theodosia Browning. Would you have a moment to talk?"

"Possibly," he said. Then, "Talk about what?"

"A former client of yours, Miss Drucilla Heyward."

Wolf-Knapp seemed to soften. "Such an unfortunate circumstance," he murmured.

"Actually more than a circumstance. A murder," Theodosia said. "A murder that I've been tasked to look into."

Wolf-Knapp's curious eyes drilled into her. "You're here in an official capacity?"

"Not at all. More like a friend of the family."

"Interesting. And you want to talk to me—why?"

"Well, you obviously know that the Renoir you sold to Miss Drucilla was stolen at the same time she was murdered."

Wolf-Knapp's head bobbed. "I spoke with the police yesterday. And just as I told them, it was the one and only time I ever worked as a fine-art consultant to Mrs. Heyward. Although I must say, she was a lovely woman. Really quite knowledgeable."

"Detective Tidwell mentioned that he'd talked to you." Theodosia took a step forward. "May I come in?"

"Of course."

Wolf-Knapp led Theodosia through a small gallery that was crammed with paintings and drawings and into an office that was also filled with artwork. Paintings hung on the walls and an entire wall of white vertical shelving held all manner of canvases and framed drawings. More pieces were stacked on the credenza behind his desk.

"As you can see, I'm up to my eyeballs in inventory."

"That's wonderful," Theodosia said, still trying to establish some rapport with him. "Business must be good."

"I get by," Wolf-Knapp said. "Please, sit down and make yourself comfortable."

Theodosia sat down in a gray club chair while Wolf-Knapp took a seat behind his white desk. She couldn't decide if he was a fusty *artiste* type or what she and her girlfriends (after a couple glasses of chardonnay) would good-naturedly call a *play-uh*.

"You mentioned inventory," Theodosia said. "So naturally I'm curious. How on earth does one go about locating an available Renoir? I would think it'd be almost impossible. That museums and private collectors would be reluctant to part with one."

"It's a little-known fact, but museums deacquisition works of art all the time," Wolf-Knapp said. "Public interest flags. A new area of interest opens up. Circumstances are constantly changing for private art collectors as well. They get bored with a certain piece or decide to move their collection in a new direction. Perhaps something more contemporary. Or their paintings have appreciated so much in value that they jump on an opportunity to cash out."

"That's interesting. So the Renoir that you sold to—"

Wolf-Knapp held up an index finger. "Technically, I was not the seller. I acted as an *intermediary* between buyer and seller."

"Okay, the Renoir that you intermediated for Miss Drucilla . . . I believe it was a still life. Where did it come from?"

Wolf-Knapp favored Theodosia with a thin crocodile smile. "If I told you that, I'd have to kill you."

Theodosia smiled back at him to let him know she understood his little joke. But inside she cringed a little because Wolf-Knapp almost looked as if he meant it.

"Seriously," Theodosia said.

Wolf-Knapp shook his head. "I'm afraid that's a trade secret."

Wolf-Knapp was being a jerk and enjoying it, Theodosia decided. She felt an urge to reach across his desk and pinch one of his ears but managed to restrain herself.

"So let me get this straight," Theodosia said. "A *seller* might contact you to see if you have a willing *buyer*?"

"That's one set of circumstances, yes."

"Does that happen often?"

"Not nearly as often as I'd like."

Theodosia knew they were dancing and jousting, and she didn't care for it one bit.

Can't this guy give me a solid answer?

Turned out, he couldn't. As Theodosia asked more questions and Wolf-Knapp skillfully deflected them, her suspicions grew. Could this hotshot art consultant, or dealer or whatever he called himself, have sold Miss Drucilla the Renoir, then stolen it back from her? And murdered her as a by-product of that theft?

She supposed it could have happened that way.

By the end of their conversation, Wolf-Knapp had revealed next to nothing, and Theodosia decided she had yet another name to add to her perplexing list of suspects.

Theodosia walked into the Indigo Tea Shop just as Drayton and Haley were turning off the lights and locking up. The aromas from scones and tea still hung in the air.

"We didn't think you'd be back," Drayton said.

"Hey," Haley said as she pulled on a black bomber jacket. "Somebody called for you."

"Who was it?" Theodosia asked.

"Don't know. He wouldn't say. But whoever it was, he was curious about *where* you'd run off to."

A hint of wariness flickered in Theodosia's brain. "You didn't tell him, did you?"

Haley shook her head. "Nope. Because, truth be told, the call felt kind of creepy to me. Like somebody was checking up on you. You know, fishing around for information."

Smokey, was that you? Theodosia wondered. *Or someone else?*

"Aren't you off to the ballet tonight?" Drayton asked as he grabbed his tweed jacket and put it on. "With Delightful Delaine?"

"Yes, but I've got to make a quick call first."

"Well, have fun," Drayton said. "Don't stay out too late."

Theodosia walked into her office, remembering what Tom Ritter had told her earlier about the Barnes Foundation.

Might they know something about a disappearing Renoir? Or about other Renoirs that have been stolen? Maybe Miss Drucilla's painting is just one in a number of thefts.

Maybe. But the only way to know for sure was to do a little fishing. She looked up the Barnes Foundation on the Internet, found their phone number, and called.

She got one of the administrative assistants in their main

office and asked to be put in touch with one of the curators, but was told that none of them was around.

"I'm sorry," the admin assistant said. "Most of our people are on vacation because of the holidays. But if one of our curators should happen to call in or drop by for some reason, I'll have them give you a ring."

"Okay, thanks much."

So much for chasing that lead.

11

❧

It certainly hadn't been Theodosia's idea, but Delaine had two tickets to *Giselle* that were burning a hole in her handbag and had insisted that Theodosia go with her.

"Why me?" Theodosia had asked.

Delaine had pursed her lips, made a lemon face, and said, "Because my regular date, Tod, *hates* the ballet and I didn't feel like inviting that drip Allan Barnaby. What a bore he turned out to be, always yapping about books and publishing, as if that's the only thing in the world a girl's interested in."

"Okay," Theodosia had told her. "I can see the logic in your thinking." *Not.*

So here they were, strolling across the lobby of the Belvedere Theatre, mingling with a glittering, black-tie-wearing, ballet-loving crowd.

"Are you sure I'm dressed appropriately?" Theodosia asked Delaine. She was wearing a short black cocktail dress with a chubby faux-fur jacket that Delaine had brought along and insisted she wear. It made Theodosia feel like a fuzzy walking burrito.

"Nonsense!" Delaine cried. "You're extremely au courant. *Alta moda*, if you will. As if you've leaped from the pages of a chic fashion magazine."

Delaine herself was wearing a black see-through blouse with a lacy black camisole underneath. The blouse had an enormous froth of feathers at the neckline that made her look like a snooty ostrich, and it was tucked into a short black leather skirt. The look was completed by studded high-heeled booties and a mink coat draped casually over her shoulders. Theodosia hoped the antifur contingent wasn't lurking somewhere. If so, they'd be in big trouble.

"Look!" Delaine exclaimed. "There's a bar set up over there. Fancy having a glass of prosecco before the ballet starts?"

"I never turn down a glass of bubbly."

They sidled up to the bar, ordered their prosecco, then wandered off to sip and people-watch. Sixty seconds later, Delaine's arm shot into the air, she let out a bloodcurdling shriek, and cried, "Sawyer Daniels! Imagine running into *you* tonight!"

Theodosia remembered Sawyer Daniels from the party. He was the one with the high voice who'd speculated that Miss Drucilla had probably "passed out" from "too much excitement." Pauline had also mentioned Daniels as the numbers guy who worked with Miss Drucilla to help her select charities, which was why Theodosia was suddenly interested in Daniels as he walked toward them, his eyes on Delaine and a smile on his face.

Though easily in his mid-fifties, Daniels had a military bearing, ice chip blue eyes, a smug Gordon Gekko smile, and white brush-cut hair. In other words, he looked disciplined. Like he was the kind of guy who jogged five miles every day, came home and chugged a protein smoothie, and never let you forget it.

"So lovely to see you again," Delaine purred, practically rubbing up against Daniels like an affectionate cat. Then she turned to Theodosia and said, "Have you two met?" Without waiting for an answer, she quickly introduced them.

"Nice to meet you," Theodosia said.

Daniels nodded back at her, but his eyes remained on Delaine.

Delaine burbled along and said, "Sawyer and I were talking the other night at the party. Right before the unfortunate, uh . . . incident."

"The murder," Theodosia said. No reason to sugarcoat it.

Delaine's eyes glazed over slightly. "Yes, uh, anyway, Sawyer was telling me about this really superb red wine . . ."

"The Benziger," Sawyer said. "From Sonoma."

"That's it. With a bouquet like ripe strawberries." Delaine's eyelashes fluttered. Probably her heart did, too.

"You remembered." Sawyer seemed beyond pleased. In fact, he seemed rather captivated by Delaine's charms.

Delaine dimpled prettily. "I never forget a good wine or an interesting man."

Sawyer Daniels gave Delaine a knowing wink. Then he excused himself, went to the bar to grab a drink, and returned.

"You worked closely with Miss Drucilla, didn't you?" Theodosia asked him.

Delaine gazed daggers at her but Theodosia kept her focus strictly on Daniels.

"Yes, I did," Daniels said.

"You manage a company that runs the numbers on charities?" Theodosia said.

"I see you're quite well-informed," Daniels said. He took a sip of wine—a stall tactic?—then added, "The name of my company is Doing the Good."

"That's such a cute name," Delaine said.

"We run analytics on nonprofit organizations," Daniels continued. "We determine how much money they're able to raise, then weigh that amount against their operating costs and what they actually spend on charitable works."

"So there's a kind of magic number where a charity is sustainable and also benefits the community?" Theodosia asked. "Or I guess what they might call their constituents?"

"That's it in a nutshell," Daniels said with a broad smile.

"So, basically, you helped Miss Drucilla invest her money wisely," Theodosia said.

"With so many different scams going on, there need to be some safeguards," Daniels said.

"And you're one of them," Theodosia said.

"We like to think so."

"I'm curious. Did your advice ever extend to Miss Drucilla's art collection?" Theodosia asked.

Daniels's brows pinched together. "I don't know the first thing about fine art, even though I do liaison with a number of local arts organizations. But I understand that Miss Drucilla had a genuine feel for collecting. She not only knew what she liked. She knew when a work might appreciate in value."

"I can appreciate that," Delaine said, batting her lashes at Daniels for about the fifty-seventh time.

Theodosia nodded. She didn't think much of Sawyer Daniels. He projected a kind of phony I'm-smarter-than-you attitude that made her wonder what Miss Drucilla had seen in him. Did Daniels give his clients a bunch of mumbo jumbo, or was he just the new breed of money guy? Probably, when Daniels presented Miss Drucilla with all her giving options, all neat and tidy on a fancy spreadsheet, she'd been duly impressed. Maybe Daniels *was* diligent and good at his job. Or maybe he was just a fast talker who was proficient at Excel.

As the chime sounded for the audience to take their seats, Delaine gave Daniels a kiss on the cheek and bid him goodbye.

"Hope to see you again real soon," Delaine said as they walked away.

"You don't think he's a little old for you?" Theodosia asked as they entered the semidark theater.

"These days, age is totally irrelevant," Delaine said. "People can be old souls or they can be young at heart." Then she giggled. "Of course, if we're talking about old family money, that's entirely different. Nothing makes a girl's heart go pitty-pat like old Charleston money."

"From what I've observed, most old Charleston families hang on to their old Charleston money rather carefully."

"Yes," Delaine said, frowning. "That does present a problem."

They settled into blue velvet seats that were located in the center section, twenty rows back from the stage.

"Not too bad," Delaine observed.

"Are you kidding? This is great," Theodosia said. Now that she was here, now that the orchestra was tuning up and the ballet was about to begin, she was suddenly looking forward to it.

"Oh my goodness." Delaine nudged Theodosia's shoulder. "Take a look at where Sawyer Daniels is sitting."

"Where's that?"

Delaine gave a nod. "Over there. Best seats in the house."

Theodosia scanned the theater and found Sawyer Daniels sitting in one of the box seats just above and to the right of the stage. Prime seats, to be sure.

"Such wonderful tickets he has," Delaine cooed. "I really must get to know the man better."

Then the lights dimmed and the music started. From there it was a whirlwind of ballet dancers, lovely music, prima ballerinas, and fabulous choruses.

Halfway through the first act, Delaine clutched Theodosia's hand and said, "Don't you just adore a tragic love story?"

"I do," Theodosia whispered back, "as long as it's not too tragic."

But the ballet was beautifully done and Theodosia had a

surprisingly good time, which meant she didn't get home until well after eleven o'clock.

When Theodosia walked in, Earl Grey was curled up in front of the fireplace (on his downstairs doggy bed), waiting for her.

"How are you doing?" Theodosia asked when he lifted his head and gazed at her sleepy eyed. "Did Mrs. Barry take you for a walk tonight?" Mrs. Barry was Earl Grey's doggy day care lady. A retired schoolteacher, she stopped by most afternoons (and some evenings) to take Earl Grey out for a walk.

"Rrowr," Earl Grey said, getting up, then shifting to a stretched-out downward-dog pose.

"Okay, you go ahead and finish your yoga. Then we'll go outside and have ourselves a good sniff."

Theodosia glanced around her living room as Earl Grey slowly composed himself. She'd left her Christmas tree lights on and they lent a warm, cheery glow. Theodosia was proud of her home decor—loved the exposed beams, the Aubusson carpet, the mixture of French and English furniture, much of which she'd had re-covered in chintz. There was also a mirrored cocktail table, an enormous sweetgrass basket filled with magazines, catalogs, and newspapers, and a vintage tea trolley that she used as a sideboard for cocktails when she entertained.

The mantel above her fireplace held a row of silver mint julep cups, all antique, though she figured that adding a row of greens, probably some blue spruce, and some mini lights would make her place look all the more Christmassy.

Theodosia changed her shoes, but kept her fuzzy shrug on as she walked Earl Grey around the block. And was glad for the warmth the jacket offered because it really had turned chilly. Trees shuddered in the stiff breeze; dry leaves tumbled down the middle of quiet streets that were lit by old-fashioned wrought iron lamps. Theodosia's neighborhood was an amalgam of mansions and cottages with the occasional Charleston single house thrown in for good measure. But it was all lovely and elegant and historic with palmetto trees fronting stately, well-preserved homes, many of which were painted in a French palette of cream, pink, and eggshell blue. Here and there were remnants of cobblestone streets and a few sprawling live oak trees added real character. Charleston also boasted a steepled skyline and Theodosia could see a half dozen or so floodlit church steeples looming in the darkness.

As Theodosia and her dog turned and walked down the back alley, she noted that the Granville Mansion, the large home next to hers, was still dark. The owner, a man named Robert Steele, a hedge fund guy, had supposedly gone off to London to do business for a year and rented the place out. But nobody had showed up yet and Theodosia didn't have a clue as to who her new neighbors might be.

Back inside, Theodosia turned off all the lights and headed upstairs. As she shrugged out of her clothes and changed into an oversized T-shirt, she checked her text messages and saw she'd received one from Riley. It said:

U still up to yr eyeballs in suspects?

It was late, but she texted him back:

Got more!

As Theodosia smiled to herself, she heard a low growl. She turned to Earl Grey and said, "What is it, boy?"

His hackles were raised and he was looking out the window in Theodosia's turret room. His muzzle was pressed close to the glass and his breath had created a tiny pouf of fog.

She frowned, mildly concerned. "What do you see, fella?"

Theodosia walked over to the window and gazed down into her side yard. And saw . . . absolutely nothing. There was no one down there, no cars were driving by on the street, and the house next door remained dark.

"C'mon, it's okay," she urged her dog. "Why don't you crawl into bed?" Not for nothing had she vastly overpaid for his orthopedic memory-foam bed.

Still, Earl Grey didn't want to abandon his post.

Okay, if you're so nervous, I'll check again.

A cold wind rattled the window in its frame as Theodosia unlatched it, gave a tug, and slid it open. She was pleased that, with the cool weather and the major drop in humidity, the window wasn't sticky as it usually was.

Theodosia gazed into darkness and listened. There was a whoosh of wind and tree branches rubbing together. But wait. Were those soft footsteps she heard walking away?

Theodosia closed her eyes and listened harder. Focused with all her might on whatever might be out there. Finally . . .

No, nothing there. Must just be the wind.

She hoped.

12

❦

As if by some pre-agreed-upon plan—or maybe a Vulcan mind meld—everyone showed up at the Indigo Tea Shop earlier than usual this Wednesday morning. Theodosia, Drayton, and Haley were all present and accounted for.

Even Miss Dimple came in early, wearing a flouncy red dress with one of those pearl-studded snap-on collars that had been so popular several decades ago. All she needed to complete her holiday outfit was a red Santa cap.

"Miss Dimple, you're a dead ringer for Mrs. Santa Claus," Haley said.

Drayton shot Haley a cautious look and said, "Dead ringer? Seriously, Haley?"

"Oops. Sorry." Haley looked suitably stricken for about two seconds. Then she said, "No, really, Miss Dimple, you look adorable."

"I thought I should dress for the occasion," Miss Dimple said, "since today's our White Christmas Tea."

"Excuse me, but we have to get through our morning tea-time first," Drayton reminded them.

"I get it, I get it," Haley said, "which is why I'm retreating to my kitchen lair."

"That girl," Drayton said, shaking his head. "If she weren't Charleston's preeminent baker, I'd . . ."

"You'd what?" Miss Dimple asked. "Fire her?"

"No, I'd probably put her in charge of the city," Drayton said. "Have you seen how Haley handles our vendors? They're all terrified of her."

"She's got a way of making people snap to," Miss Dimple agreed. "And that adorable little orange-and-brown cat of hers . . . What's its name? Teacake?"

"It's a stray Haley found in the back alley," Theodosia said.

"More like lured it in with food," Drayton said.

Twenty minutes later the tea shop was buzzing. Theodosia was offering a plated cream-tea special this morning—an eggnog scone with Devonshire cream served alongside a small bowl of fresh strawberries and your choice of spiced tea. Needless to say, it was an instant hit.

"Our customers are loving your cream-tea special," Drayton observed as he pushed a pot of Assam tea across the counter to Theodosia.

"I know. They seem to enjoy it when I make ordering a no-brainer."

"More like all-inclusive," Drayton said. He lifted the lid on the pot of Assam, frowned, and said, "No, this needs to steep an extra minute or two."

"Okay."

"So how was last night's ballet?"

"It was actually a lot of fun."

"Even though you were in the company of Madam Delaine?"

"Even with Delaine. Oh, and guess who we ran into."

"I couldn't possibly," Drayton said.

"Sawyer Daniels, the guy who runs that charity-review company."

"The fellow with the high voice."

"That's the one. And man, oh man, did he ever have fantastic seats. They were balcony box seats just above and to the right of the stage."

Drayton fixed Theodosia with a crooked half smile. "Excuse me, but those are Miss Drucilla's seats. That's where she always sat."

"No kidding. Well, somehow Daniels got his grubby little hands on her tickets," Theodosia said.

"He must have been tight with her. A true confidant."

"I guess so, although he comes across as kind of . . . mm . . ."

"Yes?" Drayton said.

"I was going to say crude, but that's not quite right. Maybe more cocky than anything."

"Well, he's a money guy. They tend to be a touch arrogant."

"I guess." Then, "Did you remember that I have to be at the Holiday Market this afternoon? Brooke set me up with a table and she says it's going to be kind of a big deal. Lots of fun vendors and jolly old St. Nick is supposed to put in a personal appearance."

"I have the tea tins all ready. They're the cute red ones I ordered last June."

"And they're filled with tea and . . . ?"

"Haley already stuck the labels on," Drayton said.

"Well, good. You guys are way ahead of me," Theodosia said.

Drayton lifted the lid on the teapot again and said, "We try." And then, "This is ready now."

Theodosia was chatting with Jill and her daughter, Kristen, when the front door popped open (for about the fiftieth time) and a familiar face came bobbing toward her.

She said, "Excuse me," to her guests and then wandered over to greet Wade Holland.

"I've heard so much about your place from Pauline that I had to drop by and see for myself," Wade said. He gazed about the bustling shop, taking it all in. "And I have to say, her assessment was spot-on. It's cute. I mean, like English-countryside cute."

"Thank you," Theodosia said. "A lot of love and hard work went into this little tea shop."

"I can see that," Wade said as they moved toward the counter. "And you're crazy busy, too. Not a table to be had. Good thing I only stopped by for takeout."

"We can certainly help you there," Drayton said, smiling at him. "How about an eggnog scone and a cup of . . ."

"Green tea," Wade said. "Always love the green tea."

"Got it," Drayton said.

"You know," Theodosia said, "I drove past your shop yesterday. On my way to check out that art consultant."

"You should have stopped in. King's Ransom is stocked to the rafters with tons of Christmas gifties. I bet you'd like our stuff," Wade said.

"Maybe I can still manage to come by, though things are pretty crazy here," Theodosia said.

Wade nodded, but his expression had suddenly turned serious. "I have to tell you—I'm truly grateful that you've been looking into things for Pauline. She's been worried sick and working herself into a grand tizzy. She thinks the police are going to grab her, toss her in a windowless room, and shine bright lights in her eyes until she confesses."

"I don't believe the police see Pauline as any kind of suspect or accessory to the crime," Theodosia said.

"You're sure about that?"

"I am," Theodosia said.

"Good. That's good to hear, because Pauline is really freaking out."

"Now that you're here, I have a question for you. One that's just this side of impertinent," Theodosia said.

"Oh yeah?" Wade said.

"In speaking with some of the party guests, it was brought to my attention that Pauline might have a gambling issue."

"Gambling?" Now Wade looked completely perplexed. "You mean like going on a—what would you call it—a junket to Las Vegas?"

"Or anywhere really."

Wade's look of consternation suddenly morphed into a boyish grin. "Gambling. That's pretty funny because I'd have to say the closest Pauline's ever come to gambling is maybe—*maybe*—going to a church bingo game or buying a raffle ticket."

"Really," Theodosia said.

"Really," Wade said.

"Okay, I'm going to take your word for it."

"Wait a minute," Wade said. "Someone actually *mentioned* this to you? Accused Pauline of being a gambler?"

"You could say that."

Wade frowned. "Wow. That's so not cool. Can you tell me who it was?"

"I'd rather not."

"Well, whatever jerk was spreading rumors, it sounds as if they're trying to throw Pauline under the bus, which I think is just plain awful. Unconscionable, really. Especially when she's been such a good and loyal employee to Miss Drucilla. And she's been staying on and working so hard to get everything in order for the estate."

"I hate to admit it, but there are some nasty people out there," Theodosia said. "People who'll make up stories."

"More like lies," Wade said.

"Here you go," Drayton called from behind the counter. He snapped a lid on a take-out cup and handed over an indigo blue bag. "Organic green tea and we dug up a nice healthy blueberry scone. Instant fortification for your busy day."

"This is terrific," Wade said, accepting the takeout from Drayton. "I'm really into wellness and trying to get Pauline to think the same way. You know, drinking green tea, practicing tai chi, earthing, that sort of thing."

"Is earthing where you walk around outdoors barefoot?" Drayton asked. "Grass between your toes and all that?"

"Yes, it's extremely healthy and connects you to the earth's vibrations. You ever try it?" Wade asked.

"Heavens no," Drayton said.

"Well, thank you anyway," Wade said. He raised his cup of tea in a kind of salute. "Hopefully, this'll see me through a busy morning."

"Come back soon," Theodosia said.

Ten minutes later, with a full house and customers waiting to be seated, a sort of crisis arose. Not exactly a life-and-death crisis. More like the delivery of a gigantic, sixteen-foot-high white flocked Christmas tree.

The deliveryman from Floradora squeezed the big tree through the front door, then eased it past a few waiting customers.

"Where do you want your tree, ma'am?" he asked Theodosia.

"How about back out on the sidewalk?" Drayton suggested. He was staring at bits of white flocking that were filtering down onto the carpet.

"Drayton!" Theodosia cried. "Don't be such a curmudgeon. We're talking about a *Christmas* tree. A gorgeous one at that."

"That's not a tree. It's an entire forest," Drayton said.

Even Miss Dimple came over to stare.

"That tree's ginormous," she said. "Lovely but ginormous. Where on earth are you going to put it?"

Theodosia had been studying the problem. It *was* a large tree. But maybe . . .

"Maybe we can squeeze it between the highboys?" she said.

"If you do that, you'll have to pull down all those decorated grapevine wreaths," Drayton pointed out. "Otherwise they'll get smooshed."

"It's no problem to move them," Theodosia said. She couldn't figure out why Drayton was suddenly so jumpy. Maybe it was something in the water (or tea)? Or was Mercury in retrograde? Or was he just being extra picky-fussy-nervous about the upcoming White Christmas Tea? Whatever.

The problem was resolved when Theodosia and Miss Dimple moved the wreaths into the office and the delivery-man was able to slide the tree into place.

"It's nice," the deliveryman said, giving it a final shove. "A tight fit but nice."

Theodosia and Miss Dimple got busy again, taking orders, pouring tea, and delivering food. Then subtly placing checks on all the tables, the better to get their customers moving so they could set up for their White Christmas Tea.

As Theodosia was cashing out a customer, Drayton took a phone call. She figured it must have been someone hoping to snag a last-minute reservation, until Drayton said, "What?" loud enough for her to hear him halfway across the tea room.

"Are you *serious*?" Drayton straightened up, his stiff body language signaling there was some sort of problem.

Theodosia edged over to the front counter, the better to hear what was going on, and saw that Drayton's ears were turning bright pink. What was the problem? Who was he talking to?

Drayton listened for another minute or so, shaking his head, looking more and more intense. "Perhaps we could . . . ," he began, but was obviously cut off by the caller. He listened some more and said, "If that's the way it is, then. . . . Well, yes, okay. Fine. Good day to you, too." The receiver wasn't slammed down but it wasn't set down gently, either.

"What?" Theodosia asked in a low voice. She was standing right at the counter now, staring at Drayton's ashen face (and still pink ears).

"We've been canceled," he said.

"Canceled how? What was canceled? Explain, please."

"That was Cordelia Manchester, the event coordinator over at the Gibbes Museum. It seems we're no longer needed to cater their annual donor's party next month."

"What!" Even as Theodosia felt shock waves rumble through her, she was making rapid calculations. "But we were *counting* on that catering event. It's always a huge deal for us and . . . and January's such a slow month."

"Now it'll be even slower," Drayton said. "I'm afraid the cancellation is a done deal. We can strike that event from our calendar."

"Did Cordelia give you a reason why?" Theodosia figured there *had* to be a legitimate reason. Must have been a change of plans. Some sort of delay.

"Cordelia said our services were no longer needed. Just like that, very matter-of-fact and not terribly polite about it."

"I wonder what happened—or, rather, what changed her mind."

Drayton peered at her. "You want to know what I think?"

"Of course I do." Drayton was usually spot-on with his ability to read people.

"I think that bully Donny Bragg got to her. We asked Bragg one too many questions on Monday night and he felt like he was being pushed around. So now he's decided to retaliate. Flex his muscle as a board member."

"You think Bragg's ego was on the line?"

"I do." Drayton nodded. "I think Bragg is majorly ticked off at us."

"You . . . could be right. Wow. And here I thought we

were doing a good thing. I had no idea a few innocent questions would make us so unpopular."

"Doesn't feel so good, does it?" Drayton asked.

"No, it doesn't," Theodosia said. Then she wondered, *Is Bragg just angry at us? Or is he guilty as sin?*

13

❦

Bing Crosby warbled "White Christmas" over the sound system as Theodosia and Miss Dimple put the finishing touches on the tables. Today they'd used white linen tablecloths, then added white lace table runners. The china was white Regency Ironstone with a swirl around the edges, and the centerpieces were large bouquets of white roses interspersed with calla lilies. Flocked pinecones and antique Christmas cards added to the decor.

Miss Dimple surveyed the tables with a practiced eye. "Maybe add a few white candles?" she asked.

"Why not?" Theodosia said. When it came to tea tables, less wasn't necessarily more.

"And toss on a few strands of those pearls?"

Theodosia nodded. "Whatever works." She walked over to the counter, savoring the notion that her tea shop gleamed like well-polished silver, and said, "What's brewing today, Drayton?"

"Since it's our White Christmas Tea, what else could we possibly serve but white tea?"

"The Emperor's White Tea from Republic of Tea?" Theodosia asked.

"For sure," Drayton said. "And probably Harney and Sons' Wedding Tea as well."

Then, because getting fired by the Gibbes Museum was still banging around in Theodosia's brain, making her feel unsettled, she said, "Do you think I should call the Gibbes Museum and see if I can smooth things over? Were they absolutely clear about us not catering their donor's party?"

"Crystal clear," Drayton said. "I wouldn't bother calling them back."

"Oh. Okay." That was disheartening.

Theodosia fussed about the tea shop for another ten minutes until their guests started to arrive. Then she was thankfully busy and all thoughts about losing the party for the Gibbes evaporated from her mind.

Theodosia had just seated a table of eight when Majel Mercer walked in. And surprise, surprise, she had Pauline Stauber in tow.

"I had so much fun yesterday, I just had to come back," Majel cooed.

"And we're delighted to have you," Theodosia said. "Again."

"You see who I talked into coming with me?" Majel said. "I was picking up some papers from Pauline and found her moping about that great big house all by her lonesome. Figured she could use some tea and sympathy. I hope you have an extra chair."

"We certainly do," Theodosia said. Then she turned to Pauline and said, "Lovely to see you again. You know, Wade was here earlier to grab some takeout."

"I thought he might drop by," Pauline said, "especially after I told him what a charming little tea shop this was. And that you also served healthy green tea."

"Well, thank you for that. We're always delighted to find ourselves with a new customer," Theodosia said.

Pauline glanced around. "Actually, I feel a little funny being here, like I shouldn't be out in public having fun. After all, the funeral is tomorrow."

"You can't mourn Miss Drucilla forever," Majel said, her voice gentle, not scolding. "She wouldn't want you to."

"I suppose you're right," Pauline said.

"She is right," Theodosia said.

Pauline gave a sad smile. "The Justice Initiative was one of Miss Drucilla's favorite charities, so I guess I am a little thrilled that Majel coaxed me along."

"It's good for you to be out and about," Theodosia said as she led them to a table. Once Pauline was seated, Theodosia patted her on the shoulder and said, "You really do deserve to treat yourself and have a little fun."

Not only was the White Christmas Tea fun; it was also a delicious menu. Eggnog scones were served with blackberry jam and Devonshire cream. Chestnut-and-mushroom soup was accompanied by a glazed ham and cheddar cheese tea sandwich. An entrée of chicken à la king on flaky buttermilk biscuits had the guests oohing and aahing about the wonderful flavors. And Haley's gingerbread cake and red velvet cupcakes were the pièce de résistance for dessert.

Drayton came through with flying colors, too, serving his special white teas, chatting with the guests, doling out little bits of tea lore here and there.

"Why white tea?" one of the guests asked him.

"Because they tend to be rather extraordinary," Drayton said. "Many white teas are grown in the Fujian province in China and the small buds on those particular *Camellia sinensis* plants are covered in silvery hairs that give the appearance of being white."

"How are they picked?" another guest asked.

"Generally by hand. Then the buds are either dried in the sun or steamed gently to give up their water content," Drayton said. "As you can see, white teas have very little color, but their taste is magnificently delicate."

When Theodosia filled Majel's teacup, she said, "Majel, tell me about the nonprofit that you head, the Justice Initiative."

"Thank you for asking," Majel said. "The Justice Initiative fulfills a critical need. We raise money to fund legal defenses for people who are unable to hire top-notch attorneys. And while we acknowledge there are a lot of great public defenders out there, there are some not-so-great ones, too."

"I'm sure."

"Which is why we have a whole cadre of volunteer attorneys who give free legal advice. Not just for a defense in court, but for real estate, wills, divorce, child custody, that sort of thing."

"You were in line to receive a grant from Miss Drucilla, were you not?" Theodosia said. "I was wondering if that grant had come through yet."

"Not yet, but I have it on good authority that we were at the top of Miss Drucilla's list, so I don't imagine there'll be a problem. On the other hand . . ." Majel shrugged. "We'll have to wait and see what happens with her estate."

"Well, good luck anyway."

"Thank you, sweetie."

Once the tea was over, the guests began to slowly shuffle out. Miss Dimple got busy clearing tables while Theodosia ducked into her office. She had about thirty minutes, if that, to pack up her goods for the Holiday Market and then hustle over to Marion Square and get set up. She was taking the first shift, from two to five; then Haley would swing by and man their booth until eight o'clock when the market closed.

Let me see. Two cases of tea and then my T-Bath products.

Theodosia had developed her proprietary T-Bath products with the idea of creating relaxing tea-based bath bombs. Those had caught on like gangbusters, so she'd expanded into lotions and potions. Now Green Tea Lotion, Chamomile Calming Cream, Rose Tea Feet Treat, Head over Heels for Hibiscus, and Jasmine Rejuvenation Oil were also part of the repertoire.

Theodosia grabbed a box of tea cozies and added them to her stash. Okay, now all she had to do was schlep everything out to her Jeep.

Propping the back door open, Theodosia made four quick trips.

Good. One more to go and then I'm outa here.

But just as she was hauling the last box to her car, Drayton came rushing outside, waving his hands.

"Wait, wait!" he cried.

Theodosia waited.

"What's up?" she asked, sneaking a glance at her watch. Now she had barely twenty minutes to get there.

"I know this is coming out of left field, but Pauline asked us to help with Miss Drucilla's funeral service tomorrow," Drayton said.

"What?" Theodosia shook her head. "You're kidding. As if we don't have enough to deal with?" Then, "Where's the service going to be held?"

"A hop, skip, and a jump away from us. Just down the block at St. Philip's Episcopal Church."

"That church is almost two hundred years old. I expect they've handled an awful lot of funerals in their time and done them rather well. Why would they need *our* input?"

"Select the music? Pick out an appropriate reading?" Drayton said. "I'm afraid a lot of details have been left to Pauline, and she's not doing all that well."

"She seemed fine at lunch. I just saw her snarfing down cake some twenty minutes ago."

"Yes, but after you went into your office to pack, a few people started asking Pauline about Miss Drucilla. That's when she had a kind of teary meltdown," Drayton said.

"I'm sorry to hear that."

"Majel was some help. But in the end, I called Pauline's boyfriend to come over and pick her up."

"You called Wade? Is he still here?"

"They just left. He was going to take Pauline home."

"To her home? Or Miss Drucilla's place?"

"I don't know."

Fifteen minutes left.

"Okay. So what are we supposed to do?" Theodosia asked. "About the church service?"

"Wait. There's more," Drayton said.

Theodosia squinted at him. "How much more?"

"They want to have their post-funeral luncheon here." Drayton held up his hands, palms out. "I know. It's a lot. But I already ran it past Haley and she says she can manage. Of course, you have final say."

"I'm fine with the luncheon, but still unsure what our contribution should be to the funeral service."

"Tell you what," Drayton said. "You go on to your Holiday Market and I'll run over to the church and try to handle things as best I can."

"Are you sure about this?"

"I'm an old Presbyterian from way back. I'm fairly sure finalizing a church service is in my wheelhouse."

"Bless you, Drayton."

Drayton might have been running on cool, but Theodosia was bubbling along at simmer. So it stood to reason she got stuck in traffic, then was late getting to the Holiday Market in Marion Square.

Luckily, the event really hadn't gotten rolling yet, so it wasn't a big deal. Theodosia located her table, really a kind of three-sided booth, unrolled a large piece of red felt, and quickly set out her tea tins, T-Bath products, and tea cozies. She also plopped down a few Indigo Tea Shop business cards.

There. Everything looks appropriately festive and cute.

In the booth to her right, a man was selling wooden reindeer, the antlers made of curly willow. To her left a woman was selling homemade beeswax candles.

"Have you had many customers?" Theodosia asked the candle lady.

"Just a few. But it's still early," the woman told her.

Just then there was a hiss of air brakes and a loud belch of exhaust as a gray double-decker bus pulled to a stop across the street from them. Minutes later, the bus's door opened wide and four dozen women from the Goose Creek Women's Club descended upon them.

Business picked up then and Theodosia spent the next hour and a half talking tea, T-Bath products, and ringing up quite a few sales.

When there was a lull in the crowd, Theodosia walked past booths selling jewelry, clothing, gourmet foods, and crafts. Following the heavenly aromas of cinnamon and spice, she found a food truck selling donuts and hot apple cider. As she grabbed a cup of cider, she turned and ran smack-dab (well, almost, though nothing actually spilled) into Sawyer Daniels.

"Mr. Daniels," she said. He looked like he'd just come from a three-martini lunch: slightly dazed expression, natty sport coat, tie that many silkworms had died for, a Burberry trench coat.

He gazed at her. "Yes?"

He doesn't remember me.

"It's Theodosia Browning. Delaine and I spoke with you last night? At the ballet?" In the light of day, she saw threads of red just below his skin. *Could definitely be a drinker,* she decided.

Recognition dawned faintly on his face. "Oh sure, you're Delaine's friend. Now I remember."

No, you don't.

"Nice seats, by the way," Theodosia said. "At the ballet last night."

"Oh yeah, only the best. Doesn't pay to go if you're not close enough to spit on the stage."

"I'm glad I ran into you today," Theodosia said as Daniels tried to edge away. "I started thinking about what you said last night and wanted to ask you a couple more questions."

"Questions?" Daniels shook his head as though he was completely confused. "Concerning what?"

"Well, you were at Miss Drucilla's the night of her party . . . actually her murder. And I've been doing some investigating. . . ."

"What? You're a private investigator?" Daniels's lips creased in amusement.

"Not exactly. I'm a private person and I investigate, if that makes any sense."

"Maybe it does. But if you're going to ask me if I *know* anything or *saw* anything unusual that night, then the answer is a resounding *no*. I'm as baffled as you are. Upset about it, too." Daniels bounced once on the back of his heels and said, "However . . ."

"Yes?"

"If you really are investigating, there *is* someone you might want to take a look at."

"Who would that be?"

His blue eyes drilled into her. "Smokey. The painter."

Puzzled, Theodosia stared back at Daniels. "Why would you call Smokey a painter? Because he paints houses?"

Daniels shook his head. "No, no, I'm talking about actual paintings on canvas. The guy is . . ." He shrugged. "I don't know what you'd call it. . . . 'Idiot savant' seems kind of harsh, because Smokey's not stupid. He's just untrained. But from what I've seen, that guy has more talent in his little finger than a lot of artists who are hanging in major galleries on King Street."

Theodosia was completely gobsmacked by Daniels's words. "You *are* referring to Smokey Pruitt? The handyman guy who lives above Donny Bragg's garage?"

"That's the one."

"And he *paints*?"

"Yeah, he paints. What did I just say? Weren't you *listening*?" Daniels asked. He was just this side of snippy.

"Yes, I . . . I was. Thank you," Theodosia said. She felt totally flummoxed as Daniels turned and walked away.

Smokey is a painter. So maybe he . . .

Theodosia's cell phone chimed in her jacket pocket. She scrambled to dig it out and said . . .

14

"Hello?"

"Was my Holiday Blend popular? Did it completely sell out?" Drayton asked.

"Almost. I think there're maybe two tins left."

"Wonderful. We're stocked to the gills back here, so I'll send another couple dozen tea tins along with Haley."

"Great," Theodosia said. "How'd things go at the church?"

"Everything's been worked out—the music, the readings, the whole shebang. So tomorrow's funeral is a go." Drayton hesitated, then added, "But a slight problem came up."

"What is it now?"

"Wade Holland called here a few minutes ago."

"More Pauline problems?" Theodosia asked.

"Not Pauline, but it seems another semicrisis is brewing. Wade received a call from the manager at Miss Drucilla's condo complex down in Hilton Head and was told something fishy was going on."

"Fishy at the condo? Like what?"

"Like maybe someone is living there?"

"Are you asking or telling?"

"Telling," Drayton said.

"What are *we* supposed to do about it?" Theodosia asked, though she figured she had a pretty good idea.

"Wade wanted to know if we could drive down to Hilton Head and check it out."

"Uh-huh." Theodosia had so many things going on, she was ready to pull her hair out. "Wade wants *us* to drive down there? That's wacky. Why can't he handle it?"

"Something about a major conflict . . . Wade called it a perfect storm between finalizing Miss Drucilla's funeral, supporting Pauline, and holding down his job at the gift shop. I know. It's an imposition and a terrible disruption, but I feel bad for him. And for Pauline, too. She was in such a sad state when she left. And we did promise to investigate. . . ."

For the first time Theodosia felt a pang of regret. Yes, they were investigating, but they didn't seem to be making a whole lot of forward progress.

"I was thinking, if we left around five we'd probably be down there by six thirty," Drayton said.

"Oh, I don't . . ." Theodosia wasn't all that eager to bomb on down to Hilton Head and check on somebody's condo. But then she paused and gave the idea a second thought. Let it rumble through her brain. Someone might be *living* in the condo? Or, rather, they could be . . . hiding out? A passing beach bum? A drifter?

Or could it be Miss Drucilla's killer? This foray could prove to be dangerous. But still . . . if we're careful, it could mean breaking the case wide open.

Yes, Theodosia was suddenly frothing with curiosity. And even though she knew that curiosity had killed the proverbial cat, her suspicions had been roused and she felt sorely tempted.

"You know what?" Theodosia said. "I changed my mind."

"So you *are* willing to go?"

"I'll come back and pick you up just as soon as Haley shows up here."

"Shouldn't be long. She left ten minutes ago."

Once Theodosia handed over the booth to Haley, she headed back to her car, dodging and weaving through a warren of booths selling candied pecans, silver jewelry, Christmas stockings, jars of jam, embroidered hand towels, sweetgrass baskets, Benne wafers, and a million other things. With Christmas carolers dressed in long plaid skirts and matching bonnets and singing their little hearts out, could the arrival of Santa be far away?

"Theo! Theo!" a frantic voice called after her.

Shoot. She was a stone's throw away from her car. Had almost managed to make a clean getaway.

Hesitating, looking back over her shoulder, Theodosia saw Delaine running after her. Or trying to run anyway. Delaine was stumbling along, looking intense and taking teensy-weensy baby steps in four-inch heels. Heels that were backless, no less. Lord knew how she kept them from flying off her feet. Maybe she curled her toes as she ran. Or there was some magical fashion shoe glue that Theodosia didn't know about.

"Delaine," Theodosia said, pausing long enough for Delaine to finally catch up.

Delaine put a hand on Theodosia's arm and leaned forward. "I'm so glad I was able to catch you," she said, her face pink, her breath coming in short gasps. "Because I—*puff, puff*—have a tiny favor to ask."

I have to do another favor? My eyeballs are starting to hurt from all this goodwill.

"What's the favor, Delaine?"

"I just got a . . . Eek, my poor toes . . . I got a call from Doreen Palmer, the executive director at the Loving Paws

Animal Shelter. You know that I serve on their board of directors."

"Yes, I know." *Because you've hit me up for donations many times.*

"Loving Paws is *such* a great outfit," Delaine said, moving seamlessly into her impassioned pitch. "Think of all the wonderful dogs we've rescued. And do you remember that *fabulous* black-tie fund-raiser we had last year, Dinner with Your Dog?"

Theodosia remembered because she and Earl Grey had attended. The dinner had been held in the courtyard of the St. Charlotte Inn, and once the steaks (for people's consumption) and kibble (for dogs' consumption) had been served, Loving Paws had staged a silent-auction fund-raiser that raised almost eleven thousand dollars.

"Unfortunately, Loving Paws has run into kind of a sticky problem," Delaine said.

"What's that?"

"In our zeal to rescue three dozen dogs from a puppy mill down in Jasper County, it looks as if our shelter is far too crowded to house them all!"

"Then you're going to have to get aggressive with adoptions," Theodosia said.

"I'm not sure that's possible this close to Christmas."

"I suppose that does present a problem," Theodosia said. After all, how many people wanted to adopt a stray dog on Christmas Eve? Probably not that many.

"I'm going to try to persuade one of our fine hotels to give us a couple of rooms at a reduced rate," Delaine said.

"Wait. You mean, book hotel rooms for the dogs?"

"Of *course* for the dogs. We can't turn them away!" Delaine's voice rose to almost a shriek. She seemed to have caught her breath just fine. "There's no way we can rescue those poor, unfortunate little creatures out of grubby cages and then turn around and tell them there's no room at the inn! For goodness' sake, Theo, it's Christmas! Have a heart!"

"I do have a heart, but . . . well, what about trying to find *temporary* foster homes for them, just until your shelter catches up with adoptions?"

Delaine scrunched her brows together and touched a finger to her cheek, as if she was contemplating Theodosia's suggestion. "Like you, I've been thinking along those same lines. Would you ever consider . . . ?"

Ah, so this is where she's going.

"I could probably take one dog," Theodosia said. She held up an index finger to reinforce her point. "That's singular, solitary, *uno*. Just one dog."

"Uh-huh." Delaine was nodding her head now, her long silver earrings swishing against her cheeks. "That'd be good."

"When do you expect to get them?"

"The dogs are in a temporary shelter in Aiken right now and our vans are picking them up Friday."

"Mmn, tricky. So close to Christmas. Well, okay. Earl Grey and I will just have to make room."

Delaine did a genteel fist pump. "Theo, you're a lifesaver!"

As Theodosia drove down Broad Street, she thought about her various suspects. Smokey's and Donny Bragg's names were melded together in a sort of slipstream that wafted through her mind. They seemed to be at the front of the pack for now. Then again, she was highly suspicious of Sawyer Daniels and Julian Wolf-Knapp.

Just as Wolf-Knapp's name popped into her brain like a cartoon thought bubble, Theodosia realized she was driving past his studio! On a whim, she pulled over—there was an open parking space after all—and decided to run upstairs. Okay, and do what? She had to have a reason to ask more questions. After all, Wolf-Knapp was no pushover. Could she quiz him about Smokey? That might be an angle she could work. After all, if Smokey was as good a painter as Daniels said he was, maybe Wolf-Knapp knew about him or was even representing him. Theodosia wasn't sure what that would prove, but if there was a connection, it could lead to some answers.

Theodosia parked and quickly ran upstairs. But when she got to Wolf-Knapp's studio, nobody was home. She banged on the door, called his name, but nada. He must have left for the day.

Back downstairs and about to give up, Theodosia decided at the last minute to step inside the Dusty Hen Antique Shop. Maybe they knew where he was?

The shop, of course, proved to be adorable: small, tidy, and absolutely stuffed with antiques, old mirrors, silver teapots, and brass table lamps. Here was an old farmhouse table topped with an array of colorful ginger jars; over there was an antique wardrobe. And everywhere were picture frames, antique china, vintage linens, gilded birdcages, and quirky side tables. As a lucky-strike extra, all sorts of new items were interspersed among the antiques: fragrant soaps, tea towels, handmade jewelry, reproductions of Paris street signs, aprons, boxes of truffles, jars of French mustard, perfumes, and wicker furniture. It was as if the Old South had staged a friendly invasion of a French *marché*.

"This is a fabulous shop," Theodosia said to a woman— the owner?—who came forward to greet her. "I love your mix of old and new."

"We try to have a little something that appeals to everyone who walks through our doors," the woman said.

"Well, you've succeeded beautifully, because I already see a market basket that I have to have."

"For your tea shop?" the woman asked. Then she smiled. "We sort of know each other. I'm Annie Dawson and I've been to the Indigo Tea Shop a few times."

"Of course you have. Annie, it's lovely to see you again," Theodosia said. Yes, she did remember Annie, now that her memory had been jogged.

Annie smiled, pleased.

"Oh, and I want that box of truffles as well. You know, I came in to see if you knew how I could get hold of Julian Wolf-Knapp, one of the upstairs tenants, but now I'm completely besotted with shopping." Theodosia picked up a blue floral tote bag and said, "Do these also come in pink?"

"They do, but we're completely sold out because of the holidays," Annie said. "But we'll be getting more in. I can let you know when they're back in stock."

"That'd be great," Theodosia said.

"So. Julian," Annie said. "I know he often retreats to his place in the country. It's a cute little plantation house with a small barn that he uses for storage."

"Do you know where it's located?" Theodosia was mostly curious.

"I think . . ." Annie walked back to her desk, picked up a spiral-bound book, and paged through it. She frowned. "I have it here somewhere." She thought for a few moments. "Oh, I know." She pulled out a drawer, picked up a green leather book, scanned it, and said, "Here it is. Julian's place is on Larkin Lane."

Theodosia thought for a moment. "That would be out in . . ."

"Dorchester County. Off Highway Sixty-one."

"Thanks so much," Theodosia said as she handed over her credit card.

"I understand Julian's place is really quite charming," Annie said once she'd rung up Theodosia's purchases. "Here . . ." She moved to a table filled with knickknacks and picked up a small drawing in a nubby gold frame. "This is a pen-and-ink drawing of his place that Kaitlin Carnes, a local artist, did. She does drawings of many of Charleston's landmark homes: Magnolia Plantation, Middleton Place, the Aiken-Rhett House. Anyway, she did this one of Julian's place."

"It's lovely," Theodosia said. "Both the drawing and his plantation home."

With her purchases tucked in the back of her Jeep, Theodosia wondered if the truffles might make a good Christmas present for Haley. She'd already bought her a pale blue cashmere scarf, but the truffles might make a nice stocking stuffer.

Theodosia's mind was now firmly on Christmas as she drove down King Street, then hung a left on Ladson. As she made her turn, mindful of some kids on the corner, she glanced in her rearview mirror and noticed that the car following her, a nondescript tan car, had also made the turn.

Huh.

At Meeting, she hooked right. As if on cue, the tan car followed her.

This is kind of weird.

Theodosia sped up and shot through the next intersection, entering as the light turned yellow, almost clipping the red.

The tan car slipped through as well.

Am I being followed? And by who?

A thought bubbled up that it could be Smokey, since he was the one with the most fingers pointed at him. So he could be feeling some unease. But it could also be Julian Wolf-Knapp. Maybe he'd been sitting in his office the whole time, listening to her shout his name and pound on the door. Then he'd—what? Decided to follow her to see what she was up to?

Without signaling, Theodosia made a fast left turn. The tan car shot past her. Didn't seem to register that she'd turned off.

How interesting. Now Theodosia wasn't sure if she'd actually been followed.

Or maybe . . . I hate to say this, but . . .

"Maybe I'm just being paranoid."

15

The minute Theodosia pulled into the alley behind the Indigo Tea Shop, Drayton ran out the back door, locked it behind him, jumped into the passenger seat, and said, "I apologize for this strange excursion that I flimflammed you into. I really do. I see now I shouldn't have been so insistent about our helping Wade."

Theodosia waved a hand. "Don't worry about it. Now I'm kind of curious."

Drayton pulled his seat belt across himself. "About . . ."

"What we might find at that condo. *Who* we might find there," Theodosia said as she took off down the alley and hooked a left.

Drayton nodded. "Ah."

"How are we supposed to get into the unit?" Theodosia asked. "Check with the manager or . . . ?"

"I have a key. Wade sent over a key."

"Then we're all set."

Theodosia drove back down Broad Street, followed it south through a fair amount of traffic, then turned onto Highway 17 and accelerated. Not so much traffic on the main highway. That was lucky; it meant they'd make good time.

"I have major news to tell you," Theodosia said.

"What's that?" Drayton asked.

"I ran into Sawyer Daniels at the Holiday Market—you know, the Doing the Good charity guy—and by the by, he told me that Smokey Pruitt is an artist."

"You mean a con artist?"

"No, a fine artist. As in painting and drawing."

"Daniels said this?"

"Uh-huh," Theodosia said. "He told me that Smokey has beaucoup talent."

"You can't be serious." Drayton sounded completely skeptical.

"Of course, this is the gospel according to Sawyer Daniels. For all I know, Smokey might be painting stick figures or doing graffiti art with cans of spray paint."

"I wouldn't classify graffiti as fine art," Drayton said.

"These days, if you can get a dealer to represent you, anything qualifies as art," Theodosia said.

"Well." Drayton looked thoughtful. "Then I suppose we need to take a second look at Smokey, a more measured look."

"I just had a weird thought," Theodosia said. "Could Smokey be doing Donny Bragg's bidding? Could he be Bragg's henchman?"

"What do you mean by that?" Drayton asked.

"Okay, if Bragg said, 'Go steal a painting,' would Smokey actually do it?"

"I have no idea," Drayton said. "But if what you say is true, that also implies that Bragg could have said, 'And while you're at it, go kill Miss Drucilla.'"

"And that suggests mind control," Theodosia said, "which is downright terrifying."

Drayton gave a shudder. "If you ask me, this whole thing is terrifying."

Theodosia watched for the tan car that had followed her earlier, but didn't see it.

Good.

They hooked up with I-95 for forty miles, then turned east onto Highway 278. This was a narrow, twisty road that took them past small country churches known as *praise houses* and roadside markets with names like Blessing Acres and Trickling Creek Farm. Apples, pecans, sweet potatoes, and muscadine grapes were all still in season. Seafood markets advertised fresh-caught shrimp, oysters, grouper, and blue crabs.

Dying rays of sun danced across shallow ponds and cypress swamps. In some places low-lying puffs of fog made the wetlands look dark and slightly ethereal.

"Early settlers called these swamps *dismals*," Drayton said.

"I think they're beautiful," Theodosia said. "They're peaceful and have a real primordial feel. And think of the wildlife that abounds in these swamps—foxes, deer, mink, cormorants, bald eagles, coyotes, and canvasback ducks."

"Osprey, too," Drayton said as they crossed a wide bridge that took them to Hilton Head Island. "Okay now, in two miles we turn onto Greenwood Drive."

"What are we looking for?" Theodosia asked as marshes and swamps slowly turned into developed land.

"A development called Shadow Dunes. There's supposed to be a gatehouse out front. But I think we've got a ways to go yet."

Theodosia made her turn, then drove another four miles or so.

"Maybe this is it right here. I see a gate with a guard and a sign that says . . . Nope, that's Montgomery Manor."

They drove on.

"Okay, we have to be getting close now," Drayton said. He

was clutching his scribbled directions and searching for Shadow Dunes. "I'm guessing it's going to be fairly upscale. . . ."

"This looks upscale," Theodosia said. She slowed as they came to a small pond with a spouting fountain in the middle.

"What's the sign say?"

"Shadow Dunes. This is it," Theodosia said as she turned into a driveway that had a gatehouse but no guard at his post. Only an enormous Christmas wreath hanging on the side of the small gatehouse.

"Pretty," Drayton said as they passed stands of tupelo gum trees, small ponds, and clusters of villa homes, "though I'm surprised there wasn't any guard."

"Lack of security is probably why there's an uninvited guest staying in Miss Drucilla's condo. What number are we looking for?"

"Three twenty-seven," Drayton said.

The condos themselves were quite nice-looking. Clustered in groups of three, all plantation style with peaked roofs, second-floor balconies, two-car garages, and abundant groves of palm trees nestled close.

"Here we are," Theodosia said as they pulled into the driveway of 327 and rolled to a stop.

"Looks deserted. Curtains are closed. I doubt anyone's there, much less creeping around and making trouble."

"Still, we promised to check it out."

"This is going to be a snooze," Drayton said as he climbed out of the Jeep, stretched, and walked slowly to the front door. Theodosia followed him closely.

Standing on an oversized sisal welcome mat, Drayton handed Theodosia the key. "Here, you can do the honors." He shook his head. "What a waste of time."

But the minute Theodosia stuck the key in the lock and pushed the door open a couple of inches, she knew someone was inside. The air felt warm and had that alive, slightly disturbed quality.

But exactly *who* had taken up temporary residence here? Some deadbeat who'd found himself a fancy deserted condo to hunker down in for a while? Or, heaven forbid, could it be Miss Drucilla's killer?

"Drayton," Theodosia whispered. "I'm going to need you to back me up here because someone's definitely inside." Theodosia nudged the door again, causing it to swing wider. Now she could see the living room, dining room, and a small sliver of kitchen.

"Wha-what?" Drayton jabbered. He took a hasty step backward, blinking hard, nerves tightening in his face. "Hold on a minute. I need to . . ."

Drayton spun on his heels and vanished, leaving Theodosia alone and feeling vulnerable. But a few moments later he was back, looking considerably more confident and brandishing a large silver flashlight.

"If whoever's in here makes any sort of dodgy move, I'll clobber them with this flashlight!" Drayton hefted the makeshift weapon high above his head.

"Good thinking," Theodosia said, even though it was doubtful Drayton would ever venture a move. When push came to shove, Drayton wasn't a hot reactor like she was. He was more about the gentle art of persuasion.

"Okay, let's do it," Drayton said.

Theodosia pushed the door all the way open, just as a young man shuffled out from the kitchen. He saw them and halted midstride, an expression of utter shock on his handsome face and a can of Gullah Cream Ale clutched tightly in his right hand.

"Who are you?" he shouted. "What are you doing here?"

"What are *you* doing here?" Theodosia yelled back.

"A better question might be, who *are* you?" Drayton asked. He thrust his shoulders back and pulled himself to his full height. He'd dropped the flashlight to his side, probably figuring there was strength in numbers. Two against one, if it came to that.

"I'm Coy Cooper," the young man said. Then he glanced at the open door and frowned. "Wait a minute. That was locked. You've got a key? Where'd you get a key?"

"Pauline Stauber gave it to us," Theodosia said.

It took a moment for the name to click in. Then Cooper said, "Ah, my aunt's personal assistant. Of course. Isn't Pauline just the perfect little indentured servant?"

Theodosia's eyes widened in surprise. "You're the nephew?"

Cooper executed a mock bow. "At your service."

"Goodness," Drayton said.

Cooper was tall and angular, maybe twenty-two or twenty-three. He had a long face and dark hair pulled into a low ponytail; he was dressed casually but expensively in a purple cashmere sweater and faded blue jeans. His feet were stuffed into well-worn driving shoes and, with his rich-boy blasé attitude, he looked as if he'd just stepped off the pages of an Orvis catalog.

"Mind if we come in?" Theodosia asked. She was already studying the interior of the condo. Nice and tasteful with lots of bleached wood and ivory fabrics that she supposed a decorator would have called "beachy" or "coastal style." There were also several oil paintings hung on the walls and a coffee table held a bronze sculpture that looked like an aardvark in agony. Or maybe it was a hunk of petrified driftwood.

"You're already in," Cooper said. But he retreated a few steps so they could come all the way in and close the door.

"Why are *you* here?" Theodosia asked him.

Cooper looked nonchalant. "I'm staying here because the funeral service is tomorrow. I was going to flake out for the night and then drive up first thing."

"You're going to attend the service tomorrow," Drayton said. He sounded like he didn't believe Cooper.

"You got a problem with that?" Cooper asked. He said it laughingly, then took a sip of beer.

"I'm fine with it unless you plan to stop at Miss Drucilla's lawyer's office and do something rash. Like contest her will," Drayton said. "Try to gain control of her estate."

"Furthest thing from my mind," Cooper said.

Theodosia wasn't sure whether to believe him or not. But for the time being, she decided to give Cooper a pass.

"We received a call from the property manager here," Theodosia said. "They were worried someone was squatting in this unit."

"Yup, that's me," Cooper said happily.

"So you have a key as well," Drayton said.

"No, I kicked in a window last night," Cooper said. Then, "Of course I have a key. My aunt gave me one a few years ago."

"And you stay here regularly?" Theodosia said.

"Nope, this is my first time," Cooper said. He pointed to the flashlight in Drayton's hand. "Hey, buddy, you going camping or something? Planning to lead a snipe hunt?"

"Just . . . being careful," Drayton said.

"You have some lovely art on the walls," Theodosia said as she looked around. She studied the paintings, but didn't see anything that looked like a Renoir.

"My aunt was a collector. So . . . she collected," Cooper said. "Now, if there's nothing else on your mind, I guess I'll say goodbye and see you guys tomorrow."

Drayton ticked the flashlight in Cooper's direction. "Count on it."

Well that was a big nothing," Drayton grumped as he climbed into the passenger seat.

"I don't know," Theodosia said as she started her Jeep, bumped down the private road, and exited onto the highway. "It's still possible that Cooper murdered his aunt, grabbed the painting off the wall, and then hightailed it down here to hide out."

"Sounds far-fetched, though I suppose it's within the realm of possibility."

"Maybe the missing Renoir was sitting in the condo's back bedroom. Or maybe it's already disappeared into the underground art market," Theodosia said.

"I read recently that today's art market is a sixty-billion-dollar business."

Theodosia glanced over at him. "That much?"

"Worldwide anyway. Lots of artists, dealers, and wealthy collectors."

"Lots of scams as well," she said.

"Probably."

They drove along in silence for a few miles. Then Theodosia said, "Drayton, I've been discounting Pauline all along. I mean as a suspect. But what if she's the one who murdered Miss Drucilla?"

"And then stole the painting?" Drayton said. "Rushed it upstairs and stashed it in some hidden nook and cranny in that great big mansion?"

"Until it was safe to move. I don't think the police went through Miss Drucilla's home all that carefully. I think they were fairly convinced that whoever killed her had escaped through the back door and disappeared into the night."

"If Pauline's the guilty party, why on earth would she ask you to look into things?" Drayton asked. "She practically begged you, right?"

"She did, and I don't know the answer to that. Maybe to keep herself in the loop? To pick up any bits of information that Tidwell might spill to me? To send us spinning in the wrong direction? Maybe . . . some kind of emotional manipulation?"

"Like tonight," Drayton said. "This ridiculous trip."

"Exactly. I'm wondering if Pauline *intended* to send us on a wild-goose chase."

"Well, actually, it was her boyfriend who called with the request."

"Doesn't matter. Pauline managed to convince Wade to convince *you* that something was terribly wrong at the Hilton Head condo."

"And we dutifully drove down here. Yes, I see what you mean," Drayton said. "Pauline does seem to be . . . pulling the strings."

16

❧

A pale moon shone down as Theodosia dropped off Drayton, then drove the few blocks to her home. Naturally, Earl Grey was waiting at the back door.

"Sorry, big guy," she said. "It's kind of late so . . ."

"Rrwr?"

Earl Grey's tail thumped the floor as limpid brown eyes implored her.

"You still want to take a run?"

Now wagging instead of thumping.

"Okay, kiddo, you're on."

Theodosia did a fast presto chango into her running gear and then they were out the door and loping down the dark alley. They took it slow the first couple of blocks, warming up, getting into their rhythm, then picked up the pace. It was a good night for running, cool and crisp, nobody around. They bounded down Ladson, running under streetlamps that delivered little puddles of warm yellow light. Light traffic noises sounded from over on Church Street; the mournful toot of a tugboat carried from Charleston Harbor a few blocks away.

When Theodosia hit Legare Street, she slowed to a trot. Then, a few paces on, she stopped altogether and doubled back in the direction she'd just come.

Theodosia wasn't sure what she had in mind—some random thought was nibbling at her brain. Something she had to do? Something she should check out?

Yeah, maybe.

Under cover of darkness, she ran down the narrow brick alley that was directly behind Donny Bragg's house.

If I want to do a little more snooping . . . there's no time like the present. But do I dare?

Running lightly, then slowing to a walk, Theodosia and Earl Grey came to a halt directly behind Bragg's carriage house. Theodosia stood there for a few moments, let her breathing quiet, and tried to decide what to do. Was she brave enough to undertake what she called a *hot prowl*? That is, sneak in and look around. And just whose place did she want to sneak into? Smokey's apartment or Donny Bragg's home?

As she stood there, the decision was made for her. Faint voices floated toward her, not a conversation she could actually listen in on—because it was hard to make out actual words—more like a faulty radio signal that faded in and out.

Creeping a little closer, hiding behind the spread of a giant magnolia tree, Theodosia peered through a tangle of foliage into Donny Bragg's backyard.

Smokey was lounging against a narrow pillar, talking to Bragg. Their voices were low rumbles, so she still couldn't hear what was being said. But they were both enjoying a leisurely smoke, Smokey flicking ashes from a cigarette, Bragg puffing on one of his contraband cigars.

And from her vantage point, they also looked relaxed. Occupied. At least for a few minutes.

Do I dare?

Theodosia looked back over her shoulder at the rectangle

of light that shone from Smokey's open door. And her decision was made in an instant. Yes, she was going to take full advantage of this opportunity. Looping Earl Grey's leash around the bottom railing and moving as quietly as possible, she bounded up the stairs to Smokey's apartment.

Rrowr?

Oops. Theodosia stopped dead in her tracks and turned around to gaze at Earl Grey. He stared up at her with questioning eyes.

Would he growl or bark and give her away? Derail her little sneak and peek? Possibly. And she surely didn't want that to happen.

Theodosia ran back down, unhooked his leash, and gave a quick tug. Earl Grey followed her up the stairs, his toenails clicking softly against the wooden steps. Reaching the top, she hesitated. So far, so good? Okay, now for the tricky part. She drew a deep breath, pushed open the screen door, and stepped inside with her dog.

Smokey's place didn't look all that different from the way it had two nights ago. Same lumpy brown sofa, large-screen TV with a tangle of wires hanging down, low lighting, and dirty dishes piled in the kitchen sink. But this time Theodosia paid closer attention to the two paintings that hung on the wall.

She didn't have a trained eye, but now that she had a chance to study them, she could see they were quite good. One was a seascape of Charleston Harbor, capturing a flotilla of sailboats with a cargo ship and Fort Sumter in the background. The other was a pastoral scene of two palomino horses. The colors, shading, and brushstrokes on both paintings conveyed a vibrant, lifelike quality. The artist—Smokey, in this case—had some talent after all.

Okay, Smokey can paint. So what?

Stepping lightly through the living area, Theodosia padded down a short hallway and ducked into the bedroom. Earl Grey followed along quietly. There was a nondescript blue quilt stretched across a double bed, a battered wooden dresser, and a ratty brown carpet partially covering a wooden floor. There were also a messy side table that held paints and brushes, and a paint-spattered easel with a half-finished painting sitting on it.

Smokey as art forger?

Theodosia tiptoed closer. No, it was a half-finished garden scene. Nothing particularly incriminating.

She crossed the bedroom floor and peeked around a doorway into the bathroom, ready to take a quick look and then get the heck out of Dodge.

Smokey's bathroom wasn't exactly a biohazard but it was close.

A narrow shelf was cluttered with shampoo, deodorant, a bottle of aspirin, some antacid tablets, and a grubby washcloth. A solitary toothbrush sat in a plastic cup. A broken wicker basket held combs, brushes, and odds and ends.

Theodosia was about to turn, when a flash of color among all the dullness caught her eye.

What? Something red? A logo on a tube of toothpaste?

No. Not quite.

An alarm pinged deep in her brain. She took a step closer.

No, it's orange. Just like . . .

Her heart thump-bumped inside her chest, then skittered wildly. It couldn't be, could it? Theodosia willed herself to calm down, to take a careful look and be absolutely sure what she was looking at. Eyes could play tricks after all.

No tricks. There were three orange syringes sitting in the bottom of that wicker basket.

Oh, dear Lord!

Theodosia ran blindly out of the bathroom, caught her toe on the edge of the carpet, bumped into a surprised Earl Grey, and almost fell down. As she flailed her arms to catch herself, she struck the painting and knocked it off its easel.

CRASH!

Theodosia froze in her tracks.

Oh, my stars, did anyone hear that?

Her heart hammered heavily inside her chest as she listened for raised voices and footsteps pounding up the outside staircase. Waited for the inevitable—the shouts, the anger, and the accusations!

When nothing happened, when no angry red-faced men appeared, Theodosia decided maybe she could breathe again. She bent down, scooped up the painting that had landed jelly-side down, and set it back on the easel. Hopefully the paint was dry enough that it hadn't picked up any nasty fuzz from the carpet.

She allowed herself a quick look around.

Did I disturb anything else?

Theodosia didn't think so. But Earl Grey was looking at her strangely, almost guiltily, as if he knew they'd been trespassing big-time. And of course they had.

"Okay," she whispered. "We'd better scram before we're really in hot water."

Jogging back down the alley, Theodosia turned and headed down Legare again. She passed directly in front of Bragg's house, not looking that way, almost pretending the place didn't exist, but all the while searching out of the corner of her eyes to see if anything was amiss.

It didn't seem to be, thank goodness.

Her heart lifted as she and Earl Grey picked up the pace.

But those syringes! Was Smokey the killer?

Somehow it didn't feel right. And yet . . . there they were. Bright orange syringes. The same type that had been used on Miss Drucilla.

Theodosia and Earl Grey stopped at the corner, waited for a car to swoosh by, then crossed the street.

Time to head home. Tonight's run felt somehow tainted.

But as Theodosia and Earl Grey started down Meeting Street, footsteps sounded behind them.

Is that Smokey? Or Donny Bragg? Did one of those goof-balls see me?

Theodosia immediately picked up the pace. She was fast and in good condition from almost nightly runs. She could probably outrun anybody if she had to. Or if she was frightened enough.

On the other hand, whoever was following behind her was running faster, too!

Anger flared.

Somebody's chasing me? I don't think *so.*

She bounded down Price's Alley, Earl Grey running beside her. This was one of the narrow hidden lanes that catacombed its way through the Historic District. Listed on the Historic Register, Price's Alley was too narrow for cars, was paved with antique flagstones, and boasted tall brick walls festooned with hanging ivy. And it was dark as a coal bin. Nobody would see her as she slipped along. . . .

BANG!

Something zinged past her, bounced off the wall ahead of her.

Theodosia was stunned.

What! Did somebody just fire a shot at me?

Like a gazelle hell-bent on escaping a hungry lion, Theodosia juked left. She and Earl Grey flew over a low brick wall, landed in a secret garden, sprinted through a forest of azaleas, dodged a marble statue of a Greek goddess pouring water, and popped out onto a well-lit street.

Two blocks later they were home, Theodosia's heart still beating out of her chest, Earl Grey figuring it had all been great fun.

She flew through the back door, yanked Earl Grey in after her, and turned the lock.

Her throat burning, chest heaving, Theodosia realized she'd just run a mile in under six minutes, which was basic qualifying time for the Boston Marathon.

Now was not the time to celebrate her personal best.

She double-checked her lock, then ran to the front door and made sure that was locked, too. And just in case, she dragged over a chair from the dining room and wedged it under the doorknob.

Okay, calm down, she told herself. *Try to get your heart rate down from a terrified one fifty to a more manageable eighty.*

She walked back into her dining room, stared into the large framed mirror that hung over her Sheraton buffet, and thought, *My hair looks crazy. So maybe I should . . .*

Her cell phone shrilled, making her jump. Had Donny Bragg seen her after all? Was he calling to scream and cackle at her? But no, it was Riley.

Theodosia wondered for a split second if she should tell him what had just happened? No, if she did that, she'd have to confess to sneaking into Smokey's apartment and then he'd jump on a plane and fly back here. Forbid her from continuing the investigation. Maybe even lock her up and throw away the key.

"Hey there," Theodosia said in what she hoped was a relaxed and happy tone of voice.

"Hey there, yourself," Riley said. "Are you still investigating?"

"Oh, you know . . ." When in doubt, Theodosia decided to hedge as much as possible. "Now and then, when I have a little free time." She certainly wasn't going to tell him that she'd run home half-crazed because somebody had taken a shot at her. Although, now that she'd had time to think about it rationally, maybe she'd overreacted. Maybe it *had* been something else. A car backfiring? A window being slammed. A rock being thrown? *Please, anything else.*

Riley snapped her out of her reverie.

"I figured as much," Riley said. "And I realize it's difficult for you to leave these things alone."

"Riley, if you could have seen that poor woman . . . dead on the floor of her home. Like some poor little creature that had been poisoned."

"I know, I know. I'm familiar with the aftermath of murder. Just remember that this investigation you insist on getting involved in is not some game of Clue. The killer is not Mr. Plum in the library with a candlestick. This happens to be the real deal and quite deadly at that."

"I've been scrupulously careful and mostly just asked questions." Theodosia squeezed her eyes shut at hearing her own little white lie.

"How can I fault you on that?" Riley laughed. But he said it like he didn't quite believe her.

They talked for another ten minutes, Theodosia trying her best to keep the conversation light and upbeat. The weather, the tea shop, his Christmas plans. Then they said heartfelt good nights and promised to talk again tomorrow night.

Wandering into the kitchen, Theodosia brewed a cup of chamomile tea—always good for calming the nerves—and carried it upstairs.

In between sips she took off her makeup, took a hot shower, brushed her hair (boy, did it ever need brushing), and changed into one of her oversized T-shirts. She walked into her tower room and peeked out the upstairs window. She listened carefully, but nothing was stirring.

Not even a mouse. Or a rat. Good. That means nobody followed me home. Nobody's lurking outside.

But just in case, Theodosia dragged Earl Grey's dog bed from his usual spot in the bedroom to the top of the stairs. He eyed it questioningly for a few moments, then plopped down contentedly.

"Good dog. Guard the house, please."

With Earl Grey at his post, Theodosia fell into a restless sleep.

BZZZ. BZZZ.

Something was buzzing around Theodosia like an angry hornet. Just edging into REM sleep, she wondered if she was dreaming about bees. She came awake halfway, decided she didn't much care for the idea, told her brain to please dream about something else, and fell back asleep again.

BZZZ. BZZZ.

Annoying. What *was* that awful sound?

This time Theodosia sat halfway up in bed. And realized . . . it was her phone making that noise. And not a buzz at all but an insistent ring-bling. Who was calling? It had to be the middle of the night, right?

Who'd call me at . . . ? What time is it anyway?

Theodosia pushed back the covers, rolled over, and squinted at her bedside clock.

Two thirty in the morning. Could it be Riley? Has something happened?

She pawed around on her night table, finally snagged her phone, and answered sleepily.

"Hello?"

It was Haley. Babbling a mile a minute, garbled words gushing out of her. She wasn't just excited; she sounded terrified.

"Theodosia, you've got to come quick and help!" Haley cried. "I think . . . Oh, this is terrible. I don't know what to . . ."

"Haley. Slow down." Theodosia was still sleep fogged and groggy. "Tell me what's going on."

"Somebody's downstairs trying to break in!" Haley cried in a frightened whisper.

"Break into the tea shop?" Now Theodosia was instantly awake. Haley's apartment, what used to be Theodosia's old apartment, was directly above the tea shop!

"Jeez. I mean . . . I think they're still in the alley, but they're *trying* to get in."

"Did you call 911?"

"No. I'm hiding in the bathroom with Teacup. Will you call them for me?"

"Yes, but I'm going to call on my landline. I want you to

lock the door—barricade it if you can—and stay on the line with me."

"Okay, okay," Haley gibbered.

Theodosia ran downstairs—thank goodness she had another line—and called 911. Told the dispatcher what was happening, gave them her name and Haley's name. When the dispatcher assured her a patrol car was on the way, she thanked them, then relayed that information to Haley.

"But what should I do now," Haley cried, "until the police get here?"

"Stay in your bathroom and keep quiet."

"Are you coming?"

"Fast as I can, honey," Theodosia said. "I'm running upstairs now to get dressed. Hang tight."

"I'll try."

By the time Theodosia came screeching into the alley behind the Indigo Tea Shop, it was all over but the writing of the police report. A black-and-white cruiser with the blue POLICE graphic was parked there, its light bar strobing red and blue, the two uniformed officers trying to calm down a very frightened Haley.

"What happened?" Theodosia asked as she jumped from her Jeep.

An officer with a name tag that read HURLEY turned to her. "You're the shop owner?"

She nodded. "Theodosia Browning, yes." Then, putting a hand on Haley's shoulder, said, "Are you okay?"

"She's mostly just shaken up," the second officer said. His name tag read BARRON.

"I'm mostly just shaken up," Haley said, repeating his words. She was wearing a down jacket over her pajamas and had little Teacup cuddled in her arms. The orange-and-brown cat looked fine, Haley not so much.

"I'm so sorry this happened. I imagine you were scared to death," Theodosia said.

"Well, yeah, since some jackhole tried to jimmy open our back door," Haley said. She shifted Teacup in her arms and pointed to a series of ugly gouges in the wood.

"Probably just kids running wild and fooling around," Officer Barron said. "We see this crap all the time. Amateur night breaking and entering. We even got a callout for a dumpster fire a couple of hours ago over on Queen Street. Behind that fast-food place Hot Diggity Dog. What a stink that made."

"Still, your door was worked over pretty good," Officer Hurley said. "Maybe you should go inside, make sure that everything's okay. You know, for insurance purposes."

Feeling deeply unsettled, Theodosia stuck her key in the lock—thank goodness it still worked—and opened the door. As she flipped on the lights and glanced around her office, she wondered what the burglar had been looking for. What had he hoped to steal? Teapots? Baskets? Christmas decorations?

On the other hand, a more critical question might have been, who had been trying to jimmy their way in? Could it be the same person who'd fired a shot at her the previous evening? Did they think she still lived here?

"Everything seems to be fine," Theodosia told the officers. "Thanks for responding so quickly."

"Yeah, thanks," Haley said, her teeth still chattering.

"We're on until six, so we'll cruise by a couple of times, make sure these clowns, whoever they are, don't decide to sneak back," Officer Hurley said.

"Thank you," Theodosia said. She watched with Haley as the officers climbed into their cruiser and pulled away, then said, "Do you want to come home with me for the rest of the night?"

"Naw," Haley said. "I think I'll be okay." She sounded much calmer now.

"Okay, but if you get scared, just call."

"Will do," Haley said. Then, "Are you gonna get the door fixed?"

"I'll call the hardware store first thing tomorrow."

Theodosia also wondered if she should call Detective Tidwell. After all, if this break-in was somehow related to the murder investigation . . .

Then she decided that no, it was late and she should let the man get his beauty sleep. She'd see him soon enough at Miss Drucilla's funeral tomorrow.

Glancing at her watch, Theodosia corrected herself. No, the funeral was actually *today*, since it was now ten after three in the morning.

Oh dear.

17

The morning of the funeral dawned far too abruptly for Theodosia. She was dog-tired after dealing with last night's break-in, feeling so discombobulated she could barely think straight, and woefully in need of a strong cup of tea.

Arriving at St. Philip's Church at twenty to nine, attired in a black jacket and slacks, Theodosia hastily located Drayton and pulled him aside so she could give him the lowdown on last night.

"Haley already told me," Drayton said as they huddled in one of the church's three pedimented porticos. "When I stopped by the tea shop first thing."

"So you know about the break-in," Theodosia said.

"Do you suppose it's because we've been investigating?" Drayton asked. He'd abandoned his normal tweedy look today and was dressed in a decorous black three-piece suit with a herringbone necktie. Because he was wearing a somber expression to match, Theodosia thought mourners might easily mistake him for one of the funeral directors.

"I'm thinking we stirred up some kind of nasty hornet's nest. Only whoever tried to break in, for whatever reason, must have thought I still lived in that upstairs apartment." Theodosia wondered if she should tell Drayton about the hypodermic needles she'd seen at Smokey's apartment. *No, maybe wait until after the funeral.*

Drayton's brow furrowed as he digested Theodosia's words. "Do you think the burglar was after *you*?"

Theodosia bit her lip. "I'm not sure it was a burglar so much as . . ."

"As what?"

"I hate to even think this, but the burglar could have been the same person who murdered Miss Drucilla." There, she'd said it. The terrible thought that had wormed its way into her brain right after she woke up and been stuck there ever since.

Drayton's face crumpled, his shoulders sagged. "That means it was someone fairly close to the investigation. Someone who *knows* we're involved."

"I suppose you're right."

"And they were intent on what? Sending a warning? Trying to stop you?"

"That'd be my best guess," Theodosia said.

"Holy Hannah, maybe we're *all* in danger," Drayton said.

"I'm sorry. I probably shouldn't have dragged you into this mess in the first place. I apologize."

Drayton raised a hand to touch his bow tie, found it wasn't there, and fluttered his fingers instead. "Never mind about me. On second thought, I'm not all that alarmed. But do you think Haley is safe? She's all by herself at the tea shop."

"She won't be for long. Right after I phoned the hardware store to come fix the back door, I called Miss Dimple and asked her to come in and help out. Brew tea, take care of customers, hang around for the post-funeral luncheon. She said yes."

Drayton glanced at his watch. "So she'll probably show up at the tea shop right about now."

"Probably."

"And we'll be back there in an hour, so I suppose we're okay." He blew out a gust of air. "For now anyway."

Theodosia hadn't heard a peep from Detective Tidwell in three days. But as she walked down the center aisle in St. Philip's, he loomed out from one of the pews like a dark avenging angel and dropped a heavy hand on her arm.

"I just heard," Tidwell said gruffly. "About the break-in at your tea shop. Is everyone all right?"

Theodosia slid sideways into his pew, his grasp a relentless tractor beam that reeled her in. "We're unnerved but unscathed," she said in a low voice.

"Any ideas come to mind as to who was behind it?" he asked.

"Well . . ." Theodosia knew she didn't dare tell Tidwell that someone might have taken a shot at her last night. If she did, he'd lock her up and call Pete Riley. Then Riley would break a leg trying to get back to Charleston and all hell would break loose. And her investigating days would be over. For good.

"Come on." Tidwell waggled his fingers at her. "For every action a reaction. What could have prompted this sinister nocturnal visit to your tea shop?"

Okay, I guess I have to tell him about the syringes.

"The thing is, I did a little prowling last night. . . ." She tried to make it sound low-key.

"Prowling where?" Tidwell demanded.

"It was perfectly innocent really," Theodosia said.

Tidwell's brows furrowed like two fuzzy caterpillars coming together. "Am I to believe you indulged in some breaking and entering?"

"No breaking, but some unauthorized entering, yes."

"A night prowl. That's enough to get you arrested," Tidwell said.

Theodosia raised an eyebrow. "You'd turn me in?"

"Consider it a friendly warning. Now tell me whose home was graced by your presence?"

Theodosia studied the church's domed ceiling for a few moments, then said, "Actually, it was Smokey's apartment."

"I *told* you not to investigate!" Tidwell hissed loudly. The sound caused a woman in a pink suit and matching hat who was sitting in front of them to turn around and frown.

"But here's the important takeaway," Theodosia said, lowering her voice to a more church-appropriate level. "When I tiptoed into Smokey's bathroom, I found needles."

"Hypodermic needles?" Now Tidwell quivered like a Boykin pointer on full alert.

"The disposable kind. And they were orange," Theodosia said. "They were exactly like . . ."

Tidwell threw up a hand to silence her.

"What?" Theodosia said a little too loudly.

The woman turned to glare at them again. But too bad for her, since Theodosia hadn't finished telling Tidwell the whole story.

"Do you think *Smokey* was the one who . . . ?"

Tidwell silenced her again as he pulled his phone from his jacket pocket and started poking at it. In his huge hands, the phone looked like a child's toy. "Be quiet. I have to make a call," he muttered.

He continued punching in numbers as the church organ started up. Two long strung-out chords, and then the opening of "How Great Thou Art."

"Gimme Glen Humphries," Tidwell snapped as he turned his back on Theodosia. Then he deftly slid away until he'd put a good ten feet between them.

As the organ music continued to build in intensity, Theodosia tried her best to listen in on Tidwell's call. But it was next to impossible. The organist was pounding out notes that sounded both majestic and a little unsettling. All she could do was wait. And hope that Tidwell would eventually tell her what he was up to.

When Tidwell finished his call, he came back, looking slightly grim.

"Are you going to question Smokey?" Theodosia asked.

Tidwell's jowls shook. "I'm stepping it up a notch. I intend to obtain a warrant from a friendly judge, search Smokey's apartment, and take him into custody."

"Whoa." Theodosia hadn't expected this kind of immediate action. "You think Smokey really is the killer?"

"Until I hear a logical explanation for those syringes, he's definitely a prime suspect," Tidwell said. He tapped Theodosia on the shoulder. "Now. Kindly step aside so I can do my job."

Theodosia turned to block him. "Before you go, I need to ask a question."

Tidwell glowered. "If this concerns my investigation, I really can't—"

"No, it's about Julian Wolf-Knapp, the art dealer. You spoke with him a couple of times, correct?"

Tidwell gave the faintest of nods.

"Did he tell you where he obtained the Renoir for Miss Drucilla?"

"He said it was from a European dealer."

"And you checked it out?"

"My assistant called a dealer in Amsterdam by the name of Vander Pflug Fine Art and had the sale confirmed." Tidwell paused, wary now. "Why? Do you know something I don't?"

"I wish I did."

Once Tidwell had left, Theodosia sat in her pew, listening to the organ music, watching the mourners continue to file in. There was a constant stream of sad-looking people, which probably attested to the fact that Miss Drucilla had been much loved. Of course, this was the perfect church in which to hold her funeral. Founded in 1680, St. Philip's was a venerable old church that had been designated as a National Historic Landmark. The church oozed grace and dignity, and during the late eighteen hundreds, the light in its massive steeple had served as a beacon to guide ships safely into Charleston Harbor.

"There you are." Drayton suddenly appeared at Theodosia's elbow and she hastily moved over to make room for him.

"Tidwell's going to take Smokey in for questioning," Theodosia whispered to him.

Drayton did a complete double take. "Smokey? Why?"

Theodosia decided she'd better tell Drayton about her foray into Smokey's apartment last night. And how she'd seen those three hypodermics.

Drayton listened carefully, his eyes widening when she got to the part about the hypodermics. Then he gave an abrupt nod. "I'd say Smokey's our man. That he's guilty as sin."

"Maybe."

"No, Smokey's the one. I can feel it in my bones." Drayton gazed at her, a quizzical look on his face. "With that kind of evidence, he *has* to be guilty. I mean, you've managed to convince me. Why aren't you convinced?"

"Because I'm not sure what to think anymore," Theodosia said.

The service was about as lovely as a funeral could be. The minister gave a warm, glowing eulogy. There was genteel music by a string quartet. And representatives from various charities that Miss Drucilla had supported took turns speaking tearfully about her caring nature and generosity.

Coy Cooper sat in the front row, looking uptight but solemn. Sitting directly behind him were Majel Mercer, Pauline Stauber, and Wade Holland. Both Majel and Pauline cried throughout the entire service, while Wade tried his best to comfort Pauline. A small gray-haired woman sat behind them.

"That's Evelyn Fruth," Drayton told Theodosia as the service drew to a close. "Miss Drucilla's former housekeeper."

"Did you have a chance to speak with her," Theodosia asked, "before the service started?"

"Are you kidding?" said Drayton. "Not only did I give Mrs. Fruth the third degree. I made sure she was coming to the post-funeral luncheon so *you* could talk to her."

"Smart thinking," Theodosia said.

"But I don't think she's guilty of anything," Drayton said as the organist launched into a crashingly loud version of "Amazing Grace." "Oops, I do believe that's the recessional hymn, which is our cue to head back to the tea shop and make ready."

"Let's do it, then," Theodosia said as she and Drayton popped up like a couple of manic gophers and slipped down the aisle. As they hit the sidewalk outside, Theodosia pulled out her phone and called the tea shop.

"Yello." It was Haley.

"The service just ended and everyone's about to leave the church," Theodosia said. "So we'll be there in a matter of . . ."

BANG!

"Haley!" Theodosia cried out. Was that a gunshot she'd just heard at the other end of the line? Oh, holy Hannah!

Then Haley was back on, her breath rasping loudly in Theodosia's ear.

"Sorry about that," Haley said. "I was juggling a hot pan and dropped my phone."

"Haley, you almost gave me a heart attack!"

"Didn't mean to."

"I'm having palpitations."

"Sorry. My bad."

Theodosia drew a deep, cleansing breath. "Well, like I said, the funeral just concluded and everyone's on their way over. Including me and Drayton."

"Okay, gotcha, bye."

18

❧

Theodosia and Drayton had all of three minutes to double-check the Indigo Tea Shop to make sure everything was perfect for lunch. And luckily, it seemed to be. Tables were set, candles glowed, and the proverbial welcome mat was out.

Miss Dimple met them at the door and said, in a calming voice, "I brewed three pots of tea just like Drayton asked, and Haley tells me the quiche and tea sandwiches are ready and waiting to be served."

"Sounds like our funeral luncheon is ready, set, go," Drayton said. He took off his suit coat and tie and hung them on the brass coatrack. Then he donned his traditional tweed jacket, bow tie, and long apron.

Miss Dimple surveyed the tea shop, then glanced back at Theodosia, a look of worry on her face. "Except for one thing. All the Christmas decorations are still up. The wreaths and angels and garlands and sparkly reindeer. Since we're hosting a funeral luncheon—which I assume should be fairly low-key and decorous—I didn't know if I should take everything down and hide it or just leave it up. I wasn't sure what was appropriate."

"I think, with the time constraints we're under, we pretty much have to leave everything as is," Theodosia said. "And since it's only a few days until Christmas, people expect a tea shop to be festive and jolly. Hopefully the mourners will understand and maybe even welcome our upbeat atmosphere."

"You think?" Miss Dimple said.

"Sure," Theodosia said.

"Not really," Drayton said.

"Curmudgeon," Miss Dimple said under her breath.

But Christmas decorations or not, the mourners dutifully filed into the Indigo Tea Shop and took their seats. Soon the place was filled with low murmurs. Coy Cooper settled at a table with Pauline and her boyfriend, Wade. Majel Mercer ended up sitting next to Donny Bragg and Mrs. Fruth, the former housekeeper. Theodosia counted another thirty or so people who also arrived for the post-funeral luncheon. They glanced around and looked pleased. Nobody lodged a complaint about sparkly reindeer.

"Many of these folks work for the various nonprofit organizations that Miss Drucilla helped fund," Drayton pointed out. "Clearly, she was generous to a fault and will be sorely missed."

"That's what I keep hearing over and over," Theodosia said as she grabbed two teapots and headed for the tables. *So why did somebody want her dead?*

Serving the food turned out to be a snap, since Haley had made the decision to plate everything ahead of time. So no multiple courses to deal with, no three-tiered trays to lug out. Just nicely arranged plates that contained two chicken-and-chutney tea sandwiches, a slice of mushroom quiche, a small bunch of champagne grapes, and a square of white chocolate bread pudding. And there was steaming-hot tea, of course.

Once Theodosia, Drayton, and Miss Dimple had distributed luncheon plates to all the guests, they made the rounds again, pouring seconds on tea.

As Theodosia poured a cup of Nilgiri tea for Majel Mercer, Majel quickly introduced Theodosia to Evelyn Fruth. She was a small, birdlike woman in her sixties who wore a tidy gray suit and a small blue velvet hat.

"Mrs. Fruth worked for Miss Drucilla for almost twenty-two years," Majel said.

"You have my deepest sympathies," Theodosia told Mrs. Fruth. "You must have been very close to Miss Drucilla."

"We were together many years," Mrs. Fruth said, her eyes misting over, "though for these last two I've been semi-retired."

"So you haven't been working at Miss Drucilla's home?" Theodosia said.

"Not really. Weeks would go by where we didn't see each other at all. But when Miss Drucilla had a major party or event, she always requested that I come in and help. Of course, by that time, she'd employed a full-time cleaning service, so I was just there to check things over. Make sure everything was perfect."

"Were you at Miss Drucilla's house the night of the Christmas party?" Theodosia asked. She realized that Mrs. Fruth was one resource she'd almost overlooked.

"Unfortunately, no," Mrs. Fruth said. "I wish I *had* been there. Maybe I could have *done* something." She shook her head and blinked as her crinkled eyes misted over.

Majel Mercer reached over and patted Mrs. Fruth's tiny hand. "You couldn't have known what was going to happen. None of us could. Sometimes tragedy just . . . well, it comes flying out of left field. Unfortunately, we're all vulnerable. Every day."

Those were the same words—a kind of sad explanation for the trials and ills of the world—that Theodosia had offered to Haley a few days earlier. But knowing you were helpless against bad luck or tragedy didn't make things any easier. In fact, it made Theodosia feel more like a helpless pawn.

As Theodosia tried to shake off her glum mood, she hurried back to the front counter to grab a fresh pot of tea. That was when Donny Bragg stood up from his table and sauntered over to talk to her.

"A moment of your time?" he said.

"Sure," Theodosia said, practically holding her breath. Did Bragg know that Smokey was going to be taken in for questioning? Had Tidwell acted fast and already hauled Smokey's sorry butt down to the police station? Turned out, the answer was yes on both counts.

"I just got word that the police picked up Smokey," Bragg said.

He loomed so close to Theodosia that she could smell cigar smoke on his clothes. Her nose twitched. He wasn't exactly threatening, but he wasn't very friendly, either.

"Did you have something to do with that?" Bragg asked.

"I'm sure Detective Tidwell has his reasons and doesn't need any suggestions from me," Theodosia said, dodging a direct yes-or-no answer. It was the best excuse she could come up with at the moment. Lighthearted, a little self-deprecating.

"I ask because I know you've been playing amateur detective all week."

"I may possess an amateur's curiosity, but unfortunately, I don't have a professional's credentials, which means I have no authority to subpoena, question, or arrest anyone. Or even issue a traffic ticket." Theodosia flashed what she hoped was a convincing smile and continued. "Look around, please. I run a tea shop. People come in, they talk, I *hear* things. That's about the extent of it and that's why I ask questions."

"Izat so?" Bragg said. "Well, thank you, Perry Mason." He looked both amused and confused, as though he didn't quite believe her.

Theodosia met his gaze calmly. "Now, if there's something I can get for you—maybe another sandwich or an extra slice of bread pudding—do let me know. Otherwise, I need to get back to my guests."

Theodosia picked up a Blue Willow teapot and brushed past him. Went to the far table by the window, poured tea, then picked up three plates and carried them back to the counter. Dumped them into a plastic tub.

"How's it going?" Drayton asked. He was standing there sipping a cup of Chinese Keemun but keeping a watchful eye on the guests as they ate.

"Okay, I guess. Donny Bragg already knows that Smokey was taken in for questioning."

"That's why he was talking to you? Well, his inquisitiveness doesn't surprise me one bit. Bragg's one of those fat cats who always seems well-connected. Gets his news on the old-boy network, if you know what I mean."

"I do. But how connected is he to Smokey?" Theodosia wondered.

"You still think Smokey might have been carrying out Bragg's bidding?"

"I don't know. Maybe we'll find out. Maybe Tidwell will push Smokey hard. Scare him half to death so he'll cough up some answers." Theodosia looked out over the tea room. "In the meantime . . ." Her eyes fell on Pauline Stauber. She was sitting there, her head down, listening to Wade whisper something in her ear.

"Pauline," she murmured.

Drayton followed Theodosia's gaze and said, "Wade seems to take very good care of her."

"He does. But like I said last night, I've grown a little leery of Pauline's motives."

"Might I remind you that you're also suspicious of Smokey, Donny Bragg, and a half dozen others," Drayton said.

"What can I say? I'm suspicious by nature."

"And I'm thankful you are. Miss Drucilla's murder is a baffling situation that even the police can't seem to figure out."

Theodosia was still watching Pauline. "She cried her way through the entire service . . . and she's still taking it awfully hard."

"Well, she did work for Miss Drucilla."

"Which also means Pauline had access to every bit of paper, password, and financial account that the woman had. So it's possible . . ." Theodosia's voice trailed off.

Drayton's eyes narrowed, as if he was reading her thoughts. "I'm no psychic, but I know you're thinking Pauline could have engineered the murder and has been crying crocodile tears ever since."

"I hate to think the worst of Pauline," Theodosia said. "But Donny Bragg did warn us she was a gambler. And that she was bad at handling finances."

"He could have been lying."

"Yes, but do *you* think there's a possibility that Pauline murdered Miss Drucilla?"

"I suppose there's an outside chance," Drayton said. "After all, Pauline was familiar with every square inch of that old mansion."

"Do we know where Pauline was when that alarm went off?"

"For all we know, she could have triggered it," Drayton said.

Theodosia nodded. "To throw us off."

"While we ran around like chickens with our heads cut off, she could have jammed a syringe full of poison into Miss Drucilla's neck." Drayton made a face and grabbed a tin of tea.

"And stole her rings and ripped a painting off the wall," Theodosia said.

Drayton paused. "That painting. It's probably the crux of the whole thing, isn't it? The real motive for murder."

"The Renoir," Theodosia said as she turned and studied

the guests again. She'd just had a thought. "You know who didn't show up for today's funeral?"

Drayton inclined his head toward her. "Who?"

"Julian Wolf-Knapp. If he could sell Miss Drucilla a pricey Renoir painting, you'd think he'd at least have the decency to attend her funeral."

Drayton measured three scoops of gunpowder green tea into a pink floral teapot and popped on the lid. "You make a good point."

By one o'clock the funeral attendees had cleared out and Miss Dimple was readying the tables for afternoon tea. They probably wouldn't be all that busy today, but Theodosia worried that Haley might be feeling kitchen stressed.

She wasn't.

"Nope, I'm okay," Haley said. She was bopping around her kitchen, wearing a chef's hat that looked for all the world like an oversized mushroom. A pot simmered on the stove while heavenly aromas seeped from her oven.

"Even though you're running on three hours of sleep?" Theodosia asked.

"Aw, Drayton keeps bringing me mugs of vanilla chai. Must be chock-full of caffeine 'cause I'm still going like gangbusters."

"I think I'd better grab a mug of that myself," Theodosia said.

She walked back into the tea room, where Miss Dimple was already setting out clean dishes and flatware. It was amazing how fast she'd been able to turn the tea shop around.

Drayton saw Theodosia looking thoughtful.

"Need something to do?" he asked.

"Actually, it looks like we're almost caught up," Theodosia said. "If you can spare me for ten minutes or so, I'm going to run down to Antiquarian Books."

"Go," he said, waving a hand. "Enjoy."

* * *

Theodosia was on a mission when she walked through the doors of the bookshop. She was hoping to find Drayton's Christmas present.

"Hey," Lois Chamberlain said as she looked up from wrapping a package at the front counter. She was a retired librarian in her late fifties who'd reinvented herself as a used-book dealer. Today she wore a red-and-black-plaid jacket, black yoga pants, and tortoiseshell reading glasses. Her long gray hair was swept up in a schoolmarm-type bun.

"Hey, yourself," Theodosia said.

"Aren't you supposed to be up to your ears in scones and Darjeeling?"

"We're not so busy right now," Theodosia said, then chuckled. "Besides, I have people working on all that."

"I have people, too," Lois said, pointing to a young woman who was busy shelving an armload of books.

"Temporary help for the holidays?"

"The very best kind. My daughter. Home on Christmas break." Lois waved a hand. "Cara, come on over here and meet the infamous tea shop lady." She grinned at Theodosia. "Do you by any chance have a 'tea lady' vanity plate on your car?"

Theodosia shook her head. "No."

"Well, you should."

A pretty twentysomething with reddish blond hair down to her shoulders came bouncing toward them. Cara Chamberlain. She extended her hand to Theodosia and said, "I think we met once before. But I was twelve and wearing braids."

"It's wonderful to see you again," Theodosia said. "And I do remember the braids. And that you were deeply into Nancy Drew books."

"A good mystery still makes me tingle," Cara said.

Lois, the proud mother, said, "Cara's just finishing up her

master's in media and communication at the University of North Carolina at Chapel Hill."

"That's fantastic," Theodosia said.

"And she's about to do an internship at Channel Eight in their Investigative News Division," Lois said.

"When do you start?" Theodosia asked, hoping Cara wouldn't get paired with Monica Garber.

Cara smiled broadly. "Right after the first of the year. And I can't wait. It's all I've ever dreamed about."

"Cara and I are looking forward to your fancy Victorian Christmas Tea on Saturday," Lois said. She touched a hand to Cara's shoulder. "We're intrigued by your so-called Grand Illumination, although neither of us is quite sure what it's all about."

"It's something brand-new we're trying," Theodosia said, "an idea that Drayton hatched. Hopefully it'll be a fun addition."

"Did you come in here looking for a special book?" Cara asked. "Can I can help you find something?"

"Maybe a book for Drayton, my tea sommelier," Theodosia said.

"So he's like a wine sommelier, only for tea," Cara mused. "Huh. Interesting."

Lois snapped her fingers. "We just got in a pristine copy of John Blofeld's *Chinese Art of Tea* though I know you already have a copy—and Drayton probably does, too."

"But it wouldn't hurt to have a backup copy," Theodosia said, "one we can keep handy at the tea shop."

"There you go," Lois said.

While Cara went to pull the Blofeld book, Theodosia took a quick spin through the bookshop. There was a delightful mix of old books, new books, and lots of great authors to choose from—Hemingway, Steinbeck, Fitzgerald, Salinger—but nothing jumped out at her. As a special gift for Drayton, that is.

"You know Drayton's taste," Theodosia said to Lois. "If you come up with any ideas, let me know."

"Will do," Lois said.

Once Theodosia returned to the Indigo Tea Shop, she discovered that afternoon tea service was leisurely at best. Seven customers at three tables.

"I have a suggestion," Drayton said as he plucked the tea book from Theodosia's hand, studied it, smiled, and set it on the counter.

"What's that?" Theodosia asked. She was thinking Drayton might want her to phone Detective Tidwell to ask if he'd been able to wring a heartfelt confession out of Smokey.

Instead, Drayton surprised her and said, "Since we're not all that busy right now, I think we should run over to the Dove Cote Inn and do a final check on Saturday's venue."

Theodosia took one look around, saw that Miss Dimple was handling tea service with ease, and said, "Works for me."

19

~❦~

Wind swirled out of Charleston Harbor, rattling the trees up and down Lamboll Street. The temperature had been dropping steadily all day and was threatening to go down to thirty-nine degrees by tonight.

Drayton struggled to wind the ends of his flapping scarf around his neck as he pulled his Brooks Brothers coat closer around him. "If it gets any colder, I'm afraid we're going to have a white Christmas."

"I've never seen that happen here," Theodosia said. Dressed as she was in short boots and a white puffer jacket, she rather liked the idea of snow. If they actually got a sprinkling of the white stuff, she and Riley could compare notes.

"The last time Charleston saw a measurable amount of snowfall was back in 1960."

"Before my time," Theodosia murmured.

"Look here," Drayton said as they stopped directly in

front of the Dove Cote Inn. "You see this winding stone footpath that leads to the front door?"

"It's lovely. Like something Hansel and Gretel might follow."

"To kick off our Grand Illumination, the lighting people are going to place two dozen six-foot-high Victorian lamps along this pathway, extending all the way up to the front door." Drayton smiled. "Can you just imagine the setting: a pinkish purple smudge in the sky as evening creeps in, and then a warm yellow glow that leads our guests to their special tea party?"

"It sounds magical."

"Of course, in the interest of historical accuracy, I selected the lamps myself—lovely six-sided globes encased in scrollwork."

Theodosia gazed at the stately bed-and-breakfast that, just six years earlier, had been a fanciful-looking Victorian family residence. Now, with new owners, it had been turned into a charming inn with twelve luxurious suites along with a wonderful new dining room addition that was sure to make it a premier entertainment venue.

"I love your idea of a Grand Illumination, but what's the story behind it anyway?" she asked. "Is it some historical thing?"

"Very much so," Drayton said. "In the eighteenth century, Grand Illuminations were 'da bomb,' as you might say today. They were all about shooting off huge volleys of fireworks and firing cannons. Today, they mainly involve lighting trees, fancy decor on homes and buildings, plus some dancing and pageants. In our case we'll have the lamps outside and actors presenting a short skit while we serve tea."

"I can't believe you already held auditions."

"It was actually quite amusing," Drayton said. "There are so many amateur theater groups in Charleston. Anyway, you didn't have time. That was the day you drove Riley to the airport."

"And you've written an honest-to-goodness script for the actors?"

Drayton gave a satisfied smile. "Of course."

"Are you going to give me a hint about this . . . What would you call it? A play?"

"More like a tableau. And no, you'll just have to wait and see."

They walked up the front path, climbed two steps to a wide front porch, and stepped into the warmth of the Dove Cote Inn's lobby. The lobby smelled of burning cedar and cinnamon-scented candles, and a blazing fire crackled merrily in a yellow brick fireplace. There were cozy armchairs and sofas in cream-colored leather with plump velvet pillows, and the Chinese carpet underfoot was an elegant shade of persimmon. Brass lamps had filmy shades, and white flocked Christmas trees decorated with sparkling white lights and ornaments completed the look and lent a festive air.

"This is gorgeous," Theodosia breathed. She'd been here once before when they'd met with the inn's catering manager, a woman named Isabelle Franklin. But back then it hadn't been decorated for Christmas.

Now Isabelle was gliding gracefully toward them with an expectant smile on her face.

"It's lovely, isn't it?" Isabelle said. "Our new owners have created a wonderful little boutique hotel." She was a small woman who wore a cocoa-colored tweed blazer and cream-colored slacks. She was in her mid-thirties, and her shoulder-length blond hair was brushed back and held in place with a black velvet headband.

Preppy, Theodosia decided. Isabelle looked preppy. And she was kind of peppy, too.

"Your inn is a wonderful addition to the Historic District," Drayton said.

"And since this is brand-new as a business, we've managed to capture our fair share of publicity," Isabelle said.

"Which is always a good thing," Theodosia said.

"Oh my, yes," Isabelle said. "And let me just say that we're thrilled you chose us to host your Victorian Christmas Tea."

"It was your Essex Room that won us over," Drayton said.

"Come and take another look," Isabelle said. "See how we've decorated for the holidays."

They walked through the lobby, down a short wood-paneled hallway hung with small oil paintings, and into the Essex Room.

It was, in a nutshell, perfect. The inn's owners had started with a lovely, fairly spacious dining room, then taken it one step further and added a large glass addition that included a curved glass roof. The finished product was light, airy, and impressive—a room that could easily accommodate seventy or eighty guests.

Drayton walked to the center of the room, tilted his head back, and looked up at gray clouds scudding by overhead. Obviously charmed, he said, "If it actually did snow, this room would become one giant snow globe."

"That's a lovely thought," Isabelle said.

"Your decorations are perfect," Theodosia said. There were three more flocked Christmas trees with white lights and ornaments, plus tons of green garland strung in the windows. On a far wall, another impressive fireplace had a large Baroque mirror above it. An elegant brass clock entwined with flora, fauna, and lounging leopards rested on the mantel. Green topiary trees hung with golden pears were perched on two inlaid cocktail tables that flanked the fireplace.

"When we first spoke, you mentioned that you were expecting around sixty-eight guests?" Isabelle said.

"That number's increased," Drayton said. "We now have confirmed reservations for seventy-five guests."

"And there could always be a couple more," Theodosia said. "Last-minute stragglers."

"So if we seat eight people per table . . . then, um, we'll

need to set up ten tables." Isabelle looked pleased. "That gives you room for a few more guests. Your so-called stragglers."

"There'll be a couple," Theodosia promised. "There always are."

"For some reason the local hotels aren't holding as many Christmas teas as they used to," Drayton said. "So we seem to be absorbing all their former guests."

"Lucky you," Isabelle said.

Drayton nodded at her. "Lucky you, too."

"Oh." Isabelle looked suddenly flustered. "I suppose you're right."

"Let's talk about the tables," Theodosia said, taking a step back and surveying the entire room.

"Just as you specified, all the tables will be covered in white linen tablecloths with lace place mats at each setting. And we're planning to use our Eternal Christmas china by Lenox and our Buttercup flatware by Gorham," Isabelle said.

"Perfect," Theodosia said. She was starting to feel her excitement build. She saw this Victorian Christmas Tea as a kind of happy culmination of a successful year as well as a fun new challenge. After all, there'd be lots of guests, a pageant to contend with, and four separate courses. Lots of moving parts to worry about!

"We've ordered plenty of flowers and candles," Drayton was saying. "To be delivered the day of. White roses in antique pitchers for every table along with white pillar candles."

"And we'll make sure all the chairs have white organza tiebacks done in a nice neat bow," Isabelle said. "You know, I think this is the biggest event we've done so far."

"And I'm confident it will be a rousing success," Drayton said.

"We should check out the kitchen again, too," Theodosia said.

Isabelle led them through a swinging door into a fully equipped kitchen.

"Just as I remember, this is more than adequate," Drayton said, looking around. "Haley will set up at the main counter of course. . . ." He stepped over to a smaller counter. "I can brew my tea right here."

"And you don't need any help from us?" Isabelle asked. "I can always bring in one of our chefs."

"We've got it covered," Theodosia said. "All you have to do is set the tables and light a fire in the fireplace, and we'll handle the rest."

"The temporary lanterns will be installed down your front walk on Saturday morning and the actors should arrive about an hour before the tea begins," Drayton said. "You can put them . . . where?"

"Probably our breakfast room will make as good a green-room as any," Isabelle said.

Drayton gazed at Isabelle and gave a wicked smile. "You're not worried, are you?"

"Not in the least," Isabelle said.

But Theodosia saw how Isabelle had twisted her hands. Yup, Isabelle was worried. A little bit anyway. Then again, so was she.

When Theodosia and Drayton arrived back at the Indigo Tea Shop, Detective Tidwell was sitting at a table, stirring sugar cubes into his Fujian white tea.

Theodosia practically broke a leg getting to him.

"Well?" she said, standing in front of him, hands planted on her hips.

He gazed at her, offered a perfunctory smile, and said, "We had to let Smokey go. There wasn't a single shred of evidence that linked him to Miss Drucilla's murder. Or to the break-in at your tea shop last night."

"You don't think paintings and syringes are enough?" she

asked. "And by the way, how did Smokey explain the syringes?" She was aware that she'd begun to wave her arms somewhat wildly, so she forced herself to stop. Folded them across her chest. Decided she could at least tap a foot to indicate her frustration.

"Smokey explained to me that he used the syringes for more intricate handyman projects," Tidwell said. "Squirting wood glue into tiny cracks, as well as filling syringes with oil for lubricating small moving parts."

"Huh," Drayton said. He was standing behind the counter, listening intently.

"But the lab is going to test the syringes, right?" Theodosia asked. "To make sure that's what they were actually used for?" She felt nervous. Nervous that she'd made a wrong assumption, nervous that maybe poor old aw-shucks Smokey had pulled the wool over Tidwell's eyes.

"Of course we'll test them," Tidwell said. Then, when he saw that Theodosia was still unhappy, he added, "I'll be the first one to admit the syringes *look* incriminating, but that sort of evidence is basically circumstantial. Nothing concrete that I can slap down on the city prosecutor's desk and say, 'Go get Smokey. Lock him up.' No, that good-old-boy prosecutor would laugh me right out of his office."

"So your suspicions about Smokey have cooled," Theodosia said.

"Tempered anyway," Tidwell said. He glanced around, trying to catch Miss Dimple's eye. She was arranging chairs and seemed to be ignoring him. So he cast a hopeful glance at Theodosia and said, "I wonder if there might be any leftover scones."

"Scones?" she said somewhat distractedly. "I suppose I could go and check."

Yes, there were still cream scones in the kitchen, so she plated one (only one), grabbed a small dish of orange marmalade, and carried it out to Tidwell.

"Here you go," Theodosia said. She set everything down without fanfare.

"No Devonshire cream? Ah well," Tidwell said. His mouth turned downward as he sliced his scone.

Theodosia slid into the chair across from him and said, "I have a question that concerns Julian Wolf-Knapp."

"Hmm?" Tidwell was occupied with troweling on as much marmalade as possible.

"When you contacted the art dealer in Amsterdam . . ."

But before Theodosia could finish her sentence, Tidwell dropped his scone back onto his plate and grabbed for his ringing cell phone.

"Yes?" Tidwell said, obviously unhappy at the interruption. He frowned, then listened intently for a few moments as his eyes roved over his uneaten scone. He said, "So you're sending someone down to . . . Oh, you already have? Yes, I'll finish here and come back. Ten minutes at the latest."

"What's going on?" Theodosia asked. From the energy Tidwell was putting out, it felt like something big had popped.

"Speak of the devil," Tidwell said as he clicked off his phone. "A very nervous art dealer in Savannah just contacted my assistant. The dealer said someone had called him about a Renoir for sale." Tidwell grabbed his scone and hastily wrapped it in a napkin, his own version of takeout.

"Sweet dogs," Drayton said from across the room. He'd overheard the exchange about the dealer from Savannah and the Renoir.

Theodosia was suddenly on high alert, too, practically quivering with excitement. "Detective Tidwell," she said, "I think I might know . . ."

"No time!" Tidwell barked. He was already on his feet and racing out the door before she was able to finish her sentence.

"But I—"

The door slammed behind him, cutting off her words.

"Doggone it!" Theodosia cried in frustration.

"What?" Drayton asked. "You wanted to tell him something?"

She shrugged. "Obviously."

Drayton walked over to the table, cupped a hand, and made a *come on* gesture. "What was it?"

"I'm fairly sure I know something that Tidwell doesn't."

Drayton beetled his brows. "That sounds awfully mysterious. I'm afraid to ask, but just what is this secret information?"

"I think I know where Julian Wolf-Knapp might be hiding out."

"*Is* he hiding out?"

"Let me explain," Theodosia said. "I stopped by Wolf-Knapp's studio yesterday on my way back from the Christmas Market. And he wasn't there—at least he wasn't answering his door. But Annie from the Dusty Hen Antique Shop downstairs told me he often spends time at his plantation house."

"And?" Drayton continued to peer at her.

"And Annie gave me his address."

"You think Wolf-Knapp might be hunkered down at his plantation house, trying to hustle up interest in a stolen painting?"

Theodosia looked grim. "If he is, that would be the absolute proof we need that he murdered Miss Drucilla."

Drayton touched a hand to his cheek. "Mercy me, you could be right. Unfortunately, we can't just waltz in and make a citizen's arrest."

"No, but if Wolf-Knapp *is* there, we can call for backup," Theodosia said.

"Theo, you realize you're not an *actual* homicide detective. You can't just snap your fingers and expect to summon an entire police contingent."

"No, but this murder business has been battering away at us all week long. Wouldn't it be nice to actually *solve* the case?"

"Tie it up with a big red bow just in time for Christmas?"

"Well, I wouldn't go *that* far," Theodosia said. "I'd settle for an arrest and assurance from the police that a stone-cold killer will be brought to justice."

"Still, we need to think twice about making any sort of move. Simply showing up at Wolf-Knapp's house unannounced would be dangerous."

"Which is exactly my point. We won't *announce* it. We'll sneak in and see what we can see."

"Sounds tricky," Drayton said.

"Where's your sense of adventure, your outrage over Miss Drucilla's murder?"

Drayton glanced at his watch as he mulled over Theodosia's words. "Tell you what. Come to my house tonight for dinner and we'll talk about this. We'll strategize."

"You're on."

20

❧

What a lot of people didn't realize about Drayton was that he wasn't just fussy; he was precise. He measured, leveled, and double-checked everything. To him, cooking and baking, tea brewing and blending were all about food chemistry. Combine the right ingredients in the proper amounts, do it with grace and care, and—voilà!—grand success.

Theodosia was standing in Drayton's kitchen, watching him work his magic with apples and pork chops. Earl Grey was also a guest tonight and he, along with Drayton's dog, Honey Bee, were romping outside in the backyard. Or as much as two dogs could romp in a Japanese garden complete with its own koi pond, bamboo forest, and display of bonsai.

Please, Earl Grey, Theodosia thought, *don't get too rambunctious and knock something over. Like a priceless windswept bonsai. And don't dip a big clunky paw into the pond and try to snag one of Drayton's prized golden koi.*

"That looks delish," Theodosia said as Drayton sizzled pork chops in a copper fry pan and added maple syrup. Then she gazed around Drayton's elegant kitchen and smiled. The stove was a six-burner range, the sink was custom hammered copper, and the cupboards were faced with glass, the better to show off his collection of teapots and Chinese blue-and-white vases. A small indoor herb garden occupied a windowsill.

"It's a simple enough recipe," Drayton said as he stood at the stove.

"Anything I can do to help?" Theodosia asked.

"Actually, yes." Drayton pulled a glass from the cupboard and a pitcher of eggnog from his refrigerator. "You can try this." He poured a tall glass of eggnog and handed it to her. "My holiday eggnog."

Theodosia took a sip. "Good."

"Just good?"

"Great. Really tasty."

"Okay, then."

Drayton added sliced apples to his pan, turned up the heat, and stirred the bubbling mixture. When it reduced to a creamy goodness, he plopped in a generous tablespoon of butter and stirred that in as well. Theodosia had learned that exact trick from watching Haley. A pat of butter added right at the end always pulled a sauce together.

"Our dinner, dear girl, is almost ready," Drayton announced. "If you grab the baked potatoes and loaf of French bread from the oven, I'll get busy and plate our entrées."

He grabbed two Limoges china plates, scooped his pork chops onto them, poured the apple–maple syrup sauce over the top, and added the potatoes. With the bread nestled in a sweetgrass basket, they carried everything into the dining room, where candles flickered on a table that was already set with linens and silverware.

As they both sat down, Drayton said, "Whoops, can't forget the wine," and reached behind himself. He grabbed an opened bottle of Château Latour from a side table and poured a glass for Theodosia.

"Are you trying to get me tipsy?"

"Just hoping to get you relaxed." He gave her a sly look as he poured his own wine. "Is it working?"

"Is it ever."

"Good. Then maybe you'll drop this nonsense about sneaking out to Wolf-Knapp's plantation house."

"He could be Miss Drucilla's killer," Theodosia said as she settled a napkin onto her lap, picked up her knife and fork.

"So could any number of people."

"This has been a tough case. It feels like every time we take one step forward, we meet a pocket of resistance and get shoved back two steps."

"I totally agree. This entire investigation has been like slogging through a vat of molasses. However, if we keep talking about it, I fear we're going to give ourselves a case of indigestion," Drayton said.

"No, we won't. We never have before. And by the way, this pork is to die for."

"Of course it is. Thank you."

"And what kind of apples are these, please?" Theodosia asked.

"They're Stayman Winesap. Sourced from Windy Hill Orchard up near York."

"Haley got them at the farmers market?"

Drayton nodded as he speared another piece of pork. "Yes. And you're right. This *is* good."

Theodosia stopped eating for a moment. "No, Drayton, this is divine," she said as she literally savored the atmosphere in the dining room. They were sitting at a Chippendale table where two silver candelabras and a bouquet of white roses served as centerpieces. A French chandelier dangled overhead and an oil painting of Charles Grey, the second Earl Grey and former British prime minister, hung on the wall. It made Theodosia sigh with happiness because, really, it was the first time she'd felt completely relaxed in almost a week.

"Hmm?" Drayton spread a pat of butter on his slice of French bread and peered at her with curiosity. "What were you saying?"

"Your lovely table, this home-cooked dinner, the wine, the camaraderie—it's almost too perfect."

"I'm sure we can think of something to spoil it," he joked.

"I can't imagine what."

"Okay," Drayton said. "How about this? Why do you think people commit murder in the first place? What's the driving force?"

"Oh . . . well." That really did bring Theodosia back down to reality. "I read somewhere that the main drivers were greed, revenge, anger, and political ideology." She took a sip of wine. "I suppose you could throw in stupidity and immaturity as well."

"Who do we know that's stupid and immature?" Drayton asked.

"My vote would be Donny Briggs, hands down," Theodosia said.

Drayton chuckled. "I can't fault you there. What about greedy?"

"That I'm not so sure about."

"Okay, moving on to political ideology," Drayton said.

"Not to put too fine a point on it, but the wealthy people who were at Miss Drucilla's party were probably mostly Republicans. And the nonprofit people were probably liberals or Southern Democrats. But to tell the truth, I didn't get a sense that anyone there was politically motivated."

"Nor did I," Drayton said. "Here." He picked up the bottle. "Have some more wine."

"I shouldn't."

"I insist."

They let the conversation wander for the rest of the dinner. Didn't mention Miss Drucilla or her murder, just talked about the tea shop, mutual friends, and about . . . everyday things.

WHAM! BAM! came from the back of his house.

Their eyes met.

"It's the dogs," Drayton said. "Banging on the back door, alerting us they're ready to come in. Probably played their little hearts out and are wondering what we're up to."

"Good thing we're almost finished with dinner," Theodosia said as Drayton got up to tend to the dogs.

Theodosia heard the thunder of paws first. Then Earl Grey and Honey Bee came streaking into the dining room. Earl Grey flopped down at her feet. Honey Bee stared at her with expressive brown eyes.

"I don't think a tiny bite would hurt," Theodosia said as she grabbed a couple shnivels from her plate and slipped them to the dogs.

"Are they being little beggars?" Drayton asked as he walked into the room.

"They're actually fairly well-behaved," she said as her cell phone chimed from her jacket pocket. "Doggone, I forgot to . . ."

"It's okay," Drayton said. "Go ahead and take it. Could be Riley calling."

But it wasn't Riley at all.

"I'm calling for Theodosia Browning," said a pleasant woman's voice.

"That's me," Theodosia said. She glanced at Drayton, whispered, "Sorry."

"Theodosia Browning? Do I have that right?" said the caller.

"Yes, what can I do for you?"

"This is Ellen Hague from the Barnes Foundation. I apologize for calling so late, but I have a message here that you made an inquiry about our Renoir paintings?"

"You're the curator?"

"One of them anyway. There are three of us who deal with the Renoirs. We write articles and press releases, arrange seminars, host visiting scholars, that type of thing."

"I understand the Barnes Foundation has an enormous collection of Renoirs," Theodosia said. She was starting to get excited.

"It's one we're exceedingly proud of," Hague said.

"I called earlier because I have a question. Now, I know this is coming out of left field, but do you know of any Renoirs, not necessarily yours, that have been stolen lately?"

There was a long silence and Theodosia was afraid the curator might be laughing at her. Or had hung up. Then she was back with an answer.

"As a matter of fact, there *was* a Renoir stolen from an Austrian auction house. Some two or three years ago," Ellen Hague said.

"Are you serious?"

"It was a fairly sensational theft at the time. A number of thieves—well, three actually; we know that because they were caught on tape—infiltrated the Dorotheum auction house in Vienna and cut a Renoir right out of its frame. The painting was titled 'Bay, Sea, Green Cliffs.' You could probably find the exact details on the Internet. Like I said, it was a huge story."

"Do you know if that Renoir was ever recovered?"

"One of the thieves was apprehended in Amsterdam," Ellen Hague said. "But no, the painting still hasn't been found. It's gone. In the wind somewhere."

Theodosia sat at the table for a few moments, digesting her dinner and Ellen Hague's words.

Finally, Drayton said, "What?"

"Have you ever heard of a Renoir painting titled 'Bay, Sea, Green Cliffs'?"

Drayton shook his head. "No, should I have?"

"Probably not. But let me . . ."

Theodosia fiddled with her phone, quickly googling "Stolen Renoir." Seconds later, the painting came up on her screen. It was a sweet painting, almost pastoral in nature. And just as the title implied, the gentle landscape painting depicted pinkish blue clouds, green cliffs, and a sparkling blue bay.

"Holy smokes, Drayton. Take a look at this."

Drayton fumbled for his reading glasses as Theodosia held up her phone for him to see.

He squinted, wrinkled his nose, and said, "Okay, I see it. Almost a painterly sketch."

"Do you think—Do you remember—Was this the painting that hung in Miss Drucilla's hallway?"

"You mean the *stolen* painting?"

"Right."

Drayton continued to study the image, then turned his attention to Theodosia.

"I can't say for sure. We were frantically busy the night of the party, so I don't know if I gave it a second glance, let alone a first one."

"I'm going to call Pauline and ask her if she remembers this piece."

"Do you trust her?"

"I think at this point I pretty much have to on this."

Drayton sat expectantly as Theodosia called Pauline. When Pauline answered, Theodosia said a quick hello, then added, "I need to send you an e-mail."

"Okay. Sure," Pauline said. Then, "What's up?"

"You'll see in a minute. Take a look at the photo I'm sending. Then call me right back, okay?"

"Okay," Pauline promised.

Theodosia sent the photo. Two minutes later Pauline called back.

"Is it the stolen painting?" Pauline was excited to the point of being positively breathless.

"Maybe. What do you think? You're the one who's most familiar with it."

"I think that might be it!" Pauline was practically shouting with joy. "You found it, didn't you? You found Miss Drucilla's painting!"

"Not exactly," Theodosia said. "Let's just say I'm hot on its trail."

Drayton gazed at Theodosia with a look of disbelief. Everything seemed to be moving a little too fast for him.

"*Are* we hot on its trail?" he asked.

"I think we are," Theodosia said. She was starting to vibrate with excitement because this could be it. This could be the break they needed. And since she was privy to Wolf-Knapp's whereabouts, knew about his plantation house, maybe they could swoop in and hopefully solve the case.

"You're convinced the thief is Julian Wolf-Knapp?" Drayton asked.

"It's sure starting to feel right. All the pieces fit. Wolf-Knapp claims to have bought the painting from a dealer in Amsterdam and that's where one of the thieves was apprehended."

"I don't care about the painting," Drayton said. "What I do care about is Miss Drucilla. Do you think Wolf-Knapp was the one who killed her?"

"He . . ." Theodosia stopped. "I think it's possible. I mean, we know Wolf-Knapp is the connection. He told me himself that he facilitated the sale of the Renoir."

"That could mean almost anything," Drayton said.

"It could also mean dealing in stolen art. Maybe 'facilitating' is one of those genteel words that kind of obscures the real meaning. Like saying 'lateral transfer' when you really mean 'stealing.'"

"You think that Wolf-Knapp somehow obtained this stolen Renoir and sold it to Miss Drucilla? Then for whatever reason, he murdered her and stole the painting back?"

"That does sound complicated," Theodosia said.

"No, it sounds positively twisted," Drayton said.

"Which is all the more reason for us to go out to Wolf Knapp's place tonight."

Drayton made a face. "And do what? Break in? Make a citizen's arrest?"

"More like do a reconnaissance," Theodosia said.

"Just you and me." Drayton didn't sound convinced.

Theodosia glanced down at Earl Grey and Honey Bee. "How about we take the dogs along for protection?"

21

❧

They took the dogs with them, but not for protection. They took them along because . . . well, because they were there.

"Honey Bee isn't exactly your trained attack dog," Drayton said as they drove down East Bay Street. "In case you haven't noticed, she's more of a lapdog."

"That's okay. She can bark, can't she?"

"Don't you know it. Like a champ."

"Once a dog gets to barking, it makes most people nervous. The old primal fear kicks in."

Drayton glanced back at Honey Bee, who was perched like a little lady next to Earl Grey in the back of Theodosia's Jeep. "Fearful of that sweet face? I don't think so."

They drove across the Ravenel Bridge, went through Mount Pleasant, and, after a few turns, ended up in a decidedly rural area.

"You know where we're going?" Drayton asked.

"Got a good idea anyway."

They swept around a tight S curve, headlights splashing

on brackish water where tupelo gum trees stood like lone sentinels. Overhead, clouds boiled, obscuring the moon and stars.

"Dark out here," Drayton observed.

That was okay with Theodosia. She figured coming in under cover of darkness was a good thing, a lucky thing, because all she really wanted was to get a feel for Julian Wolf-Knapp's place. Could he be hiding out there? Or had he already lit out for parts unknown? Or maybe the Renoir was stashed at the plantation house while he was . . . what? Busy buying airline tickets? Negotiating another sale? It was all up in the air of course. And truth be known, terribly exciting.

"How close are we?" Drayton asked. He'd been silent for the last couple of miles.

"Real close," Theodosia said. "Like we're almost . . . there."

Her headlights picked out the beginnings of a rustic ranch fence just up ahead, the wood bare and silvered. She flipped off her lights, lifted her foot off the gas, and coasted in, silent as a stealth helicopter on final approach.

"I think this is it," Theodosia whispered.

"Are you sure?"

"Pretty sure." Crunching gravel now, she drifted over to a battered metal mailbox that was perched on a pole. "What's the name on the mailbox?"

"Wolf-Knapp. Oh dear."

"Cheer up, Drayton. This is going to be fun."

"If you say so."

Theodosia parked the car by the side of the road and they got out. Took the dogs with them and crept silently down the dirt drive that led to Wolf-Knapp's plantation house. At first the place appeared as a dim, murky shadow set against a forest of shaggy willow oaks. Then, as they drew closer and could make out the actual residence, Theodosia recognized the place. It looked exactly like the pen-and-ink drawing that Annie at the Dusty Hen had showed her. Quaint, slightly sagging, and with a brick chimney set at one end. Your basic genteel Southern decay with a hint of neglect thrown in for good measure.

"This is it," Theodosia said, her heart starting to blip a little faster. It was dark as a tomb without even a glow from a single yard light or porch lamp.

"One of the old rice plantations," Drayton whispered. "Fairly typical design, though smaller than most. And not in great shape." He hesitated. "It doesn't appear that anyone's home."

Drayton was right. Even with the approach of their footsteps, which might have roused someone's interest, the place remained pitch-black.

"Maybe it's good that nobody's around," Theodosia said. "Makes it easier to snoop."

"Or maybe Wolf-Knapp is sitting inside in the dark with a shotgun balanced in his lap. And the darkness makes it easier for him to see us creeping toward his house," Drayton said.

"I love how you always see the upside of things," Theodosia whispered.

Still, neither of them backed down. They crept closer, moving from tree to tree, trying to stay in the shadows, always keeping something in front of them. A magnolia bush. A scrawny tree. A skeletal grape arbor, the grapes picked clean by birds, the vines bare twisted ropes.

When they were ten feet from the front porch, they both stopped.

"Now what?" Drayton whispered.

"I'm going to sneak up onto that wraparound porch and peek in the window," Theodosia said.

"I'll wait here if you don't mind."

"Okay, but . . . okay."

Theodosia handed Earl Grey's leash to Drayton, drew a deep breath, and started moving forward. She was stealthy as a cat, even when she tiptoed up the three wooden steps that led to the sagging porch, praying that the weathered old boards didn't creak.

They didn't.

Now Theodosia moved swiftly to a front window and pressed her face against the glass. It was dark inside, but she could see enough to satisfy her curiosity. The interior of the home looked semifurnished. Just the bare requisite of furniture—a sofa and a small dining table and chairs. A brick fireplace was set against the far wall. She padded to another window and peered in that one, too. Same thing. Sparsely furnished, wide plank floors, nobody home.

Wind shivered through bare trees, making branches clack together like old bones. Theodosia shivered, too. This not only felt dangerous; it felt creepy. She moved to another window, peered in again, saw only darkness. Must be a bedroom. Finally, she held up a hand and waved for Drayton to come forward.

Nervous, hunching his shoulders, he advanced slowly, bringing the dogs along with him. Just as he was about to step up onto the porch, Theodosia said, "I'm pretty sure Wolf-Knapp isn't here. And there's hardly any furniture inside. You ask me, the place looks practically empty. Maybe he's more of an aesthete than we realized."

"Good for him," Drayton said. "He's a less-is-more kind of guy. Now can we please leave?" He was fidgeting and anxious as the dogs strained at their leashes.

"I'd like to look around for a few more minutes."

"I doubt there's anything to see. Besides, this place has a nasty brooding feeling about it."

Theodosia jerked her head. "There are two small buildings over there I'd like to check out."

"What? You think they might be secret art repositories, that all the stolen works of the Western world are contained within?"

"You never know," Theodosia said. "And Drayton . . ."

"Yes?"

"I think you're being overly dramatic."

Theodosia took hold of Earl Grey's collar, unclipped his leash, and let him run free. Drayton shrugged and did the same thing with Honey Bee.

The two buildings backed up to woods and were locked up tight with new Schlage padlocks securing both doors. Short of a crowbar or blowtorch, there was no way they were getting inside.

"A man who likes his privacy," Drayton said. "But Wolf-Knapp's not here. Maybe he was never here." He fluttered his fingers. "He's a will-o'-the-wisp."

Then where is he? Theodosia wondered. *Winging his way to South America with a Renoir tucked in his flight bag?*

"Come on, time to go," Drayton said. He bent forward, slapped his hands against his knees to get his dog's attention. "Come on, Honey Bee."

Theodosia made a grudging decision that Drayton was probably right. Tonight was a no-go. Another wild-goose chase. Maybe they were smart to simply pack it in.

"Earl Grey," she called. "You, too. Let's go."

But all their calls, whistles, and entreaties did no earthly good at all, because the dogs, enraptured by their environs, completely ignored them. Earl Grey and Honey Bee continued to chase around wildly, sniffing out field mice, kicking up their heels, snuffling through weeds.

"These old plantations are basically doggy nirvana," Drayton said, after Honey Bee zipped by him for a fourth time. "This entire area is no doubt honeycombed with dikes and sluiceways from back when South Carolina planters grew extensive crops of rice—genuine Carolina gold."

"You can just imagine all the old levees, canals, and floodgates. Like at Aunt Libby's place," Theodosia said. Her aunt Libby lived on a similar type of plantation out on Rutledge Road. Only Aunt Libby's place was larger and in much better condition.

"Look at these little hellions," Drayton said, "running around and digging like mad." He sighed. "I'm afraid we're going to be scrubbing muddy paws tonight."

Theodosia and Drayton slogged through thigh-high weeds, marsh grass, and a few muddy patches to where the dogs had converged to snuffle about intently. Both had their heads down, following a scent that was clearly intriguing.

"Earl Grey. *Now*," Theodosia said, using her serious voice.

Strangely enough, Earl Grey didn't pay one whit of attention to her. His head remained down as he continued to sniff along a low rise that was choked with a tangle of vines and tall weeds.

"What's got you so interested, fella?" Theodosia asked. She snuck up behind him, grabbed his collar, and pulled him back. Firmly.

Theodosia was so intent at clipping Earl Grey's leash to his collar that she almost didn't see the dirty hand sticking up out of the soil.

When she finally did notice, her mouth turned dry as the Gobi Desert and her brain bonked out an imperative, screechy warning that yelped: *No. This can't be happening. Totally impossible!*

But seeing was believing, so Theodosia stole a second look at the horror. She blinked, registered the waxy-looking appendage with dirty curled fingers, and let out a strangled cry.

"Drayton!"

"What?" He was busy stumbling after Honey Bee, frustration evident in his voice.

"Get over here. Please."

"What is it?" he asked again, then threw up his hands and abandoned his chase. He turned and began to pick his way toward her. "What's wrong now?"

Her heart stuck firmly in her throat, Theodosia pointed to the solitary hand that seemed to sprout from the dank earth like some kind of unholy mushroom.

"There's a hand sticking out of the dirt."

"A what?" Drayton was shaking his head and mumbling to himself about muddying his Ferragamo loafers.

Theodosia continued to stand her ground and point, even though her nerves were firing like rockets, warning her to get out of there. To back off because this amateur semi-investigation stuff had suddenly taken a very deadly turn.

"Wait a minute. Did you say 'hand'? As in *human* hand?" Drayton scoffed. "Now who's being overly dramatic?" He honestly thought she was making a bad joke. Trying to frighten him.

"No, really. I think there's a body buried here. A dead body!"

Reluctantly, Drayton took a step closer. He stared down and let out a loud gasp. Then he slapped a hand against his chest and cried, "Hail and have mercy, I think I need a defibrillator!"

22

❦

"*Why are you* disturbing me at this time of night?" Tidwell asked in a crabby, unhappy voice. Theodosia had called 911, badgered the dispatcher, sputtered out a hasty explanation, and basically moved heaven and earth to be put through to Tidwell at home. And now he was giving her attitude? Well, that was just tough.

"Because I didn't disturb you *last* night," Theodosia responded, "when my shop was broken into."

Tidwell let out a deep sigh. "Now what's wrong?"

"It's Julian Wolf-Knapp," Theodosia said. She could hear what sounded like the *Thursday Night Football* game playing loudly in the background. Maybe the Carolina Panthers taking on . . . whoever.

"Yes, yes," Tidwell said in a matter-of-fact voice. "I had the department put out a BOLO on the man. Happy now?"

"Not exactly. That's why I'm calling."

"Watch out!" Tidwell yelped. "Don't drop . . . See, now

you've sacrificed precious yardage." Then he was back on the phone to Theodosia. "What did you say?"

"I said I'm calling about Wolf-Knapp."

"Don't tell me you found him!" Tidwell blurted out. He sounded excited and strangely curious. Suddenly, the TV noise was muted. No more football game.

"You might have found him too if you hadn't gone ping-ponging out of my tea shop like a madman this afternoon."

"Is that a yes or a no, Miss Browning? I need a straight answer. And by the way, where are you? Where exactly are you calling from?"

"I'm at Julian Wolf-Knapp's plantation house," Theodosia said. "And I need you to come, like . . . immediately. I'll text you the address."

"You've actually uncovered something?" Tidwell asked.

"I'm afraid so. Um . . . literally."

He sucked in a breath, then said, "Don't tell me you found the Renoir. The missing painting."

"More like the missing art dealer."

There was a long pause and then Tidwell said, "Could you be more specific?"

"Let me put it this way," Theodosia said. "It would help if you brought along a cadaver dog and the county coroner."

Twenty-five minutes later, Tidwell arrived like a rampaging rhino. He slalomed his old Crown Victoria to a skidding stop in the plantation's front yard, kicking up a tidal wave of dust.

"Cue the music," Drayton said. "The cavalry has arrived."

Along with his assistant, Glen Humphries, Tidwell had also brought an entire contingent of law enforcement. Two uniformed officers from Charleston, Deputy Sheriff Tom Manning of Dorchester County, two other young deputies who Theodosia thought might be twins, as well as a shiny black Crime Scene van manned by two bored-looking techs.

"Where is he?" Tidwell asked as he sprang from his car

and hurried over to where Theodosia and Drayton were standing. There was no *Hi. How are you? Thanks for helping out.* Just his typical gruff bark.

"Over there," Theodosia said, pointing at the grassy hillock that had once been part of a rice dam.

"Lead the way," Tidwell said. Tonight he'd traded his usual unstylish suit and rumpled tie for digging-up-dead-guy casual. In other words, baggy khaki slacks, a faded blue FBI T-shirt, and an oversized barn jacket.

"The dogs actually found Wolf-Knapp's body," Theodosia explained. "Earl Grey and Honey Bee. They were running around like crazy, digging up hunks of dirt and eventually exposed a hand."

"If it's really him," Tidwell said.

But some twenty minutes later, with the two sheriff's deputies poking and prodding at the shallow grave, shoveling clods of dirt with shiny new spades, Tidwell gave a knowing nod and said, "It's him."

Then it was Crime Scene's turn to move in. They set up light stanchions that gave off an amazing force field of brightness and strung yellow crime scene tape that was probably unnecessary.

Theodosia was almost afraid to ask but did anyway. "Can you tell how he was killed? Was it a drug? A hot shot in a syringe?"

"Gunshot," Tidwell said without hesitation. "Bullet to the back of his head. Clean. Execution style. There's stippling around the entry wound that indicates Wolf-Knapp was shot at extremely close range." He yelled to the techs, "Don't forget to do plaster casts of any footprints and search for shell casings." One of them nodded back.

Drayton tiptoed up behind the group, not because he wanted to look at Wolf-Knapp's body, but because he had a question.

"Why would someone want to kill Julian Wolf-Knapp?" he asked.

"Because he sold Miss Drucilla a stolen Renoir," Theodosia said. "And then—like we theorized before—he stole it back?"

"And now someone's stolen it from *him*?" Drayton said. "Your theory still sounds convoluted."

"More like a crazy, unfounded supposition," Tidwell said. "Leaving the Renoir out of the equation for now, the question remains, who killed Wolf-Knapp?"

Theodosia thought for a moment. "What if Wolf-Knapp killed Miss Drucilla for the Renoir, then someone else killed Wolf-Knapp?"

"You're saying there could be two separate crimes? Murders?" Drayton said.

"Right," Theodosia said. "Separate but related."

Tidwell looked at Humphries, noted his skeptical reaction, then shook his head. "It feels like you're reaching."

"Maybe." Theodosia edged closer to the makeshift grave. "How long has he been in the ground?"

One of the techs turned to her and wrinkled his nose. "There's lividity and the beginnings of decomp. So forty-eight hours? Maybe more?"

"Explains why Wolf-Knapp missed the funeral this morning," Drayton said.

"Because he was otherwise occupied," Theodosia said.

"You two are being awfully blasé about this," Tidwell observed.

"Take my word for it, we were definitely not calm and collected when we discovered his body," Theodosia told him.

Tidwell tasked Humphries and one of the officers to go into the plantation house and look around for the painting.

"What's the painting look like?" Humphries asked.

"Here," Theodosia said. She pulled out her phone, swiped through until she found the image of the stolen Renoir, and held it up so they could see it. "This is probably it right here. Stolen from an auction house in Vienna."

"Okay," Humphries said. "So a small landscape."

"How did you come by this information?" Tidwell asked Theodosia.

"One of the curators from the Barnes Foundation in Philadelphia called me earlier this evening," Theodosia told him. "Clued me in about a stolen Renoir." When Tidwell just stared at her, she added, "They have a collection of more than one hundred and eighty Renoirs."

"So you'd obviously been in touch with them," Tidwell said.

"I figured they'd be a good resource."

"And so they have." Tidwell gazed at her; then his eyes shifted to a point over her shoulder. "Oh no."

Theodosia turned and saw that the TV crew from Channel Eight had just pulled in.

"Damn those TV people and their police scanners," Tidwell said. "They ought to be outlawed."

"The scanners?" Theodosia asked.

"No," Tidwell snapped. "The TV people. They're jackals!"

Monica Garber and her crew buzzed around Tidwell and the Crime Scene guys like unwelcome flies, Tidwell constantly shooing them away, the TV people always sneaking back to grab a few more shots.

If the situation wasn't so macabre, it would almost have been comical.

Fifteen minutes later, Humphries and the officer came back out of the plantation house.

"Back door's been broken in," said the officer.

"Must have snuck up on the victim," said Humphries. "Hence your shot from behind."

"No sign of that painting, either," the officer said. "There are a couple of fancy horse paintings hanging on the wall, but no landscape painting."

"We'll have to search Wolf-Knapp's studio," Tidwell said.

"You won't find it there," Theodosia said. "That Renoir is long gone."

"Any ideas on where it went?" Tidwell asked.

"I wish."

Drayton looked glum. "So it's possible Miss Drucilla's murder may never be solved?"

Tidwell glowered. "Thirty-two years in law enforcement has taught me never to discount the impossible or improbable. Strange and bizarre information pops up where you least expect it. Someone blabs in a bar. A so-called friend turns suspicious. A trusted cohort dimes someone out. Last week we apprehended a carjacker. Turns out, the dunce had a list in his pocket that said 'burner phone' and 'gun.'" He looked over his shoulder and shouted, "You, get away from that grave."

Unfazed, the cameraman stepped back a measly three paces.

"Idiot," Tidwell scoffed.

"If nobody talks, if the rumor mill remains silent, we could always try to make something happen ourselves," Theodosia suggested.

"No!" Tidwell yelled. "This is where you step aside and I take complete control."

But that was not exactly how Theodosia saw it. In fact, she asked Drayton to drive them back to Charleston so she could sit in the passenger seat and make a couple of phone calls.

"I don't believe I've ever driven a Jeep before," Drayton said as he backed up carefully, then turned and headed out onto the road.

"It's a vehicle like any other," Theodosia said.

"But with a storied pedigree. Weren't these things invented during the Second World War?"

"I think the early ones were called General Purpose Vehicles, which the GIs shortened to GP and then eventually to Jeep."

"Interesting," he said. "By the way, who are you calling?"

"Pauline."

"Hmm." Still, Drayton never took his eyes off the road.

Theodosia called the number at Miss Drucilla's and got no answer.

Okay, try, try again.

When she called Pauline's cell phone, Pauline answered almost immediately.

"Hey!" Pauline said. "After you sent me an image of that painting, I figured you were hot on the trail. So . . . did you find it? The painting?"

"Not exactly," Theodosia said.

"Oh no?" Pauline's voice faded.

"Hello?" Theodosia said. Now she could hear music and a burble of conversation in the background. Was Pauline at a restaurant? A club?

"Theodosia, what . . . ?" Pauline started to say.

Theodosia cut her off. "We need to talk."

"Right now," Drayton whispered to her.

"As soon as possible," Theodosia said.

Pauline picked up on the urgency in Theodosia's voice. "What's wrong? Has something happened?"

"Better we meet in person. Tonight if you can manage it."

"I can. Wade and I were just leaving Poogan's Porch. We had a late dinner."

"Can you stay there? Wait for me there? I'm maybe ten minutes away."

"Okay, we can do that," Pauline said. "Wow. This sure sounds mysterious."

Theodosia hung up and said to Drayton, "Guess where they are."

"No idea."

"They just finished eating at Poogan's Porch."

His hands tightened around the steering wheel. "Weird," he said.

"I'll say. That's the restaurant with the giant mural titled *Renoir Redux* painted on the side of the building."

"A takeoff on Renoir's *Luncheon of the Boating Party*, right?" Drayton said.

"Yup, only it features likenesses of fourteen prominent members of Charleston's food scene."

"You think it's some kind of omen?"

"You never know."

Pauline and Wade were waiting on the sidewalk outside the landmark restaurant when Theodosia and Drayton pulled up to the curb.

Pauline lifted a hand to wave, then pulled it back down when she saw the look on Theodosia's face.

"What?" she said once Theodosia and Drayton had parked and were standing there with them.

Theodosia gave a fast rundown of the situation. Quick and terse, like ripping off a bandage. Julian Wolf-Knapp gone missing. Then found dead. Buried in a shallow grave near his plantation house.

Pauline was stunned. "Dead? The art dealer is dead?" She put both hands to her temples and pressed hard. "How?"

"He was murdered," Theodosia said. "Shot in the back of the head."

"Who would do that?" The look of utter surprise, of abject confusion on Pauline's face told Theodosia that the girl probably hadn't been the one to pull the trigger on Wolf-Knapp. She didn't think a truly guilty person could fake that much shock and amazement.

"We don't know who killed him," Theodosia said in a gentler voice. "We alerted Detective Tidwell, he came out, and the whole thing is obviously under investigation."

"His murder is related to Miss Drucilla's murder, isn't it?" Wade said.

"Yes," Theodosia said. "It's probably all connected."

"But how?" Wade asked.

"We don't know."

"This is so doggone awful!" Pauline said as tears welled up in her eyes. "Another person ending up dead. I mean . . . I didn't *know* him but . . ." Her voice broke off in a loud choke; then Pauline turned her head and let loose a series of heartrending sobs.

Wade put his arms around Pauline and pulled her close, trying his best to comfort her. "It's not your fault," he murmured.

"No, it's not," Theodosia said. *Not this one anyway.*

"You say the police are there right now? Taking charge and investigating?" Wade asked.

"That's right," Drayton said.

"A second murder like this," Theodosia said. "They'll make it a huge priority, probably go statewide, bring in as many other agencies as possible."

Wade held Pauline close as she trembled in his arms. "I don't know the circumstances that led to the art dealer's murder," he said. "But nobody—I mean, *nobody*—should end up dead and buried in a shallow grave like that poor man."

23

"This is like some kind of twisted Gordian knot," Theodosia said to Drayton. "Here I thought Julian Wolf-Knapp was the killer. Then someone snuck in stage left and killed *him.*"

It was eight o'clock on Friday morning and Theodosia had barely slept a wink all night. When she did manage to drift off and catch a few z's, her dreams had been wild and frenzied. Every bizarre event had been turned over in her runaway mind—Miss Drucilla's murder, finding syringes at Smokey's place, the break-in at her tea shop, Julian Wolf-Knapp's murder. And still she was unable to figure out a logical connection and make sense of it.

Drayton lifted the lid off a cream-colored salt-glaze teapot, peeked at the contents, and replaced the lid. "This tea is officially steeped." He poured out a cup for each of them. "High-octane Jumpy Monkey from DavidsTea to hopefully help sharpen our focus."

"Better pour me a cup, too," Haley called out. "And, guys,

I hate to say this, but we're going to need all the energy we can muster today."

They both turned as Haley approached the front counter carrying a large silver tray stacked high with candied fruit scones.

"Is there something we don't know about, Haley?" Theodosia asked. They'd already told her about discovering Julian Wolf-Knapp's body last night. Haley had been circumspect about the details, listening carefully, asking only a few basic questions. Probably because she was frightened, Theodosia decided. Who wouldn't be?

"A couple of things," Haley said. "First, here are two dozen fresh-baked candied fruit scones for take-out orders."

"Lovely," Drayton said as he eyed the scones. "So festive." They were light golden brown and landscaped with jeweled pieces of candied cherries, pineapple, and dates.

"The second thing, and the most important," Haley said. "Miss Dimple just called and said she's real sick, so she won't be able to come in today."

"No," Drayton said. He was about to take a sip of tea but changed his mind and set his cup back in its saucer. "Today's . . . it's our Old-Fashioned Southern Tea this afternoon." He sighed heavily. "This changes everything."

"Chill, guys. I already came up with a solution," Haley said.

"What's that?" Theodosia asked.

"I made what you two would call an executive decision and called my cousin Beth Ann. As luck would have it, she's home for Christmas break and staying with my aunt Alice and uncle Bill over in Goose Creek."

"Your cousin Beth Ann," Theodosia said, tapping the counter, trying to place the name. "We've met her before?"

"Maybe a couple of years ago. When she and Aunt Alice came to one of our teas."

"Is that a roundabout way of saying that Beth Ann's

agreed to come in and help?" Drayton asked, a hopeful gleam lighting his eyes.

"She'll be here by ten at the latest."

"Haley, that's wonderful," Theodosia said. "Well done. You really pulled our fat out of the fryer."

"Yeah, but I'm afraid it's a onetime deal. The flip side is that Beth Ann can help out only today. If Miss Dimple's still sick tomorrow—and I'm guessing she will be—we'll have to find somebody else to help with the Victorian Christmas Tea."

"Let's gallop across that bridge when we come to it," Drayton said.

Haley gave him a thumbs-up as she headed back to the kitchen. "Okay. Gotcha."

"Busy," Theodosia said, gazing at Drayton, who'd finally managed to take a gulp of tea and was now stacking scones into their glass pie saver.

"On the upside, we're actually in the home stretch," Drayton said. "There's our tea this afternoon and then the grand finale Victorian Christmas Tea tomorrow. After that it's *finito* and we're closed up lock, stock, and barrel for Christmas. I for one am looking forward to a well-deserved break."

"And you've earned it," Theodosia said. "We all have. Still, it feels as if time is ticking away and we're still no closer to any kind of resolution."

"You mean about Miss Drucilla's murder?" Drayton looked suddenly somber.

Theodosia frowned. "And Wolf-Knapp's, too."

"They're both crazy whodunits, that's for sure. And I hate that everything is so up in the air. But as far as investigations go, you certainly dug in and gave it your best shot."

"So did you," Theodosia said, "even though we still harbor doubts about Smokey, Donny Bragg, Coy Cooper, and even Pauline."

"Tell you what. We'll keep our ideas simmering on the back burner. But in the meantime . . ."

A loud knock sounded at the front door. They both turned

quickly and saw two smiling faces peeking in the window. Waving at them.

"I know," Theodosia said as she started for the door to welcome her early-bird customers. "In the meantime we need to focus on the task at hand."

Drayton nodded. "Which is to delight our customers as best we can."

But by ten thirty, with the tea shop humming and candied fruit scones and carrot cake muffins being served, Drayton was the one expressing utter delight.

"That Beth Ann is an absolute wonder," he whispered to Theodosia. "She's quick and intelligent, even comprehends the different varieties of tea. I mean, she actually knows a jasmine from an orange pekoe. Kindly tell me why we haven't engaged her services until now."

"Probably because she's been away at school and doesn't live in Charleston?"

"Oh. Well. Perhaps for the summer, then?"

"It couldn't hurt to ask," Theodosia agreed.

"Drayton." Beth Ann was suddenly leaning across the counter, focusing intently on him. "The ladies at table four are asking about their pot of Oriental Beauty oolong. What should I tell them?"

"That it's a Taiwanese white oolong and semi-oxidized so it needs to be brewed at a slightly lower temperature," Drayton said. "Steeping requires at least three to four minutes." He hesitated. "Do you want me to go over and explain things?"

Beth Ann, who looked like a dark-haired Haley with her shining eyes, long hair, and youthful exuberance, said, "No, I've got this. I just thought it best to check with you."

"Check with me," Drayton said as Beth Ann bounded back over to table four. "Isn't that sweet? Isn't she a darling?" He was fairly beaming.

But his words were rudely punctuated as the front door opened with a loud BANG! Now Drayton wasn't beaming quite so brightly.

"Rats," he muttered. "It's those awful TV people, come back to ruin our day."

The gang of three loped in, looking sleep-deprived after last night, but a little expectant, too.

Theodosia was about to tell Drayton to get busy and ignore them when she realized he'd already turned away and was scanning his floor-to-ceiling tea shelves. Looking thoroughly engaged and searching for . . . whatever.

So it's up to me to face off with the media monsters.

Monica Garber grinned as she hurried toward Theodosia. This morning she wore a black leather jacket, skintight jeans, and evil-looking black leather boots with silver studs.

"That body you guys discovered last night?" Monica gushed. "We were able to squeak some footage onto the tail end of the ten o'clock news. Thanks so much!"

"You're welcome," Theodosia said. "Anytime I can be of assistance with a dead body, just let me know."

Monica waved a hand. "Oh, you," she giggled. "You're kind of fun after all, aren't you?"

"Not really. Not in the sense that you mean," Theodosia said. "But I am pleased you got your big story." She hesitated. "Which begs the question, why are you here?"

In other words, why are you bothering me in my tea shop on a super-busy Friday morning mere days before Christmas?

"For one thing, Miss Drucilla's murder is a fascinating ongoing story line for our viewers," Monica Garber said, her eyes snapping with excitement. "You know, wealthy older woman with a stolen Renoir. Very ripped from the headlines in a *Vanity Fair* kind of way."

"You're telling me ratings are up," Theodosia said.

"Ratings are through the roof. Then last night . . . that art dealer turning up dead was the icing on the cake."

Garber paused, consciously wiped away the big smile that had snuck onto her face, and tried to reboot her attitude into something more businesslike. As if she were about to pitch something to Theodosia. And pitch she did.

"Because of high viewer interest, I want *you* to be our next story," Garber said.

"No," Theodosia said. She took a step backward to physically distance herself from such a ridiculous idea. "I'm not going to be your story. So really, you need to stop intruding."

Garber shook her head. "I can't do that."

"Of course you can."

"I'd hate to disappoint our viewers."

"Please, let them be disappointed," Theodosia said. "I beg you."

Garber fidgeted, looking suddenly uncomfortable. "Truth be told, there's another reason."

"I can't imagine what that might be."

"If I don't bring back a story about you, I could get fired."

"There is no story," Theodosia said. "There's just little old me. A woman with a tea shop. See?" She gestured toward tables filled with customers, the fireplace with crackling logs, the wreaths on the walls, the front counter lined with teapots. "Cute but also kind of boring, huh?"

"Maybe it is right now," Monica Garber warned. "But I'm still going to keep an eye on you."

"You got rid of them," Drayton said. "Blessings on your head."

"Don't look so hopeful," Theodosia said. "Those goofballs could come boomeranging back here any minute. They're convinced there's another story lurking somewhere."

"Heaven forbid." Drayton put three scoops of orchid plum tea into a floral teapot, added a pinch for the pot, and said, "We're still going to the Parade of Boats tonight, aren't we?"

"Oh, Drayton."

The Parade of Boats was an annual Christmas event in

Charleston. At least fifty sailboats and motorized boats, all decorated with lights and holiday figures, paraded down the Cooper River, around the tip of the Peninsula, and then up the Ashley River. It was a gorgeous spectacle and was always capped by a huge display of fireworks.

Drayton peered at Theodosia over his glasses. "It's tradition. We always go."

"You're right. Okay, but I can't stay long."

"An hour. You can spare an hour, can't you?"

Theodosia held up an index finger. "One hour to watch the boats. But that's it. And please tell me there's nothing else I have to worry about. That the torches and actors for tomorrow's tea are going to arrive on schedule."

"Everything's good to go, I promise."

"Thank you."

Theodosia stopped by a couple of tables to say hello, greeted a gaggle of new customers, then hurried into the kitchen.

"Haley," she said, "what can I do to help?"

Haley shook her head. "Nothing really. I've pretty much got it covered." She pulled two index cards from her apron pocket and handed them to Theodosia. "The first one's today's lunch. The second details the menu for our Old-Fashioned Southern Tea."

Theodosia skimmed the two menu cards. Lunch was simple enough with three choices: a tomato-bisque-and-shrimp-salad-sandwich entrée, a slice of cheddar quiche with a side of grilled brussels sprouts, and a fig, goat cheese, and frisée salad. On the other hand, Haley's menu for their afternoon tea bordered on spectacular.

"You see, I kept lunch easy-peasy because afternoon tea is going to be so elaborate."

"They're both wonderful," Theodosia said. "But I'm thinking today's lunch won't be all that busy since most of our regulars will be coming this afternoon."

Haley nodded. "No *problema*."

* * *

Theodosia's hunch proved correct. Lunch service was quick and easy. Just six tables to contend with as well as a dozen take-out orders.

"Do things always run this smooth?" Beth Ann asked Theodosia as she brushed past her.

"Just wait until three o'clock when we really get hopping. Then you'll change your mind," Theodosia said.

"You're telling me this is just dress rehearsal?"

"This is a cinch."

But with a light luncheon crowd, Theodosia was happy to find herself with a little extra time on her hands. It gave her a chance to duck into her office and check her e-mail. But as she clicked along, nothing looked pressing. An invitation to a trunk show at Hampden, a sale on silver charms at Hearts Desire, a Christmas hello from a fellow tea shop owner in Savannah, and a reminder for a dentist appointment.

She glanced at her watch. Still time to spare. Okay, then, she could try to get a start on wrapping Christmas presents. There was that cashmere scarf for Haley—ice blue to complement her blond hair—and for Drayton a collectible volume of Dickens that Lois had sent over from Antiquarian Books.

Theodosia spread out wrapping paper, ribbon, and gift bags and got started. And was cooking along fairly well until her phone rang.

Feeling chipper, she snatched it up and gave an upbeat "Hello."

There was a momentary hollow lull—maybe a long-distance delay?

"Riley?" she said. "Is that you?"

It was Riley all right. But he wasn't exactly brimming over with Christmas cheer.

"Theodosia," he said without benefit of greeting or preamble, "another dead body? Really?"

24

❧❧

Theodosia's initial reaction was *Uh-oh.* Obviously this wasn't going to be his usual *How-ya-doin'-sweetheart* type of call.

Then she pulled it together and said, "That dead body was *not* my doing. And excuse me, but how do you know what went down last night when you're a thousand miles away?"

"I have a network of spies," Riley said.

"No, you don't. Let me guess. Tidwell called."

"He did not."

"Who, then?"

"Like I said, spies. In every nook and cranny of the universe."

"Was it Glen Humphries, Tidwell's assistant?"

"Ah, clever girl, your award for a correct guess is a giant purple panda."

"Forget pandas when we've got pandemonium," Theodosia said. "If you're truly in the loop, then you know Wolf-Knapp's death wasn't my fault. That I actually did the police a *service* in discovering his partially buried body, especially when *their* investigation had completely stalled out."

"No, sweetheart, *your* investigation is now over and done with while the wheels of justice continue to grind."

"That sounds like a cheesy line from a B movie."

"Probably is. But you know what? It *is* over and done with, and I'd rather not talk about dead art dealers or dead ends or anything else. It's kind of a bore."

Not to me, Theodosia thought.

"So why don't you tell me something fun, like what's up at the tea shop today? And when I get home, are you going to whip up some of those yummy shrimp balls?"

"For a New Year's Eve treat, why not?"

"And your famous crab dip?"

"Only if you agree to pop the cork on an extravagant bottle of wine."

"You are so on."

They talked for another ten minutes and never came close to mentioning a single solitary dead body. Instead, they hashed over plans for an upcoming ski trip to Sugar Mountain in the Blue Ridge Mountains of North Carolina and joked about taking on the Boulder Dash, one of the treacherous black-diamond runs.

When Theodosia finally hung up she felt warm and happy inside. Riley would be back home in a few days and they'd be celebrating New Year's Eve together. Enjoying a romantic dinner at one of their favorite restaurants, Circa 1886. Meanwhile, the tea shop was going gangbusters, and most important of all, their holiday events were going off without a hitch. Yes, her investigation might have been slightly derailed. But except for a bump here and there (which she knew she could overcome), life was pretty darned good.

"Knock, knock," Haley called out. "May I come in?"

Theodosia hastily shoved the shiny gold gift bag containing Haley's scarf into the bottom drawer of her desk.

"Entrez," she sang out.

The door opened and Haley came in, balancing two gingerbread houses on a silver tray.

"I was going to use your desk for work space 'cause I need to put a couple of finishing touches on my gingerbread houses. But now . . ." Haley eyed Theodosia's cluttered desktop. "Maybe not?"

"Give me half a minute," Theodosia said. She leaned forward, hastily scooped up stacks of invoices, tea magazines, recipes, and catalogs, then turned and deposited the entire mess on the credenza behind her. "There. All clear."

"Thanks," Haley said as she carefully set down her tray.

Theodosia studied Haley's gingerbread houses. "Haley, these are exquisite. But when did you find time to make them?"

"I've been working on my gingerbreads pretty much all week long," Haley said, "whenever I could carve out a little extra time. Baking the gingerbread, cutting out the various pieces, fashioning everything together. Since they're nonedible, it doesn't matter if the gingerbread dries out a teensy bit. In fact, sometimes it's better that way with the larger pieces. But I do have a couple of serious cracks that need patching."

"And these gingerbread houses are for . . . what?"

Haley looked at her strangely. "They're centerpieces. For today's tea."

"I did not know that."

"Drayton didn't *tell* you? I ran my gingerbread idea past him like . . . three weeks ago. He was all for it."

Theodosia waved a hand. "Doesn't matter. These are darling and our guests will adore them. I take it there are more gingerbread houses?"

"Five more. Want me to bring 'em in?"

"An entire gingerbread community? I can't wait."

Once Haley had placed all her gingerbread houses on Theodosia's desk, she said, "I tried to make each one look like a particular style of architecture that's unique to Charleston. Like . . . that one." Haley pointed to one of her creations. "What does that remind you of?"

"I'd say it looks like a typical Charleston single home. Tall and narrow with a piazza running along the side," Theodosia said.

"That's exactly what I was going for," Haley said. "And that one there . . . the really big one?"

"Very representative of the larger mansions on Legare, especially since you made it three stories high with all those cute little balustrades and columns."

"Just like Miss Drucilla's house," Drayton said. He was suddenly standing in the doorway, staring in.

"Oh no, I didn't mean to make it look like *that* house," Haley said. Her voice conveyed her mood. "That's a sad house."

"Let me take another look, then," Drayton said quickly. He bent down and studied the gingerbread house in question. "Yes, now I see that it could definitely pass for Timothy Neville's home on Archdale Street."

Haley nodded, her good feelings restored. "Yeah, that's better. It does kind of look like Timothy's place, doesn't it?"

"Except he doesn't have actual gumdrops on his roofline," Theodosia said.

"And you need to do what with these tasty little wonders?" Drayton asked. "Because they look perfectly finished to me."

"I need to glue on a few more gumdrops and shore up a couple of roofs and foundations with vanilla icing," Haley said.

"I can identify with that," Drayton said. "Just like the constant maintenance required on most historic homes here in Charleston." He reached out and gently touched an index finger to the roof of one of the gingerbread houses. "Just like *my* home."

"Let's see now," Theodosia said. "We've got old-fashioned frilly aprons, some ruffled caps, and . . ."

"I'm not wearing a frilly apron," Drayton laughed. "If you make me, I'll quit in protest."

"How about a paisley vest and a top hat?" Haley asked.

"That's about all that's left in our all-purpose costume box. And that's scraping the bottom of the barrel at that."

Drayton pursed his lips together, thinking. "Well . . . perhaps. It *is* our Old-Fashioned Southern Tea after all."

"Beth Ann?" Haley said. "You want to wear one of these cute granny aprons?"

"Sure," Beth Ann said. She pulled a blue calico apron over her head and tied the strings behind her. "I look okay?"

"Perfect," said Haley.

"Whew." Beth Ann blew a hank of hair off her forehead. "I can see that it's no easy task getting ready for these big tea parties."

"There's a lot of prep work involved but it's all worth it," Theodosia said. "And thanks to both of you, the tea shop looks amazing."

The three of them stood back and gazed at their handiwork.

They'd selected pale peach linen tablecloths with matching napkins. The napkins had been folded into pockets to hold a hand-lettered recipe card. They'd chosen Blue Willow china (everybody's grandma had this!), nubby vintage glassware, and flatware decorated with small rosettes. Haley's gingerbread houses had been placed in the center of the tables, and in keeping with their old-fashioned theme, mason jars had been filled with old-fashioned candy sticks. Handmade pastel soaps had been placed in small peach-colored organza bags to serve as favors and sprinkles of antique buttons added to the old-fashioned flavor of the tables.

"I see you filled in with some Shelley Dainty Blue teacups," Theodosia said.

"Because we ran short," Beth Ann said. "Do they look okay?"

"They're perfect."

"What would you think about putting little tea lights inside some of the larger gingerbread houses?" Beth Ann asked. "I think it would make them look cute and glowy."

"That's a great idea," Theodosia said, "as long as the tea lights are in glass holders so the gingerbread doesn't scorch."

"I'll take care."

With five minutes left to go before their guests were due to arrive, Theodosia put on some gentle background music. It was a compilation of old-fashioned tunes that included some jazz, swing, and songs like "Walkin' After Midnight" and "Carolina in My Mind."

And then, with candles flickering, music playing, and amazing smells wafting from Haley's kitchen, the guests arrived. It was as if someone had hit a gong or shot off a cannon down Church Street. Because, suddenly, guests started pouring through the front door.

Theodosia greeted everyone, checked off their names from her master list, and then handed them off to Beth Ann, who hung up their coats and seated them at the various tables.

As the guests settled in and voices rose in spirited greetings, Beth Ann whispered in Theodosia's ear, "We've got a problem."

Theodosia turned. "Hmm?"

"We're short two place settings."

"Really?" Theodosia checked her list again. "Shouldn't be."

On the other hand . . .

"Drayton," she hissed. "Did you by any chance take a couple of last-minute reservations?"

He stopped short, put a hand to his mouth, and said, "Perhaps I forget to tell you?"

"This is easily remedied," Theodosia said. "Beth Ann, there's a small table in my office. Just bring it out and unfold it quickly while I round up two more chairs."

"I'm on it."

One minute later, the table was set with linens, plates, cups and saucers, flowers, and candles, and their two last-minute guests were happy as clams—even if their table was a little squished in.

"Okay," Theodosia said quietly to herself. "Now I've got to . . ."

She walked to the center of the room and ran through a quick mental exercise to relax and anchor herself, because welcoming guests to a special-event tea like this always put her front and center. And even though Theodosia loved being a hostess, enjoyed entertaining her guests and sharing her love of tea and tea lore, there was always a small part of her that remained hesitant.

Why is that? she wondered. Then decided, *I do not know.*

Whatever. She drew a deep breath and said, in a clear voice that rang throughout the tea room, "Good afternoon, dear guests. My name is Theodosia Browning, and I want to wish you all a very merry Christmas and extend a heartfelt welcome to the Indigo Tea Shop."

There was warm applause as all eyes turned toward her.

"As we begin our Old-Fashioned Southern Tea, you can see that my two cohorts, Drayton and Beth Ann, are already making the rounds and filling your teacups with Adagio's Earl Grey Crème Tea. Don't you love that delightful aroma? But there's lots more on tap to hopefully delight your senses and your taste buds. Because this is an old-fashioned tea, our executive chef, Haley Parker, has dug into her treasure trove of tried-and-true recipes and prepared four courses of good old-fashioned Southern food."

There was another round of applause and then Theodosia continued.

"Our first course will be fruit-and-sour-cream scones served with genuine Devonshire cream. That course will be followed by a small appetizer of fried green tomatoes and country ham corn fritters."

Theodosia paused as oohs and aahs filled the room.

"For your entrée today, you'll have your choice of either grilled duck breast drizzled with cranberry sauce or a wild salmon fillet brined in our house-brand sweet tea. Whichever entrée you choose, your side dishes will include traditional lobster hush puppies and cat-head biscuits."

Now there were audible cries of anticipation from the guests:

"Like my grandma Lolly used to make!"

"I can hardly wait!"

"All that and dessert, too?"

"Of course dessert," Theodosia said. "For that, you'll have your choice of sweet potato pie or pecan pie."

Now Drayton stepped to the center of the room to join her.

"Or perhaps a small slice of each?" he said with a mischievous grin.

"Tell them about the other teas, Drayton."

"Besides our Earl Grey Crème, I'm also brewing pots of Indian spice tea and my special Dragonwell Dream tea. I've chosen each of these blends as a perfect accompaniment to the food we're serving today. So, dear guests"—Drayton gave a short, stiff bow, like a fencing master might make—"please do enjoy."

"And if there's anything else you need or want, be sure to let us know," Theodosia said.

From then on the tea party ran like clockwork. Haley was a whirling dervish in the kitchen as she plated each course. Theodosia and Beth Ann ran the dishes out, served them, skillfully whisked away used plates, and then brought out the next course. When the numbers were tallied for entrées, it turned out their guests were fairly evenly divided. Eighteen were in favor of the duck breast; twenty opted for the salmon.

Cup after cup of tea was poured and eagerly consumed, and Drayton even had requests to brew pots of tippy Yunan and Dimbulla tea.

"These are sophisticated tea drinkers," he confided to Theodosia at the front counter. "They know what they want."

"And what they like," Theodosia said.

"Nothing wrong with that."

25

~❧~

By four forty-five, the party was winding down. Several guests hurried home to get ready for evening parties and Christmas concerts. A few guests lingered at their tables while some wandered over to the two highboys and indulged in some last-minute Christmas shopping.

Theodosia found herself gift wrapping tea towels and tea cozies, and grabbing sweetgrass baskets off the wall so she could create impromptu gift baskets filled with tea tins, jars of honey, and tea towels. No problem, she was always happy to oblige. Good thing she had plenty of clear plastic wrap and red ribbon to gussy up the gifts.

But as darkness descended, streetlamps flickered to life up and down Church Street, the last guests departed, and the party was finally over.

"I'd call that a rousing success," Drayton said as he dusted his hands together.

"Your guests *loved* every minute of it," Beth Ann enthused.

"Hopefully we can bottle some of this magical bonhomie and take it along with us tomorrow," Drayton said.

"I know we can," Theodosia said as she rolled up her sleeves and began clearing tables.

"I wish I could stay and help out at tomorrow's tea," Beth Ann said. "Today turned out to be so much fun."

"Dear girl, you're welcome back anytime," Drayton assured her. He rolled up the Oriental carpet in the entryway, then grabbed a broom and began sweeping the tea room floor.

"Thanks. I really appreciate the invite," Beth Ann said. Then to Theodosia, "Do you want me to gather up the linens before I go?"

"No, that's okay, I can take care of it," Theodosia said. "Just say your goodbyes to Haley and then scamper off. I know you've got a ride to catch."

"I think my dad might be parked outside right now," Beth Ann said, glancing out a window.

"C'mere, then. Give me a hug," Theodosia said. The two women embraced and Theodosia said, "Ditto for what Drayton said. You're welcome back anytime. As our guest or as part of the team."

"I'll keep that in mind," Beth Ann said. She ducked into the kitchen, blew multiple kisses to Haley, and grabbed her bright red moto jacket. As she shrugged into her jacket and yanked open the front door, she almost collided with someone who was coming in. "Oops, 'scuse me," she yelped, and was gone.

Theodosia looked up and said, "Uh-oh," then watched uncomfortably as Coy Cooper came walking toward her.

Cooper was dressed in a camel hair coat, a moss green sweater, and dark slacks. To Theodosia's eye he looked young . . . and rich. Almost indolently rich, which was the worst kind.

"What brings you here?" Theodosia asked him in an even tone.

Cooper's face was set in an intense scowl, as if he were on some kind of dreadful mission. He threw a quick glance at Drayton, instantly dismissed him, then focused his gaze back on Theodosia.

"Hey there," Cooper said. A small wave accompanied a greeting that was guarded.

Theodosia placed a Shelley Dainty Blue teacup and saucer in a tub that held a stack of other cups. "I didn't think you'd still be hanging around Charleston," she said. "Figured you'd run off to wherever."

"I need to talk to you," Cooper said. "It's important."

"What's important?"

"I want to hire you."

"Excuse me?" Had she heard him correctly? Or was this some kind of snarky joke?

"That dead art dealer you stumbled upon last night?"

"You know about that?"

"Yeah. You're not the only one who talks to the cops." Cooper paused. "I don't think that was the guy who murdered my aunt."

"A lot of things point to it," Theodosia said slowly.

"Not really," Cooper said. "Looks to me like somebody got his shorts in a bunch over that missing painting and murdered the art dealer. Maybe the art dealer knew something. Maybe he's the one who stole the painting. Anyway, he got whacked. And the way I see it, his killer has to be the same guy who murdered my aunt, right?"

"I suppose there could be some sort of conspiracy," Theodosia said. She didn't really believe that, but tossed it out anyway.

"No," Cooper said. "Wolf-Knapp may have been a crook and a pitiful excuse for a human being, but he didn't kill my aunt. Someone else did."

"Who do you think it was?"

Cooper rocked back on his heels. "You're asking me? I have no idea. That's why I want to hire you."

"Of course you're not serious."

"I'm dead serious."

"Interesting choice of words," Theodosia said.

Cooper frowned. "Come on, you don't think *I* did it, do you? Murdered my own aunt?" He stopped and stared at her intently. "Well. Maybe you do. Just a little bit?"

"Maybe I do," Theodosia countered.

"Then you're wasting your time. And you strike me as a fairly intelligent person who doesn't waste time on the ridiculous or nonsensical."

"Flattery will get you nowhere."

"Will money?"

"Probably not."

"Can't be bought, huh?" Cooper said, eyeing her. "I like that. I like that a lot."

"Go back and talk to the police," Theodosia said. "They're the ones running the investigation."

"Like I said before, I already had a confab with them. Can't say I'm impressed."

Join the club, Theodosia thought. Then she said, "If you've spoken to the police, they must have shared some ideas with you."

"Yeah," Cooper said. "Like the usual suspects."

"Those being . . ."

"Smokey the wild-eyed handyman seemed to be numero uno on their hot list. For a while anyway."

"But what do *you* think?" Theodosia asked.

"I don't know. I'm not familiar with the various players like you seem to be."

Drayton, who'd been wielding his broom and was almost finished sweeping the tea room, said, "I'm sorry, but we'll be closing in two minutes." He walked to the door and pulled it open. Continued to sweep in that direction.

"Giving me the bum's rush, huh?" Cooper said to Theodosia.

She shrugged. "Like the man said, we're closing."

"Sure," Cooper said. He shook his head and started for the door. As he passed Drayton, he said, "Thanks for nothing."

"You're welcome," Drayton said pleasantly. Then he closed the door, locked it, and said, "That was odd."

"No kidding," Theodosia said.

"Do you think Coy Cooper was serious about hiring you?"

"Maybe he was just making an end run, checking to see if I've figured anything out."

"Or to see if you're onto *him*?" Drayton said.

"Could be."

"Do you suspect him?"

"I didn't until just now."

"Interesting," Drayton said. "Okay, quickly changing the subject. Have you thought about who's going to help serve tomorrow?"

"I've been working on that. I've got a woman I could call or Isabelle over at the Dove Cote Inn has a couple of young ladies who help serve at their banquets."

"Your decision sooner than later would be optimal," Drayton said.

BANG! BANG! Another loud knock sounded at the front door.

"Is that pest back again?" Drayton said. "Does the man not comprehend the meaning of *closed*?"

But when Drayton peered out the front window, he discovered it wasn't Coy Cooper who was standing there banging away.

"What on earth?" Drayton said as he unlocked the door and pulled it open to reveal a second surprise guest—Donny Bragg looming in the doorway. "What do *you* want?"

Bragg wore a dark green snorkel parka, jeans, and desert boots. He looked as if he was about to run off to investigate the wilds of Alaska.

"Is this a bad time?" he asked. His cheeks had pink blooms on them, as if he'd huffed along for several blocks in the cold.

Theodosia and Drayton both responded with a resounding "Yes!"

"That's too bad," Bragg said, taking a preemptive step into the tea room. "Because I came here to say my piece."

"Which is?" Theodosia hurried to the front hallway to meet him. Not because she was being polite, but to block him from coming in any farther.

"Stop meddling!" Bragg shouted at her. "The police have been all over Smokey like stink on a dead polecat for the past three days and it's driving the poor guy nuts. Hell, it's driving *me* nuts."

"I'm sorry you've both been inconvenienced," Theodosia said. "But the fact remains, a woman was murdered."

"As well as an art dealer," Drayton said.

"Not by me. And certainly not by Smokey." Bragg dug in his coat pocket, drew out a cigar, and waved it in Theodosia's face. "*I'm* not one bit worried about the police department's so-called investigation, but I'm asking *you* to back off." He turned toward Drayton. "And you, too, friend. No more questions, no more snooping, no more nasty innuendos—you hear me?"

"Good heavens," Drayton said in a mild tone. "That sounds suspiciously like a threat. I do believe I'm quaking in my boots."

"All I want is for you people to mind your own business," Bragg snarled. "Now, I'll be flying down to the Bahamas for Christmas, but Smokey's going to hang around and look after my house. So I want you to leave him alone!" He waved his cigar in Theodosia's direction. "Ya got that?"

"You're threatening me with a Cohiba?" Theodosia said as Drayton angled his broom and deftly swept a ridge of dust onto the toes of Bragg's shoes.

"Hey!" Bragg cried as he stomped his feet and backed away. "These are expensive!"

"Should we be worried about Donny Bragg?" Drayton asked as he climbed into Theodosia's Jeep.

"I don't think so," she said.

"What if he's the one who killed Miss Drucilla? What if by warning you to stay away from Smokey, he's basically smoke-screening himself?"

"A left-handed way of putting the blame on Smokey? Of reinforcing our suspicions? I suppose that's always a possibility," Theodosia said. "But Bragg doesn't scare me. He's one of those guys who blusters up a storm but rarely backs it up with any sort of action. Like they say in Texas, all hat and no cattle."

"What if Bragg's not really flying down to Rio for Christmas?"

"The Bahamas," Theodosia said.

"Whatever. What if he plans to sneak around and see how things shake out?"

"Then we'll deal with him."

"Huh." Drayton buttoned his navy pea coat and pulled the seat belt strap across his chest. "Sometimes I don't think you worry enough."

"Oh no," Theodosia said as she pulled away from the curb. "That's all I've done this week is worry. Worry about Miss Drucilla's murder, worry about Donny Bragg and Smokey being involved . . ." She zipped around a corner, making Drayton reach out to steady himself. "Worry about stupid dead Julian Wolf-Knapp, our holiday tea parties, the missing Renoir, Pauline, and even you."

"Me?" Drayton said.

"I worry that I pulled you into this . . . mess. And that we might never find an answer."

Drayton relaxed. "Oh well. You shouldn't. Worry, I mean. We'll figure something out. We always do."

Theodosia turned down Archdale Street, heading for Charleston Harbor and the Parade of Boats.

"In case you haven't noticed, we're not exactly batting a thousand. We've been chasing our tails, spinning theories like they're cobwebs, but not making a whole lot of forward progress."

"We've made *some* progress," Drayton said. "After all, we've eliminated one of our main suspects."

"Wolf-Knapp?" Theodosia let out a bitter laugh. "I'm not sure that counts."

They rode along in silence for a few blocks. Finally, Drayton said, "It counts."

The Parade of Boats was a big deal in Charleston. As much a Christmas tradition as *The Nutcracker*, Handel's *Messiah*, and *A Christmas Carol* at the Dock Street Theatre. Which was why White Point Gardens was humming with activity tonight. Spectators lined the shoreline ten deep; food trucks selling fried oysters, po'boy sandwiches, kettle corn, and pulled pork were parked along Battery Street. And vendors selling glow sticks, Mylar balloons, and other trinkets and gewgaws worked the jostling crowd.

"Shall we get you a holly corsage?" Drayton asked as a man carrying a cardboard display board filled with red-and-green corsages strolled past them.

"Thanks, but I'll pass," Theodosia said. She had her eye on a slice of shoreline where they might get a good view of the boats as they came by. "Come on, let's try to worm our way in."

They shouldered their way past a few dozen people and, surprise, surprise, found an unoccupied sandy spot.

"Two inches closer and we'll be wading in the harbor," Drayton said. He was shifting from one foot to the other, fretting about getting his shoes wet.

"Cheer up," Theodosia said. "You were the one who wanted to come here tonight. Surely you can appreciate a prime viewing spot, right?"

Drayton edged his heels back onto drier land. "Right."

"I for one am glad we came," Theodosia said as a gust of wind caught her hair and spun it into auburn streamers. "Here we are, right at the tip of the Peninsula, where pirates used to land their frigates, where major battles were fought, where historic old cannons still stand guard."

Drayton smiled. "With the one-hundred-eighty-year-old Citadel located nearby. Nothing like a good dose of history to stir the fire in one's blood."

As if to punctuate his sentence a loud BOOM erupted from out on the choppy water.

"They're coming!" someone behind them yelled excitedly. "The boats are coming!"

Everyone pushed closer to the shoreline and craned their necks expectantly.

And then they saw it. The lead boat in the Parade of Boats was a mighty three-masted schooner. Lit with thousands of tiny white lights from stem to stern, it looked like a fairy-tale ship as it glided toward them. Appreciative shouts rang out; hundreds of people applauded. And then an armada of at least fifty boats came into view as the spectacle steamed toward them. There were yachts, sailboats both large and small, and powerboats as well. All were decorated with gleaming bright lights that reflected pixelated images in the shimmering water.

One of the sailboats had its mast draped with green lights in the shape of a Christmas tree. Another boat featured a giant star atop its mast. One boat had blue lights in the shape of dolphins carousing along its hull.

"This is wonderful," Theodosia said.

"Isn't it?" Drayton said. "Aren't you glad we came?"

Theodosia nodded. "I am. This is what it's all about: tradition, everyone enjoying a shared experience, the true spirit of Christmas."

"Goodness. If we're not careful, spontaneous Christmas caroling may break out."

"Would that be so bad?"

"Actually, I think it would be lovely," Drayton said.

Boats continued to stream past them. A Santa Claus wearing a white-and-gold skipper cap helmed one of the boats. That one elicited cheers and got a hearty wave back from Santa. Another boat had its mast decorated in the shape of a palm tree, Charleston's ubiquitous symbol of welcome. Some boats had flashing lights; others had chase lights reminiscent of theater marquees.

When the last boat had finally sailed by, Drayton said, "I know we're on a tight schedule, but there's a food truck over there selling cocoa and donuts. Care to indulge? Now that the wind's come up, it might be nice to warm our innards."

"The temp's supposed to drop down to forty degrees tonight," Theodosia said. "And it feels like it's already bobsledding that way. So I'd say hot cocoa is perfect."

They wandered through the crowd of several hundred people, no one in a hurry to leave. Boat watching had morphed into stargazing in what was a blue-black sky lit with crystalline orbs.

"Everyone's waiting for the fireworks to start," Theodosia said.

"Should be any minute," Drayton said as they approached one of the gaily decorated food trucks. "Let's see. They've got cocoa, hot cider, coffee, donuts, oh, and cream puffs. Of course they won't be nearly as delicious as . . ."

"Drayton!" Theodosia suddenly grasped his coat sleeve and pulled him aside.

"Hmm?" Drayton was still studying the menu on the side of the truck. Bouncy yellow type against a dark orange background.

"Look over there," Theodosia hissed.

"What?" Drayton cranked his head around fast, searching in all directions.

"Not there. *There*. You see those two people? Kind of whispering and almost kissing? That's Sawyer Daniels and Majel Mercer!"

26

❧

Drayton gazed at the couple who stood some fifty feet away from them. He clenched his hands, looked back at Theodosia, and cleared his throat.

"I didn't realize they knew each other so well," he said finally.

Daniels and Mercer seemed to exist in their own little bubble. They stood close together, smiling, eyes locked on each other, executing that subtle little dance that couples often do, hips and shoulders swaying and touching.

"It would appear that Daniels's company, the, um, one that makes recommendations on charitable giving, is familiar with Miss Mercer's advocacy group," Drayton added.

Theodosia was a little less circumspect. "I'd say they're more than a little familiar," she said as Sawyer Daniels pulled Majel Mercer into his arms and kissed her full on the lips.

Drayton's brows arced practically to his hairline. "Oh my, I didn't realize they were having an actual *relationship*."

But Theodosia's naturally suspicious brain was already cranking out a vivid scenario.

"Drayton, what if Daniels nudged Miss Drucilla into donating substantial funds to Majel Mercer's Justice Initiative?"

"Why would Daniels do that?"

"What if his firm's not entirely on the up-and-up? What if Daniels can be bought, or he exacts a nice healthy cut for every recommendation he makes?"

"A payoff?" Drayton said.

"Why not?" And then, because another idea had just jolted Theodosia's brain, she said, "And what if . . . just what if Miss Drucilla suddenly got wise to their little two-act play?"

Drayton's shoulders jerked spasmodically. "You think Miss Drucilla might have figured out that she was being scammed? That would mean Daniels and Mercer would both be exposed as frauds."

"Which might have inspired them to get rid of her," Theodosia said.

Drayton looked unhappy as he rubbed a hand against the side of his cheek and said, "But if she was onto them, why invite them to her Christmas party?"

"I don't know. Maybe Miss Drucilla planned to confront them. Maybe she was going to be a lady about telling them they were henceforth cut off from her largesse. Or maybe their names were on her standard guest list and Pauline simply mailed out invitations. Who knows?"

"We have to ask Pauline," Drayton said. "This is too important to ignore."

"We also have to let Tidwell know," Theodosia said.

"You think Sawyer Daniels has been conning Charleston's wealthy, well-intentioned citizens all along? Taking a piece of the action for himself? Laughing all the way to the bank?"

"Could be," Theodosia said.

"So how does the stolen painting figure in? And Wolf-Knapp's murder?"

"I'm not sure. Well . . . the painting maybe because they're just plain greedy. And Wolf-Knapp because he somehow figured them out."

"I suppose it all tracks. So when do we tell Tidwell?"

Theodosia pulled her phone from her pocket. "He's not going to be happy about this but . . . how about now?"

Now that Theodosia had Tidwell's number, she tried it, but wasn't able to get through to him. Instead she was routed to Glen Humphries. Humphries listened carefully to what Theodosia had to say about Sawyer Daniels and Majel Mercer and then replied with a no-nonsense "I'm on it."

"You are?" Theodosia was shocked that she'd gotten such an immediate reaction.

"Of course."

"Are you sure you don't want me to drop by and—"

"Really. I'll follow up on this information. We've made anything that remotely pertains to Miss Drucilla's case our top priority."

"Okay," Theodosia said as she clicked off.

"Well?" Drayton was staring at her.

"Glen Humphries says he'll make it a top priority. Maybe after last night the Charleston PD has decided to take us seriously."

"Fingers crossed," Drayton said.

They walked across the grass, hot cocoa and kettle corn long since forgotten. Overhead, fireworks were starting to light up the night sky. Hollow BAPS and BOPS sounded first; then flares streaked upward and erupted in shimmering gold and silver bursts. Onlookers shrieked with joy.

Drayton stopped dead in his tracks, as if somebody had pulled his plug.

"What?" Theodosia said.

"What if Majel Mercer and Sawyer Daniels had nothing to do with Miss Drucilla's murder? What if it really was Pauline? I mean, at several points along the way, you've leaned in that direction."

"I know, but last night she was so convincingly shocked by Wolf-Knapp's murder that I kind of let that idea go."

Drayton shrugged. "She could have been a theater major, or have an innate acting ability."

"Maybe."

"Baffling, yes?"

"Lots to stew over," Theodosia agreed.

"Still, you usually have a good nose for this sort of thing."

"Not when it comes to this case." They crunched down a gravel path, heading for her car. "What do you think?"

"I can't say I harbor the most *positive* feelings for Pauline," Drayton said.

Theodosia thought for a few moments. "What if I call Pauline about the guest list? Ask her straight out if Majel and Daniels were specifically invited. Maybe even ask her if she's aware the two of them are . . ."

"An item?" Drayton asked mildly.

"That's one way to put it." Theodosia turned and looked back over her shoulder but could no longer see Majel and Daniels. "Although maybe I'll play that close to the vest for now."

When Theodosia got Pauline on the phone, the girl was in a tizzy.

"Oh hi," she said, sounding breathless. "I was just about to skip out of Miss Drucilla's place."

"Still trying to wrap things up?" Theodosia asked. Drayton and she were sitting in her Jeep, engine running, waiting for a break in traffic.

"Working at it anyway. I feel like it's been dragging on forever."

"I need to ask you about the guest list for the Christmas party."

"I already gave you a copy." A distracted Pauline now.

"I know, but I have a question. Was that list pretty much Miss Drucilla's standard Christmas party list?"

"Oh yeah, it was all on the computer. All I did was press a button and print out labels for the invitations."

"Do you know, did Miss Drucilla add or subtract any guests?" Theodosia asked.

"Not that I recall." A pause. "Why? Have you heard something more about that murdered art dealer? Was he supposed to be . . . invited?"

"Not really," Theodosia said. "But I plan to follow up with Detective Tidwell. See if he's learned anything more from the autopsy report."

"So grisly," Pauline said, still sounding distracted. "Well, gotta run."

"Meeting Wade?" Theodosia asked out of curiosity.

"No, he has to work late. I'm off to . . . Well, I just need to run an errand."

"Okay, talk to you later," Theodosia said as she clicked off.

Drayton took one look at the expression on Theodosia's face and said, "What?"

"I don't know. Something funny. Pauline didn't sound like herself."

"Concerning Miss Drucilla's list?"

"About anything."

"Do you think Pauline might be the evil mastermind after all?" Drayton asked. "Could she have murdered Miss Drucilla, stolen the Renoir, and then tied up loose ends by shooting Wolf-Knapp?"

Theodosia pulled out onto Battery Street, bumped along, then turned down Legare.

Finally, she said, "Drayton, I have no idea."

"Then why did you turn down Legare?"

"Huh?"

"The route you're taking. We're a block from Miss Drucilla's place. Do you have some kind of hunch?"

"No, I think I'm driving on autopilot because—"

"Stop! Pull over!" Drayton commanded.

When Drayton shouted (which he rarely did), Theodosia paid attention. She juked her steering wheel hard right and bounced up against the nearby curb. When the car shivered to a stop, she asked, "What?" in a quiet voice.

"Look up there, right ahead of us. It's Pauline."

Theodosia leaned forward and peered through her windshield. It was dark and a little foggy, but she recognized Pauline all right, a slight figure wrapped in a khaki coat and a red scarf, climbing into her little blue Honda Civic.

"I wonder where she's off to," Drayton said.

"She told me she had to run an errand."

"But where? This late at night?"

Theodosia watched the blue Honda pull away from the curb; then she eased her foot down onto the gas pedal. Following along behind, she said, "I don't know. But why don't we find out?"

They drove seemingly forever. Crossed the Ravenel Bridge with Drum Island right below them obscured by poufs of fog. Drove on through Mount Pleasant and up Highway 17. Pauline kept her car at a steady fifty-five miles per hour, so Theodosia did the same, always making sure there were at least two or three cars between them.

"This is smart," Drayton said, "keeping a safe distance like this. Just like cops do in the movies."

"At least in movies there's an end point. Or an exciting chase." Theodosia tilted her head from side to side, working out a kink in her neck. "This is just plain boring." They'd driven through the center of Mount Pleasant and traversed the suburbs, and they were now out on the open road. "Where do you think she's headed?"

"I don't know, but we just crossed into Georgetown County. So your guess is as good as mine."

"What's up this way?" Theodosia wondered. Once in a while, when the road swung close to the coast, they could spot the Atlantic off to their right, a dark horizon with a bank of gray clouds hanging over it. Most of the time, there were just trees and the occasional house, retail cluster, or farm stand.

"Could she be going to Myrtle Beach?" Drayton asked.

"Myrtle Beach is a summer resort. We're three days out from Christmas. What could be happening there?"

"Christmas shopping? Restaurants?"

"Somehow I don't think so."

Drayton yawned. "Then what?"

His yawn was catching and Theodosia also yawned as she swept around a wide curve, her headlights searching the dark road ahead.

"I don't know," Theodosia said. She felt tired and a little out of sorts. Maybe this hadn't been such a good idea? "Maybe there's . . ."

"A shopping mall?" Drayton said. "I believe there's a discount mall in—"

"Whoa!" Theodosia cried suddenly. "Will you look at that?"

"What?" Drayton hunched forward and peered out his side window, trying to figure out what Theodosia was so excited about. "I don't see a thing."

"The sign. Look at the sign!" Theodosia said as she pumped her brakes hard, cut into the right-hand lane of traffic, then swerved to the side of the road. An SUV that had been on her tail tooted its horn as it whooshed by. Unhappy tailgater.

"Sign?" Drayton smacked both hands flat against the

dashboard to steady himself and stared straight ahead. "Sign for what?"

"Straight ahead. You see that ginormous red billboard with the bright yellow letters?"

He looked around, blinked hard, finally spotted the sign, and said, "Oh."

It was an enormous sign, the Taj Mahal of billboards. A brightly lit digital-powered advertisement for the Big M Casino Ship. Chase letters scampered across the bottom of the sign. They spelled out SAILING NIGHTLY FROM LITTLE RIVER.

"That has to be it. Pauline's going to a casino," Drayton said almost matter-of-factly.

"Okay, this is *très* spooky. But that's exactly what Donny Bragg told us about Pauline."

"That she's a gambler," Drayton said. "I remember." He sat there, practically hypnotized by the flickering, blinking, ever-changing lights. "Maybe he's not such a blowhard after all."

"I may have to eat my words," Theodosia said, "because, in his own way, Bragg *does* have Miss Drucilla's best interests at heart."

"Which means Pauline might be a gambler but not a murderer?"

"This changes everything," Theodosia said. "Again."

They turned around and drove back to Charleston. Arrived about nine thirty, feeling tired and a little sheepish.

"Sorry about dragging you along on yet another wild-goose chase," Theodosia said as she pulled up in front of Drayton's house.

"That's okay," Drayton said as he climbed out of her Jeep. "I'm getting used to it."

"Really, I apologize. I know I jumped the gun tonight."

"It's still good to know that Pauline was simply taking an innocent jaunt."

"As long as she doesn't come home flat broke," Theodosia said. "Or she could have . . ."

"What?"

"Pauline could have sold the Renoir and now she's gambling away the profits."

Even in the dim light, Drayton looked unhappy. "I really wish you hadn't said that."

"Sorry. See you tomorrow."

Theodosia was home for all of two minutes when she heard a knock at her front door.

"Now what?"

She looked at Earl Grey, who was just as mystified as she was.

"Who is it?" Theodosia went to the door, peered through a sliver of windowpane, and saw Delaine standing on her front stoop.

"It's me. Delaine." She saw Theodosia looking out at her and lifted a hand in a cheery wave.

"It's kind of late, isn't it?" Theodosia said as she unlocked the door and pulled it open. Then she stared in amazement.

Delaine was standing there accompanied by six dogs.

"I brought your foster dogs," Delaine said. Even though she looked as nervous as a long-tailed cat in a room full of rocking chairs, she'd managed to paste a manic grin across her face.

Theodosia frowned. "What do you mean, *dogs*? When I agreed to be a temporary foster home, you said it would be for *one* dog. Singular. I see a lot more than one dog here. In fact, I see . . ." Theodosia did a hasty head count. "Oh sweet dreams, you brought me *six* dogs?"

"You see . . . there's a problem," Delaine stammered.

"Obviously. But please don't make it *my* problem."

"Hear me out," Delaine implored. "Can we all come in, so I can at last *explain* the circumstances?"

Theodosia sighed deeply as she stepped aside and watched the herd of canines invade her house. "This is the camel inching his nose into the tent, isn't it?" she said. "This is how it starts. This is how animal lovers become the animal hoarders you see on TV. Crazy ladies with three dozen dogs, three hundred parakeets, and a herd of baby goats gnawing away in the backyard."

"You paint an overly dramatic picture," Delaine said, "when it's really quite simple. You only have to mind these sweet creatures for three, maybe four days at the most."

Theodosia raised both arms as if pleading for divine intervention. When it wasn't forthcoming, when there was no bolt from the blue, she dropped her arms to her sides and said, "What went wrong?"

Delaine offered her standard lemon face. "Some of the people who agreed to foster these dogs over Christmas weaseled out on me. So I need a teensy bit of help." She held an adorable little dachshund in her arms and was hanging on to leashes for a Doberman, a poodle, and three other large shaggy dogs of questionable origin.

"You mean, *my* help," Theodosia said.

"If you could find it in your heart, yes," Delaine said. "Now, this one's named Pumpkin." She pointed to the poodle and the Doberman. "Here are Marty and Sabrina. Those other two don't actually have names and this big boy is Gruenwald."

"He's the size of a horse!" Theodosia cried.

"No, dear. Gruenwald is simply a cross between a mastiff and a Great Dane."

"What's wrong with his fur? It's all brown and mottled and swirly." Theodosia felt like she might be edging toward hysteria. Could this be a bad dream? No, it was really happening. She could feel hot doggy breath all around her, sad brown eyes watching her. She could almost feel the hope in their hearts.

"Gruenwald's coat is a unique mixture of brindle and dappled," Delaine said. "So it might be termed *brappled*?"

"You made that up. That type of coat is not AKC recognized."

Delaine shrugged. "Whatever."

"What I really need to know is . . . is he friendly?" Gruenwald was eyeing Theodosia carefully. He seemed to have a contrite look on his broad furry face. Or maybe he was simply contemplating some kind of sneaky move.

"He's gentle as a lamb," Delaine assured her.

Theodosia reached into her jacket pocket and pulled out a Milk Bone that had been intended for Earl Grey. "Hey, Gruenwald, how about . . . ?"

WHOMP!

Like greased lightning Gruenwald leaped and his enormous jaws snatched the Milk-Bone from Theodosia's hand. A millisecond later there was a loud GUNK, which meant he'd swallowed the treat whole. No chewing, no tasting, absolutely no hesitation. It was obvious Gruenwald had not been brought up to be a gourmet.

"I should've warned you," Delaine said. "Gruenwald's what you'd call a trifle reactive. If you're holding a treat or a toy, he tends to grab it right out of your hand."

"No kidding. He's like the jaws of death."

"But basically a dear, dear boy," Delaine insisted. She leaned forward and slung an arm around the dog's wide neck. "Who's a good boy? *You're* a good boy, aren't you, Gruenwald?" She planted a kiss on his broad forehead, then straightened up. "Just be super, super careful when you stick out your hand, okay?"

"Words to live by," Theodosia said. She turned and gazed at Earl Grey, who was standing next to her, seemingly befuddled by this ruffian pack of intruding canines that had showed up unannounced. "What do you think?" she asked him.

Earl Grey stared back at her, then gave the doggy equivalent of a shrug.

So of course Theodosia took the dogs in. It was Christmas after all. And they were in desperate need of a home.

27

❧

Theodosia's phone chimed at precisely eight a.m. Saturday morning, one of Riley's preferred times to call. But Theodosia wasn't the only one roused from a deep slumber; her pack of wayward hounds began a morning cacophony.

ARF, ARF.

RUFF, RUFF, RUFF.

BARKETY, BARK, BARK.

A virtual canine symphony of barks, woofs, and howls played out all around her.

Sitting up in bed, Theodosia grabbed for the phone. "Hello?" She not only sounded sleepy and groggy; she *was* sleepy and groggy.

"Wake up, sunshine!" Riley said by way of a cheerful greeting. Then, "What's all that barking? You got the TV on? Watching reruns of *Lassie* or *The Hound of the Baskervilles*?"

Theodosia brushed away the sleep from her eyes and gazed at her menagerie of inherited dogs. They were barking, grumbling, rumbling, and stretched out everywhere as far as the eye could see. Like a great mottled carpet of fur that covered her entire upstairs. Brown, black, cream, spotted, and, yes, brappled. She'd be hard-pressed to take a step in any direction without encountering a nose, paw, or fuzzy tail.

"That's it," she said to Riley. "I'm watching the Turner Classic Movies channel while I'm getting ready. Classic old dog movies."

"Works for me. Hey, isn't today your big tea extravaganza, with all sorts of Victorian flappery and flaming scones on a stick?"

"Our Grand Illumination, yes," Theodosia said as she sank back down in bed and snuggled beneath her comforter. "I'm getting myself all psyched up even as we speak."

"You don't sound all that psyched up."

"Give me time. I'll get there."

"I know you didn't listen when I told you to stop investigating. So I might as well ask, how is it going?"

"Mine or Tidwell's?" Theodosia asked.

"Take your pick."

"I suppose we're both hanging in there. Suspects still abound but no clear answers. No arrests."

"Ah, there will be," Riley said.

Theodosia perked up. "You have that on good authority?"

"I have faith in Tidwell."

What about me? she wanted to say but didn't.

They talked some more and joked back and forth, Theodosia waking up a little bit with each passing minute. Finally, she said goodbye, hung up, and swung her legs out of bed. She regarded the seven—yes, count 'em—dogs that watched her with curiosity written on their adorable faces.

"You know what?" she said.

Four of the dogs cocked their heads; the others preferred to groom their paws.

"I have to call Mrs. Barry and seriously warn her about you guys. Tell her this isn't any ordinary dog-walking day.

With this monstrous pack, she'll have to run relays out to the backyard. Come to think of it, she might even need an assistant."

An uncertain sun hung in the sky as Theodosia pulled her Jeep into the alley behind the Indigo Tea Shop. She parked as close to the back door as possible because she knew they'd soon be loading food, decorations, and gear into the back of her vehicle. As she headed inside, the morning felt crisp as an apple with a cool breeze blowing in off Charleston Harbor. And when she stuck her key in the lock of her newly installed back door, she paused for a moment to admire it. The hardware store had made sure the door was sturdy aluminum with a double latch.

Nobody's breaking in here—that's for sure.

Inside her still messy office, Theodosia shucked off her coat and tossed it on a chair.

"Haley? Drayton? Anybody here yet?"

"We both are," came Haley's voice.

Theodosia glanced in the small mirror next to the door, said, "Eek," and walked into the tea room.

Drayton stood in the center of the room, tweed jacket, dress slacks, and bow tie perfect, looking dapper as an eighteenth-century English advertisement for a brick of imported tea. Appropriately enough he was sipping one of his morning brews from a bone china cup.

"I hate to be critical," he said. "But you have dog hair all over your slacks."

"Oh dear." Theodosia swiped a hand at her slacks. Whoops, they really did look awful. Like she'd either gotten dressed in the dark or didn't care. "Do we have any tape or one of those lint-roller thingies?"

Haley popped out of the kitchen to look. "Wow. I can't believe Earl Grey is shedding that much. Maybe the cold weather brought it on."

"It's not his fault. It's the six other dogs I have to contend with."

"What!" This was Drayton and Haley in perfect unison.

"Here's the deal," Theodosia said. "Delaine's favorite dog rescue group, Loving Paws, had what you'd call an overflow issue."

"You mean, too many dogs?" Haley asked.

"And nowhere to put them," Theodosia said.

"So Delaine stuck you with *six* dogs?" Drayton said.

"And Earl Grey makes seven. Which sets the stage for a cozy situation," Theodosia said.

"More like a veritable kennel. And I assume you have to feed them all," Drayton said.

Theodosia did an eye roll. "Are you kidding? It hasn't even been twenty-four hours and they've already cleaned me out of kibble. Do you have any idea how much food seven dogs can eat?"

"A better question might be, where do they sleep at night?" Haley asked.

"Anywhere they feel like it," Theodosia said. She brushed at her slacks some more and said, "When it rains, it pours, huh, guys?"

Drayton nodded. "I hate to bring this up, but today is our big day and we're still suffering from a shortage of personnel."

"Jeepers, Drayton, you sound like the HR department at some big honkin' corporation," Haley said.

He stared at her. "And that's bad?"

"No, it's just awfully . . . buttoned-up."

"Buttoned-up can be a good and necessary thing."

Haley made a face. "If you say so."

"I'll go call a temp place," Theodosia said. "See if we can get a warm body in here right away."

But three phone calls later and she'd struck out. Seems that tea shops weren't the only places in dire need of temporary help at Christmas. All the retail shops, restaurants, bars, clubs, and small businesses needed people, too.

Wondering if she should call Isabelle at the Dove Cote Inn and ask for help, Theodosia walked out into a half-full tea room to grab a morning cuppa.

Drayton saw her and immediately pounced. "Any luck?"

"Not yet." Theodosia leaned both elbows on the counter and said, "But I'll find someone. It's only a matter of making a few more calls."

"Then you'll need fortification. Good thing I brewed a pot of Puerh."

"I'd love some."

As he reached for his teapot, the front door opened and Pauline Stauber strolled in.

"Pauline," Theodosia almost sputtered. Why had she suddenly showed up here? Did Pauline know she'd been followed last night? Theodosia felt instantly embarrassed, as though she'd been caught doing something . . . well, not exactly illegal . . . but intrusive.

"Theodosia," Pauline said as she came up to the counter, "I didn't mean to cut you off last night when you called. Apologies."

"That's okay," Theodosia said. "I just had a harebrained theory I was noodling around."

Pauline looked hopeful. "Concerning the guest list? Did it pan out?"

"I kind of have to wait and see," Theodosia stammered just as the phone rang. Saved by the bell, she snatched up the receiver and said, "Indigo Tea Shop. How may I help you?"

"Theodosia," Miss Dimple croaked, "I'm still under the weather."

"You sound like it. Do you need anything? Should we send over a gallon of hot chicken soup?"

"That's kind of you," Miss Dimple said, her voice scratchy and barely audible. "But I'm not one bit hungry. I think I just need to stay in bed."

"Rest is the best thing for you," Theodosia said. "Good old-fashioned bed rest."

"But today's your fancy Victorian tea!" Miss Dimple moaned. "And I feel like I'm letting you down."

"Not in the least," Theodosia said.

"Are you sure?" Miss Dimple said.

"I'm positive," Theodosia said. "Don't you worry about a thing. We'll be fine." She hung up the phone, gazed at Drayton, and said, "Maybe we won't be fine."

"What's wrong?" Pauline lifted a hand. "I'm sorry, but I couldn't help overhearing. . . ."

"Miss Dimple is still sick in bed and can't help out today," Theodosia said.

Drayton poured two cups of tea, handed one to Theodosia, the other to Pauline. "And we have seventy-five people coming to our Victorian Christmas Tea this afternoon," he said, "which our dear Theodosia is acutely aware of."

"I'm not only aware. It's all I can think about," Theodosia said.

"Seventy-five people who have paid good money and are expecting multiple courses of Christmas charm and cheer. So we *dare not* disappoint them," Drayton said.

"And we *won't*," Theodosia said, meaning it.

Drayton touched the back of his hand to his forehead. "This is a nightmare."

"No, no, we'll muddle through," Theodosia said. "We always do." She wasn't sure how they were going to manage, but she realized that job number one right now was to reassure Drayton. If he hit the panic button, if he went down, all would be lost.

Pauline reached over and touched Theodosia's hand. "Sounds like you have a big problem."

"Normally, it wouldn't be. If the tea party were being held right here at the Indigo Tea Shop, we'd probably make it through just fine. But because we accepted so many reservations, we had to move it to the Dove Cote Inn."

"Why don't I come along and lend a hand?" Pauline offered.

Theodosia shook her head. "No, that's okay. We'll figure things out. I've been calling temp agencies, so something's bound to hit."

Pauline placed her hands flat on the counter and stared pointedly at Theodosia and then at Drayton. "Listen, I can't *tell* you how kind and helpful you two have been to me. So why don't you let me help out? I know my serving tea or do-ing whatever you need won't come close to repaying you for all your efforts, but it should be worth something."

Theodosia gazed at Pauline, who looked absolutely serious. In fact, in the cold, clear light of day, she also looked absolutely innocent. So maybe Theodosia had jumped to conclusions?

Drayton, who'd been listening closely, said, "You'd really do that for us, pitch in and help?"

"Of course I would," Pauline said. "In fact"—she looked around—"I could start this very minute. Help you get through lunch and learn the ropes. Like on-the-job training or an impromptu internship."

"You don't have to be somewhere else?" Theodosia asked.

Pauline shook her head. "Not today."

Drayton gazed at Theodosia. "Theo?" he asked. Worry was etched across his face.

Did Theodosia still have a few reservations about Pauline? Of course she did. But she also had seventy-five con-firmed tea reservations for that afternoon. So how awful would it be to accept Pauline's offer? After all, a bird in the hand . . .

"Okay," Theodosia said. "Thank you. Let's do it."

Drayton sprinted around the counter and gently dropped a long black Parisian waiter's apron over Pauline's head. "It looks as though you're hired, my dear."

Pauline flashed a wide grin as she wound the strings around her waist.

Then Theodosia reached over and gave Pauline a hug. "Welcome to the team."

28

One hour later, with the tea shop running smoothly, Theodosia was more than thankful to have Pauline on board. Pauline waited tables, poured tea, and served raspberry scones, orange scones, and banana muffins. She also had a nice genteel manner when dealing with the guests, and asked Drayton all the right questions—but not so many that she made a pest of herself.

"It seems to be going well," Theodosia said to Drayton as she slipped behind the counter and helped herself to an orange scone.

"Maybe we were wrong about Pauline," Drayton said. "Maybe she just enjoys a good game of poker now and then. Maybe Donny Bragg made a mountain out of a molehill."

"I hope so," Theodosia whispered back. She nibbled a bite of scone and wandered into the kitchen.

"Your orange scones are delicious, Haley. I feel like I just got a year's worth of vitamin C."

"Real orange juice along with plenty of orange zest, that's the secret sauce," Haley said.

"Anything I can do to help?"

"It's controlled chaos in here, but I think I can manage to keep my head above water. I've got my dough all mixed and plan to bake my scones and crullers in the kitchen at the Dove Cote Inn. That way everything will be piping hot right out of the oven."

"How do you feel about Pauline helping us out?"

"She's been great so far," Haley said from her post at the stove. "No wasted effort and she's a smart cookie." She leaned down, pulled open the oven door so she could check another pan of scones, then shut the door. "I can see why Miss Drucilla hired her as a personal assistant."

"I guess personal assistants get tossed into lots of different situations," Theodosia said.

"And have to figure out how to do all sorts of tricky stuff. Like arrange travel and parties and stuff." She grabbed a wooden spoon and used it to lift a lid on a simmering pot. "So Pauline's going to help serve at the Dove Cote Inn? We've got a big menu, you know . . . a heroic menu . . . so we sure could use the help."

"That's the plan."

What wasn't in Theodosia's battle plan was an impromptu visit from Detective Burt Tidwell. But like a visiting head of state, he strolled casually into the Indigo Tea Shop, glanced about with hooded eyes, then lifted his head and stared directly at Theodosia.

"Detective," she said, acknowledging him.

"Miss Browning." Slight nod. "We need to talk."

Theodosia crooked a finger. "This way, then."

Tidwell followed her down a short hallway into her office. Once he'd settled his bulk in the oversized upholstered chair they'd dubbed "the Tuffet," he said, "So I've finally been invited into m'lady's inner sanctum."

"You've been in my office before." Theodosia sat down and faced him from across her desk.

"Not really." Tidwell made a big point of studying the stacks of red hats and sweetgrass baskets, the boxes filled with teapots, tea, and trivets, and said, "Interesting."

"'Interesting' is what people say when they don't feel like giving an honest answer."

"Okay, then, it's girlie." He made it sound like an insult.

"Girlie!"

Tidwell favored her with a mousy smile. "But in a good way. A tea shop way."

"Keep digging that hole, Detective. You're doing just fine."

"Perhaps I should dispense with any formalities and get right down to business." He pursed his lips. "We've had a sort of . . . breakthrough."

Theodosia eased forward onto the edge of her chair. Yes, this was exactly what she'd been waiting to hear. Hopefully the information she'd passed on about Sawyer Daniels and Majel Mercer had led to an arrest!

She took a shot. "Please tell me that Sawyer Daniels has been arrested for the murder of Miss Drucilla." When Tidwell simply stared at her, she said, "Okay, then, was it Majel Mercer?"

Tidwell shook his great head. "Wrong on both counts. However"—he held up a chubby index finger—"thanks to your snooping, we've discovered that the two of them conned hundreds of thousands of dollars out of Charleston's most generous citizens. To say nothing of various charitable foundations."

Theodosia had a record-scratch moment. "Wait . . . What? You're telling me they're crooks?" She was so excited, she practically popped out of her chair.

"Turns out, the two of them have been in cahoots for quite some time."

But not killers. Okay, that's kind of disappointing. I thought I was onto something. Still, I was partly correct about their being involved in some kind of money scheme.

"What have they done that's so illegal?" Theodosia asked, hungering for details.

"Sawyer Daniels has been funneling as much money as possible into Majel Mercer's charity and then helping himself to a generous slice of the proceeds. Her so-called Justice Initiative? You might as well call it the Injustice Initiative, it's so crooked."

"So Daniels took a commission?" Theodosia asked.

"That would be a polite descriptor. *Kickback* is more accurate," Tidwell said. "Doesn't matter though. They're both guilty as sin."

"But not of murdering Miss Drucilla."

"No, not that."

Theodosia leaned forward, elbows on her desk. "You're positive?"

"Think about it," Tidwell said. "Why would they kill their cash cow when Sawyer Daniels had Miss Drucilla wrapped around his pinkie finger? She must have trusted him with millions of dollars to administer."

"Wow."

"And that's not the half of it. We're looking at his books, donation records, bank statements—you name it. It's already being kicked up to the state attorney general's office. Major fraud means those two are looking at serious prison time." He smiled. "I made a few other inquiries as well."

"To the people who donated to Majel's charity?" Theodosia asked.

"No, to the mayor."

"Wait a minute. You mean, the mayor of *Charleston*?"

Tidwell knitted his hands together and rested them on his ample stomach.

"I wanted to get him on board as well as our city attorney. If I'm going to investigate and prosecute two people who are involved in defrauding high-profile foundations and donors, then I want to be armed to the teeth."

"I guess it's good to know people in high places," Theodosia said.

Tidwell smiled serenely.

"I'm glad you busted them," Theodosia said. "But what about Miss Drucilla? It's been almost a week and still nobody's figured out who murdered the poor woman. With Sawyer Daniels, Majel Mercer, and Julian Wolf-Knapp out of the picture, suspects are dropping like flies."

"At this point I'm still looking at Donny Bragg and Smokey Pruitt," Tidwell said, looking grim. "Now I just have to prove it."

"You need hard evidence. Maybe I could—"

"No!" Tidwell barked. "Stay out of it."

"Okay, okay, calm down. But . . . um, I have had concerns about someone fairly close to Miss Drucilla."

Tidwell narrowed his eyes. "You're referring to the young woman who's working in your tea shop today?"

"Well . . . yes."

"She's still a possibility. As are several others."

"Care to elaborate?" Theodosia said.

Tidwell's jowls shook. "Not particularly."

"Okay, then, have you dug up—figuratively, not literally—anything new on Wolf-Knapp? I mean per the autopsy results."

"The ME concurs with me that Julian Wolf-Knapp was shot point-blank in the back of the head."

"He never saw it coming," Theodosia said.

"Murder victims rarely do."

Tidwell's words, delivered in such a cold, matter-of-fact manner, made Theodosia flinch. It made her realize that if someone got too close to this clever killer, there could be additional fallout. In other words, more victims.

"And you're still investigating Coy Cooper?" she asked.

"Looking him over, yes," Tidwell said, "though Cooper

does have an airtight alibi for the night his aunt was murdered."

"Where was he?"

Tidwell snorted. "Partying. At a club in Savannah with a dozen of his closest friends."

"As long as he was paying the bar tab and they were doing shots, nobody will remember anything."

Tidwell slapped his knees and rose to his feet, his knees making popping sounds like cracked walnuts.

Ouch.

"But don't think I'm letting Cooper off the hook entirely," Tidwell said, "because I do believe he warrants a second look." He wriggled his shoulders inside his saggy brown suit, glanced at the military watch stretched around his wrist, and said, *"Tempus fugit.* I must be moving on." With that, he executed a smart spin on what Theodosia always thought were delicate feet for a man so large and ungainly. And then he was gone.

Theodosia sat at her desk, listening to his retreating footsteps. Then she tilted back in her chair to think.

Huh.

Lots to ponder. Especially since the killer was still out there. Still in Charleston? Or off to Europe, South America, or even Asia? She knew just enough about the art market to realize there was a dark side. Billionaire buyers, plundered treasure, stolen art, and high-stakes deals all made for a lethal combination.

Were Tidwell and his crew up for this kind of chase? Or were they finally outclassed—or outsmarted? Maybe the danger was so grave that she really did have to step aside and let the professionals handle things.

Or . . . maybe not.

Theodosia stared at a vintage yellow biscuit barrel by Sadler that sat on her desk and let her mind wander. When no answers seemed forthcoming, she ruminated over Tidwell's visit. He hadn't told her much and he'd been in a hurry to leave. So maybe something supersecret was going on? And—this might be a freaky aside—but it was the first time Tidwell had visited her tea shop without trying to scam a free scone. Maybe he'd renounced his evil ways and was trying to eat healthily? No, that would never happen. He was up to something.

Two minutes later, there was a knock at her door.

"Yes?"

Drayton peered in. "I see your visitor has shuffled off to Buffalo on his swift little feet."

"That's about the size of it."

"Anything you can share with me?" He walked in, carrying a tray covered with a blue-and-white-checked cloth.

"Daniels and Mercer have both been arrested for fraud," Theodosia said. "Turns out, Majel's been pocketing money earmarked for her charity and also sharing some of the winnings with Daniels."

"Oh my. Just as you suspected."

"Daniels targeted Miss Drucilla specifically and maybe scammed as much as several million dollars from her."

"Is there any possibility of a clawback for her estate?" Drayton asked.

"One would hope so. If the money hasn't already been spent on drugs and fast cars." Then, "What's that you've got there?"

"Lunch. Haley made up a tray for you. Tomato soup, a scone, and two chicken salad tea sandwiches." He set the tray down on Theodosia's desk. "Oh, and I added a cup of Darjeeling. You need to be anchored for the afternoon ahead."

"Thank you, Drayton. And thank Haley, too."

"Of course."

"Do you need me out there, in the tea room?"

Drayton shook his head. "It's slow as molasses. And Pauline's doing fine."

Pauline, Theodosia thought as she ate her lunch. She was still kind of a wild card in all this. A person who'd been close to Miss Drucilla and might have possibly had a motive to kill her. But at first glance, and possibly even second, she did look fairly innocent.

Theodosia picked up a tea sandwich, took a bite, and toyed with her computer mouse using her other hand.

Let's just take a look-see here.

She took a fast spin through Facebook to see if Pauline had a page. She did. Okay, now she was looking to see how much information Pauline shared.

There wasn't a lot, but the information that was there struck Theodosia as startling and slightly damning.

Pauline's profile listed her as an art history major at the University of Virginia.

Oh . . . crap. Does this mean something? Why didn't I check this out sooner?

Theodosia wolfed down the rest of her lunch, then hustled out to the tea room and glanced around. It was one o'clock and Pauline was delivering luncheon plates to a table of three. Probably their last customers of the day.

Good.

She slipped behind the front counter, where Drayton was packing up teapots, and tapped him on the shoulder.

"I think we may have made a mistake," Theodosia said to him. She watched as Pauline continued serving the customers.

"What? You mean, with Pauline?" Drayton asked. "Here I thought she was a diamond in the rough. The customers seem to love her."

"That's all well and good, but I just went on her Facebook page, and guess what I found."

"I couldn't possibly. You know I don't subscribe to those Placebook things."

"Facebook."

"Whatever. What did you find that's so earth-shattering?"

"Pauline majored in art history," Theodosia said.

Drayton stared at her, his jaw working soundlessly.

"Did you hear what I said?"

He nodded. "I did. But what does that mean exactly?"

"It means Pauline might have been scamming us all along. If she's knowledgeable about art and artists, she could have easily murdered her employer and stolen the Renoir."

Drayton gave a slow reptilian blink. "And she might even know how to fence a painting."

"That occurred to me as well."

Drayton touched an index finger to his lower lip. "Did we just let the fox into the henhouse?"

"Could be. But there's no proof. We don't know anything for sure."

"What are we going to do? We've already committed to having Pauline help us at the Victorian Christmas Tea this afternoon."

"All we can do is proceed as planned and keep a careful watch on her."

"And do what? Pray she doesn't steal the paintings off the walls at the Dove Cote Inn?"

Theodosia grimaced. "Or murder someone in cold blood."

29

❧

But Pauline was on her best behavior as they packed up food, tea, teapots, trivets, cups and saucers, kitchen utensils, and Victorian decorations and gifts. Then, like a modern-day Silk Road caravan, they stuffed everything into Theodosia's Jeep and Pauline's Honda Civic.

"Wait!" Haley cried as she came running out the back door, blond hair flying. "Don't forget my cake!"

Theodosia hurried back inside and together the two of them carried out an enormous white bakery box that held Haley's Victorian fondant cake.

"Easy now," Haley said as they placed it carefully in the back of the Jeep. "Be gentle with my baby."

"It looks good enough to eat," Theodosia said.

"Bite your tongue," Haley said. "It's for display only."

"What else is left?" Theodosia asked.

"Pauline still has to bring out the last box of teapots that Drayton packed."

"You keep working here. I'll go help Pauline."

Theodosia ducked back into the tea shop and called out, "Pauline, need any help?"

"I'm good," Pauline said. She staggered into Theodosia's office, carrying an enormous cardboard box.

Drayton appeared in the doorway. "Here, let me take that heavy thing."

Pauline handed it off to him. "Whew . . . thanks."

"I think we did it," Theodosia said. "It's just a tick past two o'clock, so we've got almost two hours to get to the Dove Cote Inn and set up our tables."

"That's doable, right?" Pauline asked. She'd been a hard worker thus far, diligent and helpful. Theodosia was slowly revising her opinion. Pauline *couldn't* be a killer, could she?

"We've worked with far tighter deadlines," Theodosia said. She looked around her office and ran through a mental list. "I'm pretty sure that's everything."

"I've gotta make a quick call to Wade and tell him I'm helping you guys out, that I'll be late tonight."

"Use my phone while I grab an extra carton of honey. That's if I can find it in all this clutter." Theodosia hunted around, pushing boxes aside, mumbling to herself while Pauline made her call. "Okay, I know I just saw it. How maddening is that?" Theodosia narrowed her eyes, moved another stack of boxes, continued her search.

"Just a minute," Pauline said. "I'll ask her." She dropped the phone down from her mouth and said, "Theodosia."

"Hmm?"

"Wade wants to know if you could use an extra pair of hands over at the Dove Cote Inn today."

That stopped Theodosia dead. She straightened up, turned, and said, "Is he serious?"

"Are you serious?" Pauline said into the phone. She listened, bobbed her head, and turned back to Theodosia. "He's serious."

"Wade doesn't have to work at the gift shop?"

"He says no, not today. So . . . what's the verdict?"

Theodosia thought about all the unloading, the setting up, the making sure tables and chairs were arranged just so, then serving a four-course high tea to seventy-five guests—maybe even a few more if there were last-minute drop-ins. The images buzzed through her brain like film speeding through a projector.

Can I use the help? Yes. Should I let Pauline bring in Wade? Actually, he might be a nice, stabilizing influence on her. And if for some remotely bizarre reason she is the guilty party, he might even help to hold her in check. It feels win-win, so . . . yes.

Theodosia bobbed her head, smiled at Pauline, and said, "I can hardly say no to such a generous offer."

The wrought iron lamps were already installed when Theodosia and Pauline arrived at the Dove Cote Inn. Drayton, wearing his peacoat and a knit cap, was futzing about, making final adjustments.

"What do you think?" he asked as the women hefted and carted boxes up the front walk.

"Beautiful," Pauline said. "Like something out of a Dickens novel."

"Victorian, yes, that's the general idea," Drayton said. "And quite magical once the lamps are lit and throwing glowing little circles of light. A Grand Illumination, so to speak." Then, "I'd better give you ladies a hand with those boxes."

"There're ten more in the Jeep," Theodosia said as Drayton grabbed a box from Pauline.

"We'll get them all," he said. "You run inside and have a look at the Essex Room."

"It looks good?"

"Like I said, have a look."

To Theodosia's eyes, the Essex Room didn't just look good; it looked spectacular. The mantel held at least a dozen pots of lush red poinsettias, and a fire crackled in the large stone fireplace. Besides the flocked Christmas trees, green garland strung in the windows, and topiary trees that Theodosia had seen before, Isabelle and her crew had hung strands of frosted icicle lights from the ceiling. So it felt as if you were walking through a winter wonderland.

"What do you think?" a voice asked.

Theodosia spun around to find Isabelle, the catering manager, walking toward her. In keeping with the Victorian theme, Isabelle wore a long plaid skirt, a high-necked white ruffled blouse, boots, and a half dozen long strands of pearls.

"I think your costume is better than mine," Theodosia said.

Isabelle laughed. "It's just something I threw together. Kind of fun, I guess."

"I've never seen the room set up with this many tables."

"Ten, exactly what you asked for."

"And I love that there's still plenty of room for us to serve and for guests to move about."

"Of course," Isabelle said. "It's a Christmas party, right?"

"Which means I'd better get to work!"

First, Theodosia checked to be sure all Haley's food and equipment had made it to the kitchen. Then she took a closer look at the dining room. The tables had already been set with white tablecloths and the Dove Cote Inn's Christmas china and silver flatware, so the only thing left was arranging teacups and water goblets. Wade showed up just as Pauline began placing cups and saucers and immediately jumped in to help.

"I don't know how to thank you," Theodosia said to Pauline and Wade as they finished with the cups and saucers and moved on to crystal water goblets with gold rims.

"Just treat your guests to an amazing experience," Pauline said.

"Ditto," Wade echoed. He wore dark slacks and a long-sleeved white shirt, an outfit that said he could easily pass for a waiter.

Drayton came bounding in to watch it all take shape.

"What's next?" he asked.

"The fun stuff," Theodosia said. "Now we get to go all Victorian."

"Ooh," said Pauline, clearly impressed.

The decor was a huge undertaking but they operated like an experienced team, as if they were all old hands at it. Large silver candelabras were placed on each table, then draped with strands of pearls, Victorian lockets, and green silk vines.

Cones of floral paper were tied with ribbon and stuffed with sprigs of dried lavender and pink strawflowers. Petite rose-shaped soaps were placed in pink organza bags.

"Roses," Drayton said, "were very much favored by the Victorians."

Linen napkins were rolled and secured with vintage tags. Small silk parasols were placed on tables along with an assortment of pocket watches, top hats, and vintage postcards. Chairbacks were draped with pink chiffon tied in bows.

"It actually looks like a proper Victorian drawing room," Wade commented, "all decked out for Christmas."

"Thank goodness," Theodosia said, "since that's exactly what we were aiming for."

"Now what?" Pauline asked. She seemed jittery, eager to keep moving.

Haley, who'd just emerged from the kitchen, wiped her hands on a dishcloth and cried, "Costumes, guys! Don't forget the costumes!"

"There are costumes?" Wade said. He looked surprised that an afternoon tea party had turned into such an elaborate undertaking.

"A huge box full of them," Haley said. "They've been delivered to the library. I just took a peek—there's some pretty cool stuff."

"Where's this library?" Drayton asked.

"Right next door," Theodosia said, motioning for them to follow her.

So Theodosia, Drayton, Pauline, and Wade trooped into the Dove Cote Inn's library. It was a small room, cozy and warm, with space for two upholstered wing chairs and a dark blue velvet love seat. The walls were lined with floor-to-ceiling bookshelves and held hundreds of volumes, maybe even thousands, some of them old, some brand-new.

"Interesting place," Drayton said, pulling out a leather-bound volume and riffling through a few pages. "A fellow could lose himself in here for a few hours. Or maybe a few days."

"But not this day," Theodosia said. She was already down on her hands and knees, ripping open the box and pulling out costumes. "Let's see, we have corsets, long skirts, and pearls for the ladies. For the gentlemen, we have . . ." She grabbed a gray-striped jacket. "Hmm, looks like something you might wear to the horse races at Ascot."

"Top hats and tails," Drayton said. "I guess we're going to be authentically Victorian."

Theodosia pulled on a long mauve skirt, laced a pink-and-black-paisley corset over her high-necked blouse, and threw on a few strands of beads as well as a cameo brooch. On the way into the kitchen to check on Haley, she stopped in front of a Baroque mirror. Gathering her hair into a loose bun, she piled it on top of her head in a loose pouf and secured it with a tortoiseshell clip.

There, instant Victoriana.

"Lay out those plates, will you?" Haley said when she saw Theodosia. "They're for the scones and Devonshire cream." In her white chef's jacket and hat, Haley moved about the kitchen with authority, ducking and bobbing as she worked, looking like a manic symphony conductor. "Oh, and you look really cute."

"Thank you." Theodosia grabbed a stack of small plates and started dealing them out like playing cards. "Good thing there's a lot of counter space here."

"Yeah, this is a bangin' kitchen," Haley said. "Really easy to work in."

"So much bigger than ours."

The stove was an eight-burner Wolf stove; there were two ovens and a commercial salamander for broiling and warming. And everything—pot racks, counters, appliances—was gleaming stainless steel.

"Oh no, don't you dare go there, Theo," Haley said. "I *love* my little kitchen. Besides, you know how much I dislike any sort of change."

"I wasn't planning to change a thing at our sweet little tea shop," Theodosia said. "Heaven forbid."

"Scones are in the oven. My Charleston chowder is bubbling on the stove. Now I'll start prepping the rest of our courses." Haley jerked her chin toward the door. "How's it going out there?"

"The musicians just arrived, so Drayton should be in his element."

"I figured he'd want to hang with the actors. Wait. Are there actors?"

"There are," Theodosia said. "But their play or tableau or whatever it's going to be remains a deep, dark secret. Drayton won't reveal a thing about what's going to happen."

Haley reached up and pushed her chef's hat back from her forehead. "Seriously?"

Theodosia favored her with a mysterious smile. "It's another mystery."

"What else is new? Hey, open that cake box, will you?"

Theodosia removed the lid and said, "Oh, Haley, this is spectacular."

"You like?"

"It's wonderful."

The cake was a three-tiered masterpiece covered in buttercream frosting. Each tier was decorated with fondant crowns, royal hearts, garlands of pearls, and lace, with tiers incrementally smaller as they went up. A bouquet of pink and yellow fondant flowers adorned the very top of the cake.

"It looks like it could be Queen Victoria's wedding cake," Theodosia said.

"Isn't that interesting," Haley said, "since that's exactly what I used for reference. Now let's take that cake out there and put it on display."

Drayton had arranged the three musicians in one corner of the dining room. Three middle-aged men, all turned out in elegant tuxedos with instruments that included a dulcimer, a violin, and a cittern.

"Remember," Drayton told them, "this is a Victorian-themed tea party. So the more authentic the music, the better."

The violinist touched his bow to his instrument and played a few spritely notes. "This one's by Gilbert and Sullivan, called *Victoria and Merrie England*," he said.

"Perfect!" Drayton said.

"Drayton." Theodosia tapped him on the shoulder. Then, when he spun around to face her, she had to stifle a giggle. Drayton was truly duded out to look like a gentleman from the Victorian era. He wore a frock coat, a satin vest, and a top hat. A wide silk cravat replaced his traditional bow tie and he carried a silver-tipped walking stick.

"You look fantastic," Theodosia said, "like a proper Victorian gentleman."

"Thank you, ma'am. You look like quite the Victorian lady yourself. And I do love that cameo you added."

Theodosia touched a hand to the cameo she'd pinned to her blouse. "It was my mother's."

"Good taste runs in the family."

"Have the actors arrived yet?" Theodosia asked.

"Oh yes, and I've already given them their scripts."

Theodosia glanced around. No actors, just beautifully decorated tables along with the musicians. "Where on earth did you stash them? Oh, the breakfast room?"

Drayton touched a finger to his mouth. "Like I said before, I'm keeping it all hush-hush. But if it meets with your approval, I'd like to serve the tea and scones *before* I introduce the actors."

Theodosia gave him a probing look. "I'm curious, but I'm willing to go along with whatever you've got up your sleeve."

30

༄

Theodosia and Drayton stood at the front door of the Dove Cote Inn, watching as cars pulled up to the curb and guests clambered out. Behind them a mantel clock struck four resounding bongs.

"Showtime," Drayton announced with glee. "The torches are lit, the tea is brewed, the food is ready, the musicians are making sweet music, and now it's time to welcome our guests."

But their friendly greetings were almost overshadowed by a torrent of compliments.

"Those lanterns are adorable!"

"So *that's* what you meant by a Grand Illumination."

"With the sun going down, the inn looks so moody and elegant."

"I can't wait to see inside!"

Theodosia and Drayton shook hands, exclaimed over old friends, exchanged air-kisses, hung coats, and then passed everyone on to Pauline and Wade, who escorted the guests into the dining room.

Delaine Dish showed up wearing a long black gown with balloon sleeves and a supertight bodice. She had her niece Bettina in tow.

"Like Queen Victoria herself," Drayton murmured to Delaine, taking both her hands in greeting.

"But in a size two, dear," Delaine responded.

"I thought your sister Nadine was coming for Christmas," Theodosia said.

Delaine rolled her eyes in exasperation. "Nadine was *supposed* to come, but with her typical scatterbrain mentality, *everything* got screwed up."

Wearing a herringbone jacket with gray suede slacks, Bettina just looked sad. "Sometimes it's hard to count on Mom."

Another influx of guests arrived—Jill and her daughter, Kristen, Susan Monday (the ubiquitous Lavender Lady), and Brooke Carter-Crocket, owner of Hearts Desire. Then there were Linda, Jessica, and Judi, who'd all been at the Nutcracker Tea earlier in the week.

With half the guests already inside, Theodosia left Drayton at the front door and hurried in to see how things were going. As it turned out, most of their guests were already seated and chatting away, exclaiming over the tables and decor.

Excellent. Now to peep in on Haley.

"Haley."

Haley whipped her head toward the swinging door. "Drayton's already brewed the tea and I'm going to start plating the scones," Haley said in one long breath. "He told me he wants to serve tea and scones *before* he stages his little play."

"That's the word I got, too," Theodosia said.

Back in the Essex Room, Theodosia strolled from table to

table. They'd filled up rapidly and it was exciting to greet old friends and welcome new ones. As she skirted one table, heading for another, she happened to notice Coy Cooper pulling out a chair for Evelyn Fruth, Miss Drucilla's former housekeeper.

Seeing them together stopped Theodosia dead in her tracks.

Oh boy, did I miss something important here?

Theodosia's heart did a rapid flip-flop inside her chest and she had to grip the back of a chair to steady herself. What were these two doing here? Did they have some kind of weird codependent partnership? Was this the new, intergenerational 2.0 version of Murder Incorporated? Or maybe her mind had gone too wonky and they were simply friendly acquaintances here to enjoy a holiday tea. Maybe.

Hurrying across the room, knowing the Cooper-Fruth issue had to stay on the back burner for now, Theodosia ran into Drayton, who was looking pleased with himself.

"Once everyone's seated—which should be in the next few minutes—we'll begin serving tea and scones," he said.

"Drayton," Theodosia said a little breathlessly, "you'll never guess who's here."

"Who's that?" he asked with an abstract smile. Drayton was already thinking ahead to his program.

"Coy Cooper is here with Evelyn Fruth."

"Really?" His brows pinched together. "Whyever for?"

"I have no idea. But I find it strange, don't you?"

"As a matter of fact, yes. But there's nothing we can do short of kicking them out, is there?"

"I suppose not."

"Is that what you want to do?"

"Not without a good reason. Besides, it would be embarrassing for everyone."

"Then I suggest we proceed as if nothing is amiss," Drayton said, "and deal with them later. If we have to."

"Okay, but . . . okay."

* * *

Minutes later, Theodosia and Drayton began pouring tea while Pauline and Wade delivered plates that held scones and small sides of jam, lemon curd, and Devonshire cream.

When everyone was sipping and munching, Theodosia and Drayton walked to the center of the room.

"Merry Christmas from all of us at the Indigo Tea Shop," Theodosia said, her voice ringing out as she spoke her words. "And welcome to our Victorian Christmas Tea." Now every pair of eyes was clearly focused on her. "While you enjoy Twinings Christmas Tea with cinnamon and cloves along with your lemon cream scones and lemon curd, our tea sommelier, Drayton, has a special treat for you." Theodosia paused, then said, "Drayton?"

"To delight and sweeten your first course, we're going to usher in a few special guests from the distant past," Drayton said in his most theatrical voice. "Would you please welcome Queen Victoria herself, accompanied by her beloved husband, Prince Albert."

The music swelled as two actors, dead ringers for Queen Victoria and Prince Albert, strolled into the room. Dressed in Victorian finery of silks and ruffles, they swished about the room, much to the delight of the guests. Looking somewhat regal and haughty, Queen Victoria fanned herself with an ornate lace fan while the more sociable Prince Albert smiled and nodded to the guests.

Applause rang out like mad to welcome these realistic-looking historical figures, while Theodosia said, under her breath, "Aren't you the clever one?"

Drayton winked at her, then continued his announcement.

"And one more special guest will be joining us today—the Duchess of Bedford herself, Lady Anna Russell."

Now a slightly plumpish duchess in a long pink gown with bell sleeves wafted into the room, looking regal as well as appreciative of the guests' thunderous applause.

"As you might recall, this rather enchanting duchess was actually a bridesmaid at Queen Victoria's wedding and also became a lifelong friend of the queen," Drayton said. "I might also add that our dear duchess was the rather brilliant woman who originated the concept of afternoon tea."

Now, per Drayton's instructions, Queen Victoria, Prince Albert, and the duchess all picked up wicker baskets and began moving through the sea of tables, distributing gifts to the guests. There were cute little packets of tea, floral nosegays wrapped in lace, small jars of honey bound with ribbon, and sweet-scented sachets.

"I hope you enjoy these small Victorian gifts and favors while Drayton delivers a short recitation," Theodosia said.

Drayton bowed sharply, then said, "With slight apologies to the author Joseph Horatio Chant for lifting a verse here and there, I hope you find these words as charming as I do."

> While she sits on regal throne,
> And acts full well a regal part,
> She reigns not on the throne alone.
> She reigns in England's heart.

Drayton continued . . .

> In every land, her name is blest;
> She is beloved by old and young;
> From pole to pole, from east to west,
> The song "God Save the Queen" is sung.

With a warm smile on her face, Theodosia stepped to the center of the room and said, "And now, ladies and gentlemen, let's party like it's 1899!"

The afternoon tea seemed to go by in a whirlwind. The second course of Charleston chowder was served with shrimp salad tea sandwiches, much to everyone's delight. And once that was sipped and savored, Theodosia and company brought out the main course of braised beef tenderloin accompanied by corn bread served in individual cast-iron skillets.

"It's a major production, but we seem to be moving along amazingly well," Drayton said to Theodosia when they bumped shoulders in the kitchen.

"Speaking of productions, your idea of having actors portray Queen Victoria, Prince Albert, and the Duchess of Bedford was sheer genius. The guests were thrilled. In fact, your actors are still wandering around, staying in character, and visiting with them."

"It *was* great," Haley said. "I stuck my head out the door and caught the looks on everyone's faces when the characters came waltzing out. It was priceless!"

"But your food is the star," Theodosia said to Haley. Then she turned to Drayton. "And of course your tea."

Drayton smiled. "Of course."

"And Pauline and Wade have been a huge help," Haley added.

"You made the right decision," Drayton said to Theodosia. "They've worked their little hearts out with nary a problem."

"No problems that I've seen," Theodosia said.

"Wait a minute. Are you still nervous about Coy Cooper?" Drayton asked.

Haley glanced over her shoulder at them. "*That* guy showed up? Why?"

"We don't know," Drayton said. "So we're holding our breath in case he means to cause trouble."

"Did you ever think he could just be here for tea?" Haley asked.

"Maybe," Theodosia said. But she was suspicious nonetheless. Something about the event felt *off*. She just couldn't put her finger on what.

* * *

Their final course was praline cheesecake served with Toasted Nut Brûlée oolong from Plum Deluxe. Many of the guests groaned when they saw the slices of cheesecake accompanied by small squares of fudge, but nobody turned them down.

"You see?" Drayton said to Theodosia as they watched their guests literally scrape their plates to get every delicious bite. "We've put them into a culinary stupor."

"Wasn't that the whole idea?" Theodosia said.

She turned, walked over to Coy Cooper's table, and leaned into his ear.

"I hope everything's been to your satisfaction," she said.

Cooper gave a polite smile. "Couldn't be better."

"I must say I'm surprised to see you here." Actually, Theodosia was more than surprised. She was unnerved.

"I was hoping you might have changed your mind. About investigating, I mean."

"I think," Theodosia said, "we should leave that to the police."

Twenty minutes later, the Victorian Christmas Tea was over. Two-and-a-half hours from start to finish, with all the guests murmuring about how delicious and memorable the afternoon had been.

"My favorite part was Queen Victoria!"

"But oh, those delicious scones."

"And that cheesecake was to die for."

"You're sending them off on a sugar high," Isabelle said to Theodosia as they watched the guests practically float out of the room.

"That's exactly right," Theodosia said.

"But they loved it. You know, it would be wonderful to collaborate with you on a couple more tea parties. Bring you in as our guest caterer."

"We'd love that," Theodosia said. She watched carefully as Coy Cooper escorted Mrs. Fruth out of the room. There'd been no problems. Thank goodness. Of course, that wasn't to say Cooper was off the hook. He could still be a stone-cold killer who'd come simply to flaunt his bravado.

Theodosia focused on Isabelle again. "Now comes the hard part."

"The cleaning and packing up? It looks to me as if your people are already on top of that."

Theodosia gazed across the room, where Pauline and Wade were hard at work, stacking dirty dishes in tubs, taking special care with the china teacups and saucers.

"I've got to . . . Will you excuse me?" she said to Isabelle.

Theodosia hurried across the empty room, where candles sputtered in candelabras and flower petals and swirls of ribbon littered the carpet.

"Pauline . . . Wade," she said.

They both turned to look at her.

"You two have been fantastic," Theodosia said. "I can't begin to thank you for all the help you've given us."

"Actually," Pauline said, "it turned out to be kind of fun."

"I've never participated in a tea party before," Wade said. "It kind of opened my eyes to what's possible. I mean, going with a theme like this . . . and the costumed characters. You could just see people's eyes light up."

"We're big on themes," Theodosia laughed. "Nutcracker Teas, Rose Teas, Blue-and-White Teas, Harvest Teas, Candlelight Teas. You name it, we'll come up with something fun."

"I love that," Wade said. "It's smart marketing."

Theodosia saw Drayton emerge from the kitchen and give her a low-key wave. "Excuse me," she said. She caught up with Drayton, said, "What?"

"Haley's busy packing her things, but she's going to need help loading everything into your car."

"No problem."

Drayton glanced over at Pauline and Wade. "And I think we need to pay those two."

"That's exactly what I've been thinking. They worked their little hearts out. In fact, I'll run back over there and tell them right now."

Pauline and Wade were dumbfounded when they heard that Theodosia wanted to pay them.

Pauline shook her head. "But we volunteered."

"No, you put in a hard day's work, both of you. So you deserve to get paid."

"Wow," Wade said. "That's so generous of you." He glanced around. "If we're part of the crew, the paid crew, then we'd better pack *all* this stuff up. I see lots of candelabras and decorations that need to be transported back to your tea shop."

"Haley's got things, too," Theodosia said. "If you could help her with all the leftovers and cooking stuff, it'd be . . . amazing."

One hour later it was full-on dark as Theodosia backed her Jeep up to the Dove Cote Inn's kitchen door. They formed a bucket brigade, passing boxes from hand to hand and cramming everything into the back.

"That's it," Drayton said finally. "It's a snug fit and you're bursting at the seams, but we managed to stuff it all in. Good thing our guests loved the food. That's one thing that doesn't have to go back."

"Theo, why don't I drive your Jeep back to the tea shop?" Haley said. "I can drop Drayton on the way."

"Oh no, that's okay," Theodosia said. "I can drive back."

"You look absolutely beat," Drayton said. "Why not take Haley up on her offer? You go home and we'll unload everything tomorrow."

"That's a great idea," Wade said. "In fact, I'd be happy to give Theodosia a lift home. My car's parked out back."

"Are you sure?" Theodosia said to Wade. "I don't want you to go out of your way."

"You two go ahead," Pauline said. "I have to run over to Miss Drucilla's place and pick up a couple things, so I'll be like ten minutes behind Wade."

"Go," Drayton urged Theodosia. "The unpacking can wait until tomorrow."

"Well, okay," Theodosia said, warming up to the idea. Then to Wade, "But I do have a couple of things that should go with me."

"Let's load 'em up," said Wade.

"Your market basket?" Drayton said. "I'll stick it in his trunk."

Still Theodosia lingered. "Are you *sure* you don't want me to come back to the tea shop and help set things straight?"

"You run along home," Drayton said. "Haley and I will take care of things."

31

❧

"*Are you warm* enough?" Wade asked as they drove along in his Subaru. "I can kick the heat up a notch if you'd like."

"I'm fine," Theodosia said. "Just awfully tired."

"Long day, huh?"

"They're all long but I wouldn't want to do anything else."

"That's cool that you found your passion," Wade said. "Not everyone does." Then, "That guy who was seated at the table by the window. You sure kept an eagle eye on him."

"That was Coy Cooper, Miss Drucilla's nephew." Theodosia was so tired, she sank back in the passenger seat and closed her eyes for a moment. The warmth of the car, the hypnotic motion made her even sleepier.

"Oh right, I guess I do remember him from the funeral. I knew Miss Drucilla had a nephew because Pauline mentioned him a couple of times. So you *suspect* him? In Miss Drucilla's murder?"

"I've been suspicious of several people," Theodosia said. "But nothing's panned out yet."

"Pauline told me you're kind of an ace at this. At being an amateur detective, I mean. Solving crimes."

"Maybe not this time." Theodosia opened her eyes. "Here's my block. Hang a left and I'm the third house in."

Wade glided to the curb and peered through the dusk at Theodosia's cottage. It was hidden in shadows with just a warm glow from a small brass lamp that hung to the side of her front door. "Cute little house," he said.

"Thank you." Theodosia pushed open the car door and climbed out. She realized she was moving slow and that her neck and feet felt sore and achy. A hot bubble bath was definitely in order.

"I'll get your stuff out of the trunk," Wade said. "What did we stick in there, just those two bags?"

Theodosia walked around to the back of his tan car. "Two bags and a basket." The cool air was helping to wake her up.

Wade popped the trunk to reveal a jumble of bags and boxes. "Let's see . . ."

Leaning in, Theodosia said, "I think . . . um, that's mine right there." Her eyes darted from her basket to a bag that had fallen over to reveal a curl of blue fabric. A pale blue she'd seen somewhere before with a familiar design that seemed to touch a nerve.

Theodosia's mind was suddenly searching for a connection. Where had she seen that color? And that particular pattern of faces and gowns and skimmer hats?

Her mind lurched in one direction, then another, as an unsettled feeling descended on her like a dark, dank cloud. Then it came to her in a blinding flash. It was a Renoir scarf that she'd seen for sale in the museum shop at the Gibbes Museum. A silk scarf that depicted one of Renoir's best-known works, *Dance at le Moulin de la Galette*. It celebrated a Sunday afternoon in the district of Montmartre in Paris.

No, it can't be. This has to be a totally bizarre coincidence.

She wondered—did Wade's gift shop sell those particular scarves as well? Or was he just an avid fan of . . . Renoir?

"You okay there?" Wade asked.

He was suddenly standing right at her elbow, so close she could hear him breathing. Completely invading her personal space. And Wade was smiling, yes, but it was a performance smile only. There wasn't a single ounce of warmth.

Had he noticed her noticing the scarf? Theodosia prayed that he hadn't. And dear Lord, this had to be the tan car that had followed her earlier in the week!

"I'd better pull out those bags for you," Wade said, cold blue eyes focused tightly on her.

"Just let me grab my basket," Theodosia said, trying to keep her voice light. If she could just keep the fear out of her voice, if she could make it inside unscathed, then she could lock the door and call 911. They could probably have a car here within minutes.

"You're looking at the scarf," Wade said. "Yeah, we sell those in my gift shop. I was going to give it to Pauline for Christmas. But now, after everything that's happened . . . well, it's probably not a smart thing to do. Maybe a little too incriminating, huh?"

Theodosia stood there, rooted like a statue, as a car crept down the block toward them.

"Easy now," Wade cautioned.

It was Mr. Bentley, who lived two houses down, but it was too dark for him to see the look of terror on Theodosia's face. In fact, he didn't even glance her way.

What to do?

Theodosia racked her brain, trying to think. She needed a weapon of some sort so she could put up a fight. So she could defend herself.

Hold everything. There's a knife in my French market basket!

It was a serrated knife that Haley had used to trim crusts off the tea sandwiches. If Theodosia could get her hands on that knife, wrap her fingers around the wooden handle, and hang on tight, she could threaten Wade and get him to back off.

As Theodosia reached a hand into the basket, something hard pressed against her ribs.

A gun?

Her eyes went round as saucers as she turned to stare at Wade.

His mouth was pulled into an ugly rictus; his eyes had turned dark and shiny like a pit viper's. "I know what you're thinking," he said. "So don't do anything stupid, Miss Amateur Detective. You just *had* to put two and two together, didn't you?"

The gun jabbed harder into Theodosia's ribs. On her left side, mere inches from her heart. She wondered if Wade would dare kill her right here on the street. Would he risk it? She didn't think so. If she could only . . .

"Forget the basket," Wade said, his voice cold as glare ice. "Leave it. Leave everything and let's just go inside. We need to talk."

"Inside?" Theodosia repeated. This was not going well. She *should* have had a plan B but didn't.

"Where's your house key?" Wade asked.

"Um . . ."

"In your purse?" Another jab. "Keep stalling and I'll make it worse for you," he said in a low, threatening voice.

"Okay. Right." Theodosia dug in her purse and pulled out her ring of keys. Four keys in all. Two to her house, one to the tea shop, one to her car, all on a silver keychain with a teapot charm. She held them up. In the chill night air, they jingled like tiny wind chimes.

"Good girl. Now march. All the way to the front door. And make it snappy."

Wade perp-walked Theodosia up the sidewalk right to her front door, the gun poking her the entire time. She'd gotten a quick glance at it and knew it was a .38 revolver. No safety, just point and shoot. About as dangerous as you could get.

She looked longingly at her house. Was this the last time she'd be seeing it? The crooked walk, the Carolina pine door, the ivy climbing up the side, the slanted roof that looked as though it had been woven by nimble-fingered elves.

Theodosia fumbled with her keys as her mind raced. She thought about the stippling Tidwell had noted around Wolf-Knapp's gunshot wound two nights ago. Would they find the same dirty gray marking, the same stippling, on her? Was that what the medical examiner would write on her autopsy report?

"Come on, come on," Wade rasped.

Wade moved closer to Theodosia as, jerky and stiff armed, she fumbled to select the right key.

"There's nobody inside, right?" Wade asked.

"Just my dog."

Wade stiffened. "Dog. What kind?"

"Um . . . dachshund," Theodosia lied. "Little one."

His lip curled in disgust. "Ah jeez, probably one of those little mutts that'll bark its fool head off."

"Something like that," Theodosia said.

She fumbled her keys again, then purposely dropped them on the top step. Gazing furtively at Wade, she threw him what she hoped was a helpless female look. One that said, *Poor me, I'm such a scared little airhead that I can't even manage a simple task like this.* But behind the facade was determination that said, *I'm gonna get you, sucker, and rip your heart out if it's the last thing I do.*

Wade swore at her, then dipped down and snatched up the ring of keys.

"Jeez," he snarled. "What a ditz. Is this the one? Is this the house key?"

Theodosia maintained her act by offering a fearful nod.

Wade stuck the key in the lock and gave it a turn. They both heard a loud CLICK; then the door eased open an inch or so.

"Entrez-vous," Wade said with mock formality. Then, with the key ring still dangling in his hand, he reached out and shoved the front door all the way open.

Like a great white shark looking for its next entrée, Gruenwald's muzzle appeared as he lunged for Wade's hand. The dog's huge jaws caught him—with ease—and held tight. Then, eyes rolling back in his head, lips pulled back in a snarl, Gruenwald sank his fangs deep into Wade's flesh.

There was a terrible crunch as he bit down hard. The sound of teeth tearing into gristle. And hitting bone.

"Owwwwww!" Wade's mouth gaped wide open in a hideous jack-o'-lantern snarl, his head jerked back, and he screamed like a banshee whose wings had caught fire. "Get him off meeeeee!"

Gruenwald, trooper that he was, guard dog par excellence, held tight and shook Wade like a vicious crocodile toying with its prey.

Tendons torn and muscles shredded, Wade let out another piercing scream. A split second later, the entire pack of dogs circled the two of them in a barking, jostling, yappy tangle. Angered and upset by Wade's cries, the dogs crushed harder and closer against them, causing Theodosia and Wade to stagger and trip over their own feet. Seconds later, they tumbled to the floor in a mad tangle.

Wade landed badly, his full weight coming down on his right elbow as it connected hard with the red tile floor in the entry. He screamed as a bone shattered and the gun flew out of his hand. It seemed to hang suspended in the air for one long second, then clattered to the floor.

That was the break Theodosia needed.

She reached for the gun, arms outstretched, hoping against hope. Then her fingers brushed against cool metal and she managed to grab it. Success! Tables turned!

Gruenwald continued his brave attack. Using his giant head and powerful shoulders as a battering ram, he propelled Wade backward and shoved him into a corner.

Wade squealed like a stuck pig. "He's *killing* me, the miserable . . . *Pleeeeease,* get him off me!" His voice rose in an ugly warble, tears oozed from his eyes and spattered his cheeks.

Theodosia scrambled to her feet. "Everybody, *down!*" she commanded in a brook-no-nonsense tone. Earl Grey and three of the dogs backed off immediately while Gruenwald and the two other large dogs continued their reign of terror.

"Help me!" Wade begged as he cradled his wounded hand. Tears mingled with snot streamed down his face. "They're ripping me to shreds! My arm is broken and my hand's torn all the way to the bone. I'm bleeding to death!"

"Gruenwald, everybody, get down!" Theodosia shouted again. The three large dogs backed off reluctantly but continued their menacing growls.

"You gotta . . . ," Wade stuttered out.

Cool as a cucumber, Theodosia balanced the pistol in her hand and pointed it directly at Wade's heart. "You shot at me. Wednesday night. You shot at me and my dog."

"Help meeee!" Wade pleaded.

"Be quiet," she said. "I need to make a call."

Hunched over like a cockroach that had been swatted and squashed, Wade wept and moaned. His face had blanched white and he looked ready to pass out.

"Ambulance?" he begged.

Theodosia shook her head. "Police."

32

❧

Detective Tidwell was the first to arrive in his once burgundy, now paint-oxidized classic Crown Victoria. Theodosia's call also warranted two police cruisers, an ambulance, and your basic partridge in a pear tree. It was Christmas after all.

"Who's injured? What happened?" Tidwell shouted. He jumped from his car and sprinted for the door (as fast as a fat man can sprint). When he caught sight of Wade cowering in the entry and Theodosia pointing a gun at him, he yelled, "Stop!"

Theodosia heard Tidwell coming toward her but her gaze never wavered.

Tidwell read the intensity on her face and threw up a hand. A signal for everyone rushing in behind him to hit the brakes.

"Is that loaded?" Tidwell asked.

Theodosia moved her aim from Wade's heart to a point right between his eyes.

"Ask him," she said.

"Yes, it's loaded!" Wade shouted. His eyes were bugged out and he was shivering with fear. "Help me, Detective. I beg you. This crazy woman intends to *shoot* me."

"I doubt she'd fire on you unless it was truly warranted," Tidwell said in a low voice.

"No, no, she's out of her mind!" Wade screamed. "Kapow crazy. There's no telling what she might do!"

"I suppose you have a point," Tidwell said. "Miss Browning, are you going to shoot this man?"

"It depends," Theodosia said.

"Help!" Wade screamed again. "You're the police. You're supposed to protect me!"

Tidwell moved closer and stopped when he was within five feet of them.

"I'm well acquainted with Miss Browning's temperament," Tidwell said to Wade. "So I'm guessing there's a good reason for your current predicament."

"There's not!" Wade cried. "I've been set up!"

"You stole the Renoir and killed Miss Drucilla," Theodosia said. "Then you killed Julian Wolf-Knapp."

"There you go," Tidwell said.

"No, I didn't kill anybody!" Wade cried. "I've been set up. Framed! You have to believe me!"

Theodosia moved a step closer. "Tell us what really happened," she said in a voice slightly below freezing. "About how you killed Miss Drucilla."

"That was never my intention," Wade whimpered. "She came along and . . . well, ended up as collateral damage." He drew a quick breath. "That's it, yes. Now please put the gun down. I know you don't want to hurt me."

"Oh but I do," Theodosia said.

"Theodosia," Tidwell cautioned.

"You even took time to steal Miss Drucilla's diamond rings. Ripped them right off her fingers," Theodosia continued.

"Shut up!" Wade screamed. "You don't know anything!"

His face had puffed up like a balloon and turned an ugly shade of purple.

"I realize you're in pain," Theodosia said, "which is making you highly emotional. But why kill Julian Wolf-Knapp?"

Wade hiccupped loudly, then fought to gather his wits. Finally, in a voice dripping with scorn, he said, "Because he was a cagey old fart. Wolf-Knapp came sniffing around the gift shop, asking questions. I figured it was only a matter of time before he figured things out. He was crooked as the day is long, you know, dealt in all kinds of stolen paintings."

"That doesn't mean he deserved to die," Theodosia said.

"Give me the gun," Tidwell said to Theodosia. "And please call off those dogs." His voice had softened to a respectful tone.

Theodosia handed over the gun, stepped past a still cowering Wade, and pushed the dogs back. She blocked the entry by tipping over two dining room chairs. *Maybe* that would hold them.

"He's bleeding badly," Tidwell said. "The EMTs need to look at him."

Wade fixed Theodosia with a murderous stare. "I want . . ."

"What?" Theodosia said.

Wade practically spit out his words. "I want a lawyer."

Thirty seconds later Wade Holland was handcuffed and hauled out to the ambulance. Another thirty seconds later the crew from Channel Eight showed up in a shiny white van with a satellite dish on top.

"What happened?" Monica Garber shrieked as she jumped out. "Was it a robbery? Breaking and entering to steal Christmas presents? That would make a terrific story!"

She was vibrating like a Chihuahua caught in a snowstorm.

"Never mind. Doesn't matter," Garber said. "This setup looks great as is! Bobby, get on the horn to the station and tell them to hold a minute-and-a-half slot on the ten o'clock. Wait. Make that two minutes. We'll shoot our lead-in right here on the front lawn." She took ten seconds to study the players, then said, "Say now, this is the Miss Drucilla thing, right?"

She threw a frenzied glance at Theodosia, who nodded yes.

"Hot dang!" Garber declared. "We'll interview Detective Tidwell first. That's our lead-in."

While Garber stuck a microphone in Tidwell's face, Theodosia moved stealthily across her front lawn and sidled up next to Wade. He was sitting on the back end of the ambulance, cuffed to a metal jump ring welded into the floor. His upper arm was encased in an inflatable splint. An EMT put antiseptic and Steri-Strips on Wade's torn hand, even though his work was hampered slightly by the handcuffs.

"Am I going to get rabies?" Wade screamed. "Come on, man, you gotta help me. I'm begging you. . . . Get me to a hospital before I start foaming at the mouth!"

"Take it easy," the EMT said. He was bushy-haired and big, a teddy-bear-type guy. "Try to calm down."

But when Wade noticed Theodosia staring at him, his screams got even louder.

"Get outa here! You set those cursed dogs on me. Hellhounds. Knocked me down and chipped a bone in my elbow. Hurts like blazes! With injuries this bad, I can sue you for everything you've got."

Theodosia stepped closer, ignoring his threats, a determined look on her face. "Did she know?"

Wade's lips quivered. "What are you babbling about? Did *who* know?"

"Pauline. Did she know?" Theodosia asked in a barely controlled voice.

"What do you think?" Wade sneered.

"Stop screwing around and give me an *answer.*"

"No, she didn't know," Wade snapped. "Are you happy now? Couldn't you see for yourself that Pauline wasn't the brightest bulb in the box?"

"In other words, you used her."

"Everybody uses somebody," Wade snorted. "The hard part was putting up with her tiresome histrionics." He turned his attention back to the EMT, who'd taped his hand, and shouted, "Hey, you. Medical guy. In case you haven't noticed, I'm dying here. Are you going to give me some pain meds or not?"

The EMT's gaze shifted to Theodosia. Theodosia shook her head.

"Not," said the EMT.

"You can't treat me like this!" Wade howled. "I've got rights!"

"Wade," Theodosia said, her voice steely from between clenched teeth, "you have very few rights. Try to see it from a legal perspective—you murdered two people in cold blood. You're going to prison for a very long time."

"Go away! Shut up!" Wade screamed.

"Not until you tell me where the Renoir is," Theodosia said.

Wade turned wild eyes on her. "What makes you think I still have it?"

"Because you've been willing to *kill* for it. Twice. Once to steal it and a second time to protect it. Now quit fooling around and tell me—where's the painting?"

Looking sullen, Wade puffed out his cheeks and said, "You're so smart, go find it yourself."

Theodosia looked at the EMT, whose name tag read HANSON. "Mr. Hanson, do you have any drugs on board?"

Hanson gave a half smile. "I got a few."

"Why don't you fill up a syringe with . . . Oh, let's make it your choice. The drug du jour. Then we'll inject Mr. Holland here and see if he wants to be a little more agreeable."

Wade's eyes went round as he goggled at them. "You're gonna *drug* me?" His bravado had drained away; now he sounded frightened.

"Just a little nip to help get you talking," the EMT said. "Yeah, I can fix you up. Won't be pleasant though."

Wade held up a hand. "Wait. Don't do that. I'll tell you, okay?"

"Cooperation, I like that," Theodosia said. "The police will like that. Where's the Renoir?"

"First I stuck it in the attic at Miss Drucilla's place. There was so much crap up there, I knew nobody would ever find it. But then I had to move it."

"Where to?"

"Aw, it's in the storage room at King's Ransom. Stuck behind a bunch of boxes against the far wall. No big deal. Any idiot can find it if they know where to look."

"You two hang tight," Theodosia said.

She turned and walked back to where Tidwell was standing, conferring with two of his officers, Officer Biskens and Officer Hart. Biskens had tried to hang yellow crime scene tape in the entry, but the dogs had gotten frisky and ripped it down.

"I know where the Renoir is," she told Tidwell.

He raised a single eyebrow, his right one. It was one of his unique talents.

"Wade says it's stashed in the storage room at King's Ransom Gift Shop. Far wall, behind a bunch of cardboard boxes."

Tidwell looked at Hart and said, "Send a patrol car. Posthaste."

"Sir," Hart said, "I'll go myself."

"Here," Theodosia said. She pulled out her cell phone, flipped to the image of the painting. "This is what you're looking for."

Tidwell turned to Theodosia. "You think you could somehow call off those dogs?"

"Maybe if I close the front door, they'll settle down."

Tidwell waited until Hart had left, then said, "Tell me, what did you do to get young Mr. Holland to fess up? Threaten to bash his head in?"

She touched a hand to her chest. "You think I'd revert to violence? No, I merely suggested that if Wade cooperated, the arresting officers might go a little easier on him."

"That's not going to happen," Tidwell said.

Theodosia smiled sweetly. "I know."

"Theodosia! Theodosia!"

Theodosia heard her name being called just as she saw her Jeep career down the street and bump hard against the curb. Haley was at the wheel, driving like it was an Indy car. Drayton was hanging out the window and waving frantically.

Theodosia ran over to greet them. "What are you two doing here?"

Haley cut the ignition just as Drayton flung open his door.

"We got worried," Haley said, leaning across the seat.

"I had a terrible feeling something wasn't quite right," Drayton said. "And now, seeing the torrent of activity going on here, I'd have to say my hunch proved correct."

"I didn't want to drive over, but Drayton kept needling me," Haley said. "Badgering me. He must be psychotic."

"Psychic," Drayton corrected.

"Or have ESP," Haley said. "So . . . what the heck happened?"

"It was Wade," Theodosia said, gesturing toward the back of the ambulance, where Wade sat like an unhappy lump. "He murdered Miss Drucilla and Julian Wolf-Knapp. He's the one who stole the Renoir."

"Holy Christmas!" Drayton cried. "And he confessed all this to you? Just like that?"

Theodosia thought about Gruenwald, Earl Grey, and the rest of the dogs. "Well, I might've had a little help."

* * *

It wasn't long before Tidwell got the call he'd been waiting for.

"Sir," Officer Hart said, "I have the painting in hand, the Renoir."

"And it's in good shape?"

"Looks fine to me, sir."

"Excellent. Good job."

Tidwell clicked off his phone and turned to Theodosia. "We've done it, then. Found the painting, arrested our killer—"

"That's fantastic!" Haley cried. She and Drayton had been circling about nervously, waiting to hear the news. "Sounds like it's all been wrapped up with a big red bow."

Drayton gave a wide grin. "Just in time for Christmas."

Tidwell sighed and rolled his eyes skyward for help. But there was a faint twitch at the corners of his mouth.

Theodosia's phone rang deep in her pocket. Still smiling at the two almost perfect punch lines, she hit a button and said, "Hello?"

It was Riley.

"Hey," he said. "I called to see how you fared with your fancy Victorian Christmas Tea. Was it a huge success? Did everything go off without a hitch? No unplanned disasters?"

Theodosia tucked the phone between her ear and shoulder, smiled, and said, "You have no idea."

The Indigo Tea Shop

Haley's Fried Coffee Cake

TOPPING
    ¼ cup sugar
    ¾ tsp. cinnamon

CAKE BATTER
    1 cup all-purpose flour
    ⅓ cup sugar
    2 tsp. baking powder
    ¾ tsp. ground cinnamon
    ½ tsp. salt
    1 large egg, beaten
    ⅓ cup evaporated milk
    ⅓ cup water
    3 Tbsp. melted butter

COMBINE sugar and cinnamon for topping and set aside. Prepare a sturdy 9-inch skillet by greasing bottom, then covering that grease with a layer of heavy wrapping paper cut in a circle to fit. Also grease the top of that paper. In a mixing bowl, whisk together flour, sugar, baking powder, cinnamon, and salt. In another bowl, whisk together egg, evaporated milk, water, and melted butter. Add wet ingredients to dry ingredients, mixing thoroughly. Pour mixture into the prepared skillet and sprinkle with the topping mixture. Cover the pan and "fry" on top of stove over very low heat for 30 to 40 minutes, or until cake is firm to touch. Lift the cake out of the skillet carefully and remove paper while still hot. Yields 8 servings.

Lobster Hush Puppies

1 cup yellow cornmeal
½ cup flour
½ tsp. baking powder
½ tsp. baking soda
½ cup buttermilk
1 egg
2 Tbsp. melted butter
¼ cup onion, finely diced
1 cup lobster meat, diced
Salt and pepper
Oil for frying

IN a bowl, mix together cornmeal, flour, baking powder, and baking soda. In a larger separate bowl, mix together buttermilk, egg, and melted butter. Add dry ingredients to wet ingredients and mix gently. Gently fold in the onions and lobster meat; then season with salt and pepper to taste. Let the batter rest for 15 to 20 minutes. Heat the oil in a pot or deep fat fryer to around 350 degrees. Drop spoonfuls of batter into the oil and cook for about 3 minutes until hush puppies turn golden brown. Drain on paper towels and serve hot. Yields around 10 to 12, depending on size.

Theodosia's Famous Hot Crab Dip

    1 small onion
    1 pkg. cream cheese (8 oz.)
    1 can crabmeat, drained (6 oz.)

PREHEAT oven to 350 degrees. In a food processor, pulse onion until finely chopped. Add cream cheese and pulse to incorporate. Add crabmeat and quickly pulse for a few seconds. Place crab mixture in an oven-safe glass dish and bake for 20 minutes or until heated through. Serve while still hot with your favorite crackers. (Note: Shrimp may be used instead of crab.)

Lemon Cream Scones

    2 cups flour
    ⅓ cup sugar
    1 Tbsp. baking powder
    ¼ tsp. salt
    1 tsp. lemon peel, finely grated
    1 cup heavy cream
    3 Tbsp. milk

PREHEAT oven to 375 degrees. In a medium bowl combine flour, sugar, baking powder, salt, and lemon peel. Stir in cream and milk, using fork, and mix until dough forms a rough ball. Knead dough 4 or 5 times on a lightly floured surface. Place dough on a greased cookie sheet and pat into an 8-inch circle. Using a large knife, cut into dough halfway, marking eight wedges. Bake 20 to 25 minutes until golden brown. Cool on a wire rack and cut into wedges while still warm. Serve with lemon curd. Yields 8 scones.

Fried Green Tomatoes

1 cup cornmeal
2 cups flour
1 Tbsp. sugar
¼ cup oil for frying
4 or 5 green tomatoes, sliced ½" thick
Salt and pepper to taste

MIX together cornmeal, flour, and sugar in a shallow dish. Heat oil in a fry pan over medium heat. Working in small batches, dredge tomatoes in cornmeal mixture and fry about 2 minutes on each side or until golden brown. Drain the fried tomatoes on paper towels until all tomatoes are fried. Serve warm with salt and pepper. Yields about 4 servings.

Drayton's Pork Chops with Apples

2 pork chops, about ¾" thick
½ cup apple juice
¼ cup maple syrup
1 medium-sized apple, sliced
1 Tbsp. butter

IN a large skillet, heat pork chops, apple juice, and syrup to boiling. Cover, reduce heat to medium, and cook 15 minutes, turning pork chops once. While pork chops cook, slice apple. Remove pork chops to platter. Add apple slices and butter to liquid and heat to boiling over medium heat. Cook for about 10 minutes until apple is tender and liquid thickens. Return pork chops to skillet to heat through and coat with glaze. Serve immediately. Yields 2 servings.

Chicken–and–Chutney Tea Sandwiches

1 cup cooked chicken, diced or shredded
¼ cup celery, finely diced
3 Tbsp. onion, finely diced
¼ cup walnuts, chopped
¼ cup sour cream
1 Tbsp. lemon juice
¼ cup mango chutney
Salt and pepper
6 slices bread
Butter

COMBINE all ingredients (except bread and butter) in a small bowl and mix well. Spread butter on all 6 slices of bread; then spread chicken mixture on 3 slices. Top with the remaining 3 slices to make 3 sandwiches. Cut off crusts; then cut each sandwich into 4 triangles. Yields 12 tea sandwiches. (Hint: If made ahead of time, cover with a damp paper towel, wrap in plastic wrap, and refrigerate.)

Holiday Cranberry Sauce

1 quart fresh cranberries
1 cup water
1¾ cups sugar
3 Tbsp. orange juice

WASH cranberries and discard any that are soft. Bring water to boil and add cranberries. Cover and cook over medium-low heat until berries burst their outer skin (about 10 minutes). Add sugar and boil an additional 3 minutes. Remove from the stove and stir in orange juice. Store sauce in a jar or plastic container until ready to use. Yields about 2 cups.

Traditional Shrimp Ball

1 pkg. cream cheese, softened (8 oz.)
1 Tbsp. ketchup
½ tsp. cayenne pepper
1 tsp. Tabasco sauce
1 tsp. Worcestershire sauce
1 tsp. hot sauce
1 can shrimp (6 oz.)

MIX together cream cheese, ketchup, cayenne pepper, Tabasco sauce, Worcestershire sauce, and hot sauce until creamy. Gently mix in shrimp. Roll into a ball, wrap in plastic wrap, and chill. Serve with your favorite crackers. Yields about 1½ cups.

Drayton's Eggnog

5 fresh eggs
1 cup whipping cream
2 cups milk
½ tsp. vanilla extract
1 Tbsp. honey
1 cup sugar
½ cup rum

IN a blender, process eggs until creamy. Add cream and milk and process again. Add vanilla, honey, sugar, and rum and mix well. Pour into pitcher and refrigerate the eggnog for at least 4 hours. Serve in chilled glasses and top with a small amount of grated nutmeg or a pinch of fresh cinnamon. Yields 4 servings. (Note: Because this recipe uses raw eggs, be sure they are fresh and that the eggnog is consumed the same day it's made.)

Simply Delicious Fudge

3 cups semisweet chocolate chips
1 can condensed milk (14 oz.)
4 Tbsp. butter
1 tsp. vanilla extract

PLACE chocolate chips and condensed milk in a microwave-safe bowl and heat on high in microwave, uncovered, for 2 minutes. Remove from microwave and stir until smooth. Stir in butter and vanilla. Microwave for another 30 seconds; then pour into 12-by-12-inch pan, spreading mixture evenly.

Chill for at least 2 hours. (Note: 1 cup of dried cranberries or 1 cup of walnuts can be stirred in before pouring mixture into pan.)

Holiday Ham Glaze

½ cup pineapple chunks with juice
1 cup brown sugar
4 tsp. prepared mustard
2 Tbsp. lemon juice
1 tsp. ground cloves

COMBINE all ingredients in a food processor or blender. Yields ¾ cup of glaze. (Note: When your ham has 30 minutes left to cook, remove from the oven and score the top in a crisscross fashion. Spoon the pineapple mixture over the ham, brushing to cover the entire ham. Return ham to oven for final 30 minutes of cooking, basting frequently.)

Pumpkin–Pecan Dump Cake

1 can pumpkin (29 oz.)
1 cup sugar
1 can evaporated milk (13 oz.)
3 eggs
4 tsp. pumpkin pie spices
½ tsp. salt
1 box yellow cake mix
1 cup pecans, chopped
¾ cup butter, melted

PREHEAT oven to 350 degrees. Combine pumpkin, sugar, evaporated milk, eggs, pumpkin pie spices, and salt in a mixing bowl. Beat well. Pour pumpkin mixture into a 9-by-13-inch glass pan that has been greased and floured. Sprinkle cake mix over pumpkin mixture; then sprinkle on pecans. Pour melted butter over all. Bake at 350 degrees for 50 to 55 minutes until a knife inserted in the center comes out clean. Take care toward the end of baking; this cake can burn easily. Yields 12 pieces.

TEA TIME TIPS FROM
Laura Childs

Victorian Tea

With harpsichord music filling the air, this tea party can be as much of an extravaganza as you wish. Just like at Theodosia and Drayton's Victorian Tea, lavish decor should adorn your tea table—think candles, floral nosegays, strands of pearls from the craft store, fans, feathers, and even a top hat. Use fancy place cards and stack a few books by Victorian authors (Dickens, Charlotte Brontë, and Elizabeth Barrett Browning) on your tea table. Serve cream scones or crumpets with rose petal jam to start with, then cinnamon cream cheese and raisin bread tea sandwiches. Your entrée could be apple-chicken salad in pastry cups. For dessert, delight your guests with poached pears and almond macaroons. The perfect tea, of course, is Adagio's Queen Victoria Blend.

Candlelight Tea

Late afternoon, when the sky turns purple and shadows lengthen, is the perfect time to hold your Candlelight Tea. Make your tea table moody with linens and china in hues of blue, purple, and rich burgundy. Pillar candles, small tea lights, and even a candelabra are a must, with silver candle-holders and crystal glasses to enhance the sparkle. Serve buttermilk scones with Devonshire cream and lemon curd. Pesto-chicken tea sandwiches and Camembert-fig tea sandwiches are showy and delightful, as are pumpkin-leek tarts for your entrée. Dessert could be chocolate-dipped strawberries. For the perfect pour, choose Fireside Chat Black Tea (with chocolate and walnut) from Plum Deluxe.

Honeybee Tea

Salute our hardworking pollinators with a Honeybee Tea. Decorate your table with white and yellow flowers and tuck in some fuzzy little bees sourced from your favorite craft store. Kick off your menu with cream scones dripping with honey butter; then segue to a second course of honey-and-apple-cheese flatbread or grilled bruschetta with pears, blue cheese, and honey. Your entrée could be honey-garlic chicken or even honey-ginger-glazed salmon. For dessert, serve cake with fresh berries drizzled with honey. Serve jasmine tea with honey sticks or honey pops for a sweetener. And don't forget small jars of honey as guest favors.

Nutcracker Tea

A Nutcracker Tea is a perfect lead-in to the holidays. Drape your table with a white linen tablecloth; then lavish on the decor. Think bright red nutcrackers, sugarplum fairies, and all the pink-and-white whimsy you can find at your local craft store. Tchaikovsky's *Nutcracker Suite* is the obvious musical background as you serve candied ginger scones with Devonshire cream. Then delight your guests with tea sandwiches of smoked salmon, capers, and cream cheese on rye, as well as tea sandwiches of honey-baked ham and caramelized onion on brioche. Dessert might be fig macarons or walnut-banana tea bread. Celestial Seasoning's Sugar Plum Spice is the perfect tea.

Harvest Tea

Host a sit-down tea or a buffet tea—whatever works for you. Just be sure to decorate your table with bountiful baskets filled with apples, pumpkins, gourds, and Indian corn. Fall flowers such as mums and black-eyed Susans are perfect adornments, too. Serve a rich Darjeeling tea and cheddar cheese scones for your first course. Then follow with pumpkin soup garnished with crème fraîche and turkey, apple, and goat cheese tea sandwiches. Think individual chicken potpies for your entrée. Blackberry or apple cobbler would make a lovely dessert.

Rhapsody in Blue Tea

Drape your table in white linen, layer on some blue place mats, and add a pretty crock filled with delphiniums or blue hydrangeas. This is also the perfect time to use all your favorite blue-and-white dishes. Never mind if the patterns don't match; it's more fun that way. Start with blueberry scones and Devonshire cream. Your assortment of tea sandwiches might include shrimp salad, cucumber and cream cheese, and ham with country mustard. Serve Adagio's Earl Blue tea (with lavender blossoms), and for background music, what could be better than Gershwin's *Rhapsody in Blue*?

TEA RESOURCES

TEA MAGAZINES AND PUBLICATIONS

TeaTime—A luscious magazine profiling tea and tea lore. Filled with glossy photos and wonderful recipes. (teatimemagazine .com)

Southern Lady—From the publishers of *TeaTime* with a focus on people and places in the South as well as wonderful teatime recipes. (southernladymagazine.com)

The Tea House Times—Go to theteahousetimes.com for subscription information and dozens of links to tea shops, purveyors of tea, gift shops, and tea events.

Victoria—Articles and pictorials on homes, home design, gardens, and tea. (victoriamag.com)

Fresh Cup Magazine—For tea and coffee professionals. (freshcup .com)

Tea & Coffee—Trade journal for the tea and coffee industry. (teaandcoffee.net)

Bruce Richardson—This author has written several definitive books on tea. (store.elmwoodinn.com/bruce-richardson.aspx)

Jane Pettigrew—This author has written seventeen books on the varied aspects of tea and its history and culture. (janepettigrew .com/books)

A Tea Reader—By Katrina Avila Munichiello, an anthology of tea stories and reflections.

AMERICAN TEA PLANTATIONS

Charleston Tea Garden—The oldest and largest tea plantation in the United States. Order their fine black tea or schedule a visit at bigelowtea.com.

Table Rock Tea Company—This Pickens, South Carolina, plantation is growing premium whole leaf tea. (tablerocktea.com)

The Great Mississippi Tea Company—Up-and-coming Mississippi tea farm about ready to go into production. (greatmsteacompany .com)

Sakuma Brothers Farm—This tea garden just outside Burlington, Washington, has been growing white and green tea for over twenty years. (sakumabrothers.com)

Big Island Tea—Organic artisan tea from Hawaii. (bigislandtea .com)

Mauna Kea Tea—Organic green and oolong tea from Hawaii's Big Island. (maunakeatea.com)

Onomea Tea—Nine-acre tea estate near Hilo, Hawaii. (onotea.com)

Minto Island Growers—Handpicked small-batch crafted teas grown in Oregon. (mintogrowers.com)

Virginia First Tea Farm—Matcha tea and natural tea soaps and cleansers. (virginiafirstteafarm.com)

Blue Dreams USA—Located near Frederick, Maryland, this farm grows tea, roses, and lavender. (bluedreamsusa.com)

Finger Lakes Tea Company—Tea producer located in Waterloo, New York. (fingerlakestea.com)

Camellia Forest Tea Gardens—This North Carolina company collects, grows, and sells tea plants. It also produces its own tea. (teaflowergardens.com)

TEA WEBSITES AND INTERESTING BLOGS

Destinationtea.com—State-by-state directory of afternoon tea venues.

Teamap.com—Directory of hundreds of tea shops in the US and Canada.

Afternoontea.co.uk—Guide to tea rooms in the UK.

Teacottagemysteries.com—Wonderful website with tea lore, mystery reviews, recipes, and home and garden.

Cookingwithideas.typepad.com—Recipes and book reviews for the Bibliochef.

Seedrack.com—Order *Camellia sinensis* seeds and grow your own tea!

Jennybakes.com—Fabulous recipes from a real make-it-from-scratch baker.

Cozyupwithkathy.blogspot.com—Cozy mystery reviews.

Thedailytea.com—Formerly *Tea Magazine*, this online publication is filled with tea news, recipes, inspiration, and tea travel.

Allteapots.com—Teapots from around the world.

Fireflyspirits.com—South Carolina purveyors of Sweet Tea Vodka.

Teasquared.blogspot.com—Fun, well-written blog about tea, tea shops, and tea musings.

Relevanttealeaf.blogspot.com—All about tea.

Stephcupoftea.blogspot.com—Blog on tea, food, and inspiration.

Teawithfriends.blogspot.com—Lovely blog on tea, friendship, and tea accoutrements.

Bellaonline.com/site/tea—Features and forums on tea.

Napkinfoldingguide.com—Photo illustrations of twenty-seven different (and sometimes elaborate) napkin folds.

Worldteaexpo.com—This premier business-to-business trade show features more than three hundred tea suppliers, vendors, and tea innovators.

Fatcatscones.com—Frozen ready-to-bake scones.

Kingarthurflour.com—One of the best flours for baking. This is what many professional pastry chefs use.

Californiateahouse.com—Order Machu's Blend, a special herbal tea for dogs that promotes healthy skin, lowers stress, and aids digestion.

Downtonabbeycooks.com—A *Downton Abbey* blog with news and recipes.

Auntannie.com—Crafting site that will teach you how to make your own petal envelopes, pillow boxes, gift bags, etc.

Victorianhousescones.com—Scone, biscuit, and cookie mixes for
    both retail and wholesale orders. Plus baking and scone-making
    tips.
Englishteastore.com—Buy a jar of English Double Devon Cream
    here as well as British foods and candies.
Stickyfingersbakeries.com—Delicious just-add-water scone mixes.
Teasipperssociety.com—Join this international tea community of
    tea sippers, growers, and educators. A terrific newsletter!
Melhadtea.com—Adventures of a traveling tea sommelier.

PURVEYORS OF FINE TEA
Plumdeluxe.com
Globalteamart.com
Adagio.com
Elmwoodinn.com
Capitalteas.com
Newbyteas.com/us
Harney.com
Stashtea.com
Serendipitea.com
Bingleyteas.com
Marktwendell.com
Republicoftea.com
Teazaanti.com
Bigelowtea.com
Celestialseasonings.com
Goldenmoontea.com
Uptontea.com
Svtea.com (Simpson & Vail)
Gracetea.com
Davidstea.com

VISITING CHARLESTON
Charleston.com—Travel and hotel guide.
Charlestoncvb.com—The official Charleston convention and vis-
    itor bureau.

Charlestontour.wordpress.com—Private tours of homes and gardens, some including lunch or tea.

Charlestonplace.com—Charleston Place Hotel serves an excellent afternoon tea, Thursday through Saturday, 1 to 3.

Culinarytoursofcharleston.com—Sample specialties from Charleston's local eateries, markets, and bakeries.

Poogansporch.com—This restored Victorian house serves traditional low-country cuisine. Be sure to ask about Poogan!

Preservationsociety.org—Hosts Charleston's annual Fall Candlelight Tour.

Palmettocarriage.com—Horse-drawn carriage rides.

Charlestonharbortours.com—Boat tours and harbor cruises.

Ghostwalk.net—Stroll into Charleston's haunted history. Ask them about the "original" Theodosia!

Charlestontours.net—Ghost tours plus tours of plantations and historic homes.

Follybeach.com—Official guide to Folly Beach activities, hotels, rentals, restaurants, and events.

ACKNOWLEDGMENTS

Thank-yous all around to Sam, Tom, Elisha, Brittanie, Stephanie, Sareer, Talia, M. J., Bob, Jennie, Dan, and all the amazing people at Berkley Prime Crime and Penguin Random House who handle editing, design, publicity, copywriting, social media, bookstore sales, gift sales, production, and shipping. Heartfelt thanks as well to all the tea lovers, tea shop owners, book clubs, bookshop folks, librarians, reviewers, magazine editors and writers, websites, broadcasters, and bloggers who have enjoyed the Tea Shop Mysteries and helped spread the word. You are all so kind and you help make this possible!

And I am forever filled with gratitude for you, my very special readers and tea lovers, who have embraced Theodosia, Drayton, Haley, Earl Grey, and the rest of the tea shop gang as friends and family. Thank you so much and I promise you many more Tea Shop Mysteries!

Keep reading for an excerpt
from Laura Childs's next
Tea Shop Mystery . . .

A DARK AND
STORMY TEA

*Available now from
Berkley Prime Crime!*

1

༺❧༻

At five-thirty on a Monday afternoon it was full-on dark when Theodosia Browning, proprietor of the Indigo Tea Shop, stepped out the back door of the Heritage Society. Pushing back a lock of curly auburn hair, she scanned the western sky, hoping for a faint smudge of orange to light the way home. When she didn't find it, she set off at a fast clip, chiding herself for staying so late.

Still, Charleston's venerable Heritage Society was sponsoring a Maritime History Seminar this Wednesday and, as luck would have it, Theodosia and her team had been tapped to cater an afternoon tea for visiting scholars.

Gotta hurry back, Drayton will be waiting, Theodosia told herself as she snugged her coat collar up against a cold wind. Overhead, trees thrashed as rain began to pelt down, stinging her face like icy needles.

Awful weather for early March. Especially when Charleston should be bursting with azaleas and pink camellias.

Now thunder rumbled overhead, low and slow, as if pin after pin was being knocked down in a cosmic bowling alley.

Theodosia hurried across King Street and hesitated. She glanced around at enormous two-hundred-year-old homes that sat on their haunches like nervous cats; then she shivered as sheets of rain slashed down. Because the shortest distance between two points was a straight line, she knew a shortcut down Gateway Walk, a tangled trail that wound through the backside of the Historic District, would save her an entire block of slopping through puddles. And with this weather system blowing in so hard and strong, the decision was a no-brainer.

Of course, Gateway Walk was probably deserted right now, Theodosia told herself as she hurried through a pair of ancient wrought iron gates and headed down a narrow, winding path. With this foul, unseasonable weather there'd be no tourists snapping photos, none of the usual ghost walk tours with guides spinning eerie tales about haunted graves and wafting white specters.

Tall boxwood hedges closed in as Theodosia skimmed along slippery cobblestones. Great gray wisps of fog rolled across her path like ghostly ocean waves, driven in by wind off Charleston Harbor a few blocks away. Charleston, a city that was already slightly ethereal due to high humidity, salt-laden sea air, and antique glowing streetlamps, became positively spooky when the fog swirled in.

Of course it's spooky, Theodosia told herself. *Even this pathway is purported to be a prime viewing area for ghostly phenomena. Which, by the way, I don't happen to subscribe to.*

Theodosia had traveled these hidden paths and walkways dozens of times, always reveling in their sumptuous gardens, Greek statuary, hidden grape arbors, and pattering fountains. But tonight she had to admit the atmosphere did feel slightly different.

And for good reason.

Always a gracious and posh dowager, Charleston was on

edge right now. A dangerous killer the local press had dubbed Fogheel Jack had been skulking down its hidden lanes and alleys. After a seven-year hiatus, this madman had suddenly reappeared in Charleston to strangle an unsuspecting young woman with a twist of sharp wire.

Now residents hurried home from work in a wash of blue twilight and locked their doors before total darkness descended. Visitors who'd come to languish in luxury at Charleston's historic inns and feast at four-star restaurants that specialized in grilled redfish, blue crab, and fresh oysters were warned not to wander too far from the relatively safe confines of the Historic District. Around the City Market, Waterfront Park, and White Point Gardens, Charleston police had stepped up patrols and officers rode two to a cruiser.

No. Theodosia shook her head to dispel the notion of danger and told herself she'd be fine. Better than fine. Even though she was surrounded by live oaks, palmettos, and crumbling stone walls, she was only three blocks away—actually, make that two and a half—from busy Church Street and the welcoming warmth of her tea shop. And once she reached the front door of that cozy little establishment, she'd be perfectly safe. Drayton Conneley, her dear friend and tea sommelier, would be waiting with a fresh-brewed pot of Darjeeling, eager to hear final details about their catering job. Haley, her young chef extraordinaire, would probably be tucked upstairs in her apartment along with Teacup, her little orange-and-brown ragamuffin cat.

Theodosia could almost feel the warmth of the Indigo Tea Shop settle around her shoulders like a cashmere blanket, could practically inhale its rich aromas. So nothing to worry about, right?

Then why do I feel so unsettled?

Theodosia knew the practical, rational answer. It was because of Fogheel Jack. He was the mysterious, unknown killer who'd murdered two women some seven years ago and was apparently back for a return engagement. Even her customers, sipping tea and nibbling fresh-baked scones at her quasi-British, slightly French-inspired tea shop, furtively whispered his name.

Who was he?

Where was he?

When would he strike next?

The *Post and Courier* had made no bones about last week's murder, a headline boldly declaring *Fogheel Jack Is Back!* That murder had taken place in a small park over near the University. The strangling an almost exact reenactment of the two seven-year-old, still-unsolved crimes.

Fogheel Jack. That's what rabid journalists had called him back then. And the name had stuck. Obviously.

Some of the TV stations had gone so far as to speculate that this brutal killer had been roaming the country and returned to Charleston because he found it to be more to his liking, a kind of preferred hunting ground.

Enough of that nonsense, Theodosia told herself as she chugged along. Last week's murder had happened miles from here. So there was no way . . .

A faint sound up ahead. The scrape of shoe leather on pavement?

Theodosia slowed, listened carefully, then stopped dead in her tracks. Cocked her head and listened harder.

But the only thing she heard was the constant pounding of rain and the occasional whoosh of cars over on Archdale Street.

I'm being silly. Acting like a fraidy-cat.

Resuming her pace, Theodosia headed down the final passageway. This was normally a gorgeous place to sit and watch sunlight play on palmetto trees and purple wisteria. To watch butterflies and honeybees cavort. Not happening today. Instead, she hurried past fog-strangled clumps of azaleas as thunder rumbled overhead and rain pelted down.

Blinking, wiping her eyes, she found it difficult to navigate the narrow path let alone avoid its deepening puddles.

Theodosia cautioned herself to hold steady. After all, St. Philip's Graveyard was just ahead. After that she'd be home free.

Unfortunately, she had to contend with this blinding rain and doggone fog.

Theodosia ducked her head and continued on as damp vines clutched at her ankles. Finally, through a scrim of shifting fog, a moldering tomb came into view. Then another seemed to pop up. And even though this was most definitely a creepy graveyard (ghost hunters claimed they'd seen glowing orbs here), Theodosia had never been so happy to see it.

The brick path doglegged left and Theodosia followed it around a square marble tomb with a kneeling angel on top. Cold, wet, feeling like a drowned rat, she couldn't wait to . . .

Another noise.

Theodosia's shoulders hunched reflexively as she came to an abrupt stop.

Is someone besides me wandering around in this miserable weather? A graveyard visitor or lost tourist?

She waited nervously as electricity seemed to thrum the air like so many high-tension wires.

What to do?

An answering slash of lightning lit the boiling clouds overhead. And illuminated a strange tableau taking place some thirty feet in front of her.

Two figures. Locked in some kind of unholy embrace. As if caught and buffeted in the eye of a hurricane.

Then utter darkness enveloped the scene and rain drummed down even harder.

Her heart practically blipping out of her chest, Theodosia wondered what she'd just witnessed? Lover's quarrel? Crazy horseplay? Someone being attacked?

Lightning strobed and crackled again, yielding a startling

revelation. One of the figures was now stretched out atop a low tomb.

Behavioral experts say that faced with imminent danger, most everyone has an immediate fight or flight reaction. Theodosia didn't opt for either of these. Instead, she shouted, "Hey there!" Tried to make her voice sound loud and authoritative.

A hooded figure in a long black shiny coat rose slowly and turned to face her. The image suddenly struck her as somber and frightening, like a creature out of a horror film. Or the Headless Horseman character from *The Legend of Sleepy Hollow*. She stared, trying desperately to make out the man's face—she thought it was a man—but was only able to discern dark hollows for eyes and a horizontal slash of thin lips.

"What are you . . . ?" she shouted again, even though it was difficult to make herself heard above the onslaught of the storm.

Then Theodosia was struck silent as the man lifted a gleaming blade and tilted it in her direction. It was a strange gesture. He could have been threatening her, he could have been offering a benediction.

The air felt charged with danger as Theodosia slowly spread her arms wide, as if in surrender, and took a step backwards.

That's when the man turned and slipped away into the shadows.

Unnerved, Theodosia waited a few moments and then crept forward. Really, what *had* just happened? What had she witnessed?

Slowly, cautiously, her heart beating like the wings of a frightened dove, Theodosia advanced on the small dark figure that had been flung carelessly across the tomb. It looked . . . almost like a bundle of rags. Was it a person? She thought so.

Peering at the crumpled figure, she said, "Hello? Do you need help?"

There was no answer.

She took another step forward.

That's when it all changed for Theodosia. That's when she saw streaming rivulets of blood mingled with rain as it hammered down.

2

❧

Flustered and trying to fight off the blind panic that threat-
ened to engulf her, Theodosia fumbled for her phone and
managed to punch in 9-1-1. When a dispatcher came on the
line her words poured out in a torrent.

"There's been a murder! At least I *think* it's a murder. In
St. Philip's Graveyard. I need help!"

"Where are you?" the dispatcher asked. A male voice, all
business but concerned-sounding too.

"I just told you. St. Philips Graveyard."

She heard mumbling in the background, several voices all
merged together, and someone saying *ten-fifty-three* and *a
possible one-eighty-seven*. Police codes, she guessed. Then
the dispatcher was right back with her.

"An alert's been sent, help is on the way," he said. "But
you *must* remain on the line, do you understand?"

"Okay . . . okay," Theodosia said. She was trying to stay
calm, to sound as if she was in control of her faculties, but it
was difficult. Rain continued to pour down, seeping under

her collar and running down the back of her neck, chilling her to the bone. She was also standing in total darkness, surrounded by ancient, crumbling statuary and tombstones. A carved skull stared at her with hollow eyes. A lamb with a missing head stood guard just to her left. And of course there was that poor body. With so much blood leaking out.

"Are you still there?" the dispatcher asked. "Talk to me. I need to know that you're okay."

"I'm here, I'm okay." Theodosia said as she clutched her phone with a cold, death-like grip.

"There's a cruiser two minutes out, so you need to hang in there as best you can." Against the constant drip, drip, drip of rain he sounded worried.

Theodosia nodded, even though she knew the dispatcher couldn't see her.

"Okay," she said finally. "I'm still here."

"Are you in any physical danger?"

Theodosia looked around. "Right now? I don't think so. But . . ."

She ground her teeth together as her curiosity reared up hard and fast, getting the better of her. Clouding her judgment.

She crept forward, the heels of her loafers sinking into soft, dark moss as she edged across soggy ground. Then she stopped and peered speculatively at the woman. She'd been flung haphazardly across a low pockmarked marble tombstone, almost as if she'd been put there on display. As if her killer wanted to say, *Look what I did.*

The scene was macabre. The woman's face and arms looked bleached white, like bones picked clean. And every time lightning flashed, and wind ruffled the woman's clothing and hair, it was like watching a herky-jerky old-time black-and-white movie.

But wait . . .

It took Theodosia a few moments to become fully aware of the khaki book bag with a purple emblem, sodden and half-hidden under the woman.

"Dear Lord," she said, her voice low and hoarse. "Could it be Lois?" Lois Chamberlain was the retired librarian who owned the Antiquarian Bookshop a few doors down from the Indigo Tea Shop. She sold khaki book bags that looked a lot like this one.

Theodosia lifted her cell phone and spoke into it again. "I think . . . I think I might know her."

"You recognize the victim?" the dispatcher asked. Surprise along with a hint of doubt had crept into his voice.

"I recognize the book bag anyway."

"Uh-huh."

"I'm afraid it might be Lois Chamberlain from the Antiquarian Bookshop," Theodosia said. Then the lightning strobed again, set to the tune of a kettle drum thunderclap, and she saw long reddish-blond hair hopelessly tangled and streaked with blood.

"Or maybe . . . her daughter?"

Could that be Cara? Theodosia wondered.

"Officers are thirty seconds out," the dispatcher said in her ear. "Two cars coming." He seemed more concerned with their timely arrival than the dead body Theodosia was staring at. "Are you hearing sirens yet?"

As if on cue, dual high-pitched wails penetrated her consciousness.

"I hear them, yes. They're getting close."

Then they were more than close. Gazing across a tumble of moss-encrusted tombstones through swirls of fog, Theodosia saw the first cruiser turn off Church Street and bounce up and over the curb. Without cutting its speed, the car skidded across the sidewalk, maneuvered around the side of the church, and churned its way toward the graveyard. Slewing across wet grass, the car rocked to a stop just as its reinforced front bumper hit a tilting tombstone with a jarring *clink*.

A second cruiser followed as lights pulsed, sirens blared, and a crackly voice yelled at her over a loudspeaker.

It was kind of like Keystone Cops, only it wasn't.

Guns drawn, serious-looking uniformed officers sprang from both vehicles.

"Here. Over here," Theodosia called out. She raised her hands in the air to let them know she was an unarmed civilian. "I'm the one who called it in." *So please don't shoot me.*

The EMTs arrived right on their heels. Siren screaming, red lights flashing, jumping from the ambulance and rushing to tend to the victim. They cleared her airway, used a ventilator bag, did chest compressions, administered some sort of injection to try and jumpstart her heart. Nothing seemed to work. The woman—Cara?—appeared to be dead.

"Soft tissue trauma compounded by a hyoid fracture," one of the EMTs murmured. "Ligature cut deep. Not much we could do."

One of the officers, a man who'd been holding a flashlight so the EMTs could work, walked over to Theodosia. His name tag read DANA.

"You're sure she's been . . . ?" Theodosia touched a hand to the side of her own neck to indicate a strangulation.

"Looks like," Officer Dana said.

Theodosia's face was a pale oval lit only by bouncing flashlights and the glowing blue and red bars on the cruisers. "So it could have been . . . ?" Her voice trailed off again.

Officer Dana aimed suspicious cop eyes at her. "You're thinking Fogheel Jack? Let's hope not."

But Theodosia knew it probably was. She'd been born with masses of curly auburn hair, blue eyes that practically matched her sapphire earrings, an expressive oval face, beaucoup smarts, and a curiosity gene that simply wouldn't quit. Right now her smarts and her curiosity gene were ramping up big-time, telling her this was definitely the brutal handiwork of the killer known as Fogheel Jack.

Another officer, Officer Kimball, walked over to them as he spoke into his police radio. He said "K" into the radio, then looked at Officer Dana. "We need to lock down the scene until they send an investigator."

Theodosia took a step forward. "Pete Riley?" Her voice sounded soft and muted amidst the clank of activity and barked orders.

Officer Dana looked at her sharply. "You know him?"

"He's my boyfriend."

"I don't know who got the call out tonight," Officer Kimball said. He sounded unhappy and resigned, as if he'd rather be anyplace else. "We'll have to wait and see." He sighed. "Anyhoo, Crime Scene's on its way."

"I'll get some tape from the vehicle," Officer Dana offered.

Halfway through stringing yellow and black crime scene tape from a grave to a mausoleum and then winding it around another grave, Officer Dana glanced up at a large figure that was bobbing toward them. The figure slipped behind a tall obelisk, then reemerged again.

"Looks like the big boss himself came out," Officer Dana said.

Theodosia peered through dark swaying strands of Spanish moss and decided that could mean only one thing.

"Detective Tidwell," she murmured, just as Detective Burt Tidwell, head of the Charleston Police Department's Robbery and Homicide Division, appeared. He was dressed in a baggy brown suit the color of sphagnum moss. What little hair he had left was acutely disheveled, his eyes were magpie beady, and his oversized belly jiggled. As he drew closer Theodosia saw a soup stain marring his ugly green tie.

"You," Tidwell said when he caught sight of Theodosia. Clearly they knew each other.

Theodosia gave a half shrug. "I was taking a shortcut back to my tea shop and I . . ." Her voice trailed off as Tidwell held up a hand. Then she cleared her throat and said, "I think I know her."

That grabbed Tidwell's attention. He peered at Theodosia from beneath heroic bushy eyebrows and said, "You *recognize* the victim?"

"I think it might be Cara Chamberlain, Lois's daughter."

"The bookstore lady," Tidwell murmured. Besides being a meticulous, boorish, ill-tempered investigator, he was extremely bright and well-read. "You're sure it's Lois's daughter? Are you able to make a positive ID?"

"I think so."

His head shook setting off a jiggle of jowls. "You need to be absolutely sure before we do any kind of notification."

"Then I don't—"

Theodosia's words were once again cut short by the arrival of the Crime Scene team. Their shiny black van pulled up next to the police cruisers. Men in black jumpsuits got out and immediately established a hard perimeter—setting up lights on tripods and even more yellow crime scene tape. When the entire graveyard glowed a ghastly yellow, they began to record the scene, using still cameras as well as video cameras.

"Anybody touch her?" one of the techs asked. He aimed his question directly at Theodosia and Tidwell. They both shook their heads.

"Good. Step back, then," he said.

"Any footprints?" Tidwell asked. "Can you pull plaster casts?"

The tech looked skeptical. "Dunno. There are a few prints but they're already mushy and filled with rain."

Theodosia stood there feeling helpless and bedraggled. Her normally curly hair was plastered to her head and she'd crossed her arms in a futile attempt to stay warm. Still, a keen intellect shone in her eyes as she watched the proceedings.

Strangely, the night was shaping up for even more action. A shiny white van with a satellite dish on top had just rolled in. Theodosia figured it was TV people who'd tuned in on their scanner and gotten wind of the murder.

"Oh, hell's bells," Tidwell said when he saw the van. "The media jackals have arrived."

"What have we got? Lemme through, lemme through," came the high-pitched, semi-authoritative voice of Monica Garber. She was the lead investigative reporter at Channel Eight, a tenacious pit bull of a woman who lived for the thrill of sinking her teeth into a fast-breaking story.

Officer Kimball held up a hand and tried to block her, said, "Ma'am, you need to stay back."

"Stuff it," Monica Garber snarled as she sailed right past him. She was mid-thirties—around Theodosia's age—attractive in a hard-edged way, and always projected her own brand of on-air sassiness. Tonight she was tricked out in a form-fitting hot pink blazer, tight black jeans, and short black boots. Her long dark hair flowed freely about her shoulders.

Theodosia didn't think Monica Garber would be particularly thrilled when she discovered who the victim was. Cara Chamberlain was a journalism student who'd taken the semester off to do a news internship at Channel Eight. Thus, she was practically one of their own.

How would Monica Garber handle her emotions when she realized the victim was Cara?

Turns out, not very well.

Once Monica pushed her way past the police line and registered that it was Cara lying there, she promptly fainted. Would have fallen and split her skull open on a hump-backed tombstone had not Bobby, her cameraman, lunged forward and caught her at precisely the last second.

"Nuh, I'm okay," Monica protested when she regained consciousness a few moments later. Then, as she looked over at the body, her eyes rolled back in her head and her knees wobbled like a Jell-O ring being passed around a Thanksgiving table.

"Get her out of here!" Tidwell shouted.

Bobby the cameraman and the young man who'd been manning the boom microphone got on either side of a shaky, protesting Monica Garber and half carried, half dragged her away.

"Good," Tidwell said. "Now, if only this tedious rain would let up. I have additional personnel on the way and we need to . . ." He half spun, noticed Theodosia again, seemed to seriously study her, and said, "Miss Browning. A favor if you will."